LOVE
and
DEATH
in
BALI

Novels by Vicki Baum

GRAND HOTEL
RESULTS OF AN ACCIDENT
HELENE
SECRET SENTENCE
MARTIN'S SUMMER
FALLING STAR
MEN NEVER KNOW
CAREER
A TALE FROM BALI
NANKING ROAD
CENTRAL STORES
THE SHIP AND THE SHORE
GRAND OPERA
MARION ALIVE
ONCE IN VIENNA
BERLIN HOTEL
THE WEEPING WOOD
HEADLESS ANGEL
DANGER FROM DEER
THE MUSTARD SEED
WRITTEN ON WATER
BALLERINA
I KNOW WHAT I'M WORTH
MORTGAGE ON LIFE
FLIGHT OF FATE

LOVE

and

DEATH

in

BALI

VICKI BAUM

With a new foreword by
NIGEL BARLEY

TUTTLE Publishing

Tokyo | Rutland, Vermont | Singapore

"Books to Span the East and West"

Tuttle Publishing was founded in 1832 in the small New England town of Rutland, Vermont [USA]. Our core values remain as strong today as they were then—to publish best-in-class books which bring people together one page at a time. In 1948, we established a publishing outpost in Japan—and Tuttle is now a leader in publishing English-language books about the arts, languages and cultures of Asia. The world has become a much smaller place today and Asia's economic and cultural influence has grown. Yet the need for meaningful dialogue and information about this diverse region has never been greater. Over the past seven decades, Tuttle has published thousands of books on subjects ranging from martial arts and paper crafts to language learning and literature—and our talented authors, illustrators, designers and photographers have won many prestigious awards. We welcome you to explore the wealth of information available on Asia at **www.tuttlepublishing.com**.

Published by Tuttle Publishing, an imprint of Periplus Editions (HK) Ltd.

www.tuttlepublishing.com

This title was first published in 1999 as *A Tale From Bali*.

Library of Congress Cataloging-in-Publication Data
Baum, Vicki, 1888-1960.
  [Ende der geburt. English]
  Love and death in Bali / Vicki Baum; with a new foreword by Nigel Barley; [translated by Basil Creighton].
    382 p. ; 21 cm.
  "This title was first published as A Tale From Bali"--T.p. verso.
  ISBN 978-0-8048-4180-1 (pbk.)
  I. Creighton, Basil. II. Title.
  PT2603.A815E5313 2011
  833'.912--dc22

                  2010051926

ISBN 978-0-8048-4180-1

Distributed by

North America, Latin America & Europe
Tuttle Publishing
364 Innovation Drive
North Clarendon
VT 05759-9436 U.S.A
Tel: 1 (802) 773-8930
Fax: 1 (802) 773-6993
info@tuttlepublishing.com
www.tuttlepublishing.com

Japan
Tuttle Publishing
Yaekari Building 3rd Fl, 5-4-12 Osaki
Shinagawa-ku, Tokyo 141 0032, Japan
Tel: 81 (3) 5437-0171
Fax: 81 (3) 5437-0755
sales@tuttle.co.jp; www.tuttle.co.jp

Indonesia
PT Java Books Indonesia
Jl. Rawa Gelam IV No. 9
Kawasan Industri Pulogadung
Jakarta 13930, Indonesia
Tel: 62 (21) 4682 1088
Fax: 62 (21) 461 0206
crm@periplus.co.id; www.periplus.com

Asia Pacific
Berkeley Books Pte. Ltd.
3 Kallang Sector #04-01
Singapore 349278
Tel: (65) 6741-2178; Fax: (65) 6741-2179
inquiries@periplus.com.sg
www.tuttlepublishing.com

26 25 24 23   9 8 7 6 5   2309VP
Printed in Malaysia

Contents

Foreword

Vicki Baum was born into a wealthy but dysfunctional Jewish family in Vienna in 1888 and trained initially as a concert harpist. By the time she came to Bali in 1935, however, she had laid her harp aside in favor of a typewriter and already enjoyed a considerable reputation as a popular and stylish writer, both in German and in English translation, and had established herself in print and in person on both sides of the Atlantic. Although a prolific author and Berlin journalist, she would always be remembered most for her first 1929 best seller, *Menschen im Hotel,* (*Grand Hotel*), which went on to storm the stages of European theatre and triumph on Broadway until it was finally filmed in the United States in a version that featured Greta Garbo and Joan Crawford and won the Academy Award for best picture in1931. This was a turning point in her life. She was famous around the world, yet, as she noted somewhat sourly in her autobiography, a successful book may be harder to live down than a failure and, throughout her professional career, Vicki Baum would struggle both for artistic independence and to be regarded as anything more than a light "women's writer" of the kind whose work appeared in magazines. Later, with her usual disparaging and ironic wit, she would describe herself as "a first-rate writer of the second rank." So, while *Grand Hotel* allowed her to make the transition from Germany to America and move into Hollywood scriptwriting, she would not know real literary success again until the appearance of *Love and Death in Bali* in 1937.

By the mid-30s Vicki Baum was disappointed in her lack of definitive success in Hollywood and tired of the interference that was part of the studio system. "Fifty people were using my toothbrush," as she put it. She embarked on a series of voyages to distant parts, in search of inspiration and experiences that she would draw on in her books for years to come. In 1935 she visited Egypt, Mexico, New Zealand, the South Seas, Japan and China, and was in Bali from May 1935 until the following April, arriving in the company of the artist Walter Dreesen and his lover, photographer and dancer Fritz Lindner. There she was guided around the island by the charming and charismatic German, Walter Spies since, as a former musician and the wife of a well-known German conductor, she was already familiar with several members of Spies's own highly musical family. She was also a fervent devotee of dance and Spies was coincidentally engaged, at that time, in planning and writing his own collaborative book on Balinese dance and drama, as well as organizing cultural displays for a visit of the Dutch Governor-General. Vicki saw an intense version of Bali specially arranged to impress outsiders. After her short visit she returned to America, but was haunted by the memory of Spies and Bali and a book that was lurking in her mind. A year later, at the start of the rainy season, she returned with Dreesen and Lindner and, while they moved on, she would stay a full nine months with Spies in his house at Campuan in Ubud. So it was here, in a riverside guest house he had built for Barbara Hutton (at that time the world's richest woman) that she would sit down to write *Liebe und Tod auf Bali*. (This was originally translated as *A Tale from Bali* but is now, more accurately, rendered as *Love and Death in Bali* in the present edition). The book was finished, despite attacks of malaria and diphtheria, before she returned to America in October of that year. *Love and Death in Bali* is just one of several works associated with Walter Spies and the Ubud of the late 20s and 30s for, before the Second World War unleashed itself upon Southeast Asia, the little house in Campuan was at the centre of a bohemian community of artists and scholars who sought to explore and fix their experience of Bali in writing, music and painting. Spies was himself an accomplished musician, painter, ethnographer, cinéast, choreographer and natural historian and became a bridge between the West and the Balinese to such an extent that even the Dutch, the colonial ruling power, could find no alternative to using him as Director when they wanted to establish their new Bali Museum. Charlie Chaplin, Noel Coward, Miguel Covarrubias, Colin McPhee, Leon Stokowski, Margaret Mead and Gregory Bateson—and others famous at the time as artists, opinion-formers and academics but now forgotten—all served their apprenticeship in things Balinese at the feet of Spies and spread his vision of Bali as an enchanted island across the world. From being seen as a place where the inhabitants were primitive and violent, and to which Dutch officials might be relegated as punishment, Bali became a site for Western fantasies about a tropical paradise.

Vicki Baum was exactly the sort of woman that Spies adored—literate, clever, independent, open-minded and very funny and, in the evenings beside the river at Campuan, their friendship blossomed and flourished. The selfless Dr. Fabius of Baum's spoof introduction—a device shamelessly lifted from Conrad's *Heart of Darkness*—is a tribute to him and his scholarship. We know that she was so taken with Spies as a character that she later began another work of fiction based upon him and entitled *Portrait of an Unknown Man*; alas, it was never completed. It is significant for understanding the relationship between her experience in Bali and her writing about it that, when subsequently asked to compose a memoir about Spies, she declared that this was now impossible, as her fictional Spies had completely eradicated the historical one from her mind. Whereas in the introduction of *Love and Death in Bali* the author edits the rambling manuscript of Fabius, in real life that relationship was reversed, and it was Walter Spies who painstakingly amended Vicki Baum's text to correct the ethnography and provide the confident local color that makes it such a vivid read and such a convincing introduction to the Balinese way of life. Vicki Baum was deeply affected by Bali for the rest of her life and attributed to it a sort of personal spiritual awakening, so that the title page of the book bears a quotation from the Bhagavad Gita. Perhaps this deep personal involvement explains why it has gone on to become an unquestioned classic and continues to shape the Western encounter with Bali.

Love and Death in Bali skillfully intermeshes several different stories that all come together in the infamous *puputan*, the slaughter and mass suicides that brought the old Bali to an end in 1906 and finally extended Dutch rule from the north over the south of the island. The invasion, triggered by the looting of a Chinese ship cast up on the beach at Sanur, brought the Dutch the military resolution they sought but at the price of worldwide condemnation for the blood shed as they finally crushed out the anomaly of southern Balinese independence. Hereafter, they would have to handle Bali with special care. The structure of the novel—interwoven, apparently unlinked persona who nevertheless end up impacting each other—is a literary technique that Baum has used with repeated success since her *Grand Hotel*. Bali is usefully ambiguous in that it blends the egalitarian democracy of the village community with caste hierarchy radiating from the royal palaces, and this contradiction is exploited in the contrasting characters of her narrative and their different attitudes to authority. The principal figure, Pak, is a simple casteless peasant who both owes allegiance to a feudal lord and resents it following the cruel exactions made on him and his family and sees no reason to embrace a fight between rulers that is none of his concern. So, instead of marching fearlessly into the Dutch guns with his father and his raja, as tradition and his ruler demand, he decides to look after what is left of his own family instead. Raka is a noble dancer, famed for his beauty, who comes to a final acceptance of the apparently unjust punishment that the gods have unleashed upon him and finds release and redemption in the self-sacrifice of a willing death. For him, to embrace the end of Bali is a way to ensure that it lives on. And throughout the book, it is the love of beauty that stalks the pages in several of its divine forms, the love of Pak for his second wife, for his cheap and worthless china plates and for the fighting cock whose confiscation finally poisons his heart; of Raka for the beauty of his lord's wife, for the beauty of the dance, and, finally for his own fair face. The Balinese characters here are very far from being the naked savages that the Dutch declare them to be but, rather, are thinking, sensitive, cultured people who might have stepped out of a hauntingly idyllic landscape painted by Walter Spies.

Baum seems often to have drawn her characters from life and was not unwilling to enter into the minds of locals in a way that seems strikingly unpatronizing for the time. So while Fabius is clearly Spies, even at this remove, it seems likely that the character of Raka, the beautiful but adulterous and finally leprous dancer, is borrowed from that of Rawa, Spies's favorite male performer from the village of Pagutan, who was notorious for his infidelities and whose otherwise perfect face and body were marred by bad teeth. Spies regularly took his visitors to watch his performances. More generally, the male-male relationships in the story and the resolution of the conflict in the rescue of Oka, the Balinese youth, by Dekker, his Dutch enemy who is then overwhelmed by the sheer physicality of his male beauty, seem to owe more than a nod towards the homoerotic milieu of Campuan in which Spies himself moved and to which Baum herself was accustomed since her Berlin days.

And yet, despite her informed empathy for local people, Baum does not fall into the mistake of casting the plodding Dutch who oppose the comely Balinese as mere monsters. While she shows Bali as a very special and enchanted place, it is not without its flaws that build up to gradually erode the idyllic state of her opening, and she is careful to declare in her introduction her admiration for Dutch rule. In her book, the Dutch are devious and ambitious but their belief in their own civilizing mission, while overblown, is no mere empty pose. The burning of widows and the physical mutilation of criminals, both part of traditional Balinese life, were as repugnant to a wider world then as they are now elsewhere and the same arguments were bandied back and forth then as are deployed now. Vicki Baum never embraces uncritically the romantic and exotic notion of Bali as a paradise on earth, as did some others of the Ubud set, and remains, to the last, an independent and critical thinker.

Love and Death in Bali was well received when it first appeared in German in 1937. It would be several more years before the National Socialists proscribed Vicki Baum's books and consigned them to the flames. The English translation enjoyed modest success in Great Britain where the *London Times* remarked coolly that "The characters that emerge from this earthly paradise are appropriately attractive" and the *Observer* was not alone in noting, "As a novel, although it is often vivid and powerful, and although it is readable throughout, ...[it]... is of less value than as a brilliantly sustained record of unfamiliar ways; but the record is deeply interesting." Its greatest success was undoubtedly in the U.S., where it was listed as a best seller by the *New York Times*. Their reviewer probably hit the nail on the head by noting of the author, "Not only has she chosen for her setting that enchanted South Sea Island which has lately been so overpublicized, but she has written it in terms remote from the maunderings of crooners and the ecstasies of casual tourists." For Bali was far from being unknown, and its imagined attractions were very much in the fashionable air, with commentators of the time remarking on "the Bali craze" that was sweeping the West. By the 1930s over a hundred tourists regularly passed through Bali each month in organized groups, on a pilgrimage initiated by the exotic images of the artist Wijnand Nieuwenkamp just after the turn of the century, and the suggestive, bare-breasted photographs of Gregor Krause in the twenties. Walter Spies had been associated with a dramatic film set on the island and called *Island of Demons (1933)* while Denis and Roosevelt's steamy tale of forbidden love, *Goona Goona*, had enjoyed widespread success in the West in the previous year. The term, *goona goona*—magic—even briefly became a euphemism amongst the New York glitterati for sexual allure, and Cole Porter included "a dance in Bali" as one of the listed endearments of his "You're the Top" hit song of 1934. Miguel and Rosa Covarrubias, similarly guests in Ubud, had shot a film there that was widely publicized in New York, and one of Miguel's Balinese paintings was chosen for the cover of *Vanity Fair* in 1936. It was voted the best cover of the year. As a well-known designer as well as an artist, he was even able to arrange a sort of extended Balinese promotion in the windows of the Franklin Simon department store, complete with Balinese-inspired textiles and an outrigger canoe, before he released his own book *The Island of Bali* in 1937, the same year as Vicki Baum's. All this ensured that Baum's novel fell on well-prepared ground and was enthusiastically received. "By far the best book which Miss Baum has written in years," roundly concluded one reviewer. Given subsequent developments, it is ironic that Vicki Baum notes in her own preface that the real Bali contains no Bali bars, Bali bathing costumes and Bali songs. Life, since then, has imitated art.

Vicki Baum had been astute enough to see which way the political and artistic wind was blowing in Europe and moved herself and her family to the United States in 1932. In 1938 she became an American citizen. *Love and Death in Bali* was one of her last books to be written in German rather than the English that she later embraced. She died of leukaemia in Los Angeles in 1960, having successfully concealed the true nature of her illness from her family until the very end, a ploy she allegedly borrowed from the plot of one of her own novels.

Nigel Barley

Preface

It must, I think, have been in 1916, a time when Europe was too much preoccupied to remember the existence of a little island called Bali, that I came by chance into the possession of some very beautiful photographs. One of my friends had got them from an acquaintance—a doctor who lived in Bali. They made such an impression on me that I begged my friend to give me them; and I kept turning again and again to these pictures of men and beasts and landscapes, whenever the horrors my generation was exposed to—war, revolution, inflation, emigration—became unbearable. A strange relationship grew up between these photographs and me; I felt that I should one day come to know those people and that I had actually walked along those village streets and gone in at those temple doors.

It was not until 1935 that I was able to make the voyage to Bali. My first visit was the realization of a dream without a hint of disillusionment. The privilege I enjoyed of seeing the real and unspoilt Bali instead of merely the modernized and tawdry fringes which tourists skirt in comfort was due to a letter of introduction to Doctor Fabius.

It was Doctor Fabius whose now faded and yellowing photographs had played so great a part in my life. He had the reputation of being the oldest Dutch resident and an eccentric with an unrivalled knowledge of Balinese life. The other Dutch officials on the island had a great respect for his professional ability, his knowledge and his influence over the natives. At the same time they were inclined to laugh at the way he lived and said of him that he was half Balinese. He was a white-haired, lean, silent old gentleman, of an ironical turn of mind and rather averse to visits from persons like myself. In spite of this a peculiar sort of friendship developed between us in the course of time, and this resulted in his taking me with him to more and more distant villages and allowing me to see the real life of the Balinese.

When I returned to America I had a strange feeling of homesickness for Bali; I wrote several letters to Doctor Fabius which remained unanswered. I went back to Bali a year later for a second, and this time a long, visit, and found that he had died of pneumonia. The works of art, which had filled his house to overflowing, had been bequeathed to various friends; but for me Fabius had singled out one of those cheap, funny little Japanese tin boxes. I received this legacy with a feeling of perplexity and surprise. The box contained papers, some written by hand, some typewritten. There were pages from diaries, notes on customs and ceremonies, memoranda of all sorts, and also a long novel, the theme of which was the conquest of Bali by the Dutch. With them was a letter, in which Doctor Fabius authorized me in a few rather ironical sentences to reduce this jumble of manuscripts to order—"a task in which I have always been hindered by my Balinese laziness," as he said—and to publish what I thought worthy of publication.

Love and Death in Bali is the book I have extracted from these papers after trying to discard what was redundant or too involved. It is concerned with a historical event which is known in the story of the colonization of Bali as "Puputan," that is, roughly, "The End." Nevertheless, it is not in the strict sense a historical novel, but rather a free rendering of actual occurrences.

Names and characters have been altered and the order of events is sometimes arbitrary. For example, the burning of widows at Tabanan took place three years and not three months before the dispatch of the punitive expedition. The Dutch officials of that time are nearly all still living and were, as I know, good friends of Fabius, who spoke of them with the greatest esteem. Men like Liefrinck and Schwarz are renowned for their knowledge of Bali and they love the island dearly. The officials in Fabius's book have not only been given other names but are fictitious characters, who have no connexion with the real persons they represent. When I went through his manuscript I came upon many liberties of this kind, which I have no doubt were intentional. So I left them as they were. Clearly it was his aim to present the truth from the inside, even at the cost, when he thought it necessary, of sacrificing outward accuracy.

Similarly, I have taken the liberty of ending the story with the conquest of Badung. Fabius's interminable manuscript goes on to the final colonization of other districts as well, where very much the same events occurred as in Badung. The Lord of Tabanan committed suicide with his son when he was taken prisoner and in Klungkung there was the same wholesale recourse to self-inflicted death—a puputan—as at Badung. Moreover, it seems to me that in Fabius's eyes the simple and, in the deeper sense, pacifist existence of the peasant Pak was perhaps of more importance than the collisions in Bali between the vigorous *Realpolitik* of Holland and a heroic and medieval pride of arms.

Since then the Dutch have carried out an achievement in colonization that reflects the highest credit on them. Scarcely anywhere in the world are natives free to live their own lives under white rule so happily and with so little interference and change as in Bali; and I would like to believe with Doctor Fabius that the self-sacrifice of so many Balinese at that time had a deep significance, since it impressed upon the Dutch the need of ruling this proud and gentle island people as considerately as they have, and so kept Bali the paradise it is today.

The introductory chapter, put together from diary notes of Doctor Fabius, is concerned with the present day. The tale itself embraces the years from 1904 to 1906. For help and encouragement in sifting and examining the mass of material my thanks are due to: The Resident of Bali and Lombok, Mynheer van Haaze-Winckelman, Mrs. Katharane Mershon of Sanur, Herr Walter Spies of Oeboed, and many other of my Bali friends.

Bali has become the fashion. When I came back from the island, where in many places life and customs have remained unaltered for thousands of years, I found an irruption of Bali bars and Bali bathing costumes and Bali songs. I need not say that Doctor Fabius's book has nothing to do with this Bali—if only because this Bali does not exist.

Vicki Baum

Introduction

When I got home from the little Government hospital, where I had spent the whole morning attending to various cases of fever, severe bamboo cuts and tropical ulcers, I found a bicycle leaning against the wall at my gate. I hurried across the courtyard, for I was curious to know who my visitor was. My Dutch friends like to make fun of me because my place is built in the native style—a house of whitewashed daub with a portico, surrounded by a number of smaller buildings or balés. Balés are raised platforms with roofs of alang-alang grass resting on posts. Many balés have one or even two mud walls and they can be sheltered from sun or rain by matting. Life is cheerful and pleasant in these balés and only the house itself has real walls. The whole plot is surrounded by a wall above which palms and fruit trees grow as high as a forest

On the steps of the open portico sat Ida Bagus Putuh and a step higher squatted the sculptor, Tamor. They were from the village of Taman Sari, near the coast and several hours distant from the foothills where I lived. Both clasped their hands and raised them to their shoulders in greeting. Ida Bagus did it with punctilious ceremony, but Tamor, who had modern ideas, did it with a laugh, showing his white, evenly filed teeth, as though he did not take the ceremony quite seriously. Tamor was a good-looking and talented fellow, who sometimes carved figures of quite astonishing beauty. He was fond of wearing brightly colored sarongs and beautiful head-dresses, which he wound round his small Egyptian skull with an air all his own. He had a red hibiscus flower stuck behind his ear and was smoking a maize-leaf cigarette which had a sweet smell of spice and cloves. His fine torso was hidden by a dirty, cheap Japanese shirt, for that was the height of fashion with the younger generation. "Greetings, Tuan," he said cheerfully. Beside him was a coconut-fibre bag, in which, I knew well, he had a new carving to show me. "Greetings, Tuan," Ida Bagus Putuh said also. "Greetings, friends," I said, and looked at them both.

Putuh, who knew that I was somewhat old-fashioned, was dressed in the old Balinese style, and was as smart as though he were paying a visit to a raja. He was naked to the waist, with long, beautiful muscles beneath his light brown skin. He wore a gold-threaded saput round his waist and hips girding his hand-woven silk kain. He had even stuck his kris in his girdle behind his back and its beautifully made wooden hilt projected above his shoulder. Putuh, too, wore a flower; it was in his head-dress above the middle of his forehead, but it was not an hibiscus flower but a yellow champak blossom. Its stronger, sweeter and more aromatic perfume pervaded the whole portico—the perfume of Bali—and it was already beginning to fade. Ida Bagus Putuh had a quid of sirih, betel, lime and tobacco, in his mouth, which was not so becoming, and at intervals he skilfully spat a jet of red liquid clear of the steps right into the courtyard.

"How long have my friends been here?" I asked out of politeness.

"We have only just come," was the reply, and this, too, was merely a polite formula. The two of them might very well have been sitting on the steps for five hours, squatting and smoking contemplatively with the inexhaustible patience of their race.

Ida Bagus is the title of those who belong to the highest caste of Brahmans. I had a suspicion that Putuh, though not half my age, was quite as old-fashioned in his way of thinking. In earlier days his family played a great part in his village and far beyond it. It produced many great priests or pedandas up to the time when the great disaster overtook Putuh's father. Now they were poor and lived quietly in Taman Sari and Putuh labored in the rice-fields like any sudra. But he had a dignity beyond his years, and, as I have said, he was of a conservative turn of mind and kept to the fine manners of the older generation. The Balinese in general have very little idea how old they are. Their mothers, after six or seven years, get the dates mixed up (and no wonder with the complicated Balinese Calendar) and then they give up counting. But certain events, of which more will be said later, occurred when Putuh was two; and since these events became a landmark in Dutch colonial history it was a simple matter to reckon Putuh's age. He was thirty-two years old at this time according to our reckoning and nearly twice as old if the days of the year are reckoned as two hundred and ten according to the Balinese Calendar.

Although Putuh was a modest man, and Tamor's intimate friend, he had taken care to sit a step higher, as was due to his caste.

I sent for coffee and lit my pipe, which never failed to excite astonishment and amused admiration in the Balinese. Both men now stared at me with open mouths. These people are adepts at registering wonder: their upper lips, arched in any case, curve right upwards, their nostrils dilate and their elongated eyes, which look sad even when they are laughing, take on a fascinated expression. "Mbe!" they say, full of amazement. "Mbe!"

Conversation began to flag, as it was meant to do. We circled round the object of their visit in many an elaborate phrase. As for Tamor, it was clear from the start that he had carved something which he wanted me to buy; but whether Putuh had accompanied him merely out of a liking for me was not so easy to discover. He sat and chewed, keeping his mouth open and smiling all the while—a rather complicated exercise—and now and again an anxious and intent look came into his eyes.

Tamor announced that he had brought Putuh with him on the back of his bicycle, and Putuh added to this that he had really intended coming by the motor-bus but fortunately Tamor, too, was going to my house on business of his own. The Government had made good roads by which the few cars of the Dutch officials and the native rulers could travel in all directions, as well as an occasional, fully loaded, rackety prehistoric bus. The natives, however, love their Japanese bicycles, and even women may be seen on them in their bright-colored kains with little packages precariously balanced on their heads.

"What has my friend got in his bag?" I asked Tamor at last, when I thought that full honor had been done to preludes and politenesses.

"It is nothing," he said modestly. "Only a bad carving."

"May I see it?" I asked.

He slowly opened the fibre bag, unwrapped a carving from a
piece of rag and put it down on the step near Putuh's naked brown
feet. It was a simple and vigorous piece of work—a doe and a stag
in the moment of coming together. An arrow had pierced the male
in the flank and both their necks were arched back in a way that
expressed anguish and the pangs of death. I looked at the two beasts
with emotion. Suddenly I was aware that I had once seen something
like it many, many years before. Then I remembered. It was Tamor's
uncle who had tried to carve them—in defiance of the style of his
day. The memory came back with a rush as I felt the smooth finely
worked satinwood in my hands.

"Has my friend ever seen a carving like this before?" I asked.

Tamor smiled in surprise. "No, Tuan," he replied.—"I must therefore beg forgiveness."

I had fallen in love with the piece on the spot and knew that I
should have to have it. But first there were many ceremonies to be
gone through. I praised the carving, while Tamor maintained that
it was bad and worthless, unworthy to stand in my house and that
he was a wretched beginner and bungler. Joy and pride in his work
shone meanwhile in his honest eyes, in which there was the inno-
cence of an animal. I asked him the price and he assured me that he
would take whatever I chose to give and that he would be happy to
be allowed to offer me the piece as a present. I knew that Tamor was
a good salesman and that, like all Balinese, he loved nothing better
than earning money to gamble away at cock fights. He was merely
counting on the fact that I would offer more than he would venture
to ask—and so it proved.

The deal concluded, Tamor knotted the money in the folds of
his silk girdle; but still Putuh had said not a word about the motive of his visit and it would have been impolite to ask him straight
out. Perhaps he had been unable to pay his taxes and wanted to ask
me for a loan, but in that case he would have come by himself and
secretly, not with Tamor. The conversation dribbled on. The rainy
season would soon be here. The heat had been bad for some days
on end, particularly when you had the sawahs (the rice-fields) to
plough. There had been a corpse-burning at Sanur, the next village
to Taman Sari, nothing to speak of, only simple folk who shared

the cost among them, about thirty bodies in all. There were a lot of squirrels among the coco palms and they had had to get together and frighten them off for a night or two with torches and clappers. The Lord of Badung had taken a girl of Taman Sari as wife, a Gusti from the lower nobility of the Wesjas. At next full moon there was to be a three-days' temple feast at Kesiman. The rice-fields did not yield as much as they did in the old days. The rainy season would soon be here and then there would be an end of the heat.

After we had canvassed all these little village topics, the conversation completely dried up. The Balinese think nothing of squatting through an hour or two in silence, and the gods only know what goes on meanwhile behind their placid foreheads. But I was still smelling of the iodoform and carbolic of the hospital and was eager for my bath. I begged to be excused. That was really only a joke, for properly speaking it was for my visitors to beg leave to go. They clasped their hands and raised them to their left shoulders and I withdrew to my little bath-house.

I had my bath and drank my home-made arrack. My servants brought me my meal to another balé—cooked rice and roast sucking-pig bought in the market, vegetables colored yellow with kunjit and flavored with various strong spices—papayas and pisang. After that I lit my pipe and lay in a bamboo chair to read the latest magazines. As Bali has a direct air-line with Holland, we are only ten days behind the rest of the world with our news. Sometimes it almost puts my brain in a spin when I think of our little island, so ancient, so unique, so like paradise in spite of every innovation, so unspoilt, being linked up so closely with the rest of the world by aeroplanes and large steamers and tourist agencies.

I read myself into a doze and did not wake up until my little monkey, Joggi, jumped on to my shoulder and began gently searching through my hair. The sun meantime had moved across the sky and the palms and bread-fruit trees in my garden threw long shadows. My cook's mother was crossing the courtyard with a palm-leaf basket containing offerings. I watched her—a lean figure with shrunken breasts—as she busied herself at my house altar and did those reverences to the gods which I, as a white man, did not know how to do. Now my house was assured of divine protection. The air had grown cool and the doves cooed in the cages suspended from the eaves.

An hour or two had gone by when I returned to the other house. It still smelt of champak flowers and Putuh still sat on the step chewing sirih. Tamor appeared to have gone. I went to the gate and looked for the bicycle. It had gone. I was sure now that Putuh wanted to borrow money of me. If you did not pay your taxes within two years, your fields were taken from you and put up for auction. I put my hand on his shoulder to reassure him. "Had my friend something to tell me?" I asked. He took his sirih out of his mouth and put it down on the step.

"I ought not to burden the Tuan with my trivial affairs," he said politely. "But I know that the tuan has a good medicine for sickness and I hoped that the tuan would give me medicine for my sick child."

"Which of your children is sick?" I asked, forgetting to address him with the formality beseeming his caste. Perhaps he took it for the familiarity permitted among equals, for his face brightened.

"It is Raka, Tuan," he said. "He has the heat sickness."

"Why didn't you bring him with you?" I asked severely. "You know that anyone who is sick can come to me in the sick-house."

Putuh looked at me with brimming eyes. His smile took a deeper meaning. It was the saddest smile imaginable.

"The child is very weak, Tuan," he said. "He would have died on the way. His soul is no longer with him."

Putuh had three wives, one of whom had left him. Of these three wives five children had been born. Raka was his eldest son. I knew Raka well. He was a slender little fellow, six years old, and a wonderful dancer. The Guild of Dancing of his village paid a celebrated teacher in Badung to give Raka lessons in dancing. They were proud of this child in Taman Sari and they hoped he would become a great dancer and be an honor to his Guild. And now Raka had malaria and was delirious; his soul had left him, and his father had been seven hours at least in coming to me and telling me about it.

"You are Raka's father," I said sternly. "Why did you not come to me before? Will you people never learn that you must go for the doctor while there is still time?"

Putuh let his head fall with an expressiveness peculiar to the Balinese. "Raka's mother is a stupid woman," he said. "She has no more sense than a buffalo cow. She sent for the balian and he gave

the child medicine. It is good medicine, but the child wishes to go
to his fathers."

The hopeless fatalism of this put me in a rage. I rushed for my
bag, and seizing Putuh by the arm I dragged him to my car, heaping
reproaches on him all the while. I could scarcely refrain from calling
the village doctor, the witch-doctor, the balian, a stupid old buffalo.
The native doctors can cure many ailments with their exorcisms
and herb lore, but in the case of many others they are powerless.
For malaria they decoct a brew from a bark which contains quinine,
but not enough quinine to be efficacious. Many balians came to me
in secret for quinine pills, which they then reduced to powder and
mixed with their brew. But the doctor of course was not so clever a
conjurer as that. As we rattled along in my battered Ford it occurred
to me that Raka might very well have died meanwhile and that the
soul of this child who was to have been a great dancer might by
now be astray in the darkness of the unknown. I could hear myself
upbraiding Putuh on and on without restraint and at the top of my
voice as we went noisily over the bridge which spans the abrupt
gorge at the end of my village. Putuh listened to me quietly and
when I had done he began to smile once more.

"What the gods will must come to pass," was all he said.

Raka was not to me just an ordinary patient. I had seen the child
dance the kebjar at a temple festival a short time before. What in-
tentness in his small face, what ancient wisdom in his eyes! On that
occasion the thought came to me for the first time that he must, as
the Balinese believe, have already lived many lives. I suddenly felt
that I could realize what ancestor was born again in the little Raka,
and who it was who had once more been made manifest in order to
return to the island once more and to live again—to live a new life
with the same sweetness and bitterness as the old, but with fewer
mistakes and aberrations and one step nearer perfection, and that
Balinese heaven whence there is no longer the necessity to be born
again. For moments together during that dance it seemed to me
that the little figure in the golden robe was not the child Raka, but
the older Raka, his forefather, the radiant, glamorous Raka of other
days—the man whom everyone loved, who had erred and been
punished and who had been purified by his own efforts, so that he

came back to earth not as a worm or a scorpion, but as a child and a grandson and a dancer as he himself had been. I loved little Raka as I had loved the other in earlier days; and the old car went far too slowly to suit my impatience.

My thoughts might be high-flown and beautiful, but my words to Ida Bagus Putuh the while were full of vulgarity and good Dutch curses. I saw nothing of the road and the landscape, although as a rule, even after thirty-five years in Bali, I never tired of gazing at the terraced rice-fields, the gorges and the distant vistas of palm trees. Putuh had put a fresh quid into his mouth and was silent for very shame at the white man's lack of control.

We passed through the town of Badung, which is also called Denpasar from its street of shops where Chinese, Indians, Japanese and Arabs have their funny little booths. We went by the hotel. One of the five radios of the island could be heard through the entrance which was on a level with the road. It sounded like Sunday in a Dutch provincial town and I shut my eyes in disgust. Putuh laughed and tried to imitate the sound of it, which seemed comical to him. "The white people's gamelans are not good," he criticized. As we passed the two great wairingin trees at the entrance to the main street, my thoughts were caught back into the past. The trees were still there, standing where they had stood years ago before the wall of the Puri, the palace of the lords of Badung. This was the spot where Bali had changed the most. There, where the palace court-yards had sprawled abroad their clutter of buildings and people, white-skirted girls were playing tennis and, farther away, Moham-medan salesmen from Denpasar were practising football. An auto-mobile full of tourists was coming round the corner.

I don't know whether it ever occurs to the Balinese that in this spot their lords, together with all their dependants, died a grim and proud death. They are forgetful folk, and perhaps it would be im-possible to be as happy as they are unless one had their talent for forgetting. The Dutch, however, do not forget how the lords of Ba-dung and Pametjutan, of Tabanan and Kloengkoeng went to their death. They remember it with admiration. Perhaps it has helped them to understand the soul of the Balinese and how carefully they have to be treated if they are not to be utterly destroyed. I like to believe that the death died by its lords has helped to preserve the island's liberty and its ancient laws and its gods.

A hundred yards or so from the hotel women were again to be seen bathing naked in the river, the houses again retreated behind their walled enclosures and the palms reared their tufted tips. Poultry, pigs and dogs scattered before the car. We turned into the next village and reached the expanse of rice-fields beyond it. North of Sanur my gasping conveyance was brought to a stop and we set off for Taman Sari across the rice-fields. I pulled off my shoes at the edge of the fields, for on the foot-wide banks of moist clay that part the sawahs it is easier to get along barefoot. In front of me yellow-green vipers darted rapidly into the water of the sawahs, where planting had just begun. The sky and all its clouds were reflected in the water among the tender green tips of the young rice plants. Taman Sari does not lie on a large road and so life there goes on as in the old days. Putuh walked behind me and the tread of his bare feet was noiseless and sure.

The sign woven of palm leaves that there was sickness in the house hung at the door of Putuh's dwelling. In the niches on either side of the gateway there were offerings to the evil spirits—sirih and rice and flowers—so that they should not enter the courtyard. Putuh and I entered, followed by my servant carrying my bag on his shoulder as though it was a heavy load.

The courtyard, surrounded with its various smaller buildings and balés, was clean and silent. Two or three well-grown black porkers scampered away in front of me. I had not wasted time putting on my shoes, although the village people laughed at me when I came along barefoot like a Balinese; but I was too impatient to spare time for formalities. Putuh, with punctilious politeness, murmured the usual excuses: his house was poor, dirty and stinking, and he begged me to forgive it. I was relieved when I saw only the sign of sickness at the gate and not yet the sign of death. Putuh called across the courtyard for his wives. One of them, the younger, came out of the kitchen with a baby in arms astride on her hip. Two little girls naked but for wooden pins in their ears stared at me, finger in mouth. The fighting cocks crowed from bamboo basketwork cages farther away in the yard. Putuh led me to a building of bamboo standing on a stone foundation, which was clearly the balé where his second wife lived with her children. A very old woman, probably Raka's grandmother, squatted on the bamboo bench with the sick child in her lap. Near her knelt his mother; she was a woman with a rather faded, Indian face, such as you often find among Brahmans, and young, firm breasts. Both women smiled anxiously as I bent down over the boy.

Raka looked bad. His lips were dry and cracked with fever and his flickering eyelids were closed. His arms were emaciated and the small dirty fists were limply clenched. He muttered ceaselessly in delirium. His forehead and forearms were smeared with a yellowish ointment, no doubt a remedy of my colleague, the balian. His pulse was quick and thin and his breathing was light and difficult. I saw at once that it was not malaria, or in any case not only malaria. As always with the sick in Bali, he was naked and only lightly covered with his little kain. The grandmother said something in a low voice to Putuh, who repeated it to me: it was not fitting that the woman should address the white tuan. "The child has not sweated yet. He is hot and cold, but he cannot sweat," Putuh said, smiling. It took me years to understand this Balinese smile. Sometimes it is seen on blanched lips and then it signifies great sorrow and perhaps even despair.

I soon found that Raka had double pneumonia. "How long has the child been sick?" I asked. The mother and grandmother took to their fingers and reckoned with a great effort. They came to an agreement on nine days. The crisis would soon be reached. "How did the sickness begin?" I asked, so as to be sure of my ground. Putuh hesitated before replying. What I wanted to know was what were the first symptoms, such as shivering, vomiting. I might have known what Putuh's reply would be. "Somebody cast an evil spell," he said in fact in a low voice. In Bali there are no natural causes of sickness. The sick must have been bewitched, plagued by evil spirits or punished for the misdeeds of an ancestor. Again the memory of the other Raka passed through my mind, while I tried to get medicine down the child's throat, and chivvied the women away to heat water and to fetch kains to wrap and cover the hot little body with and a kapok mattress for the couch. "Who would bewitch a little child?" I asked. "Raka is a beautiful dancer; everyone loves him."

"There are witches in the village," Putuh whispered. "I name no names."

He fixed me with an agonized expression as I got the needle ready in order to give the child an injection.

"If he is bewitched I will break the spell. You know that," I said in a rage.

"Everyone says of the tuan that he has great power," the grandmother said with awe; she came carrying a heavy earthenware vessel carefully in her arms. The sinews of her thin arms were like taut whipcord. The mother brought kains and cloths, bright in color but not too clean. I rubbed Raka's feet with salt, made him a hot compress and wrapped him up in everything I could lay hands on. Then I laid him down on the couch and the old woman crouched down again beside him. On the right of the house there was a smaller open balé, such as you see in every courtyard, where the daily offerings are prepared. Raka's mother cast one more look on the child, who had now ceased muttering, and then she squatted down there and began weaving palm-leaves together. It might be necessary to make more offerings than had been made so far—great and powerful offerings to the gods, so as to enlist their aid; and offerings to the evil spirits, so as to appease them. There are witches in every village of Bali. These are women, mostly old, but sometimes young, who league themselves with the powers of darkness by means of certain secret spells, handed down from generation to generation. They take the left-hand road, as the saying is. They acquire the power of changing themselves into lejaks, strange and sinister beings, who roam abroad by night, doing mischief and spreading misfortune. Often, while their bodies are asleep in their homes, the evil souls of such witches, transformed by magic, haunt the night as balls of fire. Nearly every Balinese has seen lejaks. One may smile—but I have myself more than once encountered such fire-balls at night, strange apparitions, that breathe and hover, and there are other white people in the island who have had experience of these inexplicable spooks. I did my utmost as a doctor to help little Raka; but I was not quite sure that it was only an inflammation of the lungs which I had to fight.

An hour went by in silence. Putuh had squatted down on the steps at my feet and I sat on a mat near the improvised sick bed and waited. There was some strong and inexplicable bond between this child and me. I had to stay until the crisis had passed, for better or for worse. Time came to a stop, as it sometimes does. My servant squatted at the far end of the yard near the basket cages containing the cocks, and hummed a tune which consisted of five notes and sounded melancholy, though it was intended to be gay. He was passionately fond of cock-fighting. The Government banned all but a few officially authorized cock-fights, since it wished to protect the Balinese against gambling away all they possessed. Nevertheless, many a secret cock-fight took place on the sly in the close-cropped meadows behind the villages. Absentmindedly I watched my man take a white cock out of its basket and caress it. Time had ceased to move. After an incalculable interval I heard a sound from the bundle of cloths on the bed. I got up quickly and looked at the boy. He had come to himself. His eyes were open and almost clear. Sweat was pouring in trickles down his face and washing the dirt from his light brown skin. With dry lips he asked for something to drink. Putuh himself jumped up and came back with half a coconut shell fitted with a handle. He put it to the child's lips and he drank the water eagerly. Putuh looked questioningly at me. "It is all right now," I said with relief. The grandmother raised her hands and murmured with thankfulness that the tuan could break any spell. She called across the yard and the boy's mother came and stood shyly near the bed, as though it was not her own child at all. She looked quietly at the boy. Raka smiled at her. Putuh did not speak to her, for he could not so far forget what was due to his dignity as to address his wife in the presence of a visitor.

"My little prince, you will soon be well again now," he said to the child. The grandmother stood up and embraced my hips with both arms—a mark of devotion which only an old woman could allow herself. "Raka will soon be dancing the kebjar again," I said with satisfaction. I freed the wasted little body from its hot wrappings and rubbed it. The fever was broken. His grandmother helped, while his mother merely stood there limply as though worn out by extreme exertion. His grandmother gently touched my hand when I bent over and looked at the child's face. "The tuan, too, has noticed whom he is like?" she asked with a knowing smile. Yes, I replied, I had.

"The tuan knew his forefather. The tuan is old too, he has come to the evening of his days as I have," the grandmother said. I was taken by surprise, for I had never noticed that I was old. I had forgotten, as the Balinese did, to count the years as they passed. Yes, I, too, was old and the past was dearer to me and nearer and clearer than the present. I put my hand on the old woman's shoulder, a sign of great affection which made her titter like a young girl.

It was already dusk by the time I had given them all the necessary directions and left the courtyard. My servant carried my magic bag tied to a bamboo pole and also a bottle of sweet rice wine which Putuh had given me. The village street was now full of life and movement, for the hour before sunset is a busy time. Men were taking in their cocks after having left them all day long outside the walls of their compounds to enjoy the sight of passers-by. Women returned from some errand or other with square-shaped baskets on their heads. Boys with long poles tipped with a bunch of feathers drove waddling ducks back from the fields. Girls put offerings in the niches at the gates. Everybody was intent on being safely home and settled down before darkness fell and released the demons and spirits. Men with sheaves of rice on bamboo poles, men with great bundles of hay, men with sleek, light-brown cows coming in from the fields. Idle young men with flowers behind their ears, hard-working old men, wise and wizened, all came along, one after another, with necks erect and bodies naked to the waist, walking with their incomparable rhythm. I am never tired of watching these people, and the way they talk and sit on their haunches and rise to their feet and work and rest. The bark of a dog, the smoke of the open kitchen hearths, the smell of cigarettes and champak flowers. The girls came with smooth wet hair from bathing, adorned with flowers. Here and there an oil lamp was already alight in a shop. A sound hovered in the air like the chimes of many bells in tune—it was the gamelan, the Balinese orchestra, which makes such finely woven music. The orchestra were practising their programme for the next festival in the large balé, the village town-hall and meeting-place. At the end of the village there stood a sacred tree, an ancient wairingin, as large as a church, with a dark dome of foliage and thousands of arching roots exposed to the air that gripped like iron and looked like iron. Beneath its huge cupola stood one of the six temples of Taman Sari; a double gateway, crowded with images of gods and guarded by demons, led into the first of its three courts.

Temples in Bali are not buildings: they are open enclosures surrounding sacred places which have been revered since the dawn of time. The great stone and wooden chairs and thrones stand there, and on them the gods invisibly seat themselves when the priests call upon them. I stood for a moment at the temple gate to let some women with large baskets of offerings on their heads pass by. The music of the gamelan sounded as I left the village and set off again across the rice-fields. I saw the Great Mountain in front of me now, veiled with bars of drifting cloud. The first bats were already on the wing and the cicadas made a merciless din. I looked forward to being at home again. I would sit and look at Tamor's deer and marvel at this piece of work which his uncle had begun and failed to carry out and his descendant had brought to completion. I remembered how the old woman had called me old and how it had made me laugh. But it was true that I had lived in the island a long time and seen a lot. I had known many people who were now dead and many who had been born again. I realized that I was harnessed to the cycle of things and a part of them. I had known the island when it was still fighting for its liberty, and I was there when it was conquered and got new masters in place of the powerful and cruel rajas of the old days. But it had altered little. There were bicycles now and motor-buses and a little modern rubbish in a few wretched little shops. There were a few hospitals and schools, and there was even an hotel where tourists were dumped for a three days' stay and then carted off again after seeing a few sights they didn't understand. But Bali had not changed. It lived according to the old law, resisting every encroachment. The mountain, the gorges, the rice-fields, the palm-clad hills were the same as ever. The people were the same as ever. They were the same people, from one generation to the next, cheerful for the most part, gentle and quick to forget; we should never understand them quite and never learn the secret of their placidity and resignation. Many of them were artists and they would always make new music for the gamelan and carve new figures in wood and stone and write new plays and dance new dances. But the gods did not change, and as long as they were throned in a thousand temples and inhabited every river, mountain, tree and field, Bali, too, would not change.

Yes, it was true. I must be old to think such thoughts. I stumbled barefoot along the low banks between the sawahs as I meditated on these things. In the midst of the fields there was a small temple, built when disaster and blight fell on the sawahs. At the gateway sat a man wearing a large round hat he had woven himself. I thought I recognized him. He was an old man and he waved his hand to me.

"Greeting, Tuan," he called out, in the sing-song of the old-fashioned folk.

"Greeting, friend," I said. "Greeting, my brother."

It was Pak, the father of Tamor, the sculptor. He was as old as I, gray-haired and toothless. He had to break up his sirih with a knife, because he could chew no longer.

"How are you, Pak?"

"I am content," Pak sang out. "My feet are content, my hands are content after my work. My eyes are happy when they look out on the sawah, and life is sweet."

I stood talking with him for a short time, chatting about this and that. My servant waited nearby, just a little impatient, for he wanted to go into the village that night and see the Shadow Play. He was in love and the girl would be there, and he would be able to make eyes at her and perhaps whisper a word in her ear. I am coming soon, my friend—just one moment. I am just going in through the temple gate to look out over the fields. They shone more brightly now than the sky itself whose reflection gleamed on the surface of the water. The first frogs were already croaking and from Sanur could be heard the dull regular beat of the kulkul, the wooden drum which calls the men together. I saw the shrine of the deity in the last rays of the sun. Three plates of cheap pottery, with a rather hideous pattern of roses, were let into the stonework at the base of the shrine and caught the light. Yes, there they were still and still well-preserved— these three plates which had played so great a part in Pak's life. I stood a moment longer, listening to the cicadas and the thud of the kulkul. The cool green smell of the growing crops came from afar. Raka will get well, I thought to myself. Pak raised his hand and waved me a friendly good-bye as I went.

"Peace on your way," he sang out.

"Peace on your sleep," I replied.

My automobile was waiting with a trusty and patient air on the road north of Sanur. A crowd, twenty strong, stood round it, eyes, mouths and nostrils expressing delighted expectation and astonishment. They were the young people of the village, and they cheered as my old bus grunted huskily and started off.

The moon was high in the sky when I got home. There shone the constellation of Orion, which they call the Plough here, and the Southern Gross. The night air of my garden quivered with the chirping and humming of insects and the zigzag flight of fire-flies. The air was cool and there was a sheen on the palm-leaves which made them look like narrow kris blades. My little monkey sat on my shoulder and went to sleep. The tjitjak lizards on the wall made a smacking noise and a large red-spotted gecko uttered its cry in a husky baritone. I counted—eleven times, that meant good luck. After that there was silence, the vibrant silence of tropical nights. As soon as I closed my eyes I saw Raka's little fevered face. Beyond it appeared the face of his ancestor—and Putuh and Pak and the cheap plates still unbroken on the little temple among the rice-fields. The old, old stories, touching and droll and proud and bloody. Many have died, but Pak lives on, the old peasant on the edge of his sawah.

I lit my pipe and got out some paper. Now I would tell all I could still recover of the days gone by.

He who is wise in his heart, sorrows neither for the living nor the dead. All that lives, lives for ever. Only the shell, the perishable, passes away. The spirit is without end, eternal, deathless.

(From the Bhagavad-Gita)

The Wreck of the Sri Kumala

PAK woke up when the cocks crowed at the back of his yard. He shivered under the blue kain with which he had covered himself and his eyes were still heavy with sleep. The room was dark, although Puglug, his wife, had left the doors open when she went out. Pak gave a deep sigh. He got up unwillingly and unwillingly went to his labors. But the day was favorable for ploughing, according to the calendar, and Pak got up from his mat just as the kulkul of the village sounded the seventh hour of the night. An hour more and the sun would step from his home and bring the day with him out of the sea.

The cocks still crowed lustily and Pak smiled as he picked out the voice of his favorite, the red one. He was still too young, but Pak could already see he had the makings of a fighter. Pak girded his kain about his hips and pulled it through between his legs so that it made a short loin-cloth. He groped about in the darkness for the beam and took down his knife and the sirih pouch and tied them to his girdle. His kain was moist and cool with the heavy dew. He had a hazy recollection of a confused dream. He felt his way to the other mat on the bamboo couch which stood opposite his own. The children were asleep—Rantun, who was seven years old, Madé, the next in age, and in the corner the bundle containing the baby, who had no name as yet.

Pak and his wife had made sure that they would have a boy this time. They had paid the balian eleven kepengs when the child began to stir in its mother's womb and he had promised them a boy. Pak had begun to build castles in the air and had thought out a fine name for him. He wanted to call him Siang, the light and the day. Then when Puglug disappointed their expectations by giving birth to another girl, they did not know what name to give the child. Probably they would simply call her Klepon, a name that several girls of his family had been given.

Pak sighed once more as he left the room and after hesitating a moment in the open porch went down the steps into the courtyard. The kulkul had stopped.

The women had lit a fire in the kitchen balé and Pak's father came following his lean shadow across the yard with a bundle of dried palm-leaves on his head and went across to the wall. Pak's uncle lived on the west side of the plot and his first wife, who could never be at peace with anybody, could be heard quarrelling already. But Puglug was unclean for forty-two days after the birth of her little girl and could not prepare any food for Pak. He had good reason to sigh. He was as sick of Puglug as if she had been a dish of which he had eaten too much. Three daughters she had borne him and not one son. She was useless and not even good to look at. He sat on his haunches on the steps and looked down ill-humoredly at his wife, who was sweeping the yard with a besom. The sky by now was a little lighter behind the tops of the coco palms and Pak could distinguish her heavy shape, as she bent and got up again.

Then he caught sight of Lambon, his young sister, coming from the kitchen and carrying a pisang leaf heaped up with cooked rice. Pak took it eagerly, sat down again on the steps and felt better. He put three fingers into the rice and crammed his mouth full. His spirits rose with every mouthful he swallowed. Puglug paused in her work for a moment and watched her husband, for whom she was not allowed to cook any food, while he ate, and then went on sweeping. She is a good wife, Pak thought to himself, now that his belly was contented with rice. She is strong and can carry thirty coconuts on her head. She is hard-working and goes to the market and sells sirih and foodstuffs and earns money. It is not her fault that she cannot bear a son. Our forefathers decided it so. He wiped his fingers on the emptied pisang leaf, threw it down on the ground and began carefully wrapping his sirih in betel-nut and adding a little lime to it. As soon as he had the strong quid in his mouth, so strong that the spittle ran down from the corners of his mouth, the world seemed a good place. He got up to fetch the cow from the shed and the plough from the balé where all the implements were kept.

Lambon, who had sat at his feet watching him eat, went back to the kitchen. Her small face looked pretty in the light of the blazing fire and Pak looked back at her for a moment and was proud of her.

Lambon was a dancer; she danced the legong at the festivals with two other children, in a dress all of gold and a crown of yellow flowers in her hair. She was beautiful; Pak could see that, even though she was his sister. She had not celebrated the festival of ripe maidenhood and yet the boys of the village stood in front of the house and drew in their breath with nostrils dilated when she passed. The whole family hoped she would marry a rich man when she was old enough.

But now that Pak stepped into the yard in the dawning light, he stopped still with open mouth. It looked as though the demons had made their home there all night. In many places the straw had been torn from the wall, which he had thatched with such care after the last harvest. Not far from the gate on to the road yawned a hole. A heavy branch had been broken from a bread-fruit tree and lay on the ground like a dead thing. Half the roof of the shed had been carried away. Pak stared at all this in terror. He could not understand it. He had never seen anything like it. He ran quickly to his father, who was old and knew more than he did. "Who has done it?" he asked, out of breath.

The old man was both lean and feeble, for his strength had been drained away by many attacks of the heat sickness. "Who has done it?" he repeated in a sing-song, as his habit was. It gave him time to think and to hit on a shrewd answer. Pak stared at him in an agony of suspense. He could positively feel the evil spirits about his ears. It was they who had played havoc with his yard by night.

"There was a storm from the west last night," his father said. "That is what has done it. I lay awake all night and there was lightning in the sky and a great uproar in the air." He began to smile with toothless gums and added, "The sleep of the old is light, my son."

At this Pak's terror gave way a little. "Perhaps we ought to make a special offering to Baju, the god of the wind," he murmured, staring at the gap in the wall. The old man pondered this at his leisure. "Many years ago," he said, "there was a storm like this. That time the pedanda ordered every household to kill a chicken for Baju. There were great offerings made and next day the sea cast up a ship, laden with rice and coconuts, which were divided up among all of us."

Pak listened in astonishment. "Mbe!" he said, deeply impressed. He examined the gap in the wall. "Shall I kill a fowl?" he asked. It occurred to him that now all the demons and spirits of the underworld could come thronging into his unprotected yard. The old man, who often knew what people were thinking without needing to be told, said, "Call your brother. We will mend up the hole with straw while you are on the sawah. When you come home you can build it up with earth. There is still some lime here too, to whiten it with. You must kill a fowl and we will offer it to the gods. But after that, go out to the field, for today is a good day to plough."

Pak turned about obediently, feeling consoled by the old man's measured sing-song. "The wife is still unclean and may not offer sacrifices," he muttered, however.

"You must kill the fowl and your sister and my brother's wives will make the offering and I will ask the pedanda what we must do."

Pak's heart was lighter, for the pedanda, Ida Bagus Rai, was almost the cleverest man in the world and nearly infallible. Even the Lord of Badung sent for him when he wanted advice. Pak spat out his sirih and went to the kitchen. "You must get a present ready for the pedanda," he said to the women. "It need not be anything very much, for the pedanda knows that we are poor. Lambon shall take it. And bring me a white fowl to kill."

Puglug, whose ears were sharp, had come up and stood leaning on her besom. Suddenly, without waiting to be asked her opinion, she burst out, "Why do you want to go taking great presents to the pedanda when the balian gives just as good advice for three papayas? Perhaps I, too, could tell you what happened last night if I was asked. I could have told you beforehand, for Babak was here only the day before yesterday and told me what the market women were saying.

The sister of Babak's mother saw a man with only one leg and a great pig's face and anyone with any sense knows what that means. If the balian were asked he could say what would be best to do. He would say that every man in the place should take a big stone and go with it to a certain house and stone a certain person, who is the cause of it all, to death. Killing a white fowl! And taking presents to the pedanda! You might think we were rich folk with forty sawahs. Or perhaps my husband has five hundred ringits buried under the house the way he runs to the pedanda just because there is a little hole in the wall. Naturally Lambon is glad to go to the pedanda's house, for perhaps she will catch sight of Raka there. I have noticed myself how her eyes darken if Raka only passes by, and that is a disgrace for a girl whose breasts have not grown yet——"

What Puglug went on to say was drowned in the squawking of the fowl which Lambon was carrying. Pak took it by the legs and went with it to the south corner of the yard. He would have liked to strike his unmannerly wife, who spoke without his permission, but he did not. She talked and talked—like a flock of ducks in the sawah, quack, quack, quack, whether she was asked her opinion or not. Oh, how sick he was of Puglug and how obvious it was that he ought to take a second wife.

He took his broad-bladed knife from the wooden sheath, which was stuck in his belt, and lifted the fowl high in the air.

"Fowl," he said, "I must now kill you. I do not do it because I wish you evil, but because I must offer you up in sacrifice. Pardon me, fowl, and give me your permission."

When this formality was concluded he held the knife level with the ground and swung the fowl so that its neck collided with the blade, and then he threw the bleeding creature down. It gave one cry and died. In the sudden stillness, a regular battle could be heard going on between Puglug and the uncle's first wife in the kitchen. They were a good match in their passion for chatter and gossip and in fluency of tongue, and Pak could not help laughing outright as he listened to the unintelligible clatter, which suddenly ended in loud peals of good-natured laughter. He had almost forgotten his fears. As he went past he gave his two younger brothers, who slept together on a mat in an open balé, a shake to wake them. "You must shovel out some earth and mix it with lime so that I can mend the wall properly tonight," he said, feeling that he sat aloft as master of the house.

Meru was wide awake at once. "As you command and desire, my lord," he said in the lofty language used to a raja. Pak gave him a friendly clap on the shoulder. He had had a great liking for his good-looking, light-hearted brother ever since the days when he had taught him to walk. Since then Meru had in a sense left him behind, for he could carve and had even made a doorway for the palace of the Lord of Badung. "Who is going to give you your sirih today, you idler?" he asked good-naturedly, and went on to joke about Meru's many adventures with girls. "Someone who is better looking than your wife," Meru replied, and this, too, was said in fun. "We shall see yet who brings home the best-looking wife," Pak said grandly. And as he spoke he was thinking of a particular girl, who had been in his mind for some time.

His spirits were quite restored as he led the cow by her halter out of the ruined shed, lifted the plough on his shoulders and set out. The old man, tottering at the knees, was already busy at the wall with great bundles of straw. It was late; the sun was rising. "Will my father think of feeding the cocks?" Pak called out to the old man politely. He was answered merely by a reassuring wave of the hand and a lift of the forehead with eyes closed—a gesture of friendly assent. And so Pak, with mind at rest, turned his back on the strange occurrences of this extraordinary morning and left the yard by its narrow gateway, peaceably preceded by his cow.

In the village street, where the walls of the compounds formed a long line, broken only by the high gateways, life was by now in full swing. The rays of the sun in the smoking morning air lay like silver beams athwart the tops of the palms and the dense fruit trees. A thousand birds sang at once. The large ribbed leaves of the pisang were transformed by the rising sun into bright transparent discs of green. Red hibiscus flowers bloomed round the house altar behind every wall. Women went by with baskets and mats on their heads, one behind the other, preceded by their lengthened shadows; and the one in front spoke under her breath without caring whether the next heard what she said. They stopped when they came to the wairingin tree and helped one another to lower the loads from their heads. Then they spread their mats on the ground and displayed their goods on them to the best advantage—sirih, cooked rice, ducks' eggs, garlic and spice. Puglug as a rule went to the market too, but now she had to wait until the days of her uncleanness were over before she might work again. Pak, as he went quietly along, shook off the thought of Puglug as though it were an ant. He loitered a moment in front of the house of Wajan, who was a man of wealth, and the cow came to a stop and began pulling at the short grass at the edge of the road. She was used to having to wait for Pak here. He stopped as though to see to his large round hat which he wore on top of his head-dress, and at that very moment a boy came out bringing

Wajan's cocks, which he put down on the grass to cool their feet.
Wajan had eighteen cocks and Pak only four; even this was more
than a man in his poor circumstances ought to have and Puglug
made many peevish comments on the fact. Since there was nothing
but the cocks to be seen Pak gave a tug at the cow's halter and said,
"We must get on to the sawah, sister," and went on his way.

Pak's father had been given two sawahs by the old lord of Pametjutan and he himself had got two more from the young lord Alit of
Badung. His were situated on the northeast side of the village and
the old man's on the north-west. As his father had not the strength
now for heavy work in the fields, Pak had to cultivate all four
sawahs himself; he had only one cow and his relations could not
give him enough help. The lord's gift of land had made a serf of Pak
in so far as he had to pay half the yield to the overseer of the lord's
land. Also he had to do any work required of him by the household
of the lords in the puris of Badung. But in return for all this he had
four sawahs, rich and well-watered land, heavy sheaves at harvest
time, green and fragrant silk before the ears formed. If he worked
industriously, the four sawahs yielded two hundred sheaves, with
two harvests every fifteen months. That brought in, for his share,
enough food for his family, enough rice for the festivals and taxes
and offerings, enough to pay friends of his for occasional help. And
in good years there was still a little over which he could sell to Chinese traders when ships put in at Sanur to take in a cargo. Pak had
prayed to the goddess Sri that the harvest might be a good one and
the earth kind and the ears full. He had let the water into the eastern
sawahs three days before, and that was why he had to start ploughing that day, for so it was laid down. Meanwhile the fields on the
west were nearly ripe; the water had already been drawn away from
them, and thus ploughing and planting on one plot alternated with
reaping and binding on the other.

Pak met other men from the village, who had come to work on
their fields, all along the narrow balks. They shouted a word or
two to each other—about the night's storm and the jobs they were
going to and coming from—without stopping to talk. His eastern
fields lay some way from the village and Pak had to get his cow and
his plough down the steep bank of a river and across the ford. The
path, trodden by bare feet, was slippery and the cow jibbed. Pak

called her "sister" and "mother," begged her pardon and tried to explain that the descent was unavoidable. Suddenly he heard girls' voices from the river and stared with open mouth. He had forgotten that he was later than usual and that he would meet the women on their way back from bathing. They climbed the steep bank one after the other, laughing and twittering like birds at sunrise. Pak's heart stopped. He had caught sight of Sarna among them.

He gave her a quick glance as she passed him, but he did not see whether she returned it. She smiled, but he did not know whether it was to him or at him. I ought to have put a red hibiscus flower behind my ear, he thought. But no, he thought immediately after, that would have ruined everything. It did not do to show the girls all you felt for them. He stood on the grass and grasshoppers jumped about him and he gazed after Sarna. She was young and strong and beautiful. Everything about her was rounded—her face, her breasts, her hips. Round, but tender and charming. His liver and his heart were big and full of sweetness when he looked at Sarna. Her hair was wet and her sarong too. She had a moist and heavy lock of hair hanging from below her headdress, as a sign of her maidenhood. She wore large earrings made of lontar leaves in her ears, like the rice-goddess Sri. When Pak made offerings to the goddess and prayed to her for a good harvest, he always saw her in his mind's eye as Sarna, rich Wajan's daughter.

He got his refractory cow to the bottom by the time that the girls had reached the top. They stood there in a gaily colored row shouting down to him and laughing, but he could not catch the drift of their jokes. He looked after them till they vanished across the rice-fields, and then went on, shaded by his large hat. The cool water refreshed his feet as he forded the river, and he was happy.

After ascending the other bank he soon reached his sawahs. They were deep in good muddy water, and although Pak had got up in a bad temper for work he now rejoiced in it. He got the plough in position, attached the cow to it and put his own weight, too, behind it. With bent knees he pressed heavily down to make the plough dig deeply into the soft, moist earth. The soil made a dull sucking noise as it rose and fell from the ploughshare. Pak loved this sound. He loved this earth. The mud splashed up and sprinkled him and the cow with cool drops which soon dried to a gray crust. White herons flew over and alighted to fish on stilt-like legs for the slender eels which throve in the sawahs. Dragonflies flickered past. The earth sucked and threw up noisy mud bubbles and was eased....

So the hours passed. When the sun was at its highest and the first four of the eight hours of the day had gone by, Pak stopped ploughing. His thighs ached, so did his arms. Sweat ran into his mouth. He felt a great emptiness in his stomach. Yet it annoyed him to have to leave his work to go home to fill his empty stomach with food. He put a fresh sirih into his mouth to appease his pangs.

Then suddenly he saw a small figure coming across the rice-fields with a small basket on her head. He screwed up his eyes. The white herons rose at her approach. Pak began to laugh—it was Rantun, his daughter, bringing him his dinner, though really she was still too small to undertake the tasks of a grown girl. She came along looking very solemn, dressed in a little sarong which flapped about her feet. She had little earrings in her ears and a long lock of hair fell straight down her forehead. It had not been cut yet, for Pak had never yet had enough money by him for the festival that he had to give when the pedanda cut this lock for the first time and blessed the child. Why, he had not even had his own teeth filed, though he was a married man and a full member of the village council. These festivals were put off from year to year in Pak's family. Perhaps in time he would be able to save enough money to get it all done at one go—the filing of his teeth, Lambon's ripeness, the cutting of the lock and the first birthday of the newly born child. Pak had a little money buried under his house, fifty-two ringits in all; it had been fifty-five before the last cock-fight. Puglug had made sharp remarks about men who gambled away their money instead of seeing to the burning of their mothers, and Pak had listened with a stolid face, knowing in his heart that Puglug was right. His mother had died five years ago and it was high time her remains were burnt. Pak was often secretly afraid that the unreleased soul of his mother would make itself felt in ways disastrous for the family. He had searched everywhere to find where Puglug hid her own money, her market earnings; but he had never found any of it and Puglug maintained that she had to spend it all to feed him well, as it was the duty of a wife to do.

While Pak's thoughts had been running on all the cares of which Rantun's uncut hair reminded him, the child had come up. Now she knelt down at the edge of the sawah and opened her basket. Earnestly and a little timidly she handed him a pisang leaf of rice and another of roast beans. Pak rinsed his hands in the water which ran from the neighboring field down into the sawah and began to eat. The cow cheerlessly pulled the grass on the narrow balk. When he had eaten his fill he gave Rantun what was left and she modestly ate it up. Rantun was a quiet gentle child and Pak was very fond of her in spite of her not having turned out to be a son. He put his hand on her shoulder and they sat thus for a time, motionless, silent and perfectly happy.

When he was rested and had enjoyed long enough the comfort of a full belly, Pak got up. "You are a good little woman and one day I'll give you a fine new sarong," he said, putting his hands round her. Rantun snuggled tenderly against them. Pak was grateful to his little daughter, but he had a great longing for a son. He could squat for hours picturing to himself all that he would do if he had a son. Daughters belonged to their mothers and later to the man who carried them off. A father had to have a son for companionship and to give him descendants. With his hand still on Rantun's tender little body he reflected that he needed a second wife to bear him sons, since Puglug bore only girls. At last he let go of the child and helped her to cut a long thin wand to catch dragonflies, which, roasted, are a great delicacy. Then with a sigh he turned again to the plough and the wet earth.

The sun was already declining when Pak heard a sound that made him stop and listen. The kulkul, first from Sanur, faint but insistent, and then from Taman Sari too, could be heard in deep rapid beats. Pak finished his furrow, but he paid little attention now to his ploughing. He was wholly absorbed in wondering why the kulkul was beating at that hour of the day. He could feel his liver swelling with curiosity. Hurry up all of you, come and help quickly, was the message beaten out by the village drums, as they reverberated over the sawahs. Work had ceased in every field. "What does that mean?" the men called to one another. "They're calling us in," others said. Pak was already unloosing the cow. "We have got to go," Krkek shouted across to him. He was an elderly, intelligent man, much respected in the village, and the head of various committees to do with the supply of water to the fields and the harvesting of the rice-fields. Pak, like the rest, left his work and drove his cow as fast as he could along the dyke and across the river to the village. The ford was thronged with gray buffaloes, light-brown cows and mud-caked hurrying men, eager to know what was up. Half-way up the river bank they met another lot of men coming from the village. "Turn back," they shouted. "We have to go to Sanur, we're wanted, something has happened." Most of them had brought the pointed bamboo poles, used as a rule for carrying loads, and some even had a kris in their girdles or a spear in their hands. "Is it a tiger?" Pak asked excitedly. Krkek laughed scornfully through his nose. "You can grow to be a very old man in the plains without ever seeing a tiger," he said patronizingly. "There are still some in the hills. I helped to kill one up in Kintamani." Pak made a sound of polite admiration with his lips. The cow pulled him back to the river; she wanted to be washed down after her labor as she always was. For a few minutes everything was turmoil, shouting and confusion. Then Krkek told some children to drive the cows and buffaloes to the pastures, and the men fell into single file and set off at a quick pace for Sanur.

There the roads were crowded with people, all making for the shore. At every yard gate stood old women carrying astride on their hips the infants entrusted to their charge. The younger women hurried along with the men, laughing and chattering, followed by their daughters. The boys of the village were a long way in front, kicking up a cloud of dust. Pak learnt from the clamor all round him that a boat had been wrecked on the coast. He laughed in amazement—this was just what his old father had said. He was as wise as the pedanda himself.

"The old man at home told me that already," he shouted to the man nearest him. Another burst out laughing at some thought that suddenly crossed his mind and the laughter spread. They could not go on for laughing, they shut their eyes and slapped themselves on the knee. They had all been frightened and now it appeared that Baju, the god of the wind, had wanted to do them a favor and had cast up a ship on the coast for them. They all had visions of rich wreckage, cases of goods, rice and dried coconut. Pak, who was hurrying along faster and faster, secretly felt that he had a good deal to do with the wrecking of the ship. His father had foretold it and he himself had killed his finest white hen for the god. He saw cause and effect in close and most happy sequence and he bothered no more about his broken wall.

The crowd parted for a moment to make way for the head man of the coast villages, the punggawa, Ida Bagus Gdé He was a handsome man, rotund and stout, with round eyes and a moustache. A servant held a Chinese paper umbrella above his head, although the road was completely shadowed by palm trees.

Pak could hear the surf before he saw it. Big waves were crashing on the beach, for it was high tide. They ran the last part of the way and then they all abruptly stood still and gazed at the sight that met their eyes.

The sea was breaking over a large ship, which appeared to be helpless. It had once had three masts, but two had gone overboard. The sails hung down in shreds. A few men could be seen on her, waving their arms and calling out; but the people of Sanur could not understand what they said. The waves broke in foam between the ship and the shore, and with each wave the ship was flung crashing upon the reef with so deafening a roar that some of the women put their fingers to their ears. Although the reef was only about a hundred paces from the shore it was impossible to wade out to it. Sarda the fisherman and two other men carried a jukung down the beach and launched it. They rowed out head-on to the waves, but they were flung back time after time and at last gave it up. As each wave retreated it left on the beach small packages of unfamiliar objects which had a strong and unpleasant smell. Some boys ran down and picked them up and ran back again screaming before the next wave thundered in. The women fell on the booty, laughing in their eagerness to know what it was. It was buffalo hides, wet through and softened by the water and stinking, and dried fish which the water had almost turned to a jelly. Pak picked up one of these dripping fish and wondered whether it could be dried again and still made use of.

And now the Chinaman, Njo Tok Suey, pushed his way through the crowd. He had a house in Sanur and traded with the boats that put in there. People laughed as they made way for him. He wore a sarong, as they did in Bali, but also a jacket and cap, like a real Chinaman. His cap was crooked and showed his shaven head. The crowd shouted with laughter. They had heard that Njo Tok Suey had a head as smooth as an egg, but they had never seen anything like it before. The Chinaman paid no attention to their merriment but pushed his way, puffing and blowing, to the punggawa. The two men were at once surrounded, for of course everybody wanted to hear what they said. Pak was disappointed at not being able to understand. "What are they talking?" he asked the knowing Krkek. "Malay," the other replied with the air of knowing every language in the world.

After speaking for a short while with the punggawa, the China-man stepped back and made a low bow. The punggawa, addressing the crowd, called out in a loud voice, "Bring everything you find and lay it down before me here. It belongs to the men on the ship and nothing of it must be taken."

There was a low murmur from the crowd. If the gods of the wind and sea cast up wet buffalo hides on the shore it was clear they meant them as a present to the people of the coast. Pak surrendered his fish rather unwillingly. He laid it reluctantly down on the heap of drip-ping objects which rose at the punggawa's feet. "It is only a heap of stink," cried out Pak's friend, Rib, who was a wag, and the murmurs of the crowd turned to laughter.

But the laughter died away when the punggawa ordered them to rescue the men from the ship. The punggawa had great power over the people of Taman Sari and Sanur and it was not an easy matter to defy him. His eyes were fiery and he had a loud voice that no one could disregard. The front ranks of the circle surrounding him un-obtrusively melted away, and a few of the older men muttered that they had no courage. It was not for poor sudras and rice cultivators to have courage; courage was the business of warriors and rajas of the Ksatria caste and self-sacrifice might be the duty of a Brahman, as Ida Bagus Gdé was. This at least was what Pak thought and the majority was of his way of thinking. Meanwhile the ship's timbers could be heard groaning and rending every time it was thrown on the rocks. The crew had stopped crying out and their silence showed the danger they were in. The Chinaman, Njo Tok Suey, stood beside the punggawa, not behind him as good manners enjoined, waiting patiently with his hands buried in his wide sleeves.

A small knot of men who had been standing together higher up the beach now came running up. They were the unmarried and younger men of the two villages and Pak saw his brother, Meru, among them. His youngest brother, Lantjar, was there too; he had got hold of a spear from somewhere and was waving his lanky arms. Suddenly all the men turned their heads, and a cry, started by the women, spread from mouth to mouth. "Raka," they shouted, "here's Rakal Raka, what are you going to do?"

Pak elbowed aside the man next him and then saw with a momentary shock that it was the wealthy Wajan whose ribs he had dug with his elbows in order to make his way to the front.

Raka had put himself at the head of the young men and was now knotting his kain into a loin-cloth. Raka was the handsomest man in all the five villages round and the best dancer in the whole lordship of Badung. He was the eldest son of the revered pedanda, Ida Bagus Rai, and all this combined to make him the hero of the villages. The girls' eyes darkened when he passed and the men could not help smiling and wishing him well whenever they saw him. When he danced he looked like the young god Arjuna himself, splendidly dressed, proud and beautiful.

At this moment indeed there was nothing of the glamour about him, except for the fine build and beauty of his body. He looked like any peasant with his kain knotted between his thighs as he darted into the sea behind a retreating wave which left only its froth on the sand. "Who will come bathing with me?" he called out laughing, and some did actually follow him up to the edge of the foaming breakers. Meru was one of them, Pak saw, and he had only just time to seize Lantjar and drag him back as the next wave was breaking on the beach.

A universal shout went up when the young men vanished in the water, for the people of Sanur were afraid of the sea where there were sharks and sword-fish. Only a few fishermen were on intimate terms with it and its unreliable god Baruna too, who exacted many offerings from them. Pak stood perfectly motionless, his arm about Lantjar's slender shoulders, which were quivering with excitement. Everyone was motionless as they gazed dumbly at the water. When the wave had spent itself they saw Raka and his companions already some way out wading towards the wreck. The ship's sides were stove in by the next sea that struck it and a man climbed to the highest part of the ship that was still above water and waved what looked like an old faded flag.

"What is that he's waving?" Pak asked the omniscient Krkek, for it might well be a cloth endowed with magic powers.

Krkek screwed up his eyes and considered the matter. "It is the sign the Dutch carry in front of them when they fight," he said at last.

"Mbe!" said Pak, impressed by the extent of his knowledge. Even he had heard of the white men who ruled the north of the island and even on the south of it had overthrown the lords of Karang Asem and Gianjar. Far-travelled men who passed through Taman Sari had surprising things to tell of these Dutchmen. Pak had never yet seen one and he knew that the sight of them would terrify him. It was said that the white men were as tall as giants and tremendously stout and strong. Their eyes were without color, but they could see quite well, although they moved about like blind men, as stiffly and clumsily as figures of stone. It was uncertain, too, whether they had souls and whether any part of the divine nature dwelt in them as it did in every living creature in Bali. They had come years ago from Java, the only foreign land Pak had ever heard of. They were clever and powerful beyond measure, probably because they had fair skins like many of the gods. Although this was all in the highest degree strange and alarming, it appeared that the Dutch did not do any harm. They respected the gods of the island and the ancient laws. They could cure sickness and were unwilling to have people killed. It was even said that they would not allow the rajas on the conquered territories to carry out death sentences. They were immeasurably rich and occasionally one of their ringits got as far as Taman Sari. On it was stamped the picture of a long-nosed, full-breasted but not unpleasant-looking goddess.

Pak ran over in his mind all he knew about the white men, while Lantjar's trembling body leant against him. He plucked up his courage, for it was possible that some of them might come to land from the wrecked ship and that he would before long have to face the sight of them. In a few minutes he even forgot his anxiety for his brother Meru, who was struggling on through the water, although he had nothing to gain there.

A great cry rose from the crowd when Raka and the handful of men with him reached the ship. The force of the waves had decreased, for the tide seemed to have passed its height. The sea had fallen already and revealed the vessel's battered hull. Two jukungs put out; one was Sarda's and the other belonged to another fisher-man, Bengek, who owned the neglected sawah next to Pak's.

The people laughed when they saw what Raka was about now he had reached the ship. He and some of his companions each took one of the shipwrecked men on their backs and then waded through the surf and foam of the ebbing water to the shore. The laughter grew louder and louder as they came nearer and ended in general uproar and stampeding when they reached the shore. Pak's extreme apprehension was relieved when he saw that the men who were carried ashore on the sandy beach were not white men after all. They were Mohammedans and Chinese and in wretched plight. The women uttered cries of pity, particularly over the youngest and handsomest of them, who was bleeding from a wound on the forehead and seemed to be unconscious. They came round him in a circle, but made way when a woman who was taller than the rest went up to the wounded man and crouching beside him took his wounded head on her knee.

It was Teragia, the only wife of the beautiful Raka; she was greatly revered in the village, though she was still young and awaiting the birth of her first child. The good powers were so strong in her that many could feel them radiating from her. She had the gift of healing and of finding springs, and sometimes the divinity entered into her and spoke through her mouth. She was of high caste, as Raka, too, was, and the doctor of the village was her father and had taught her many formulas and magic prayers. She wiped the blood away from the young man's forehead with the corner of her sarong and look-ing round murmured a few words to her servant who knelt beside her. The girl folded her hands in token of obedience and ran off. She quickly returned with a small basket out of which Teragia took a number of large leaves. She put them on the wounded man's fore-head, whereupon the bleeding ceased and the man opened his eyes and sighed. The women uttered exclamations of astonishment and admiration and pressed closer.

Meanwhile Njo Tok Suey had taken charge of the other newcom-ers. They had brought a few saturated cases with them which they put down on the beach. One of them was a Chinaman too, and he gave a few brief orders in Malay. He was clearly the master of the ship, although he was in a wretched state; his clothes were torn to

rags and his chin trembled. Njo Tok Suey supported him and conducted him to the punggawa. The men of Sanur and Taman Sari
crowded round, eager not to miss a word. Unfortunately the interview between the punggawa and the two Chinese was carried on in
Malay. Krkek pressed forward as near as he could, and even put his
hand to his ear to hear better. He translated bit by bit what the three
men said for the benefit of his fellows.

"He says his name is Kwe Tik Tjiang. He says he is a merchant
from Bandjarmasin. He says his ship is called *Sri Kumala*."

There was some laughter at this, for they thought it funny that a
ship should have a name like a person. Krkek motioned to them to
keep silent so that he could hear.

"He says they anchored yesterday off Bijaung. The storm came
up and beat against the ship and broke the anchor cable. He says
the ship was tossed to and fro like the shell of a coconut. He says
they have been in great terror. They did not think they would ever
reach land alive."

Krkek paused to listen attentively as the Chinaman raised his
voice and embarked on a long sentence.

"The Chinese Kwe Tik Tjiang thanks the men for rescuing him
and begs leave to retire. He is in pain and very tired," Krkek then
went on.

The crowd murmured its sympathy. The Chinaman stood a moment longer in silence, and looked at the people round him with
inflamed and swollen eyes. They stared back at him, for it was not
every day that they saw a shipwrecked merchant from Bandjarmasin. The Chinaman tottered as he turned to go, and Njo Tok Suey
quickly gave him his support and led him away in the direction of
his house.

"He looks like a dead sea-urchin," the wag Rib said as soon as
their backs were turned. There was some laughter at this and the
punggawa turned round in annoyance.

"Men of Sanur and Taman Sari," he said, "I order you to mount a
guard to see that nothing is taken from the ship. Whatever is thrown
up on the shore is to be stacked up here, so that the Chinese, Kwe
Tik Tjiang, loses nothing. Any man who acts contrary to my orders
will be severely punished and fined a heavy penalty."

"So be it!" the men murmured obediently.

The punggawa searched the crowd with his eyes. "Where is Raka?" he asked. Everyone turned round to look for him.

Raka was standing behind Meru, Pak's brother, the carver, with his arms affectionately about his shoulders, resting after his exertion. The water ran from his long hair, and though he laughed he looked exhausted. The punggawa stepped up to him, followed by his servant with the indispensable umbrella. "Raka," he said in a loud voice for all to hear, "I shall inform your exalted friend, the lord of Badung, of your gallantry and readiness. His heart will rejoice to hear a good report of you."

The men again expressed their assent. Raka raised his clasped hands to his shoulder to thank the punggawa, who then left the beach. The crowd was already dispersing. Some had followed the Chinese to Njo Tok Suey's house, where they now stood gaping inquisitively over the wall. Others followed the women, who took the young Javanese into the village. Pak stood irresolute. He was proud of Meru for the part he played in the rescue and for the friendly way Raka had leant upon him. Nevertheless, he resolved to warn his younger brother as soon as he got home.

"What we want now, brother," Raka said to Meru, "is a big jar of palm wine."

"My belly feels as cold as if I had drunk the whole sea between Bali and Lombok," Meru replied as they went off hand in hand. Just as Pak was about to follow them, he felt a hand on his shoulder.

"You, with a few more, had better mount guard here," Krkek said. "You are honest and sensible and I can trust you. I will send you food and firing, and perhaps I can pick out a few friends of yours to join you, and then you won't need to be afraid of the darkness. You shall be relieved at the first hour of the day."

Pak's heart sank as he heard this, but Krkek was the most important man of his village and president of the water committee. He was not a man to gainsay. Even the raja had no power over the subak and had to accept its distribution of irrigation water. Nevertheless, Pak attempted a feeble excuse. "I am too tired to stay here as watchman," he said. "My eyes will shut whether I like it or not. I was at work in the sawah since sunrise. A tired man makes a poor watchman."

But Krkek would not listen, for it would have compromised his authority if he had revoked his order. "We have all worked in the

sawah, brother," he said mildly as he walked away. "My wall has a
hole in it, big enough to let in all the demons, if I don't mend it up
before night," Pak muttered in an aggrieved tone, but Krkek shut
his ears and vanished behind the palm trees that bordered the village. Pak looked round about him. He was almost alone on the
beach. There was only Sarda, and a few more with him, crouching
beside his boat and chewing sirih. But they were fishermen of Sanur
and used to the sea. A few of the ship's crew were lying down about
two hundred paces away. They looked strange and ill-disposed. The
natives called out to the foreigners and invited them to join them,
but they shook their heads and a little later got up and went away.
Pak sighed. He was horribly afraid of the night. Already the sun was
sinking in the west. The tide had gone out and the sand extended
nearly as far as the wreck and only tiny wavelets nibbled at the
shore. A group of children had waded out to the wreck, where they
frolicked about with a great show of daring and kicked the water up
with their feet. No more hides were floated ashore, but the smell of
them pervaded the air and made the watch still more unpleasant.

Pak now felt for the first time how tired he really was. His thighs
ached as he squatted beside Sarda. His eyes were haunted by all he
had seen and whenever he closed them he saw the ship being battered against the reef. The sky was as green as a ripening rice-field
and then as red as the gums of a child at the breast, and then darkness fell. The kulkuls in the villages announced the beginning of the
night with short rapid beats.

Pak chewed sirih. His mind wandered, and his head felt empty.
A long time passed in this way. Then the women, whom Krkek had
sent from the village, arrived with ample supplies of food—rice and
vegetables and meat roasted on spits. The light of torches shone
out behind them among the palm trunks, and men came with palm
wine in hollow bamboo stems. Pak was glad to drink the sweet tuak,
for his throat was dry. Dasni, a Sanur girl, squatted in front of him.
She had looked at him more than once at the Temple festival and the
last rice harvest. She was not exactly ugly, but she had a dark dirty
complexion and her breasts were too heavy. She crouched submissively before him and handed him food, gazing attentively while he
chewed to see whether he enjoyed it. "I hear you have got a child,"
she said. "I hope it will be strong and beautiful and like its father."

Pak muttered a word or two in acknowledgment and after wiping his fingers threw away the empty pisang leaves. Dasni remained where she was while the other women got ready to go. At the last moment she took something from her girdle and thrust it into Pak's hand. Then she vanished with the others. Pak looked to see what she had given him. It was a bulb of reddish garlic. He smiled. So Dasni was anxious about him and wanted to be sure that he would be safe during his watch.

When the women had gone, the men continued discussing the day's events as they sat on their heels round the nearly burnt-out torches and at last they began to yawn. Sarda collected broken coconut shells and driftwood and made a fire. The night was lonely, cold and perilous. Pak crossed his arms and put his hands round his shoulders to warm himself. Some of the watch had vanished and others fallen asleep. Pak stared into the darkness and his fears gained on him. He drew nearer to Sarda. After a time the fisherman fell asleep with his head on his knees and Pak succumbed also. If lejaks or evil spirits emerged now from the darkness he was defenceless. He quickly felt for the garlic in his girdle which Dasni had given him and rubbed himself all over with it, so that the smell should keep away the evil spirits, and finally stuck the rest in the bored lobe of his ear. Now he felt safer, for it was well known that the demons could not endure the smell of garlic. He gave Sarda a cautious shake, but it did not wake him, so he left him alone; it was not right to be too tough with people when they were asleep, for then their souls might not have time to return to their bodies. He felt a great longing for his sleeping bench safe within the walls of his house and for the warmth of his wife Puglug, who was good even though not beautiful, and for the little girls on the other bench. Nobody came stealing stinking fish or going off with the stranded wreck. I told Krkek, thought Pak, that my eyes would refuse to stay open; and he let them close. He dreamt of the gap in his wall and saw it mended again and better than before. He heard a great noise in his dream coming from the battered ship. He also saw men going by in the light of the watch fire and the face of the Chinese, Kwe Tik Tjiang, bent over him and his foot in a black shoe kicked against him. Pak turned unwillingly on to the other side and ceased dreaming. He heard the cocks crow and opened his eyes. The kulkul beat the last hour of the night. He thought he was at home and groped about him, but the things he touched were unfamiliar. He was chilled to the marrow and biting cold nipped his feet. It was this that woke him and he sat up. Now he recognized Sanur beach where he had been when he fell asleep. It was still dark but for a strip of greenish light where sky and water met. This was the herald of Suria, the sun-god, who would soon leave his house bringing the day with him. The tide was high again and sang with a loud voice and flung the waves up to Pak's feet. He jumped up in terror, and looking round for the others saw that they had vanished. The fire had burnt out; there were only a few embers in which Pak warmed his hands. His limbs ached, his stomach was empty and his heart had gone small. He pondered for a minute or two and then decided to go home. Even Sarda had gone. He had his sawah to see to; that was his job—not watching over the battered ship of a Chinaman who looked like a dead fish and left the smell of dead fish behind him on the shore. The spirits had already retreated and all wandering souls had returned to every sleeper's body. Pak felt full of courage again as he set off on his way home.

But his heart stood still when he saw a light coming over the water. His feet became as heavy as stone and he could no more move them than if he had been bewitched. He tried to remember the incantation his father had taught him when he was a child to protect him if he encountered lejaks or spirits. But his head was as empty as a pot with a hole in the bottom. The light came nearer and he heard the sound of a laden boat grating on the sand. Pak was relieved to see a man get out of the boat and come towards him with a light in his hand: it was at least nothing supernatural. It was just an ordinary lantern, a wick in the hollow of a bamboo stem, covered with a dried pisang leaf. Pak waited. At first he thought it was Sarda, but when he recognized who it was he began to feel afraid once more.

The man with the light was Bengek, the husky fisherman. He was a hideous man with a bad throat which prevented him speaking out loud, though he was not dumb. On the contrary he had a quick and bitter tongue. His mother was reputed to be a witch, with the power of turning herself into a lejak, and for that reason people avoided her son as far as possible. Yet no one dared to offend Bengek, for all feared him and his mother.

"Peace on your coming," Pak therefore said with trembling lips, and Bengek stood still and shading the light with his hand peered into the darkness.

"Is that you, Pak?" he asked in a hoarse whisper. "Are you not on your sawah yet, you industrious neighbor?" he asked again. Pak decided not to notice the sarcasm, but to behave as though this encounter at the edge of the sea in the last hour of the night was nothing out of the common.

"Where are you coming from?" he asked therefore—the usual question on meeting anybody.

"From my mother's house," Bengek replied.

"Were you not on the sea? I saw your light on the water," Pak said.

"Why do you ask, then, you clever Pak?" Bengek said.

"I was told to keep watch over the ship," Pak said. It sounded more imposing than he had meant it to. Bengek came close up to him and shone the light in his face.

"And have you kept good watch to see that no one stole the ship and went off with it in his sirih pouch?" he asked hoarsely. Pak stood his ground in the odor of garlic and felt fairly safe.

"Had you been to the Chinaman's ship?" he asked.

The fisherman made no answer. He turned back to the shore, where the outline of his boat grew slowly more distinct. Soon he returned with a wet box on his head as though he were a woman. As he passed Pak he remarked casually, "And if I had been to the Chinaman's boat, what would you do then?"

Pak caught him up, for he felt his liver grow hot with anger.

"I should denounce you to the punggawa," he said breathlessly.

"No, no, my brother, you would not do that," Bengek replied. Pak felt for the knife in his girdle, and standing in the husky fisherman's path he commanded, "Put the box down. I must see what is in it."

"Fish I have caught," Bengek whispered in a sing-song. He put the box down at Pak's feet contemptuously, as though to say: I dare you to open it. Pak did in fact feel that poisonous sea-serpents and things with prickles might bite his hands as soon as he groped under the lid. "Take up the box and follow me to the punggawa," he said all the same, trying to speak in Krkek's authoritative manner. Bengek caught sight of the knife in Pak's hand and squatted down beside the box. "Come, brother, let us consider the matter," he said. "I tell you it would be very mistaken if you denounced me to the punggawa. And you know why, too."

"Why?" Pak asked with a tremor, for he knew the answer already.

"Because it would do you and your family no good. If I choose, your cow will fall sick, your fields will dry up and your children die."

Pak raised his hands in horror and shut his eyes. He knew how Bengek and his mother got power over people and money from them by such threats and how some who had not given way had suffered for it. He did not know what to say and he wished his father was there, for he had the wisdom of the evening of life.

"You have seen me come from the sea with a basketful of fish I have caught," Bengek said. Pak considered this and said nothing. What were the Chinese foreigner and his miserable ship to him that he should put his family in peril?

"I have seen you come from the sea with a basket of fish you have caught," he said obediently.

Bengek laughed and caught hold of his hand to pull him down to the ground beside him. "Wait a moment," he said. "As you are my friend I'll show you what I have caught in my net."

Pak could not resist his curiosity. He crouched down and watched open-mouthed while the fisherman opened the case. Bengek lifted out three bundles of seaweed from which he slowly and carefully unwrapped three plates. Then he held his lantern close to them and let Pak see the treasure in all its splendor and beauty.

What he saw was white plates with a garland of roses on them, so life-like that you felt you could take hold of them. Pak put out his forefinger and touched the flowers timidly. The plate was cold and smooth and the roses were painted or rather, in some magic way, united with the white porcelain.

Pak had seen plates before. The Chinese, Njo Tok Suey, had two hanging on the wall of his house and it was said in the village that they were worth more ringits than could be counted a thousand times over on the fingers of one hand. Plates like these were let into the base of two shrines of gods in the Temple of the Sacred Wood. And the lord of Badung had had the back wall of the large balé, where he received important guests, adorned with them. Pak had heard of them first from Meru, and then he had himself gone with many other men from Taman Sari to Badung to marvel with open mouth and round eyes at this priceless treasure. But plates like these three had never been seen by anyone in Bali.

"Have you any more?" he asked incredulously as he looked into the box.

"No," Bengek answered, and shut down the lid. But with that one fleeting glimpse Pak had seen the gleam of silver, as though of fishes' scales or of many ringits. Bengek lifted the case on to his head and turned to go. "The plates," Pak called out. The fisherman did not look round or pause.

"The plates are for you because you are such a good watchman. And the fish I caught are for me," he said, and his hoarse whisper mingled with the sound of his bare feet on the sand.

Pak stayed crouching over the plates. My soul is wandering in a dream and sees things that are not real, he thought. Then—how long after he did not know—the kulkul beat the first hour of day. Daylight had come without his knowing. He cautiously put his hand out to the plates. He was wide awake and they were real. The birds sang and soon the road would be full of the people of Sanur. Pak snatched up his treasure in a panic and hid it within his dew-soaked kain and then took the nearest path that led to the rice-fields. It skirted the village and not a soul was to be seen. It seemed to him that a whole year had passed since he left his sawah the day before. He did not know yet what Bengek's present portended. Squatting down at the edge of his sawah he took the plates carefully from his kain and breathed on them and polished them. The rising sun was reflected in them and the roses looked like real flowers. Only the raja possessed anything like it. His chest throbbed and thudded like a gong, as he turned the plates about in his hands. There were some marks on the back which he examined closely, straining his eyes and wrinkling his forehead. They had no resemblance to the letters in the lontar books he had learned to read. Probably they were characters of great magic power. Otherwise how could such delicate and fragile ware have come whole and unbroken to Bengek's net, when a great ship like the Chinaman's burst asunder and broke up? He did not know whether the powers of good or of evil dwelt in the plates. Pak considered this and looked about him. His eye fell on a mound in the corner of his sawah on which some offerings lay, dried by the sun. He had heaped up the mound the day he let the water into his field, bringing shovelfuls of earth from three points of the compass in turn to form an altar for his offerings and prayers.

This spot was under the protection of the Goddess. The earth of his field, blest by her, was of sufficient power to break any spell that might, for all he knew, be inherent in Bengek's gift. Taking his knife from its sheath he began digging out the earth at the foot of the mound. It was soft and muddy and easy to dig out. When the hole was large enough he bedded the plates into it and closed the earth round them and smoothed it down.

"O Goddess," he said, "I offer you these precious plates. Make them pure of evil influences and bless my field so that its soil shall be fertile and the ears full and heavy."

The tjrorot sounded its hollow wooden note in the distance. Pak set off home to fetch his plough. He had left home a poor man yesterday. It was as a rich man he returned. Richer than Wajan, Sarna's father. His secret lay big and warm in his heart, like a steadily glowing fire.

The Puri

A FLOCK of white pigeons rose from the ground and circled high above the puri of the lord of Badung. The silver bells on their feet gave out a whirring tinkle of metallic sound, like the voice of a white cloud at noon. The gray pigeons in their red cages cooed as they tripped to and fro. A large kasuar, which had been searching the grass for food, extended its long neck, thrusting it this way and that as though it had too tight a collar. Muna, the slave-girl, laughed and let her hands fall for a moment. Bernis, the most beautiful of the lord's wives, bent back her head and looked up into the sky. She shook out her hair. "Well?" she asked, without taking her absorbed and dreaming eyes from the flock of pigeons up in the sky. Muna began zealously combing her mistress's long hair again. She drew it back strand by strand; it was sleek and fragrant and shone with coconut oil.

"Then she was clever enough to arrange matters so that she was bound to encounter him," Muna went on quickly. "She put herself right in his path as he went to his cocks. He did not so much as glance at her. She said: 'Greetings, my lord and master,' turning her eyes away. 'Greeting, Tumun,' he said, and walked on. She ran after him and pulled at his sarong. 'My lord and master has had no sirih from me for a long time,' she said. My mistress ought to have seen how the lord behaved then! He paid no attention at all—he looked straight through her, like this"—Muna copied the lord's contemptuous look and squinted with the effort—"he paid no more attention to her than if she had been a dead dung-beetle in his path. He simply went on and left her standing there—the vain, silly creature. All the women laughed her to scorn."

"What a shameless woman," Bernis said, "to make herself cheap. You can tell that she is a beggar's daughter."

Muna had ended her task. "I have heard," she said, "that she was a whore at Kesiman and had to go about with her breasts covered until the Anak Agung Bima brought her into his palace." She drew a palm-leaf basket towards her, in which were white cambodia flowers, tinged with pink. Taking here and there a single hair she wound it about a petal to hold it fast. It looked as though the flowers were scattered carelessly over her black hair. "My mistress is the most beautiful of all. She will bear a strong and fine son and the lord will raise her up to be the first of his wives," she chanted.

"Hold your tongue and don't talk nonsense," Bernis broke in. Muna went dumb with fright and cowered down with the instinctive movement of one who was used to being beaten.

"Go," said Bernis. "Leave me alone, I cannot endure your chatter." Muna took the comb and basket and vanished down the steps. Bernis laid her head in her hands, for she wished to give rein to her sadness. She had been wedded to the young lord Alit for twelve months and still she had not had a child. In her last month, too, her hopes had been dashed and it was long since her lord had visited her. It was a strange thing that all his twenty-two wives were childless. And yet the courtyards and all the other dwellings of the puri swarmed with children; all the court officials, the servants, the slaves and all the numerous retinue of the palace—they all had children. Only the dwellings of the lord's wives were silent; only in them there was no sound of small feet. Bernis caressed her own skin to sooth its longings. She held her breasts in her hands to still the ache of an unfamiliar pain. Then she let her hands fall and restlessly pulled her sarong tighter. "Muna," she called out. Apparently Muna had been watching her from a distance, for the next moment she was once more on the steps of the portico. "What is my mistress's wish?" she asked with a virtuous expression. Bernis drew the girl towards her and put her arm round her. "You are growing up," she said cajolingly. "It will soon be time to look out for a husband for you. Have you been looking about yourself yet?" Muna giggled and looked coy. "Is it the gardener, Rodia? Or the keeper of the white cocks? Yes, it is he, I know. He has a moustache and looks like a noble. He blows out his nostrils like a horse whenever he catches sight of you." Muna hid her face in her mistress's lap and murmured shyly into this secret recess. "Who is it?" Bernis asked, lifting up the girl's head with her hands on her hair.

"Meru, the sculptor," Muna whispered with lowered eyes.

Bernis reflected on this. "Your taste is not bad," she said slowly.

"He has no eyes for me—he has too many girls," Muna whispered. She had the face of a little monkey and the prettiest and nimblest of hands.

"You are too young. Wait a year," Bernis said chillingly. There was silence for a time. Muna took Bernis's hand and played with it.

"With whom did the lord spend last night?" her mistress asked abruptly. Muna's mouth twisted in a droll grimace, but she did not reply at once. She left her mistress on tenterhooks.

"With Ida Bagus Rai, the pedanda of Taman Sari," she said at last while her eyes danced with amusement. Bernis did not appear to see the joke.

"The pedanda is a nice man and a very holy one," she said with a sigh of relief. "And Raka's father," Muna threw in quickly. Bernis looked at her reflectively to see what lay behind this. "It is taking a liberty to gossip about the lord's friends," she said loftily.

Muna pouted and said no more. The pigeons wheeled and alighted with a rustle of wings in one of the eastern courtyards. Bernis watched them absent-mindedly. All this part of the puri had been built by Chinese and was roofed with Chinese tiles. The back wall of the portico where they were sitting was lined with large greenglazed tiles, the same as those which adorned the wall round the palace. Bernis's dwelling was one of the most splendid of all. It stood on a tiny square island enclosed by runnels of water and flowerbeds. The lord honored the most beautiful of his wives in every possible way, and gave her the position that became noble birth. But he had not chosen his first wife, who had to be of his own caste. Muna tried to read the expression on her mistress's face. "There are men who are fonder of the old lontar books than of women," she said meaningly. Bernis was not angry; she merely sighed. Boredom descended upon her, like a gray bird with widespread wings.

"What can we do to pass the time?" she asked idly.

Weave, Muna suggested. Go to the pond and look at the waterfowl. Turn out the chests and try on all the sarongs. Fetch palm-leaves and plait dishes for the offerings. Sleep until it was time to dress and watch the dancing in the chief court. Bernis shook her head. Muna pushed the gilded stand towards her on which were all the ingredients for making sirih—the silver casket of sirih-leaves, lime in a little wooden box, a box of beaten silver containing tobacco, chopped betel-nut on a pisang leaf. Bernis pushed the tray away again. For some reason the lord did not like his wives to chew and make their teeth brown, as other women did. And so Bernis denied herself this consolation, in which even the poorest of women indulged. "I did not know there was to be dancing tonight in the puri," she said listlessly. Muna began at once upon all she had heard about it. "It is the dancers from Taman Sari," she said eagerly. "They are coming to dance the baris. The lord has given them new robes and they are dancing to express their thanks for them. Over three hundred ringits the robes cost and they say that there is real silver on the baris crowns. They say, too, that a girl is going to dance at the same time as the men, but that I cannot believe. It would be improper," Muna said primly. "The nymph ought to be played by a small boy as she always has been. But the Taman Sari dancers always must invent something new, and that is why such an idea came into their heads. We shall see what the lord will have to say to it if Raka really brings a girl with him."

"Who is the girl?" asked Bernis.

"Lambon, a poor sudra's daughter. No bigger than a gnat. I saw her dance the legong at the feast of the Coral Temple," Muna replied. Bernis scarcely heard her.

"A crown with real silver . . ." her mistress said slowly. "Raka will look beautiful with a silver crown," she added.

"Yes, he will look beautiful," Muna said. Then they both fell silent and gazed at the runnels which enclosed their island.

A thousand people went in and out of the puri. Buildings were crowded together in innumerable courtyards; balés full of household articles, weaving stools and sacrificial vessels; the dwellings of the wives, relatives, officials, servants, slaves and their families. Watch-towers flanked the entrance to the main courtyard in which visitors had to wait until the lord received them. His own house was in the second court, and the large reception balé in the back wall of which were the plates, that excited such great and universal

admiration. The house temple in the north-east wing was a beautiful building with images of stone in its wooden shrines and with
carved doors showing Vishnu on his bird, Garuda. Here, too, was
an island surrounded by running water and bridges on three sides
leading to the temple doorway. There was a mosaic of shells on the
steps. Everywhere there were trees, coco and betel palms, cambodia
trees with gray branches and bright flowers, champak trees, dark-
leaved and tall. Tall grasses were planted between the paths, and
flowers too. A balé in the fourth court was given up to the fighting-
cocks, of which Lord Alit alone possessed forty. The whole place
was alive with birds and beasts that were kept as pets. There were
the kasuar and his mate, vain and ridiculous creatures, pigeons of
every sort, small green parrots with red breasts, which were caught
in the west of Bali, and white cockatoos from the neighboring island of Lombok. Monkeys tugged at their chains or roamed about
free to work what mischief they liked. There was a large number of
small, rough-coated horses in open sheds, and buffaloes for drawing
waggons rubbed themselves against the palace walls. Black swine of
alarming fecundity ran loose with their litters and dogs, poultry and
ducks were beyond counting. A large leguan and three huge turtles
were in cages near the largest kitchen balé in readiness for the next
feast. There were rice barns and threshing floors for threshing the
grain; there were numbers of cooking balés and provision stores and
balés for preparing sacrificial offerings and balés in which were kept
the figures for the Shadow Play.

The lord Tjokorda Alit was seated cross-legged on a couch in his
house. It was fairly light there, for the door on to the portico stood
open and the Chinese architect had had large glass windows put in
the opposite wall, like those in the palaces of the great sultans of
Java. On the cross-beam of the roof lay offerings and many books—
writings engraved on narrow strips of the leaves of the lontar palm.
An oil lamp hung nearby, with a fringe of blue glass beads round the
shade, a present from the Dutch Controller, Visser.

The lord was only of middle height and there was a flabby and
unfinished look about his face as well as his body. As his skin was
remarkably light in color, his courtiers and his wives told him that
he was handsome. But his looks did not please him and he knew

that he was ugly, uglier even than a simple sudra, to whom hard labor gave strength at least and muscular limbs. The lord was often over-whelmed by a vehement disgust with himself, particularly when he had his handsome friend Raka with him.

Alit's eyes were half closed and he was pulling at his opium pipe. A boy of about nine years of age crouched at his feet. He was called Oka and was a distant relation of the lord's, the son, by some father or other, of one of his wives, a woman of no caste. He had adopted the boy. Oka's small face was bent over the flame of the opium lamp at which he was carefully roasting an opium pill, ready for the next pipe. The drug's bitter-sweet smell filled every corner of the room, and the fumes made the child's heart thump and his forehead drowsy. Without opening his eyes Alit handed the smoked-out pipe to be filled again. He kept Oka almost constantly at his side because the child was quiet and seldom spoke; and the lord loved above all things to be silent and to think. It was this, no doubt, that gave his eyes their strange and almost suffering expression, like that of people who know too much. But for the moment Alit felt happy and lightened of care, borne aloft by the soothing opium trance. An ever-widening clarity opened up new perspectives before his closed eyes and it seemed to him that he could now comprehend those mysteries over which he had pondered with the pedanda of Taman Sari the night before. "One says: I have killed a man; another thinks: I have been killed! Neither one nor the other knows anything. Life cannot kill, life cannot be killed." Long series of verses in the noble language of other days passed through his mind, echoing their wis-dom in resounding words. "End and beginning are only dreams. The soul is eternal, beyond birth and death and change." He gave his pipe to the boy to fill once more. It was the fifth and last, for he never exceeded this number at one time. So long as he smoked all was good and his mind at peace. At other times he was often over-come by a melancholy for which there was no real cause. He was young, rich, powerful. He had many and devoted wives, many loyal and gifted advisers and rice-fields stretching farther than the eye could see. His only trouble was that sometimes he found no object in his life—as though it had stopped still or as though he had been bom with a soul tired out by too many reappearances on earth.

A shadowy figure with clasped hands appeared in the open door-way. It was one of the gate-keepers from the first courtyard. "What do you want?" the lord asked with annoyance.

"The punggawa of Sanur is waiting in the outer balé with two Chinese and requests an audience."

"Send him and his Chinese to Gusti Wana," Lord Alit said irritably.

"I did so, master. The minister heard the punggawa and told him to bring the matter to the lord's own ears. He sent me here." And now there appeared in the portico behind the gate-keeper several bent figures and a murmur of voices could be heard from which Alit understood that his high officials had come to beg him to receive the punggawa. He gave his pipe to Oka and rose to his feet. The punggawa is a busybody, he thought. He thinks himself a tiger, but he is no bigger than a cat. In one corner of the room there was the figure of a courtier carved in wood and painted in sombre colors, designed to hold the lord's kris. Oka took the kris from the hands of the wooden figure and gave it to his master, and the lord put it through the back of his girdle and then advanced into the portico among his counsellors. Gusti Wana was there with the rest, a little man who easily became excited; also Gusti Nyoman, the steward of the yield from the rice-fields and the lord's revenue, Dewa Gdé Molog, captain of the guard, garrison and arsenal of the puri. The last was a man of fine words and very proud. There were further three of the lord's relations, who had gained admittance to the family through one or other of his wives and claimed kinship as cousins or brothers-in-law. They had long-winded titles, fine names and no influence. Alit looked over the company with a smile and silence fell. Suddenly they all began talking at once and explaining the punggawa's predicament. The lord put up his hand and again they were silent.

"Why did you not send the punggawa to my uncle? You know well enough that village disputes of his do not interest me.

"The Tjokorda Pametjutan is old and sick and complained of being in great pain this morning," Gusti Wana said. "No one could ask of him to deal with difficult matters."

"Is it then a difficult matter that the punggawa wishes to intrude on me?" the lord asked, still smiling. The best he could hope was to find the zeal of his officials entertaining and rather funny, but as a rule it wearied him to such a degree that he yawned until his eyes watered. He sat down on a raised platform which Oka had spread with a finely woven mat. "Bring the punggawa and his Chinese here," he ordered the gate-keeper. By receiving them in the portico of his own house instead of in the large reception hall, he showed that he did not take their business seriously. The courtiers placed themselves cross-legged behind him and the punggawa entered the courtyard followed by the two Chinese. All three advanced with bodies politely bent and stopped at the foot of the steps. Just as the punggawa was about to speak, an aged little man flitted past him and crouched at the feet of the lord. This was Ida Katut, the lontar writer and storyteller of the puri. He had the face of a field-mouse and an insatiable curiosity to hear and see and note all that went on. Afterwards when he came to recount what he had gleaned, the lord often laughed aloud as he recognized the people Katut had, so to say, devoured and whom he now reproduced with all the peculiarities of their walk or voices and the vanity or submissiveness with which they entered his presence.

The punggawa came this time without his umbrella, for he had left his servant behind in the first court. The two Chinese were dressed for this solemn occasion in the dress of their country, long robes of gray silk and short coats without sleeves. It was apparent that Njo Tok Suey had lent his friend a dress to put on, for it was several inches too long for the merchant of Bandjarmasin.

Njo Tok Suey, in order to make himself more impressive, had put spectacles on and they excited great astonishment, for the courtyard had meanwhile filled with people who, unable to resist their curiosity, seemed to beg condonation by the humble and submissive way they drew near. They squatted all about, the fathers with their children between their knees as though they were watching a play.

When the punggawa began in sonorous tones to make a set speech, Ida Katut winked and blew out his cheeks. Alit caught his drift and suppressed a smile, and then listened absent-mindedly to the punggawa's account of the wreck of the *Sri Kumala*. But after a time the words fell on his ear merely as empty sound and the verses of the Bhagavad-Gita again took possession of his mind: "He who is wise sorrows neither for the living nor for the dead . . ." A murmur from his retainers reminded him that he sat in council, and his attention was finally recalled to the matter in hand by a nudge that Ida Katut roguishly gave his feet on the sly. He was just in time to hear the punggawa's summing-up: "And therefore I beg your lordship to give ear in your goodness to the complaint of the Chinese, Kwe Tik Tjiang, and to resolve the matter, for I am only a stupid man and incapable of giving judgment."

The two Chinese now stood forward and began to talk rapidly. Njo Tok Suey, who was already known to the lord, spoke for both, since the merchant from Borneo spoke an unfamiliar Malay dialect. Ida Katut unobtrusively pointed to his left cheek. Alit saw what he meant. This other Chinese had a large wart on his cheek from which grew five long hairs. Once more he suppressed a smile. He was grateful to Ida Katut for trying to enliven the tedious duties his position imposed.

"Your Highness," Njo Tok Suey began, "my friend has a complaint to make against the people of Taman Sari and Sanur. He asks that they shall make good the damage they have done him. He begs that the people who rifled his ship shall be punished for it and made to pay a fine in compensation."

The lord with an effort brought his attention to bear on this tiresome business. He was enraged with the punggawa for confronting him with these smooth, unfathomable Chinese, who made him think of the yellow vipers on the sawahs. "We have heard already from the mouth of the punggawa that your ship was a wreck before it struck. It was the god's pleasure to handle you roughly and it would be better if you asked your own priests the reason for it. The people of Taman Sari and Sanur have nothing to do with your misfortune."

"My friend went back that very night to relieve the watch, although he was sick and weak. When he boarded his ship again he found that much was missing from it. Many people must have been there with axes and knives and have carried away everything of value," Njo Tok Suey said in a submissive voice. The other Chinese grinned at this account of his misfortune and his forehead contracted in wrinkle after wrinkle below his black outlandish cap. Something about this exaggeratedly smiling face displeased the lord. He knew his fellow-men and his heart either went out to them or turned away from them at first sight.

"The punggawa reports that he had a watch put over the ship, although he was in no way bound to do so," he said with a note of impatience in his voice.

"The punggawa's watch were sleeping like armadilloes when my friend arrived on the beach," Njo Tok Suey said modestly.

The punggawa expanded his chest and said, "I posted a watch because I knew that Badung long ago agreed in an important letter to the Dutch to waive its right of salvage and to respect the ownership of wrecked ships. But I cannot prevent the watchmen sleeping when they are tired."

A spasm passed over Alit's face at this reminder. It was true, he reflected, that he had given the Dutch power over the laws of his kingdom. He had put his name to many letters under pressure from the white men's envoys, who were as ready with the tongue as with the pen. They had threatened him with armed force, persuaded him with smooth words and promised him protection against attacks of hostile neighbors. The knowing Gusti Nyoman from Buleleng had befogged his brain with a mist of words. The lords of Tabanan and Kloeng-kloeng had submitted to the same demands. Even his uncle, the Tjokorda of Pametjutan, with whom he shared the rule of Badung, had persuaded him that it was better to make small concessions to the white men rather than have them invade the country with cannon and armed force. Alit had signed his name and tried to forget. But whenever he was reminded of it, it gnawed at his heart; it was like a tiny invisible worm eating into his pride. The courtiers stirred resdessly to and fro and spoke in low voices. Only Wana, the minister, and Katut, the lontar writer, understood the foreigners' language. The rest did not know what the Chinese wanted, but they saw clearly that it was something unpleasant.

"You Chinese, whose names I have not retained," the lord said loftily, "I have heard what you said and now I speak to you. The men who live on the shore brought you out of danger on their backs. They watched over your ship and your goods were stacked on the beach and not touched by anyone. If they took wood and iron from your dead boat, they were only exercising a right that my forefathers gave them and that has been theirs for many hundreds of years. And as for you," he said in his native language, turning to the punggawa, "you would do well not to remind me of the Dutch. Badung has not submitted to the foreigners. You are my father-in-law and my friend and the head of five villages, and you ought not to make yourself the spokesman of these foreign Chinese and their paltry affairs."

"That is so," the courtiers said, but the punggawa's lips went white with anger; though he folded his hands and inclined himself. The two Chinese whispered hurriedly together. The lord relaxed again after he had spoken. Sometimes he felt he was a weakling in the sight of his forefathers, and his heart, in spite of his resolute words, was feeble and incapable of great wrath. He no longer listened as Njo Tok Suey began to speak again, for his ear had caught the sound of a tumult in the outer court, the pattering of many bare feet and merry shouting and loud laughter. He bent down and whispered in Oka's ear, "Go and see whether Raka has come." The boy slipped away with hands clasped. When Alit turned to the Chinese again Njo Tok Suey had ended his remarks and was silent. Ida Katut stole a look at his master, and Alit turned a questioning look to his first minister.

"The Chinaman says that he sailed under the Dutch flag, with his ship's papers in order and under Dutch protection. He repeats his request to be compensated for his plundered ship. That at least is his expression. He is an impudent rascal and has two faces," Gusti Wana ended on his own account.

"At what do you put the damage you have suffered?" the lord asked with a frown. It was obvious now that the Chinaman from Borneo needed no interpreter. Putting his hands in the sleeves of his robe he said fluently:

"My loss cannot be estimated. I must return to Bandjarmasin a ruined man, without ship, money or goods. My boat was still good enough and I could have made her seaworthy again with a little labor and trouble. The people of the coast have completed its destruction. My losses are greater by far—but I will be content with two hundred ringits in compensation."

When he had spoken, there was a brief pause, during which Oka resumed his place with an embarrassed air at Alit's feet. The lord bent over him expectantly. "The people of Taman Sari have come with their gamelan," Oka whispered. "And Raka? Is Raka in the puri?" the lord asked quickly. "Raka is not with them," Oka replied, laying his hand on his master's knee as though he needed comfort-

ing. The sun already marked the last quarter of the day and dusk
drew on.

"Kwe Tik Tjiang," said the lord, suddenly remembering the name
of the impudent and unpleasant petitioner, "as you had the Dutch
flag on your ship and as in spite of this the gods allowed you to be
wrecked, you can see for yourself that it is not holy and has no power
whatever. But if, as you say, the Dutch are your friends, I advise you to
go to Buleleng and ask for your two hundred ringits from them."

With this the lord stood up, for his patience was at an end. The
Chinese, however, took a step forward and said, "I am only a poor
humble trader and cannot enforce my rights. But the Resident of
Buleleng is well disposed towards me. He will use his power to see
that I have my rights, for he has been put over the island by his
queen and what he commands is done."

Such insolence as this, accompanied by bows and submissive
grimacing, sent the blood to Gusti Wana's head. But before he could
speak, the Dewa Gdé Molog leapt to his feet, and, losing all control of
himself, sprang from the platform and stepped up to the Chinese.

"Our kings are inferior to no kings in the world," he said in a loud
voice. "Whoever insults them shall be punished with death. No one
gives us commands and no one is allowed to smirch our honor. We
are not afraid of the Dutch! Let them come with their cannon and
their guns. We have cannon, too, and our soldiers can shoot, and
when the Tjokorda sends out his holy kris and they see the sign of
the lion and the snake, more than six thousand warriors will come
with their spears and fight for Badung."

Dewa Gdé Molog was endowed with a loud and resonant voice,
he was a warrior of the Ksatria caste and a rash, hot-tempered man.
He could read no lontars and his jokes, when he had been drinking
palm wine, were broad and unrestrained. But his strength and his
boastful talk gave him influence over the men. He had spoken in Balinese, or shouted rather, and to the farthest walls of the courtyard
the men stirred and murmured their agreement. Even Ida Katut's
hand went involuntarily to his kris. But he soon let his wrinkled
hand fall and looked at the ruby-adorned hilt which projected
above the lord's shoulder. It was the holy kris, Singa Braga, with
the signs of the Lion and the Snake, on which Molog had called. It

made his lord's irresolute face seem even more irresolute. Alit's face showed that his captain's outspoken words had wounded him: his own pride lay deeper, encased, hard and difficult of access. "It is foolish to waste proud words on a Chinese pedlar," he said wearily. Gusti Wana looked disapprovingly at his lord. Where can Raka be? Alit wondered impatiently. "The council is ended," he said, and turned to go. The whole affair, which turned on such a trifle as two hundred ringits, seemed to him so utterly unimportant and petty. Where can Raka be? he thought. His heart was gripped with suspense; the whole day would end in nothing unless the sight of his friend gave it radiance and meaning. He was almost inclined to pay the Chinese the money merely to be done with it. But at that very moment he heard Kwe Tik Tjiang saying, "I will tell his Highness the Resident of Buleleng what the lord says."

It was a humble but unmistakable threat. The Chinese bowed, smiled and waited. All looked at the lord and waited for his reply.

At this moment the gate-keeper crossed the court and whispered a message to Oka which he repeated to his master. The lord turned away impulsively and walked quickly through the gate leading to the outer court.

"My minister, the Gusti Wana, will resolve the matter," he said over his shoulder to the punggawa who stood irresolute. Raka appeared on the steps and bowed to the lord with folded hands.

"Will my lord forgive me for being late?" he asked in the formal style. Alit quickly laid his hand on his shoulder.

He had forgotten the Chinese as completely as if they had never existed. His eyes shone and he expanded his chest with relief. "It does me good to see you," he said familiarly, and putting his arm round Raka's shoulder he led him away. "Tell me what you have done all day," he said. "I have been terribly bored and only waiting for the evening."

"Are you in a bad mood?" Raka asked with the same familiarity, for the ceremonial style was merely a joke between them, which they kept up for the courtiers' benefit. By the time they entered the house, in front of which the tiresome conference had taken place, the Chinese and the punggawa, too, had vanished as though the earth had swallowed them up. Only Ida Katut still lounged on the steps, humming to himself. The lord took Raka in and Oka shut the door.

"Tell me something," Alit said, sitting down cross-legged beside Raka on the couch. "In the puri the day is empty and the air stands still. What adventures have you had meanwhile?"

"I went to the temple," Raka said. "We all took offerings, so that our dance may go well. Before that we rehearsed a long time, for we are doing something out of the common, and the gamelan players were all astray."

The door opened and the servants brought in sirih and young coconuts with the shells cut off them. They drank the cool milk which had a delicate sourish taste, and Alit himself prepared the sirih for Raka.

"And so you have done nothing all day but make offerings and rehearse the dance?" he said with a smile.

"No," Raka replied at once, smiling also.

"Why were you so late?" Alit asked abruptly. "In your life something is always happening. I want to have my share in it."

"You need not envy me. I had troubles at home which detained me," Raka said. The word "troubles" sounded oddly from his smiling lips.

"What kind of troubles?" the lord asked.

"My wife has miscarried of the child we were expecting. She bled and I had to stay with her."

The lord was silent. Then he said, "You will beget another child."

"Many children from many wives," Raka replied gaily.

"What does your wife look like?" Alit asked suddenly.

"She is taller than most women, nearly as tall as I am. Her face, too, is large and her hands. But she has eyes like a roe deer's and there is great power in her."

"I have heard that," Alit said. "She found out where the punggawa should dig his well. Do you love her very much?"

Raka laughed and clapped him good-naturedly on the shoulder. "Love is a word from the old poems you read. In real life there is no love. Men come together like apes and birds. It is sweet sometimes to play with a woman, but the wind blows and there is an end of it. I cannot imagine what you mean when you speak of love."

"And your wife?" Alit persisted. There was a frown on his brow and his eyes were unlit beneath the heavy lids.

"I married her because my father wished it. She is a great help to me now that my mother cannot see well. Also our families have always been connected. I respect her very highly—almost as if she were a man on the same level as oneself. She would please you," Raka added with a smile. "Besides, she understands the old ways of speech and reads about times past in the lontar books."

Alit considered Raka's answer for a few moments. He appeared to be pleased with it. He signed to Oka and the boy fetched his pipe and began preparing the opium. Alit took the first pull and then of-fered the pipe to Raka. He shook his head. "Before dancing I must not eat nor indulge in the joys of opium," he said.

"Like a priest before the morning prayer?" said Alit, laughing. Raka made a face. He imitated a pedanda muttering Mantras and moving his fingers. Suddenly he broke off and became serious.

"To think that I might once have become a pedanda," he said uneasily.

Alit quickly put his hand on his knee. "You are still young and no drop of knowledge has ever penetrated your brain," he said con-solingly, with a trace of condescension and also of envy. He signed to Oka. "Bring the baris dress for Ida Bagus Raka. He shall change his clothes in my house," he ordered. The boy slipped from the room. It was invaded for a moment by light and sounds from without as the door opened and shut.

There was coming and going all the time in the courtyard. The inquisitive spectators of the conference had gone and others had come and squatted down in their place. At one moment some fowls had strayed in, too, and been shooed away with laughter and clap-ping of hands. Now a crowd of servants appeared, carrying halves of coconut shells with wicks burning in the oil. They hung the lamps here and there along the walls and from the eaves and chased away the shadow of night. Below in the first court there was already a gay and expectant crowd in the light of row on row of lamps, for the people were streaming in from many villages to see the dance, news of which had been borne on the breeze. Old men and young; women with flowers in well-combed, oiled hair, accompanied by all their children and with babies on their hips or in their arms; young girls, in a state of eager excitement, with gay shawls over their shoulders against the chill of the night. The men of Taman Sari set up the instruments of their gamelan orchestra at one end of the space reserved for the dance and the gilt carving shone whenever servants went by with more lamps. Those who could find no room in the courtyard crowded in front of the main entrance of the puri. Small boys with flowers stuck behind their ears, cigarettes in their hands and much finery on their sarongs climbed up on to the walls. Women vendors spread their mats and their provisions outside in the light of the small lamps, and many of the people ate, and when they had done threw away the leaves, which were immediately licked clean by the dogs. Ida Kutut threaded his way through the crowd like a wood-beetle. He kept his ears open and his wrinkled face beamed with the joys of eavesdropping.

The dancers were already waiting up in a balé screened by hangings. It was besieged on all sides by an inquisitive crowd, surging and swaying and spying in through every gap or hole in the curtains. Mothers lifted their children up and showed them the two dancers who played the minister and his funny servant to give them a foretaste of the laughter to come. In the middle of the balé, shielded from view by the men, sat Lambon, bolt upright in her gilded robe, like the small wooden image of a goddess; she was delighted by the prospect of dancing and by the fragrant smell of the champak flowers she wore on her crown. Her aunt sat beside her; she seemed to have left her volubility at home. Probably she was overcome by the splendor of the palace. From time to time she plucked at Lambon's robe or said something to her in a whisper. The famous teacher from Kesiman, who had taught her dancing, sat on Lambon's other side. His long hair, already going gray, was knotted up under his head-dress and he wore a short black coat with sleeves, which gave him the air of a courtier in ceremonial dress. He seemed to be anxious and chewed sirih to compose his mind, although it was rather hard work for his toothless gums; but he was too vain to grind his betel-nuts beforehand, as old people did.

Among the gamelan players sat Pak in a state of eager suspense. He had put on his best kain and wore a hibiscus flower behind his ear. He had, too, a new red saput about his hips, a present from Puglug. As he did not possess a kris, he had brought with him a short knife in its sheath, which he had stuck in his belt at the back. But all this was nothing to the splendor of his head-dress, for the gamelan guild had bought new ones from their common purse, purple and richly embroidered with gold flowers, which rivalled the gleam of the instruments, and made the players feel that they were quite as smart as the dancers in spite of their new and costly dresses.

Pak squatted expectantly beside the large gong which it was his part to beat. His fingers were stiff and clumsy from his labors in the field; they were not adapted for the delicate bells and other metal instruments on which the melodies were played. Nor was his ear true enough to beat the large drum which led and gave the time to it all. But he loved music with a slumbering love, just as though its notes were a soft cushion he could fall asleep on. The gong was easy to manage, and he had learnt how to beat it when he was still a little boy who sat between his father's knees.

Once he got up and went to the dancers' balé to see his little sister, on whose account he felt a throb of agitation, for among the older members of the gamelan there were persistent undercurrents of disapproval of a girl's dancing in the same dance as the men: it was wrong and unseemly because it had never been done before. He pushed the hangings aside and tried to attract her attention over the shoulder of her teacher, but she did not smile; she merely returned his look with a solemn gaze as though she actually were the nymph she represented in her gorgeous dress. Even to Pak she seemed no longer to be the same girl who brought him his rice that morning and carried water in her torn sarong. He loved his sister with almost the same paternal love as he felt for his daughter Rantun.

The arena for the dance was marked off by spears and flag-poles from which hung lamps of a foreign sort that Pak had never seen before. They were not made of wood and had no basin to hold the oil and wick; they were made of glass and cast almost too brilliant a light. He regretted that Krkek was not at hand to explain the phenomenon to him.

Instead he now caught sight of his wife Puglug squatting in the front row of the spectators with her two daughters in front of her. They had a piece of sugar-cane which they sucked alternately in a sociable way. Puglug was very smart in a new yellow sarong with a pattern of large birds. Pak wondered where she had got the money for it. It annoyed him to see that her breasts were uncovered, which meant that bats and vampires could suck her milk. Apparently she had left Klepon, the newly born infant, at home in its little hammock crib, in which it had been laid on the Twelfth Day festival. Then Pak suddenly caught sight of Sarna and his heart gave such a jump that his breath failed him. Her hair was combed tightly back and adorned with flowers, as though she were a woman of noble birth, which was not all in keeping with her station, for after all she was only the daughter of a sudra, however wealthy he might be. She wore silver earrings instead of rolls of lontar leaves. She looked very beautiful and Pak could not take his eyes from her face. After a time his mind was made up; he got to his feet and squeezed his way through the throng. "I'll only buy sirih," he muttered to himself as his pretext, although his sirih pouch was well filled. He did not succeed in getting anywhere near Sarna, so he went outside the gate where the women vendors sat. "Are you not going to buy from me?" a woman called to him. Turning his head he recognized Dasni, the Sanur girl who had brought him his food to the beach. As she had called to him he squatted down in front of her mat and looked at her. She had a white head-dress wound through her hair and her dark honest face was covered with little pimples. "Do you want sirih?" she asked, with a sidelong glance which did not become her. "Two kepengs' worth," he said. She eagerly made up a quid for him and he took the money out of his kain and held it out to her. She looked full in his face and refused it. Pak stared blankly. Without thinking what he was doing he had asked her for sirih. That meant: "I want to sleep with you," and she had understood it so. A girl who refused payment for sirih implied thereby that she gave her consent. The wag Rib, who was squatting near, laughed aloud. "Take care you don't get lost on your way home," he said pointedly. Pak beat a retreat. "Peace to you," he said hurriedly, and vanished.

This time he was successful in his attempt to get near Sarna. He waited until she saw him and then ventured a look which told all. And Sarna—he could not be deceiving him-self this time—answered his look by quickly raising her long eyelashes. Pak's hands tingled; he longed to go straight to her and seize her from behind. He bit his lips. Someone gave him a nudge and said, "They are beginning." Pak came out of his trance; he worked his way back through the crowd and bent again over his gong.

But now his eyes were caught by a sight which worked more powerfully on him even than Sarna. The large reception balé, which rose above the walls of the second court, had been illuminated in the meanwhile with many lamps, and female servants were busy laying down finely woven mats for spectators who could find no room below. The light shone and danced on the tiled wall at the back, and there, let into the wall, Pak saw plates. There were many plates and they were beautiful. Pak strained his eyes and even got on to the wall of the courtyard to see them better. There were no flowers on these plates; they had only a pattern in blue streaks that seemed to him Chinese. On the plates which Pak had let into the earth of his sawah there were flowers. His plates were whiter and there were roses on them, whose fragrance you could smell if you looked at them long enough. Pak had dug up his treasure twice already to feast his eyes with the sight of it. He felt for one dizzy moment of overweening pride that he was richer than the raja himself. The possession of the plates had made another man of him. But for them, he would never have dared to look with meaning eyes at the daughter of the wealthy Wajan and to dream of her as he did.

Next there was a surging and heaving as a gilded chair came along on the shoulders of six bearers above the heads of the crowd. On it sat an old man with white hair and beard. This was the Tjokorda of Pametjutan, the uncle of the lord Alit and co-regent. His numerous retinue followed him and assisted him, as the chair was put down, to rise totteringly to his feet. He sat down on a raised seat in the middle of the large balé and began talking to the other spectators there. Several men ran off excitedly to announce to the lord that his uncle had arrived.

The wives had already left their balés and were assembling in front of the lord's house, followed by their serving-women. They were splendidly dressed in trailing sarongs and silk breast-bands. Black lace shawls hung over one shoulder. They wore many jewels and their hair was smoothly drawn back from their foreheads and adorned with flowers. They looked like bright exotic birds as they rustled along, laughing, talking, jealously inspecting one another or clinging together softly in mutual admiration. They felt each other's dresses appraisingly and their eyes shone, for it was an exciting break in the routine of life in the palace to show themselves to the eyes of other men.

The burble of their eager voices ceased as the lord, accompanied by Raka, emerged. The women held their breath. Raka was already arrayed for the dance and a magnetic force seemed to radiate from him. He was clad in a white undergarment that enclosed his slender legs and from his shoulders fluttered bunches of bright-colored ribbons gleaming with gold. He wore a kain of stiff gold-painted material and at his waist was a kris with a sparkling hilt. He had a tall head-dress, triangular in shape, on which hundreds of silver discs on short stems quivered and gleamed. This lofty plaited helmet made him look very tall and erect and war-like.

He paused for a moment in the portico as though he was aware of his own beauty and wished to give the women time to admire him.

The lord lingered at his side for a moment with his little finger hooked in Raka's; then he let go of him. He smiled on his wives, who formed up in a rank, and called out a greeting to them. They were beautiful and his eye took in their beauty with satisfaction. "You smell like a flower-garden," he said with a smile. This joke of their lord was greeted by a loud titter. Tumun, whom the others considered cheeky and forward, approached him with a roguish look. "One does not know which is the handsomer, Raka or our lord," she said audibly to her serving-woman. Bernis turned on the pert creature with a contemptuous look; and then she looked at the lord until she had caught his eye and drooped her eyelids and smiled at him with an expression that betrayed a previous intimacy with him. He returned her look and her smile. Her hungry heart fluttered and she felt that now there was an understanding between them. Muna, the slave-girl, whispered over her shoulder. "The lord will not read his books tonight." Bernis pressed her lips together and took her place in the procession down to the first court. Alit looked after his wives. "Of all the things," he said, resuming the discourse about his ill-humor which had just been interrupted, "of all the things I had to promise the Dutch the one that will trouble me least to have renounced is the burning of my widows. I do not care for the thought of making myself at home in heaven with a bevy of wives. Their chatter and their jealousy would make residence there a trial."

Raka laughed loudly, but a moment later his expression changed. "The gamelan has begun playing," he said hastily. The notes which ushered in the first passage of the music could be heard coming from the outer court; and when Alit looked up again, Raka was already through the gate. He saw him once more as he emerged into view in the outer court among the group of dancers in the arena which was marked off by two men holding up sacred umbrellas.

The lord, now joined by his impatient dignitaries, stood a moment longer in the gateway leading down to the outer court. He smiled without knowing it as he surveyed the dim brilliance below, the throng arrayed in all its finery, the naked children with large shining eyes. He knew many of the people and loved them all.

The gamelan played a freely moving tender melody alternating with the loud, quick and warlike notes given out by the beat of the drum. He loved these moments of expectancy before the dance began, when a prickling of suspense ran over his skin. Sometimes merely to hear the overture made him feel that he could shrink and become a child again. His eyes had feasted on the golden splendor and movement of the dance from his earliest years: before he could even speak he had sat on his mother's lap and watched it, and something of the dreamy delight which had gripped him in those days lingered with him still. He looked forward with almost painful impatience to seeing Raka dance and he felt his heart, that often seemed asleep, beating fast. Ever since, as naked five-year-old children, they had learnt to know north from south and east from west, they had always been together. Although he was a year younger than his friend, he felt far, far older. He had seen Raka grow up, happy and impetuous and endowed with a tempestuous soul. No one could laugh as Raka could, nor be so unhappy, nor so wildly excited at a cock-fight, nor so still and silent when the sun went down. No one in all Bali could dance as he could.

Raka, surrounded by the other dancers, advanced with his hands on Lambon's shoulders. He felt her tremble and bent down to her. "You are afraid, aren't you?" he asked. She did not reply, but only silently shook her head. "You have only not to forget to turn away when I come with the kris."

"I am not afraid of you," Lambon answered, glancing up at him over her shoulder. It was her part to represent Supanaka, the sister of Rahwana, the demon-prince, who was sent by him to seduce Laksmana in the form of a beautiful nymph. He, however, cut off her nose and sent her back to the dark regions whence she came. They had rehearsed again and again that moment in the dance when Laksmana raised his kris above her head, for the dance had to go smoothly on and a false movement on Lambon's part might cause her to be wounded by the blade.

Raka walked round her to see if her dress sat rightly. He adjusted one of the many cambodia flowers in her crown of gilded leather pierced with a lace-work pattern. He went behind her and tied the zone of gold which enclosed her body down to the hips and drew it tighter. The gamelan played. Lambon's face smelt bitter-sweet of flowers, kunjit powder, and the lamp-black which framed her forehead. As Raka wound the zone about her he felt her budding breasts. It made him smile. To think that this was little Lambon, flowering already. He looked in her face, astonished. It seemed only yesterday that he had taken her to her master and held her consolingly between his knees. His hands were warm from the touch of her body, as though she was a bird he had caught. He let go of her and pushed her from him. She stood in front of him with lowered eyes. The gamelan played on. Lambon stood swaying inwardly, as young pisang leaves often do when there is no breath of air.

Raka turned away and sat down on the mat beside the other four dancers. Lambon took her master's hand and crouched beside him. The first dancer stood up and with eyes fixed advanced in the solemn rhythm of the dance through the hangings and up to the two umbrellas which flanked the space marked off as a stage. The gamelan played on. The second dancer got up after a long interval; he was a better dancer than the first and the loudly talking crowd was hushed.

Servants came and knelt before Raka, offering him young coconuts filled with cool, thin, sour-tasting milk. He refused them, although his throat was parched with excitement. This always happened to him before he danced. He did not know why. He got outside himself and knew himself no more. He felt his heart beat and his sinews stretch as taut as a rope tied to a heavy weight. Yet he felt light and without weight at all. The old teacher called this state "having other thoughts." Raka felt himself enveloped in a blue veil which made people's faces grow pale. Soon he saw nothing but this blue haze. He was alone within it as in a cloud. The gamelan played on and on. He heard nothing of the joke of the comic servant, or of the applause of the audience shouting with delirious delight, greeting every joke and allusion with peals of laughter, signalling their enjoyment from one to another, while the young lads took the opportunity of pressing against the wall of girls as though this would help them to hear better. The lord's wives, sitting cross-legged on mats in a small balé, were as skittish as young animals released from confinement. Their laughter rose and fell like a breeze.

Raka knew nothing of all this. He heard the gamelan call him and now he saw a point of light rise in the blue vacancy like a crystal ball. His eyes were fixed in a stare as he rose to his feet. "The way is prepared," the narrator chanted in front. "My lord will soon appear. He walks in the forest and flowers grow beneath his feet. He threatens and tigers tremble for fear." The gamelan was playing, the drum beat furiously. Raka stood between the two umbrellas which flanked the entrance to that other world, the world of fantasy in which he was transformed into a god. He felt himself stretch and grow, far beyond his real height. Then he stepped forward into the light of the lamps.

The lord sat with his chin propped in one hand and his eyes never left Raka for one moment. "Our master devours the dance with his eyes," Ida Katut whispered to his neighbor who nodded and made a grimace that said much. He was called Anak Agung Bima, the child of the great. He was one of the three relations of the lord who affected to be important persons in the puri. Bima had arrogated to himself an office of his own. He confiscated horses, women and cocks that took the lord's fancy. He had procured the plates which adorned the reception balé and paid nothing for them. He received the presents which were brought to the puri and often kept some for himself. Semal he was often called, which means squirrel, because he was always hoarding and nibbling. But above all he considered it his office to guess Alit's unspoken desires and to fulfil them, whether for better or worse. He was short and stout and he followed his master and cousin wherever he went, never letting him out of his sight and sticking so closely to him that Alit sometimes felt that he was caught in a spider's web. Bima got on to his knees to see what interested the lord, for he had just made an involuntary movement.

It was Lambon, who had just appeared on the scene. She looked small and slender and her child's face was profoundly serious. She advanced with knees and thighs tightly pressed together. Her hands fluttered like birds. Her slender neck quivered under her large crown. She glided towards Raka in faltering zigzags. It was an utterly artistic, almost inhuman dance in which feeling had been left behind and everything was precisely timed and measured movement of an extreme aesthetic perfection. Her small bare feet raised the dust from the ground and her hips swayed as cool as the stem of a water-lily. Now she was close to Raka and he moved with her. Her arms enclosed in tight and gleaming sleeves described tense arabesques in the air. "Look, she approaches the god," the narrator chanted. "She winds herself about him, like a snake, and as a creeper embraces the upright trunk. Beware, Laksmana, beware of the nymph." The gamelan played on. Raka and Lambon glided past one another, their faces drew near for a moment and then separated and again drew near. It was like the play of butterflies before their mating.

The lord leant forward with his eyes fixed on the dance. His eyes drank their fill, as Ida Katut had said. He clenched his fists as a servant drew Raka's kris from the scabbard and gave it him. The love-play turned to earnest. The kris flashed over Lambon's head and she quailed beneath it—and vanished. The gamelan played. The drums beat in a tumult. Then Raka ran towards the other two dancers in the battle of Laksmana with the two demons.

Many of the children had fallen asleep. They clung fast to their mothers like little monkeys in their sleep. Many of the slave-girls of the palace-women slept too, with their heads leaning upon one another. Even some of the courtiers, with the sirih still in their mouths, let their heads fall forward. The old Tjokorda Madé had fallen asleep, wearied out with age and much suffering. Only Alit was alert and wide-awake to the very end.

With the last note of the gamelan the crowd broke up and quickly dispersed. They set off home by the light of the torches, keeping together, so that they need fear no demons or lejaks. Many of the women held knives, with onions speared on them, a certain defence against the dangers of the night. The men of Taman Sari bore their instruments on their shoulders. The newfangled lamps round the arena, which did not last out so long as the coconut lamps, were dimmed with their own smoke. The lord's wives stood wearily lean-ing on one another, and the faded flowers in their hair smelt all the more strongly for being faded. They waited on their lord's pleasure. Bernis stood apart, impatient for what the night might bring. The lord remained seated on his mat, lost in reflection. He smiled as he looked after the retreating dancers. Ida Katut squatted near, trying to read his thoughts. The Anak Agung Bima approached him with clasped hands, though he was of the same blood as Alit.

"I noticed you found the little girl dancer beautiful," he said tentatively yet officiously. The lord raised his eyes heavily from the vacant arena and stood up. He stretched and took a deep breath of the cool air which fell dew-laden from the tops of the palms.

"She is still a child," he said, "but one day perhaps she will be a beautiful woman."

Buleleng

IT was hot in Buleleng. A sluggish breeze wafted the heat south-ward from the equator and it hung heavy along the shores of Bali. The Chinese sat in front of their shops with their jackets unbut-toned and perspired. Two traders from Bombay sat cross-legged be-side their balés of cloth and played dominoes. Three sailing-ships from Macassar were anchored in the roadstead and the crews roamed the few streets of the town, brown-faced, black-fez'd and bold.

A Javanese servant ran along the gravel path to the office. He was carrying, with an anxious expression on his face, a white tunic which creaked with starch. The Controller in charge of inland affairs, Myn-heer Visser, stood impatiently in the office. He was in shirt-sleeves and the sweat ran in three small trickles down his neck. He stamped his feet, drummed on his desk and gave every sign of angry impa-tience. At last the servant appeared with a tunic, which he held out to his tuan with bent, submissive back. Visser cursed a little in flu-ent Javanese, though this language does not lend itself well to curses. He hastily put on the uniform and buttoned the high collar up to his double chin. The gold epaulettes gleamed. Visser ended with an honest Dutch Godverdamme and the Javanese began to laugh. He knew this signal: it meant that his master's rage had cooled and that peace and quiet were restored.

"What's up?" Boomsmer asked from the door leading to the sec-ond office. He was a tall sandy-colored Dutchman with tousled hair and blue eyes.

"This buffalo of a servant of mine hadn't ironed my tunic and the Resident wants to speak to me immediately," Visser said as he but-toned in his paunch with an effort.

"At nine in the morning? There must be something up. Perhaps the Russians have been smuggling their superannuated breech-loaders into South Bali again."

Visser snatched up a few official papers and put them under his arm and took a quick drink from a bottle of gin which dwelt in a small cupboard on the wall just below the portrait of the Queen and her consort. He looked plaintively at Boomsmer, who looked like a shelled egg in his tight white jacket and appeared to find something to laugh at in his heated colleague.

"You don't feel the heat, man," he said reproachfully.

"That is a matter of will-power," Boomsmer replied, drawing himself up.

Visser went out. "I know one thing: once I'm old enough to draw my pension I'll go about in a sarong," he said from the door.

"That's just about your mark!" Boomsmer called after him as the door shut. Visser had the reputation of being too easy with the natives. No sense of discipline, in Boomsmer's opinion. It was essential, in his view, to keep a tight hold on that refractory island. But the Resident doted on Visser apparently. Visser knew the natives and understood their complicated lingo. He was sent out to conduct friendly palavers, which he sometimes brought to a successful conclusion. But for Visser's interposition they might never have got the concession in South Bali. Cannon were better than concessions, Boomsmer considered. He had a ticklish sense of honor and in his opinion the Dutch Government was too easy-going. The mere mention of Bali made them all grow sentimental, he thought irritably. He himself had no enthusiasm for the island. Life in Buleleng was not the height of comfort and he regretted Surabaya. There was not even a club, as there was even in the most godforsaken colonial settlement. The natives were dirty and spat out their betel-juice even on the office stoep. They were eaten up with scabies and ringworm and fever and were too stupid to have themselves cured. They had innumerable superstitions and tabus, and the higher castes were even worse in that respect than the lower ones. The petty rajas, who after all were no better than bare-footed peasants, squatted about among the litter of their puris and thought themselves the most mighty sovereigns on earth because they could have the heads and hands of their subjects hacked off when they had the mind. But when one of them died, then he was wrapped in white linen and kept in the house till the stink rose to heaven. Boomsmer shuddered at the recollection of this charnel stench and took a quick nip of gin in his turn. The portrait of the Queen, youthful and in full regalia, looked down amiably from the wall.

Boomsmer went up to Visser's desk and took the uppermost paper lying there. There was nothing on it, however, of political interest, but only a series of childish drawings of gentlemen in top-hats, such as Visser was in the habit of scribbling when he pondered a problem. Boomsmer sighed and returned to his own office, where a Javanese clerk with long thin hands stood at a desk, copying documents.

"What's all this about that Chinese?" the Resident asked the Controller, who was seated opposite him in a cane chair. They were on the verandah of the large house, as it was coolest there. Berginck, the Resident, had his empty breakfast-cup at his elbow and also a large pile of papers waiting for his signature.

"The Chinese to whom the people of Citgit have mortgaged their fields?" Visser asked.

"No, that's done with. The Chinese whose boat was wrecked." The Resident searched about among his papers. "Kwe Tik Tjiang, the man's name is," he added, and looked the Controller full in the face.

"I thought that was done with too," Visser replied, after recalling the name and the circumstances. "The man calmed down and went back to Banjarmasin."

"So you thought, but it is not the case. The fellow turned up again the day before yesterday, and this time he has the gusti behind him."

"Gusti Nyoman? What has he to do with the Chinese?"

"In the first place, they see in him a sort of raja and think he can get more done than we can. And in the second place, they know that he was appointed by the Government and it seems they prefer to palaver with a Balinese rather than with us."

"May I have a look?" Visser asked, taking the paper from the table. It was not unlikely he had forgotten the details, for this claim was only one among hundreds which had to be disposed of in the island. The Resident undid two buttons of his tunic and waited. He was a tall powerful man with fine brown eyes, to which short sight gave a look of concentration.

"As your Excellency will see, I had good grounds for refusing his claim," Visser said, returning the papers to the table. "He had bad luck, it is true. But how does that concern our Government? His boat was wrecked on the coast, but his life was saved and the people there even fished his goods from the sea and returned them to him. I cannot understand why he comes to us for damages. We are not an insurance agency, after all. Moreover, the Resident initialled the case himself before it was dismissed." And Visser gave the paper a flick nearer the Resident's short-sighted eyes.

"You did not draw my attention at the time to the fact of the boat's being wrecked on the coast of Badung," the Resident said, without looking down at the document. Visser made no reply to this.

The three refractory provinces in the south were a thorn in the side of the Government officials. It was an unsatisfactory situation that the Dutch should be masters of the island and yet not masters of it. Also Klungklung, Tabanan or Badung might at any moment kindle a spark and rouse the already subdued lords to rebellion. There were treaties, so old that they smelt of mildew, with additional clauses and signatures which gave the Government a certain influence over these territories. So far, so good. But it was not a satisfactory solution and the Government in Batavia gave Buleleng to understand from time to time that their officials in Bali had had ample time to bring that colony to heel. Visser knew all this as well as the Resident did, and it sometimes robbed him of his sleep. He had done his bit. He had gone alone into the lions' den; again and again he had ventured unarmed and unprotected into the puri among a thousand warriors armed with their krises and tried to bring their rulers to reason. He had drunk their horrible sweet rice wine and ruined his stomach with their over-spiced dishes. He had with infinite patience won the regard of several lords and tried calling himself their elder brother, to whose counsel they ought to give heed. But when he heard the word Badung he knew at once that there was unpleasantness to come.

"On the whole I got the impression that the Chinese wanted to make a deal out of his shipwreck. It is money he is after, that's all."

"It never for a moment entered my head that it was for us to compensate him," the Resident said. He pushed his empty coffee-cup aside with a clatter. Visser, too, felt the blood go to his head. He wiped the perspiration from his neck.

"As your Excellency seems to feel a particular interest in the case I would suggest summoning the gusti here together with the Chinese, Kwe Tik Tjiang," he said in his official manner, expecting to hear the suggestion turned down.

"Yes, Visser, will you see to it?" the Resident said, however. "I shall be at home until two. In any case there is no occasion to be upset yourself," he added in a conciliatory tone.

Visser crossed the expanse of grass on which were a few old Balinese stone statues and the flag-staff. It lay hushed in a drowsy stillness. An attempt had been made to give it a homely air by getting seeds from Holland and growing them in the borders. They flowered with difficulty and unwillingly in the moist heat in which groves of palms and the tropical creepers of the forests throve with indescribable luxuriance. A few Balinese were loitering along the garden railings and farther along the road were to be seen the trim villas of the Dutch settlers, all exactly alike, all painted a bright yellow and all with a hanging lamp and two imitation Delft plates in the stoep. At the edge of the road immediately in front them stood a little girl, brown and stark naked but for four brass bracelets round her arms and ankles and rolls of lontar leaves in her ears. Visser gave a deep sigh and returned to his office. He took a nip of gin and, sitting down at his desk, drew three more little gentlemen in top-hats on the uppermost sheet of paper. *"Opas!"* he roared out suddenly. *"Tuan?"* came the dutiful echo from without. The uniformed orderly entered with a frightened expression on his face. "I am now writing a letter which you will take at once to the gusti Nyoman," Visser said, and Opas squatted in a corner to wait for the letter to be written. Before many moments had passed Boomsmer's sandy head appeared round the door.

"Well, what did the tuan Besar want with you?" he asked.

"Nothing, nothing at all," Visser said. "Only the usual nonsense."

"So you say," Boomsmer observed. "The first commandment in the Colonies is that nothing is without consequence."

"And so forth," Visser said. "I know all you're going to say by heart. Our honor is at stake, we are the masters and we insist on obedience, we think only of the good of the natives and this country belongs to the Netherlands. And now I will tell you something: that sort of talk merely inflames the situation. For heaven's sake, leave the natives alone, and if they don't care about corrugated sheet-iron and bicycles, why make them? They're no use as plantation coolies either. It's all a lot of damned nonsense."

"You're an anarchist," Boomsmer said, and as Visser made no reply to this he withdrew again to his own room.

An hour later three two-wheeled vehicles drew up before the Residence, with a loud clinking of shining harness. In the first sat the gusti Nyoman himself. In the other two were Kwe Tik Tjiang and several of the gusti's retinue. Nyoman walked quickly, though with dignity, up the garden and was greeted courteously on the stoep by the Resident. He took the proffered hand loosely and with some embarrassment, for he was not yet quite at home with the manners of the white men. His escort squatted on the stone steps, which gleamed with the true Dutch cleanliness; and this dissuaded the men from spraying them liberally with red betel-juice. The Chinese stood patiently at the foot of the steps; he was smiling and he looked hot in his silk robe.

The Resident offered the gusti a chair and the gusti sat on it cross-legged just as though it was his usual bamboo bench. He was a good-looking, strongly built young man, whose eyes showed that he was intelligent and energetic and resourceful. Also, with his silvery green sarong and brown bare feet, he wore a white tunic, buttoned to the chin, as the Dutch did. "The tuan sent for me and I am here," he said in Malay. The Resident offered him a cigarette. "Ask the tuan Visser to come here," he told the orderly who was crouching on the steps. "My friend Nyoman can tell him what the complaint of the Chinese is."

Gusti Nyoman came of a noble family, but of a branch of it that was not quite without taint. He had gained his position in Buleleng by coming to an understanding with the Dutch. The other native lords called him a traitor behind his back and there was no love lost between him and them. They had treated him as a man of lower caste and an upstart until the Dutch put power in his hands. "I set no store by this Chinaman," he said arrogantly, although Kwe Tik Tjiang was listening, "but since his complaint is with the lords of Badung and Pametjutan I thought it best to bring it to the ears of the tuan Resident."

Visser at this moment stepped on to the stoep and after greeting the gusti sat down in silence at the table. He had brought his Javanese clerk, who squatted on the floor ready to take a minute of the proceedings. The Resident signalled to the Chinese to come nearer and plead his case; and Kwe Tik Tjiang, who was by now quite used to being his own advocate, opened out with great fluency.

When his boat struck, so his story ran, he was not for some hours in possession of his senses, since his head had struck the mast in the violence of the storm. Therefore the first mate had been in sole charge during that time. He himself asked the punggawa of Sanur to set a guard over the boat and in addition he left two of his own men on the beach. Also he had returned to the ship with the rest of the crew towards morning and had found about two hundred of the people of the coast breaking it up and plundering it. It was not in the power of him and his men to stop them. On boarding the ship at ebb-tide he found a large part of the cargo missing, including an iron chest containing ringits and several bamboo baskets in which were strings of Chinese kepengs, a thousand to each string. Next day, when the cargo was unshipped, further thefts came to light. Thereupon he made his complaint to the court of Badung, but was scornfully refused redress. It had occurred to him that in his first suit to the Resident he had not been sufficiently clear as to the extent of his losses. Now therefore he submitted a correct list of them and a report showing how they came about.

With this and a low bow he laid several sheets of paper written in Malay characters before the Resident.

The Resident read them through, passing each sheet when he had read it to the Controller. Visser went redder and redder in the face as he examined them, and now and then he whistled aloud without himself observing this breach of etiquette. The gusti sat and smoked with an air of sleepy amusement.

The document consisted of a long list of all that the merchant of Banjarmasin had lost, beginning with the chest containing 3,700 rix-dollars and ending with the cooking utensils of the cook Simin, of Banjarmasin, valued at five Dutch guilders. Then followed the sworn testimony of the crew, given in the presence of, and signed by, the harbor master of Singaraja.

The Resident reached for the document and read it through twice more and finally sighed. "Is that all?" he asked ironically. The Chinese bowed several times and produced another document from his wide sleeve, which he handed to the gusti, watching with expectant eyes as it pursued its course into the Resident's hands. "Still more?" Visser muttered.

"A letter from the Chinese, Tan Suey Hin of Sanur," the gusti said in a bored voice, "to the Chinese, Kwe Tik Tjiang."

"Is it usual for Chinese to write each other letters in Malay?" Visser asked, after glancing hastily at the letter and seeing the Arabic characters. The Resident smiled pensively. "It announces that Tan Suey Hin can no longer buy up the wreck as marauders removed the copper plates and the shrouds after Twe Tik Tjiang left Sanur, leaving the wreck on the beach," the Resident said to the Controller, winking as he spoke.

"Bad, too bad," Mynheer Visser sighed hypocritically. The Chinese looked from one to the other and observed that they were not taking him seriously.

"The people of the coast of Badung behaved like wreckers," he said bitterly. His disaster took on even larger proportions as time passed and, in any case, lying was part and parcel of his tortuous Chinese mentality.

"All this is quite new," the Resident said. "There was nothing of all this in your first claim." Visser bent forward to hear better. The Chinese did not reply. The Resident produced the earlier document and began to compare it with the new one. He shook his head and finally produced his spectacles, although he was loath to admit his short sight, and began again. At last he put the whole bunch down on the table and looked the Chinaman up and down.

"So you had three thousand seven hundred rix-dollars on board and two thousand nine hundred kepengs besides. How was it that nothing of all this money was rescued?" he asked.

"Kepengs to the value of a hundred and seventy-five guilders were recovered from the sea," the Chinese said. "I have only entered my actual losses."

"I see. The actual . . ." the Resident said abstractedly. "I read in your first statement that the crew when they were rescued carried some cases ashore with them. What did they contain?"

"Sugar," the Chinese said.

"Oh—the sugar was rescued and the money left on the wreck," the Resident observed. Gusti Nyoman laughed loudly. It seemed to him a good joke.

"Salt water destroys sugar——" the Chinese said. "I cannot say exactly what happened—I had hit my head on the mast——"

"One moment," Visser said, stepping up to the Chinaman. "Are you certain that the case with all that money was on board when you left the ship? Or is it not possible that it went overboard in the storm?" Kwe Tik Tjiang considered this. He weighed the pros and cons. If it was more to his advantage not to lie, he was quite ready to speak the truth.

"It is possible that the chest went overboard. But I know nothing. I saw nothing," he said smoothly. Visser was satisfied and sat down again.

"Your claim has gone up a good deal from the five hundred ringits it started with," the Resident remarked after a pause, during which he had been totting up the figures with the point of his pencil and trying to make a rough calculation. Kwe Tik Tjiang looked at the gusti, as though seeking his advice. The gusti went on smoking; the smell of cloves was wafted on to the verandah and he complacently surveyed his long finger-nails.

"Tuan Resident, your Excellency," the Chinese said, "how could I presume to make a definite claim? I am a simple man and now a ruined man. My boat was good, it had a new cabin, it has been plundered and broken up and the copper stolen; now there are only a few planks left. I have specified my actual loss under oath. His Excellency will decide what compensation shall be paid me."

The Resident sighed. The matter was even more troublesome and unpleasant than before. He almost regretted he had ever dug it up again. The gusti threw away the stump of his cigarette.

"The Chinaman says they told him at the court of Badung that they had a perfect right to do as they did and that thirty per cent of the wreckage went to the lord of Badung," he said, without raising his voice. The Resident took off his spectacles and his eyes narrowed.

"Did the lord of Badung say that?" he asked quickly.

"One of his relatives, Tuan Resident, your Excellency," Kwe Tik Tjiang said. There was a pause. Visser did not appear to be listening.

He had collected all the papers in his rather informal way and was studying them; a broad smile came and went over his perspiring face.

"I have given you a hearing and will give your suit my closest attention," the Resident said, rising to his feet to show that the hearing was concluded. The Chinese again glanced at the gusti to see what he ought to do next. Then with a low bow he withdrew. His long robe swept the dry ground of the garden as he returned to the waiting carriage.

"It would be best to make an investigation on the spot in Badung," the gusti said. "The Chinese have slit tongues, it is true. But the people along the coast of Badung are brought up by their fathers to be robbers. That is true also."

Visser broke into a laugh as he read. "He had a gold watch and chain too. And chain——" he repeated. "It must have been no common watch. A hundred and seventy-five guilders our friend wants for it."

"A watch?" the Resident asked absent-mindedly. He was reflecting that the ship had sailed under the Dutch flag. Impossible to overlook that. "What were you saying, Visser?"

"The whole business stinks to heaven, Resident. This letter in Malay of the other Chinaman is a put-up job. You can see that a mile off. And the list of his losses is a pure invention, in my opinion."

"What do you propose?" the Resident asked. The gusti stood by, thoroughly enjoying himself. How these white men perspired and how seriously they took everything. Visser tried to guess his superior's wishes. He suppressed a sigh.

"If your Excellency thinks fit, I can of course go to Badung and see what really happened. The punggawa of Sanur is a supporter of ours. He will give me all necessary information. But, as I say, it is a fishy business, very fishy indeed. We would do better to steer clear of it."

"The question turns on whether Badung has broken Clause II of the treaty by which it renounces the right of salvage," replied the Resident. "I don't see how we can steer clear of that, my dear Visser."

The People of Taman Sari

WEEKS of hard work followed for Pak and his muscles grew hard and the sweat ran off him in streams. The rice was ripening in his west fields, the ears hung heavy on the stalks, whose green became first silver and then gold. Even his old father often came out in the late afternoon and sat on the narrow dyke and rejoiced in the sight. Life is sweet when the rice ripens and the heart is content. Pak made many clappers which he fastened to long poles and set up in his fields; they scared the birds and at the same time made enough din to excite his neighbors to fury. There was a festival in the rice temples of the subak on the day before the harvest, with many offerings, and the old women wound black kains about their thighs, with golden ones beneath hanging down in a train; they wore yellow shawls over one shoulder and had many flowers in their gray hair. They danced before each shrine with the offering-vessels held high in the left hand and the children sat nearby in great delight. Pak's aunt danced, too, with a rapt expression, for though her breasts might be withered, she had been a temple dancer when she was a child, as Lambon was. Puglug went with her mat and took her place in the row of vendors at the temple gate and made more than two hundred kepengs. Pak took them from her, for the three ceremonies after the birth of little Klepon had cost a lot in rice and money and on the third day of the festival there was to be a cock-fight to which he looked forward with the greatest excitement.

Pak's father was a great connoisseur of cocks, and on the cross-beam of his balé there were three old lontars, where it was written in which corner of the cock-pit and against what sort of cock on any given day a bird had to fight in order to win. On the day before each

cock-fight many people came to Pak's place to ask the old man's
advice. He pretended to be reading out of his old books, although
his eyes were dim and he had long ago forgotten how to read. But
he knew the lontars by heart, for he had learnt them from his father
when he was still a boy. The visitors brought presents with them of
ducks' eggs and coconuts and papayas, and Pak was proud of having so knowing a father. Altogether his family was distinguishing itself, although they were only poor people of no caste. The eye of the
raja had looked with favor on Lambon, and when she danced the legong with two other children on the evening of the harvest festival,
Pak could see that she delighted everybody, though no one said so.
Meru, his young brother, moreover, was summoned to the palace to
carve two new doors for the eleven-storeyed tower of its temple and
he went out and bought himself a kris on the strength of it.

Pak dug beneath the floor of his house when Puglug was at the
market and took out three ringits for the cock-fight. He gave only
a little food to his red cock, so that he should be light and nimble,
and putting him in a wicker hamper went off to the cock-pit. He
hesitated a long time before deciding which cock to challenge and
rejected a large black-and-white one, although his red bird was frantic to fight him. He went over in his mind all the advice his father
had given him—to take the west corner and to pit his cock against
a white bird without a single black feather. In spite of this he lost his
cock and two of his ringits besides. The winner took his beautiful
red cock away dead and Pak's heart was heavy, though he gave no
sign of it; he laughed and slapped the other man on the knee and
made a number of jokes which he thought very good indeed.

He tried to make good his losses by staking his last ringit on the
lusty black-and-white cock he had passed over as an opponent, and
won. His courage rose and he made bet after bet and lost and soon
there was not a kepeng left in his kain. He felt a strong inclination
to stake his loin-cloth, Puglug's present, but at the thought of her his
courage failed him.

Early next day they began harvesting, Pak and his friends who
belonged to the same harvest guild and his brothers and uncle. The
women and children joined in, too, and there was much singing, although the work was hard. The sun blazed and the ears were prickly. Pak wore his large hat and a sleeved jacket woven out of fibre as

a protection against the haulm. He saw to it that he worked all day long near Sarna and he asked her when she would go to the river to fetch water. Yes, Sarna was helping in his field, for her father belonged to the same guild and the members had to help one another. Sarna sang well but was not much good at reaping. But Pak was in love and the blood pulsed in his veins, and little he cared whether Sarna was quick or slow with her rice sheaves.

Puglug came out to the sawah, bringing food for all the people, and they ate a great deal from politeness, and said what a good cook Puglug was and that Pak was a lucky man. Pak, too, was polite, and poured scorn on his wife and her cooking, and his face shone with sweat and happiness. But Puglug was cross and spoke less than her custom was. At night when the two fields were harvested the men went back to Pak's house and ate once more. The old man squatted among them and told old tales and generally forgot how they ended. The rich Wajan sent his son home for palm wine in bamboo stems and Krkek praised the harvest and Pak for the way he had tilled his land. There was a great deal of laughter and drinking and it was one of the happiest nights of Pak's life.

They had forty-eight sheaves from the one field and fifty-three from the other, and this was seven more than Pak had hoped for. When he had given half to the lord and three-tenths to the guild, there remained forty-five for himself, and this was more than his family required for the next half-year, by which time the next fields would have ripened on the soil in which Pak had buried his treasure.

"Father of Rantun," Puglug said, addressing him by the name of his favorite child, as she did when she wanted something, "Father of Rantun, the work is becoming too hard for me. My back pains me since the birth of the last child, and the aunt, the old besom, is no help to me. I have to go to the river three times a day for water because I cannot any longer carry the large pitcher. What are you going to do to lighten my labors?"

Pak muttered that his household was full of women; there were Lambon and the two daughters and his uncle's wives. This brought a torrent of words from Puglug. "Lambon," she said, "thinks no doubt that her hands are too good for work now that she dances the legong. She is off to Kesiman to her teacher and does not come home for the rest of the day, like a strayed dog. She runs after Raka, who spends half his time at Kesiman too, practising new dances. She is no good in the house and only one more idle mouth to feed. Rantun has enough to do looking after her little sisters and gathering dried coconut shells for the fire. Besides, she has the heat sickness every three days and her arms are tired out with carrying Klepon around. I don't believe you know what goes on in your own house."

All Pak's peace of mind was shattered and he let his head sink. "Wife, that is not a seemly way to speak and if I did what was right I should beat you," he said to preserve his dignity; but in his heart he was ashamed of himself. Ever since the harvest he had been meeting Sarna secretly, at night under the wairingin tree, where it was pitch-dark, or near the old temple on the outskirts of the village where the grass grew high between the balés. Merely to think of Sarna was worse than hunger and thirst and yet he could not stop thinking of her.

"Rantun, come here," he called, and Rantun came running across the yard from the kitchen to her father. He took her by the shoulders and held her in front of him and looked at her. It was true that her little arms were thin and her eyes too bright. She was carrying Klepon on her hip—a thriving happy little girl, who had no idea of being an unwanted child. The brass rings round her wrists and ankles were almost lost to sight in rolls of fat. She was clearly too heavy for Rantun to carry about. Madé, finger in mouth, clung to Rantun's sarong. Rantun had a broad leaf in her hand with offerings on it and a glowing coconut shell. It would soon be evening and she had to place the offerings at the gate and a light, so that the evil spirits would see to find them and not need to come into the yard.

"Are you quite happy, Rantun?" Pak asked as he stroked the little girl's hot neck.

"Very, father," Rantun said, and this stirred Pak's heart as though with the touch of a hand. "Give Klepon to me, I will carry her, your mother has no time," he said, and he took the plump little girl on his own hip. If she had been a son he would have proudly stationed himself outside the gate to excite the admiration of his neighbors. But as she was a daughter he preferred to keep her within. "Go and put the offerings outside," he said with a playful slap on her thin little flanks. Rantun smiled at him, almost as though he needed comforting, because she had the heat sickness, and went off with her

lighted coconut shell. Puglug stood near meanwhile, her arms folded
on her breast, for which little Klepon stretched out her arms.

"What have you been thinking I ought to do to make your life
less hard?" he asked Puglug. She was a good wife and had not made
such a very great fuss when he lost the three ringits. The worst of
Puglug was that you could keep nothing secret from her. She came
home on market-days stuffed to the brim with news and other people's secrets, which tumbled out of her like potatoes from an over-
filled basket. She had found out all about the cock-fighting to the
last detail, even though women were not allowed to be present.

"I have been thinking that it was time you took a second wife,"
Puglug said, confident of being on the right tack. "I have the right
to ask that you should give me a younger sister in the house to share
the work and help me when I am not well. Also she could look after the house and cook the meals when I am at the market making
some money."

When he heard this Pak felt as he had that time when a large coconut fell on his head. He blinked his eyes. "You are not half as stupid as I thought," he said amiably. "You are right. I will look about
in the village and bring home a second wife as soon as I have found
the right girl." His head went hot and dizzy. It overwhelmed him
that Puglug herself should direct him how to appease his hunger for
Sarna. He took her hand in his and patted it.

"There is someone in Sanur who is the very one for you and who
would be glad to have you. Everyone in the village knows that you
have not much eye for the girls. But there would be very little difficulty in persuading this Sanur girl I am speaking of. She would
suit very well in the family, for her sister's mother married a cousin
of your father's. You won't remember that, for she went a long way
away, to Krobokan." And Puglug took up the child from his hip as
it was showing signs of beginning to cry.

"In Sanur?" Pak said in amazement. "Who is there in Sanur who
thinks of marrying me?"

Puglug squatted down beside him with the child at her breast.
She always did this when she had news to impart and Pak knew that
a lengthy talk was to come.

"I mean Dasni, if you want to know, and I could not ask for a
better sister in the house. She can carry forty-five coconuts on her

head, and if you think I am exaggerating ask anyone in Sanur. She can carry three sheaves of rice on a pole like a man and last harvest she threshed more rice than any other woman. As it happens I know that she has had her eye on you for a long time past, but of course you have never noticed that. But long ago she asked me to bring her two earthenware jars when I went to Badung market. When she came for them we had a long talk. And if you like to be spared the trouble I was going in any case to Sanur for Sweet Wednesday and I can talk it all over with her then."

A second whacking great coconut seemed to have fallen on Pak's head. "Dasni," he said, almost speechless for disappointment. "And why should I want Dasni of all people as a second wife?"

"I am just beginning to tell you the reasons. Dasni can weave baskets and padang mats beautifully, and I could take them to market and sell them. And in her family there are always three sons born to every daughter, and the balian has read in his books and told her that she will soon have a husband, who is a better man than people think," Puglug went on volubly. The child had fallen asleep on her breast, and she crouched in front of Pak and her ill-favored face looked up into his with entire devotion. Pak was confounded by her last words. A better man than people knew. He was certainly that. A man who had treasure buried in his rice-field, which he could dig up any day and turn to money. True enough, Pak was a better man than people knew. Nevertheless, the balian's prophecy did not please him. "There are plenty of good men in the two villages," he said. "And Dasni has pimples on her face."

"That is a ridiculous objection," Puglug said. "Rich Wajan has many sugem pigeons. You have only to go and ask him for some of the droppings, so that the balian can make the remedy, and in three days her skin will be clean."

Pak started once more at the mention of Sarna's father. He winced at anything that reminded him of Sarna and there was nothing that did not remind him of her apparently. He looked down on his wife in silence and thought it over. What am I to do with two ugly women in my house? he thought. I am not a pig—to be contented as long as I have all the food I want. My eyes want to be fed, too, and I want to be envied for a wife with beautiful breasts, and who is a delight to me. But he was sorry for Puglug and refrained from saying anything to wound her.

"I will speak to Krkek about it and ask his advice. He is a clever man," he said evasively.

"Shall I mention it to Dasni in the meanwhile and take her the remedy for her skin? The balian would mix it properly for me in return for a basket of pisangs, and you need only give rich Wajan a present if the droppings of his pigeons do good."

"If I ask rich Wajan for anything at all, it will be for something better than pigeon-droppings," said Pak. He bit his lip as soon as it was out of his mouth. Puglug looked narrowly at him and said no more. He would have given much to know whether she had already heard at the market about his secret meetings with Sarna. But Puglug was silent and her face showed no sign.

"We have talked enough for one evening," he said. "I am tired. Tomorrow we shall know better."

Puglug followed him obediently into the house and laid Klepon down in her cot. Rantun and Madé were already rolled up on the other bench. Pak took the oil lamp down from its hook and looked at the little girls. Rantun even in her sleep had her arm protectingly round her younger sister. Pak smiled, pinched out the wick and lay down on his mat. Puglug had lain down already, but that was no concern of his. He lay awake until she had fallen asleep; then, feeling it hot and oppressive in the little room, he got up and went out into the yard. The moon was shining and the palm-tops were black against the brightness in the sky. He walked aimlessly to and fro, driven by the unrest in his blood. Then he squatted down and let the night air and the dew cool his body, but it was no good. It is a fever that destroys the flesh, he thought sadly. If it goes on, it will take me three days to plough one furrow and I will get behind with my work, and they will shut off the water from my sawahs and I shall be punished. He went out through the gate and crouched in the sluice that flowed along the wall and through the village. The water cooled but did not calm him. I must take Sarna into my home, he thought, so that I can see her and be with her whenever I wish. Sarna is a rich man's daughter and spoilt. She will not be the second wife and do as Puglug bids her when she has to pound the rice. He tried to imagine Sarna doing the housework in a dirty kain and getting ugly as Puglug had. That cannot be, he thought. If she is spoilt, she can go on being spoilt. I am rich enough. Besides, it is well known that the second wife is for the husband's pleasure as a rule. He went back into the moonlit yard and knotted up his kain again around his wet hips. Thoughts surged in his wretched head, which was not used to thinking. The dogs had woken up and looked at him with surprise. Then he heard light footsteps in the yard, and looking up he saw the old man there. "Why do you not sleep, my son?"

"I don't know, father. I am overcome by a great restlessness and the narrow walls of my rooms suffocate me," Pak replied. The moon shone brightly and every object and every building cast black shadows. The old man, who had shrunk together in the last years, so that Pak was now taller than he, looked sadly up at him.

"I thought the cow must have broken loose," Pak muttered. "It is nothing else, father——"

"I have heard you creeping home just before cockcrow for three nights past. Are you going secretly to a woman?" the old man asked, and Pak realized with relief that there was nothing the old man in his wisdom did not know and understand.

"What is it that tortures a man like a sickness and puts him beyond his own help? It is a woman—and I must have her or else my whole life will be brought to nought."

His father considered this for a while. "I will speak to my old friend, the pedanda," he said. "In all probability this woman has used sorcery and the spell must be broken. You know that the mother of the husky man of Sanur is a witch and the women go to her for such things. Now go to sleep and tomorrow I will see how to heal you of this sickness."

Pak hung his head at this. He had no desire to be healed. He wanted to have this fever for ever in his blood and Sarna with him in his house to appease it. He tried in vain to imagine that she took the dark way to the witch and mixed a witch's brew with his food. But she was always at the back of his eyes, and he could see her at every moment, and her face was always sweet and faultless, full of laughter and roguishness; it was inconceivable that she should have anything to do with the black arts of magic. He followed his father's bent and withered form across the moonlit yard to his balé "May

I sleep with you, old man?" he asked familiarly as if he was still a child. The old man nodded. Pak lay down beside his father's emaciated form which took little room on the couch and his father spread half of his own kain over his son. Lantjar, the youngest of the brothers, was asleep on the floor. Pak felt calmer to be lying close to his father as in his childhood. His eyes closed. It would be sensible to take Dasni, he thought. But I do not want to be sensible, but happy, he thought again as he fell asleep.

Raka and Lambon were coming over the rice-fields from Kesiman. They were on their way home after a three weeks' stay in the house of the old teacher of dancing. They were a long time on the way, because in all the villages they passed through Raka was hailed and stopped and invited into the houses and pressed to take at least some fruit or sirih. Laughing and light-hearted he went on his way, taking as a matter of course the love people felt for him. As his dancing delighted them and it made them happy to offer him hospitality, it would have been impolite to decline what they were glad to give.

The basket on Lambon's head was soon full of fruit and sirih and at last Raka was carrying on his bamboo pole a hamper containing a little black pig. Someone had given it to him for his wife, Teragia, in gratitude for her care of a sick child. Raka was in no hurry to be home. He sat down on the steps leading up to the doors of houses and talked to the old women, who were always eager for news of neighboring villages. He squatted at the road-sides with the men who were fondling their fighting-cocks and weighing one against another and even letting them fight one another for practice and the fun of the thing. It was the idle hour of the day when field labor was done and there was leisure for amusement.

In every village the young unmarried men, who were as yet of no importance whatever, assembled in their open balés, smoking, chewing and boasting of their latest conquests. Raka sat with them and chaffed them and slapped them on the back. But when they asked him about his own adventures he laughed and said he had nothing to tell them. He was said to be all the more a favorite with the girls because of his reticence. Whenever he passed a mother with her little children beside her, he called out his congratulations and admired the beauty and fatness of the babe at her breast. He jokingly helped the young girls to hoist the heavy pitchers on to their heads when they had drawn water. He talked to children, cows and ducks he met by the way and let no one pass without asking them whence and whither. And so it was that they had been a good two hours on the way before reaching the river that flowed at the back of Taman Sari.

Lambon kept always a pace or two behind Raka, for he was her elder and almost her teacher and married and of the highest caste. She was proud of going in his company through the villages and seeing how beloved he was; and she knew that girls older than her, who already had big breasts, were envious of her. She strode on with a nervous look and felt in every inch of her the joy of Raka's presence and of being Lambon, the dancer, on whom the raja himself had smiled when he saw her dance.

When Raka loitered anywhere she knelt down by the roadside and wiped the little beads of sweat from her face. She had plenty to do, too, with her hair and her head-dress while waiting for him, for she had just reached puberty and now there was to be a neat coil of hair on her head and a fringe, as sign of her maidenhood. Apart from this, not much fuss had been made of it, a few offerings had been offered up, her brother Pak had given her a new sarong, and one or two of Puglug's friends had brought some sweet rice cakes which they helped to dispose of over a good gossip without paying much attention to the little ceremony. Lambon was not eager to be home again. It was a life of poverty and her brother's and uncle's wives were always having words over the little there was to eat. She had been spoilt at Kesiman and she had become estranged day by day from the life in her own family.

Her teacher's home at Kesiman could almost be called a puri— there were so many balés and so many people living on his rice and everything was so fine and open-handed. It was at Kesiman, too, that Lambon had her friends, not at Taman Sari. There were two, younger than she was, with whom she danced the legong, and three others, who helped her to dress for dancing and looked with admiring eyes at her beauty. They confided all their secrets and there was no end to the giggling and laughing when they were together. Lambon's favorite was little Resi, her master's granddaughter, who was like a sister. Sometimes they sat a whole morning together hand in hand without speaking. Lambon was glad to be silent, for then she could think about Raka undisturbed. Now and then there were differences of opinion between the old dancing master and Raka. The master was a noble of a wealthy family and devoted his life to handing down the old dances and steps, as he himself had learnt them from his own master fifty years before in Sukawati. But Raka was daring: he suddenly did something in a dance that had never been seen before, and when the master took him to task, he was not even aware that he had danced in any but the traditional way. Lambon, on the other hand, executed every movement zealously and scrupulously in the way she had been taught, without departing from it by a tremor of her neck or a quiver of the little fan in her hand. She had fingers that could be bent right over the backs of her hands and fine mobile wrists. She could roll her shoulders as if they were balls and give her eyes a dazed stare or dart them like lightning from corner to corner of their sockets, just as the dance required. Raka had taught her how to touch her heels with the back of her head when dancing the legong. The old teacher was horrified at the sight of this unseemly innovation, but Lambon loved to do it and she practised it in secret, with Resi to support the small of her back. Now that she was a girl Lambon often found herself doing and wishing things she could not quite understand. She did not want to annoy the old dancing master; and yet to bend her supple body backwards with closed eyes gave her pleasure even though her head felt dizzy afterwards; for it was Raka who had taught her how to do it. Sometimes, too, she could not stop laughing at silly jokes of her friends. But above all, her heart was big with suspense, for now that she was growing up she would have to consider which man she would not refuse to sleep with if he asked her.

She knew that she was beautiful; it was as obvious as that she had two legs. Her old teacher had impressed upon her that the gods were actually present, seated on their thrones, when she danced at the temple festivals. It was obvious that the gods could not be asked to look on at any but beautiful dancers. So when her old teacher, too, was pleased with her and her friends were full of admiration and Raka praised her, she was content to ignore the village youths who stood and looked after her as she went by. She wanted none of them. She wanted Raka. But Raka, as far as she could see, thought as little of her as she did of the little fan she used for dancing.

Everything she knew came from Raka. He showed her every movement which her teacher was too old and stiff to show her. He stood behind her, holding her hands firmly and making every movement with her until she got it right. He put his fingers on her neck and made her aware of all its vertebrae separately until she could move them one by one. He clasped her round the hips and glided to and fro with her until she gained the right speed and agility and could do it alone. Other girls all grew up with their mothers, far removed from men. But she had been used from childhood to having the hands of her master and Raka on her body. And for some time now it made a lot of difference whether it was the old guru's or Raka's.

When they reached the shadow of the palms which fringed the top of the river bank, Raka stopped. Lambon stopped too, politely in the rear. "Let us rest a little," he called to her. "This son of a pig gets heavier the longer I carry it." Lowering the bamboo pole from his shoulder, he put the hamper down on the grass. The little pig grunted its satisfaction. Lambon dropped to her knees and took the basket from her head. Raka looked idly at her. "My stomach feels empty again," he called out to her. She brought him the basket and knelt in front of him. He lazily took a pisang and began to eat it. Lambon watched with veneration in her eyes. He had gleaming white, evenly filed teeth. When he had done he turned over on his back with his arm under his head and looked up into the tree-tops.

"The lord wants us to dance the baris again in Badung next week. He has visitors from Tabanan," he said drowsily.

"That will be lovely," Lambon said delightedly. She loved the glamour of the puri, and the baris was the only dance in which she could dance with Raka. The old teacher, certainly, thought it unseemly, but the Taman Sari dance guild had held out on this point, and the success which had attended the innovation of a girl's appearing with the male dancers had justified them. The teacher had assembled his pupils and told them the story of the baris dance. Lambon never attended to what the narrator chanted during a performance, but she sat full of awe while her teacher told the stories of demons and gods, although she forgot it all again directly. All she retained was the impression that the dancing belonged to another world than that of the village and her brother's household. A world of princes and princesses and demons, with gods coming down from heaven to fight with them, of women who were likened to flowers and wild birds and deep ponds, in which gold-fishes swam.

It was not the same, either, in the house of Raka's father, the pedanda, as it was in her own home. Lambon sometimes went on errands there for her father or was sent for by Raka. She was always a little afraid of Teragia, although she was never anything but kind to her. She smoothed Lambon's hair with her large hand and also brought her bright-colored fruit-juice in the half of a coconut shell and little rice cakes tasting of palm sugar. Yet Lambon always felt embarrassed in the priest's house, everything there was so spotless; and flowers of every color, which Raka's father, the pedanda Ida Bagus Rai, needed for the daily offerings, grew there. Raka's mother went noiselessly about the courtyard—a tall, erect old lady dressed in a black kain and with the breasts of a young girl. As she was blind it was her custom to acquaint herself with persons and things by touch. It seemed funny to Lambon when the old lady's cool hands explored her face as though she was a piece of carving or a figure in wood. But you could not laugh in the priest's house as you could elsewhere. Even Raka was not the same in the presence of his parents and his wife.

Lambon's thoughts went from one thing to another as she sat beside Raka on the grass, following the direction of his eyes. All he could possibly see up there was a little cloud slowly sailing to join her sisters near the Great Mountain. Raka pulled a stalk of grass and began chewing it. Suddenly he laughed aloud and turned over and stared in Lambon's face. "What are you laughing at?" she asked, taken aback.

"Not at you," he replied, still laughing. He waved his left hand in the air to disclaim the idea. Only nobles and artists might wear their nails so long. They were pointed like the spur of a fighting-cock and the color of mussels.

The little pig gave a loud squeak. Lambon aimed a blow at it. "Don't——" Raka said, holding her hand tightly. She wrenched it free and said, "You hurt me." It was a lie. It pleased her when Raka held her hand, even if it did hurt. Now her hand lay on the grass like a, pisang rind someone had thrown down and Raka once more gazed into the sky.

The faint outline of the new moon could be seen rising in the east, scarcely visible, for the sky was still bright. Lambon looked impatiently at the sky that detained Raka's eyes.

"Is it true that there used to be seven moons?" she asked. Ever since she had put on her first kain and begun to dance she had been accustomed to ask Raka everything.

"You always forget everything you are told," he said. "There used to be seven moons, until one of them fell down and now it hangs in the Temple of Pedjeng as a giant gong. Since then there have been only six, and that is why the year has only six months now. It used to have seven," Raka said drowsily, without taking his eyes from the sky.

"Is the woman who lives in the moon very beautiful?"

"Yes, she is very beautiful."

"What does she look like?" Lambon asked importunately. Raka at last took his eyes from the cloud and sat up. "How am I to know?" he asked in a moment. "I have never paid her a visit yet."

"Do you know any girl who is like what you imagine her to look like?" Lambon asked. She would have given her new sarong to hear Raka reply: "You, you, Lambon." But he said, "No."

Lambon decided to talk of something else.

"Are there any other countries beside Bali?"

"Yes," he said, "there is Java, where our ancestors came from." It was wonderful how Raka knew everything. But his reply left her as unsatisfied as before. "And who made the stars?" she asked.

Raka sighed, for Lambon's mania for asking questions was exhausting and replies were thrown away, for she forgot all she was told. But after a look at her parted and expectant lips he decided to answer this too.

"You must imagine heaven just like Bali. Just the same. There are the same villages and temples and puris. Only that in heaven everything stands on its head, as though reflected in a river. Yes," he said, "Bali is a reflection of heaven. You can understand that. Up there there are sawahs just as here below and what you see sparkling as stars are the tips of the young plants hanging down towards us."

Lambon looked about her at the young plants gleaming in the water of the sawah and then looked again up into the sky. Raka's explanation made her feel a little dizzy.

"Some people say all the same that the stars are simply there to ornament the sky at night," Raka added.

"I don't believe that," Lambon said with decision. She thought it over for a moment and then reached for her basket and arranged the fruit in it.

"Sambeh is going to have a baby soon," she said meanwhile, without looking at Raka.

"Who?" he asked in surprise.

"Sambeh, the servant in your house," Lambon said. She paused, and as Raka made no reply she went on, "She is going to have a baby, and then she will be unclean for forty-two days, and won't be allowed to cook any food or be of any use at all about the house."

"It seems the gods will it so," Raka said piously. He did not know what Lambon was driving at.

"Teragia will want another servant," Lambon said.

Raka had nothing to say to this. He took hold of his pole and tied the hamper with the little pig to it. The little pig squealed like a baby.

"I should love to be a servant in your house," Lambon said. "I thought perhaps you would ask Teragia to take me as a servant when Sambeh has her child . . ."

She came to a stop and could not go on. Her heart pounded. She could feel the blood rush to her face and was angry with herself. Raka put two fingers under her chin and lifted back her head and looked at her face with curiosity. "No," he said. "No, Lambon, I can make no use of you as a servant."

"Not? Why not?" Lambon whispered in dismay.

"You are too forgetful for a cook, too clumsy to carry water," Raka said severely. She looked at him miserably and he began to laugh. "Lambon," he cried, "you are too beautiful by far for a servant, particularly in a pedanda's household."

Lambon sat motionless and her hands went limp. She looked down at herself and then up at Raka. His skin was much fairer than hers. Raka was fair-skinned and handsome and she had a brown skin and thin arms and her father was a poor man of low caste.

"You are not to laugh at me," she said angrily.

Raka looked at her in astonishment. "What things you think of while you sit there with your eyes going dark," he said teasingly.

"My eyes do not go dark, not when I think of you," she said, almost bursting with rage. He laughed out loud. "You can't see your own eyes. But I can and they are dark," he shouted.

Lambon turned her head away in mortification, when he took her by the hands and drew her towards him and stared in her eyes. She pulled her head-dress down over her face and then, feeling that this was not concealment enough, she buried her head in her arms. Raka let go of her and shrugged his shoulders; then he got up, stretched, put the pole across his shoulder and walked on. Lambon raised her head, and when she saw that Raka had gone on she, too, took up her basket and followed him down the steep river bank. On the way she picked a little purple flower and put it in her hair above her forehead. The load on her head did not sway. Raka looked round at her and laughed.

"Let us have a bathe before we go home. We are hot and dusty," he called to her. There was no one at the bathing pool yet, for the sun had not set, though the moon was visible. The water looked cool and the sand gleamed in the river bed. Raka did not wait for her answer. He had already undone his kain, and covering himself with one hand, as he had learnt to do as a child, waded into mid-stream. There was a small rock there, on which the women who had bathed that morning had laid offerings—now withered. Lambon put her basket down, girded up her sarong and followed his example; only she kept at a distance and went farther downstream, away from the rocks, to the spot where women always bathed. She heard him splashing and blowing higher up and saw him forging through the water, turning it to milky foam. When the water was up to her waist she took off her sarong and threw it on to the bank. Her legs were much lighter in color than her breast, which was always exposed to the sun. It was a never-ceasing tribulation to Lambon that the very parts of her that Raka saw were tanned and coarse. Kneeling on the sandy bottom she plunged her hair into the water to wash it. The water was cool and clear and the current was stronger there than elsewhere. Lambon's spirits rose; she shouted for joy and smacked the water with her hands. Raka was just wading ashore; his body shone wet as he wound his kain about his waist, Lambon played about a little longer in the water, but Raka took up his pig and went on, as though he had forgotten all about her. As soon as he had turned away, she scrambled hurriedly out of the water, slipped on her sun-warmed sarong and began smoothing her hair. She looked about for some flower, and finding two more of the violet-colored ones, adorned herself with them. She felt cheerful and happy now and the wind blew refreshingly against her moist body. She looked down at herself and was rather better pleased with the sight. Then she picked up her basket and hurried after Raka. She caught him not far from a wairingin tree that shadowed a small rice temple. He stopped and waited as she came breathlessly up with him.

"Do you really mean you want to come into my house?" he asked, just as though they had never stopped talking together.

"Yes," she said eagerly, supporting the basket on her head with her left hand. Raka looked her up and down, he looked at her hair, her face, her neck, her breast and her hips and the cheap new sarong of which she was so proud.

"But I want no second wife in my house," he said jokingly, and yet with just a hint of earnest. Lambon stared at him in alarm. The next moment his arms were round her and his face pressed to hers. The wairingin tree rose high and dark above them. A bird sang and ceased again. Lambon's knees failed her and the nipples of her breasts hurt. She pushed Raka away with all her strength. He picked up the pole and his pig, which he had let fall on to the grass.

"Be quiet," he said to the little beast which had begun to squeal. "We are going straight home now."

He had vanished from sight while Lambon was still collecting the fruit which had been scattered from her basket. It is his fruit, she thought, running after him. She caught him up only at the edge of the village. "Here is your basket," she called out breathlessly. "Keep it," he called back. But she ran on and caught hold of him by his kain. He turned round and stood close to her with a laughing tender look in his eyes.

"You will not be able to dance much longer, Lambon," he said. I never noticed it until today, he thought. Lambon is too old now for the legong.

Lambon gazed at him without understanding at once what he was saying. It had never entered her head that her dancing was over when she arrived at puberty.

"Too old——?" she murmured. "But what shall I do when I cannot dance any longer?"

He felt sorry for her; not very, for she was charming and he knew that he could have her when he wished.

"It is time you looked out for a husband," he said. "There are plenty of men in the village who would like to sleep with you." He took her head in his hands for a moment, her warm hair in his warm hands. The three purple flowers were still in her hair, but crushed, when he turned and left her. Lambon stood looking after him until he reached the gate and disappeared.

His wife looked up from the loom as he came in, for he had been three weeks away from home; but he said nothing as he went past her to the sty with the little pig. "Has Raka come home?" his mother asked, for her eyes had grown dim. "Yes, he is here," the pedanda, Ida Bagus Rai, called out to her, and went on chiselling a raksasa in stone which was to be set up as guardian at the cross-roads at the entrance to the village.

Teragia stood for a moment beside her weaving loom and then followed her husband to the pigsty.

Teragia was always the first to rise in the priest's house-hold. She left Raka still fast asleep and went out softly. The morning was dewy and loud with the songs of birds. She returned to the house again to get a clean kain and she put another ready for Raka when he woke. She paused a moment to look at his sleeping face. Raka the beautiful. His hair fell over his cheeks and he breathed deeply and evenly. Raka, Teragia thought, my husband, my handsome brother. She never got over her amazement that the gods had given her Raka. Beside his beauty she felt herself ugly, and stiff and dead beside his life. She spread out her hands over his breast, but did not venture to touch him.

When she went out into the courtyard again to get water from the large earthenware vessel and wash her face and hands, she heard her father-in-law, the great pedanda, Ida Bagus Rai, coughing in the big house; and so she went quickly to the kitchen quarters and roused the two servants. Soon after the fire in the hearth was fanned to a flame and the smoke curled out through the thatched roof.

Teragia bowed low as the pedanda descended the steps. She knew that he meditated in the mornings and disliked speaking before he had prayed. Also he might not eat, drink or chew sirih until he had blessed the holy water for the day. She stood humbly to one side as he passed without seeing her. Ida Bagus Rai was a tall man whose hair was turning gray and the bridge of his nose was as thin as the blade of a knife. He walked on to the balé, where he prayed and sat down on his cushion with legs crossed and folded hands to meditate. The day before Teragia had woven small platters of palm-leaves of the kind prescribed for the daily offerings. She fetched cooked rice from the kitchen and sirih from the basket, and she went into the garden to pick flowers for the offerings and arranged them in the correct manner in the platters. Then she stepped over the bamboo grating which separated the precincts of the house temple from the rest of the courtyard, to keep the pigs out.

There were many beautiful shrines. The pedanda himself had chiselled the stone figures of gods and demons on which the altars rested. Teragia folded her hands over her forehead, knelt down and then laid the offerings on each shrine. The fowls came and pecked up any grains of rice that were left over. The sun was now up and a blue moist haze rose from the palms and mingled with the acrid smoke from the kitchen hearth. Teragia's next task was to put the loom ready for Raka's mother. The old lady could still weave quite well by the mere touch of her skilled hands without the use of her eyes. But Teragia had to put the strands of yarn ready for her with the colors in the right order. When this was done it was time to go to the spring to fetch water for the pedanda to consecrate.

Teragia would not leave this task to a servant; it was her own treasured and sacred duty. Also the women of the village believed that the water which Teragia herself fetched had a double virtue. Therefore she raised the heavy pitcher to her head, after placing over its mouth a basket with a few little offerings, and left the yard.

She soon joined the procession of women who were on their way to the spring to bathe. They were mostly pious elderly women who were not content to bathe in the river but took the longer steeper path up the river gorge where a very ancient and incredibly large wairingin tree gripped with its roots the mossy rocks whence the spring issued. Every day when Teragia, alone and unaccompanied by a servant, mingled with them as though she were one of themselves, it was a feast of joy to them. They touched her dress and her hands to show their pleasure and crooned old-fashioned blessings on her in long-drawn chants—happiness for the day, joy on her path, stillness of mind and a son, or many, in due time. Some of them who were grandmothers brought their grandchildren with them to let Teragia see the cuts they had got from bamboo splinters or from coral on the beach.

Teragia loved these early morning hours when everything glistened as though created afresh overnight. She took off her two kains and stood beneath the spring which spouted from the mouth of an old, mossy stone serpent. She looked like a boy among the other women, for she was taller than they and her breasts scarcely showed. After washing her hair and smoothing it down she wound her kains about her again. Then she joked with the old women and took the children between her knees and rubbed an ointment of yellow kunjit on their sore places. She did not fill her pitcher until peace fell again on the spring. But first she laid her offerings on the little wooden altars which stood in the gorge above it. Her knees shook as she hoisted the full pitcher on to her head, but she was strong and carried her load with back erect.

When she reached the river again she did not take the usual path by the ford but went about a hundred paces upstream, where a small basin had been hollowed out among some rocks. Lower down, the river was already approaching the sea and sluggish, but here it rushed turbulently in small rapids. As Teragia crossed it, she caught sight of the pedanda at the edge of the river a little higher up. He was cleaning his teeth, washing his long hair and bathing. He was accompanied only by two pupils. Teragia too called herself a pupil of her father-in-law's, for though she was not initiated into the secrets of the sacred Mantras and Mudras, he taught her to read the old books and imparted the knowledge by which one could tell which days were auspicious and which of all the thousand different offerings to offer up.

When Teragia got home again Raka was still asleep, but his mother was already seated at her loom. "Greeting, daughter, peace on your coming," she chanted. Teragia stroked the old lady's hands and put a flower in her smooth hair. "Peace on your work," she replied, smiling.

The two servant-girls were laughing happily as they swept the courtyard and fed the pigs. Teragia carefully poured out some of the spring water into a silver vessel, which she then replaced on the tripod in the prayer balé She fetched spills of sandalwood to burn and lit the sacred fire in a small brazier. She poured more water into a jar, ready for the priest's washings. She brought flowers from many bushes and trees, red for Brahma, blue for Vishnu, white for Shiva. She tied a flower to the silver staff which was used for sprinkling the consecrated water and put the long-handled bell ready in its silken holder. She put on one side the basket containing the high crown which the pedanda wore at high festivals and arranged his cushion. When all was done she surveyed her work with satisfaction. While standing thus she felt what seemed to be a light touch on her neck. She turned quickly round with her hand on the place where she felt the touch. No one had touched her. But Raka was on the portico of the house and it must have been his look she felt as he looked at her from behind.

"Here is an empty stomach shouting for cooked rice," he called to her. He patted the fine network of muscles over his diaphragm. Teragia laughed. "I was coming, hungry man," she called back, and then, after quickly and rather hurriedly putting sirih beside the cushion, she ran to the kitchen.

She came back to Raka with a heaped-up leaf and found him sitting comfortably on his heels. The sweet clove scent of his cigarette pervaded the courtyard. Raka is at home again, Teragia thought happily. The rice was steaming hot and Teragia held the leaf while he ate. It pleased her to wait on him, though her palms hurt with the heat. She went for a second supply when she saw that he had still not had enough; also, as a surprise she brought him strong coffee in the only glass the household boasted of. Then she stood watching while her husband ate and drank and smoked again. "Come, eat too," he said affectionately, and gave her what was left.

She sat turned away in a corner, for it was not the right thing to eat in a husband's presence, and ate gladly.

Now the pedanda entered the courtyard and walked to the house with unseeing eyes and mind absorbed. Teragia left her husband, although she would gladly have stayed on enjoying these happy moments with him for ever. She went instead to give the priest his comb and the oil to comb out his hair. When it was smoothed to a close helmet round his refined and slender skull, he tied it in a tight knot at the back of his head, as a sign of his rank.

Teragia walked behind him as he went to his balé. He turned to the west, rinsed his mouth three times, poured water over his feet and again smoothed his hair. Then he took up the kain of white linen, which is the vestment of a pedanda, and put it on instead of his ordinary dress. Cleansed thus for his sacred duties he turned his face to the east, towards his domestic altar, in order to speak with the gods. The fowls assembled expectantly beneath the balé, waiting for the grains of rice which fell to the ground in the course of the ceremony. A particularly impudent, youthful and ill-bred fowl made a great clatter which almost drowned the priest's murmured words.

When Teragia looked about for Raka she discovered him leaning against a tree watching his father with a mixture of awe and amusement. He was now wearing a cloth wound rakishly about his head and the sunlight flashed from his teeth. Raka, Teragia thought again, that is Raka, my husband, whose child I bear within me. He knows nothing of the darkness upon which floats the world. Raka grimaced as the little monkeys in the garden always did, and vanished with a wave of the hand behind the kitchen. Teragia collected herself and followed the prayers with an earnest face.

Holding a champak flower between the forefinger of his clasped hands, with his priest's ring on his thumb, Ida Bagus Rai spoke to the gods. He called on each one singly and for each one he cast a petal into the holy water and threw flowers to each of the four points of the compass. He took up the bell and rang it to call the attention of the gods and he moved his fingers, with all the grace of a dancer, in the ancient manner prescribed in the Mudras. From time to time he ceased from his murmured prayers and sank into a mute and concentrated supplication, with clasped hands raised to his forehead. Then he sprinkled himself and the flowers with water and put a tiny fan of flowers in his hair, as ordained for the priest. The fowls stood by and looked on. Teragia waited below the balé to be of service to him, but Ida Bagus Rai saw no one. The prayers went on and on, for the gods were many and each had to be summoned and addressed by his name as Lord and King and Prince and Raja. Teragia kept a look-out for Raka out of the corner of her eyes. He was sitting now on the balé where the implements were stored and busily employed. The servants' children stood leaning against him, and two sons of their neighbor as well, and he was making kites for all of them. I will give you a fine son, and his kites will fly the highest, Teragia thought happily. She left the prayer balé and joined the group. Raka did not even see her. He and the children were now pulling hideous and comical faces at each other and their laughter rang through the courtyard. Teragia went closer to them; she was aware of the weight in her womb and felt that her hands were empty. She put them on the shoulders of one of the children and the boy looked round at her and his laughter died away.

"There is a good wind for kite-flying today," Raka said. "We will go on to the stubble fields later on and fly them." Beasts of various shapes and colors lay scattered about his feet, great long-tailed fishes, birds and legendary creatures, for Raka was a welcome visitor in many villages and could construct kites of strange shapes, not only the square ones of Taman Sari.

"Yes, that will be grand," Teragia said.

"Will you come with us?" Raka asked. She looked at him in surprise. "Perhaps——" she faltered. It scarcely seemed possible for her to go out kite-flying with a herd of children. It was all right for Raka. She stood there beside him a moment longer and then went back to the pedanda. No sooner had she turned her back than the laughter burst out again.

Ida Bagus Rai, as soon as his last prayer was ended, flung himself on the sirih he had resisted for so long. He smiled at Teragia, but it took a little time before the solemn expression left his eyes. The first supplicants for his counsel were already collecting in front of the house. Teragia saw Pak's father and rich Wajan among them. "Where has Raka gone?" she asked his mother. "To the palms," the old lady replied. Teragia followed her husband there, for she wanted to be with him as long as he was at home.

She could not find him at first. It was only when the cry of a betitja bird came from the top of a tree that she discovered him. He was
up there, gripping the trunk with his feet as though he were part of
the tree, imitating the bird's note. A young and unpractised betitja,
who had not yet learnt to sing properly, answered with a false note
or two. "Come up, Teragia," Raka called down jokingly. She clasped
the trunk in her arms—it was always something—and waited. Raka
took his knife from his girdle and cut the large palm-leaves which
were used in the household. They fell down with a loud rustling
noise. When he had got enough he came down. Teragia let go of
the tree and bent to pick up the heavy leaves and put them over her
shoulders. Raka watched her for a moment, then took her load from
her—it was no load for him. "Pity," he said suddenly. "What is a pity,
my brother?" she asked. "That you aren't a man," Raka said, smiling.
"It would be fun to have you for a friend if you were a man." Teragia
smiled too. "But then I could bear you no sons," she said with bent
head. He was silent for a moment and then began to whistle like a
betitja and went off with the leaves. It is true, Teragia thought, letting
her hands fall to her sides, I have let two children escape too soon
from my impatient womb. But this time she felt safe, for her father,
who was a great doctor, had uttered powerful blessings over her.

The morning was taken up with work in house and garden. Everything was bright and radiant, for Raka was at home. She felt his
presence everywhere, even when she did not actually see him. In the
kitchen the servant girls squealed with delight over everything he
said and did. Later she saw him sitting with his father and eagerly
telling him something. Next he ran across the courtyard, taking his
mother a fresh skein of yarn. Then he was up on the roof of the balé
in which the offerings were got ready, mending the thatch, accompanied by two children, and a moment later the rope of the well near
the house altars rattled and ran. He played with the wild pigeons,
which he had taught to curtsy to him. Then she saw him busied with
leaves of lontar palm as though he were going to write a book, as his
father did. It was not that, however. When she bent over him to see,
he was cutting beautiful fishes out of the leaves; then the children
came back from the beach bringing a particular variety of mussel
which they heaped up at his feet. Raka looked up at Teragia and
stopped in his work. "I am making a chime for the temple," he said

almost defiantly. "It will be used for the New Year's Festival." "That is right," she said. There were still three months until the festival of the Galangan Nadi. She left him to his task of tying the tinkling mussel shells to the leaves. Why do I always seem to be interrupting him? she wondered. She went away, but stopped in the next court-yard and looked at him over the bamboo fence; her eyes could never have enough of him. He did not know she was watching him, but he shook his head as though an ant had been annoying him. Teragia walked quickly away. She felt uneasy and, asking the old mother's leave, took a basket and went into the village. She paid her father, the doctor, a visit, went to the market to make purchases and looked in at several houses where there were old or sick people to attend to. The whole time she felt restless and knew that it was only strength of will that kept her away from Raka. His hand rested on my heart at night, she thought, but she did not believe it all the same.

On the way home she heard from a distance shouts and jubila-tions coming over the walls. There was a miscellaneous crowd at the gate looking through, and they, too, held their sides for laughing, and more and more people came up to see what was going on. Tera-gia pushed her way through and entered the yard. There she found a circle of people who might have been watching a play. In the centre was Raka walking to and fro, giving a performance. He had folded up his head-dress into a little cushion, as women do to carry loads on their heads, and on the top he was balancing a flat basket of the kind used for offerings, piled up with indiscriminate articles as offerings and covered with a red cover. His loin-cloth was bound round his chest, and he was obviously imitating a woman who was very proud of her beautiful offerings and walked with mincing steps to the temple. His face beamed with delight over his performance. From top to toe he was a woman: his hips rolled, his hands fluttered with refined affectation, his half-closed eyes expressed unashamed depths of feminine self-consciousness.

Teragia put her basket down and stopped in the gateway. She ob-served Raka's father among the spectators, wiping tears of laughter from his eyes. His mother was there too; she could not see but was being told all that went on by a neighbor. "Now he is twisting his neck," she announced, almost weeping with laughter; "now he's afraid the offerings will fall down as he goes up the steps; now he's

wobbling his hips just like old Dadong, who thinks she's so beautiful; now he's stumbled, but he only puts on a sweeter expression."

Raka was utterly absorbed in his impersonation and the more
people laughed the more new turns occurred to him. Just as he was
about to take the basket from his head and give it to his father, who
often took the offerings from the women at high festivals, and just
as the pedanda was entering good-naturedly and heartily into the
joke, Raka suddenly saw his wife.

Teragia stood on the top of the steps leading up from the road
watching him. Her mouth was open with amazement. She thought
she was smiling, but not a smile crossed her face. Raka went on for
a moment and then stopped abruptly. He pulled the loin-cloth from
his chest, gave the make-believe pile of offerings a kick that sent
them flying, and became a man again. The laughter ceased. The pedanda, as though he had forgotten something, took up his chisel with
an almost embarrassed air and turned again to the figure he was at
work upon. The gathering dispersed and in a moment the courtyard
was empty. Only from the kitchen at the back there were still sounds
of tittering.

Raka stood in the middle of the yard putting on his headdress,
and it seemed he was waiting for Teragia to speak to him. "How long
have you been here?" he asked at last, just as though she was a visitor. And like a visitor she replied, "I have only just come."

"Why did you not laugh?" he asked. Teragia said quietly, "I did
laugh. I laughed a lot, it was very funny." Raka looked at her with
annoyance. Suddenly she caught sight of a flower under his turban
above his forehead and she went quickly up to him. "Oh, Raka," she
said softly, "what have you got there?"

It was a large-flowered orchid, seven blooms on one spray, fluttering like butterflies over his forehead.

"Isn't it a beauty?" he asked. "I found it in the garden. Would you
like it? If you'll only laugh I'll give it you perhaps."

"Oh, Raka," Teragia repeated, "you ought not to have taken
it——"

He pouted like a scolded child. "Aren't you pleased when I adorn
myself?" he asked, but then taking the spray from his head he held
it out to her. Teragia did not take it.

"We went right to the forests of Besaki, three days' journey, for them," Teragia said slowly. "He wants these orchids for the first day of the Galangan. We waited until they would be in flower. They belong to Shiva. You ought not to have taken them. There are plenty of other flowers to decorate yourself with——"

Raka's head hung down sorrowfully, but the next moment he looked up defiantly.

"You are a pedanda yourself——" he said. "Much too holy for me."

He looked down in her face, hoping to see some response there to his joke But Teragia looked grave and upset and only repeated, "Oh, Raka——"

He still held the white orchid in his hand and at last he forced her to take it.

"How is it you cannot even laugh?" he asked abruptly.

Teragia stared at him. "Can I not laugh?" she said incredulously. He shook his head. "Forgive me," she said slowly. When he looked at her he saw that her eyes were shining, but she was not crying.

"Has your father never told you what happened to me?" she asked.

"Did someone hurt you?" he asked impulsively.

"Oh no," Teragia said. "Oh no, no one has hurt me, my brother——"

He drew her down beside him on the steps and held her hand in his. Warmth flowed in and over her. She let her eyes fall to the white orchid in her hand and began to speak hesitatingly.

"We lived far from here then, at Abeanbase in Gianjar," she said. "And that is why you have never heard about it. I was a child, eight years old perhaps. My grandmother fell sick and then my mother, and in a short time they both died. Then I fell sick, and for all his prayers my father could not cure me. He could cure all the people in the village, but not me. My skin broke out into hideous sores which ate my flesh away to the bone——"

She felt Raka's hand draw back involuntarily, and this hurt her, but she had to go on. "My father put himself into a trance, but no god appeared to him to give him advice and he remained hollow and vacant. The months went on and I only got worse, until there was not a healthy spot left on my body; my blood burned with the poison and my strength was wasted away; at last my heart grew weak and scarcely beat any more. Again my father put himself into a trance and this time Durga, the goddess of death, entered into him and told him he ought to take me to the Temple of the Dead and leave me there to die, alone and in her protection only.

"My father did so. Before sundown he carried me in his own arms to the Temple of the Dead, and he has often told me that I weighed no more than a fowl that he might have been taking as a sacrifice. He took offerings with him too, and the few women of my family who were still alive mad offerings. My father sat with me holding my hand—as you are holding it now, my brother—and waited till the sun had gone down. He called once more to the goddess to take me to herself, and he listened for my heart and it beat no longer. Then he said farewell to me and went away.

"They had laid me in the balé where the offerings were prepared and had spread a white kain over me. I was so weak that I saw my father only in a mist when he left me, and then I knew no more. In the middle of the night I woke up and the court of the temple was a blaze of light. I saw all the altars in a light brighter than sunlight, and the temple was full of forms. But no, I did not see them, but I felt their presence, and I knew that I was surrounded by many invisible beings. I had no fear, only joy, and then I lost consciousness again and fell asleep and knew no more."

Teragia stopped for a moment and looked at the orchids in her lap. She noticed that Raka breathed uneasily.

"When I woke up," she went on, "it was bright daylight. The birds sang and my heart was very light. A gray goat with two kids was scrambling about in the court of the temple, eating the flowers from the offering plates, and I looked at the kids and laughed, for they pleased me. Then I looked at my hands—and they were clean. All the sores had healed. They had healed so completely that I had forgotten the pain; and never since that day have I been able to remember what the pains and the sickness were like. When the sun rose above the trees my father came to bury me. And he found me healed and without a sore on my whole body, and I was playing with the two little kids."

"And then?" Raka asked when Teragia was silent for a time. She looked at him in surprise.

"What more shall I tell you, brother?" she asked softly. "Since then it has been granted to me to heal sick children, and sometimes the gods speak through my mouth. You say that I cannot laugh. But I know I am very happy. There is not a happier woman than I am, and you must forgive me if I am sometimes burdensome to you. Perhaps I am fashioned of stone and not of bamboos that float on the water . . ."

When Raka bent over his wife to look into her face he found that she was smiling after all. And it was, as she said, the smile to be seen sometimes on the stone statues in the temples, an enigmatic smile and quite without mirth.

She took the white orchid from her lap and put it back under Raka's head-dress. "There," she said, "you were quite right to pick it. It looks beautiful on your forehead and you shall wear it. There will be more of them in flower when your father needs them. Forgive me for troubling you . . ."

❋   ❋   ❋   ❋   ❋

Pak was ploughing for the third time on the eastern sawahs, and now the soil was soft and kindly and replied with a light rustle when he went over it with the lampit to break it down. The labor had been heavy, and if his legs were weary they ached no longer. The sawah lay ready to receive the seedlings.

Pak had set aside the best of his sheaves, part for the temple dues and part for seed. Now at last the time had come when he could gather up in bundles the little green seedlings, which he had grown from seed in a corner of the sawah, and his brother Meru helped him with the planting.

While he planted Pak thought of Sarna and talked to her in his head all the time. My little pigeon, he said, my white roe, my young mangis fruit. He never knew before that such words existed, but they came into his mouth of themselves. When he met Sarna in secret and held her in his arms he said things like that to her. My little pigeon, my white roe, my young mangis fruit. Sarna did not laugh at him, although she loved to laugh and teased him a great deal.

She did not seem to dislike his strong brown body, for she met him as often as she could; but though she gladly gave him her bloom and fragrance she would hear nothing of marriage. "What should I do in your home?" she asked mockingly. "You have not even room for a second wife. Should I have to cook for Puglug and do her work, while she was at the market enjoying herself?" Or else she said, "How can you think of marrying me? Why, you have not even had your teeth filed." And Pak was ashamed. Or else she said, "Where would you get the money from to buy me plenty of new sarongs? I'm vain, you know, and I like always to be beautifully dressed. Someone has promised me five foreign gold pieces to make five gold rings with."

"And I can buy you ten gold pieces," Pak bragged. "But perhaps you expect the raja to send for you and make you his wife."

"And why not?" Sarna asked coquettishly, and Pak felt he was seething in boiling oil like the sinful souls in hell. He was not a very prudent lover and the whole village knew his secret. Puglug, in spite of her volubility, held her tongue and this weighed on him. He would have preferred hearing her rail at him when he had spent the night away from home, or decked himself out with new head-dress or loin-cloth. He always now wore hibiscus flowers behind his ear and the little bush beside the house altar was stripped bare.

"Brother, who eats our hibiscus flowers overnight?" Meru asked him, for Meru, too, wanted a flower behind his ear when he went to Badung to carve the temple door for the prince. "We have no more flowers left for the offerings," Puglug said curtly. "It has come to this—that I have to pay money for them at the market or barter sirih for them."

"Yes, it is a scandal that we haven't flowers enough of our own for the offerings," their aunt agreed, being for once of the same opinion as Puglug. "Look at him strutting about like a cock that has won twenty fights."

The heavy field labors were done and Pak had nothing to do but wait while the western fields lay fallow and the young plants grew tall in the eastern ones. He only went out now and again to weed and look to the edges of the fields and see that the water was deep enough. At this stage no woman might set foot in the sawah, not even Sarna, who sometimes came along as though by accident. The sawah was now imbued with good, rich strong male force, which begot increase, and no woman might intrude.

"I will build you a house such as not even the wives of the raja have," Pak said to Sarna one night under the shadow of the wair-ingin tree.

She let her fingers stray lightly and caressingly over his face. "How many ringits have you got buried under your house to make you talk like that?" she asked, laughing. Her laughter came from her throat like the coo of wild pigeons. It made Pak's blood pulse in his veins whenever he heard this laugh. He bit her throat as young horses did when they had done with play and wanted to come together.

"If I had many ringits buried, would you like me better?" he asked breathlessly. But it was impossible to get Sarna to answer a serious question.

"You can't be dearer to me than you are," she said, and clasped her hands behind his neck in a warm, untiable knot.

Pak went and dug up the plates from his field and took them home and buried them in secret under his house where his ringits were. Puglug was at market and had no suspicions. But it did not escape the old man, who knew everything. "Son," he said, "I have asked my friend the pedanda and he has given me some holy water to mix with your food. I have been to the balian, too, and given him eleven kepengs and a large offering and he will break the spell. But you keep grubbing about in the earth like a dung-beetle burying his ball of dung, and you are driven round in circles day and night. You know that your mother must be burnt soon so that her soul may be freed. What are you looking for in the earth under the house? Are you digging up your savings and taking them to the woman who has bewitched you instead of thinking of your mother's soul?"

At this Pak could keep his secret no longer, but dug the plates up again and showed them to his father by the light of the oil lamp. The old man held them up close to his dim eyes and stroked the smooth porcelain and looked at the roses and pondered over them for a long time. "Where did these come from?" he asked at last.

"They came from the earth in our eastern sawah when I was ploughing deeply," Pak said. It was not actually a lie and his con-science was clear.

"Plates such as these came to us long ago from the countries beyond Java, from China and countries whose names are not known," the old man said, and Pak marvelled, as so often before, at the extent of his father's knowledge.

"Are they worth a lot of money?" he asked deferentially.

And his father said, "More than you can count. Someone must have buried them in the raja's sawah long ago."

One day Pak wrapped the plates in a freshly washed kain and tied them to a bamboo and set off for Sanur.

"Where are you going?" he was asked by everyone he met.

"To Sanur," he said without stopping.

"What are you going to do at Sanur?" they asked.

"I have something to sell the Chinese, Njo Tok Suey," he replied with an important air as he walked on. The whole village was left buzzing with curiosity and that was just what he wanted.

When he arrived at the Chinaman's house he had to pluck up his courage, but at last he went in; he did not crouch on his heels on the ground but stood upright, for Njo Tok Suey was a Chinaman without caste.

"If you have pigs to sell you had better go to Kula with them," the Chinese said. "The boats that put in here want no more pigs. But if you have any copra, we could talk about that."

"I don't want to sell either pigs or copra but something far better, something you have never before set eyes on," Pak said, puffed up with pride. "Show me," the Chinese said. Pak undid the clean kain with ceremony, wiped each plate before taking it out and then displayed the three plates.

Njo Tok Suey at first said nothing at all. Then he went into the house for his spectacles. Pak quailed slightly, but not too much, when the Chinaman emerged wearing the spectacles. A man who had less hair on his head than a pig on its back could not make much impression on him.

"Where did these plates come from?" the Chinese asked.

Pak was ready with his story of having turned them up in his field when he was ploughing deeply. He told him also what his father had said. "They came from China long ago and must have been buried as a great treasure in the raja's fields. Perhaps they were an offering against bad harvests and mice," he added on his own account, for this had just occurred to him and struck him as being a remarkably acute observation. Njo Tok Suey shook his head as he turned the plates over in his hands. "They are not old and they do not come from China either," he said. Suddenly something appeared to have come into his head, and he went quickly into the house and came back with a voluminous document. Pak looked over his shoulder, but he could make nothing of it.

"It occurred to me that somebody had stolen from the ship and buried them in your sawah," Njo Tok Suey said finally. "But they are not on the list." This sounded Chinese to Pak's ears, but nevertheless he gave a slight start. He had contrived to forget how the plates came into his hands, and now he shuddered when he remembered the night he had kept watch and encountered the husky man. "Why do you come to me with these plates?" Njo Tok Suey asked.

"I want to sell them and you are the only man with enough money; also you know better than other people the worth of such treasure," Pak said confidentially. Njo Tok Suey again looked the plates over. "You have not any copper to sell?" he asked abruptly.

"What is copper?" Pak asked with an innocent expression.

"I can easily tell you that," the Chinese replied. "Copper is what you people stole from the ship which was wrecked here. Kepengs are made of it."

"I stole nothing," Pak replied in an injured tone. "I was one of the watch." Whereupon Njo Tok Suey looked at him for some time in silence.

Pak had heard talk in the village of this and that having been taken from the wreck, but nobody bothered about it any longer. He had even been to the beach himself with his younger brother, Lantjar, who deserved a little fun now and again, and was of use besides helping to carry home nails and wood and whatever else they might find.

"I want to take a second wife and I must build her a house, for she comes of wealthy parents and is beautiful enough to ask that and more," Pak said, deciding to put all his cards on the table. "That is why I want to part with my treasure and sell the plates which the Goddess herself sent me. It costs money to marry a second wife, as you know, sir."

Njo Tok Suey removed his spectacles as though the plates were not worth further inspection. "I have no use for the plates," he said. "You would do better to bring me copra. But to oblige you I will give you ten kepengs for each of them."

Pak laughed bitterly. He knew that dealing with a Chinese was worse than having leeches behind your knees. But this was going too far. "Ten ringits each," he shouted. "And even then it is making you a present of them."

They bargained on and on, but the Chinese was hard-headed and it came to nothing. Twelve kepengs each was the utmost he would bid, and this was no more than Pak sometimes spent in one day on sirih alone. He wrapped up his plates again and returned to Taman Sari. He was not downhearted, far from it. He buried the plates again, this time near the wall, so that Puglug might not find them, and carefully trod down the soil.

Next day the whole village knew that Pak had turned up some plates in his sawah, and a number of inquisitive people turned up on one pretext or another and stood about in his yard, keeping their eyes open for a sight of the plates. This was just what Pak wanted. It might be all to the good if the wealthy Wajan heard that Pak, who was poor, had something that no one else in the village had so much as set eyes on.

From now onwards Puglug talked of nothing else, and she turned up every yard of earth in the courtyard in the hope of finding the plates, and seeing them with her own eyes and touching them with her own fingers. His aunt and uncle brought him tid-bits to wheedle his secret out of him. And Pak was aware from all sides how greatly he had grown in importance. Sarna alone asked no questions. She merely gave him a sidelong look now and then, while her tongue roamed over her upper lip—a sign that she was thinking something over. Pak himself had to introduce the topic.

"There are some people in the village who seem to think I have turned up treasure in my sawah," he said. He was having rather a restless time of it, for as soon as Puglug left the house, he dug up the plates and buried them again somewhere else so that she should not find them. Also, now that the Chinaman had refused to deal, he did not know what to do but bury them in one place after another and content himself with the riches of secrecy and the importance it gave him.

"The people in the village seem to think you offered yourself for the low job of scaring squirrels and gathering coconuts, like any other poor man," Sarna said, and her words were like a douche of cold water.

"There are some things women do not understand," he replied with dignity. Sarna pinched his ears and laughed, but before he left her she asked when they would meet again, and the lover's fever in his blood burnt more fiercely than ever.

It was true that he was working hard at gathering coconuts; he wanted more than his own twelve trees yielded. By rights he ought now to be taking it easy after the heavy labors of ploughing and planting. Instead of that he had to climb up and down the palm trees, skinning his calves on the trunks, and then load himself up with coconuts. When he got home he set his brother Lantjar and his sister Lambon to work to cut up the nuts and dry them in the yard, so that he should have copra to sell the Chinaman.

"It's a shame," Puglug broke out. "Soon we shall not have a drop of coconut milk to feed Klepon on when she teethes and we shall have to buy coconuts for the temple dues and we shall forget what grated coconut tastes like."

"Which only shows that there is more sense in many a coconut than in the heads of some people I know of," her aunt said, bristling for battle. Pak said nothing at all. He took his four cocks to the place where most of the men forgathered at that time of day. He wanted to hear no more for a good while about women, coconuts and buried crockery. Even his little sister, Lambon, was not the same ever since she had grown too old to dance the legong. She sat sullenly in front of a pile of coconuts, which were destined to become copra, and forgot even to lift her knife for half an hour together.

And so it came to that Friday when all Pak's perplexities were submerged for an hour or two in the excitement of an event which went beyond anything he had ever experienced.

It started with the beating of the kulkul to summon all the men of the village to the house of the punggawa of Sanur. They lost no time; from Taman Sari and from the neighboring four villages along the coast they hastened over the rice-fields strung out in single file. It was the same as on the day when the Chinese ship struck. "What can it mean?" Pak asked the wise Krkek. "I had the news yesterday," he replied carelessly. "A great punggawa of the white men has come in a ship from Buleleng to ask questions of us."

"Ask questions of us? What does he want to ask?" Pak cried out, and his knees gave way beneath him with fright.

"We shall know soon," was all Krkek said.

The punggawa's courtyard was like the entrance to a hollow tree inhabited by, bees. It was one surging jostling crowd and women vendors had already spread their mats on its fringes, for there was the promise of doing a brisk trade. Pak squeezed his way into the yard behind Krkek, and as most of the crowd was now squatting down he made room for himself between two half-grown lads. And now he saw the white man.

The sight was not nearly so bad as he had imagined it would be. In the first place, the white man was no taller than Pak himself, and he sweated like any ordinary man. All the same, there was something frightening about his face, for it was not white, as you might have expected, but pink, as light-colored buffaloes were beneath their bristles. The white man was enclosed in unbecoming and solidly constructed clothing, though this certainly was white, and he sat on a kind of seat Pak had never seen before.

"What is that he is sitting on?" he whispered in Krkek's ear.

"A chair. All white men have them," Krkek said. Pak clicked his tongue in amazement.

"Is he lame?" he asked next, when he had considered this strange apparatus from new points of view. "Or why do his legs hang down like that?"

"Be quiet," Krkek said testily. "White men cannot sit in any other way. It is the sign of their caste." This satisfied Pak for the time. He could tell that the white man was of high caste by the fact that his chair was higher than the punggawa's mat. Also the punggawa's servant held the indispensable umbrella over the white man and not over the ruler of the coast villages.

"Silence," the men in the courtyard called out, and stirred expectantly to and fro. "He is going to speak to us."

All opened their mouths in order to hear better and a murmur of wonder ran through the crowd when the Controller addressed them in their own tongue. "He speaks like anyone else," Pak said, quite taken aback. Rib, the wag, was sitting near him. "Did you expect him to grunt like a pig?" he asked audibly, and there was laughter from behind. The punggawa stood and looked over the heads of the crowd. "Silence," he said severely. "Listen to what the tuan Controller has to say to you and answer when you are asked."

"People of Sanur, Taman Sari, Intaran, Renon and Dlodpekan," the Controller said, "you all remember that on the second day of the third week of the second month a ship, the *Sri Kumala*, was wrecked on your coast?"

"That is so," the people murmured readily.

"Now I want those of you whom the punggawa appointed as a watch to step forward."

For a time the courtyard looked like a rice sieve when women shake it and the grains roll this way and that. But at last twelve men pushed their way to the front row with their hands clasped. Pak was one of them and Sarda, the fisherman, and his waggish friend, Rib, and several other of Pak's neighbors. "It is true then that a watch was set," the Controller said to the punggawa. Krkek made himself the spokesman for the rest.

"It is," he said in a voice that trembled slightly. "There was a watch set for several days, two and two, good honest men."

The Controller pondered this, wrinkling his forehead meanwhile. "Punggawa," he said.

"Tuan Controller," said the punggawa, and clasped his hands as though he were a man of no caste in comparison with the white man.

"The punggawa told me yesterday that he set no watch because he did not wish to accept any responsibility, and that the watchmen of the Chinese were overpowered and the ship plundered. This morning, when questioned by the raja himself, the punggawa took all this back. I am now convinced that a watch was set. But what am I to make of these two different stories, and what am I to say to the tuan Resident?"

"There was a watch set, tuan Controller," the punggawa said, and his voice sounded small and hollow. "But as our watchmen were tired and sleepy men who did not keep good watch over the boat, I thought it better to say that I had not provided a watch."

"Which of you kept watch the first night?" the Controller next asked. "I want to speak to them."

Krkek gave Pak a push in the back which landed him straight in front of the Controller. Clutching about him in alarm he encountered Sarda the fisherman's arm and gripped tight hold of it. The Controller seemed to smile and Pak felt relieved. He ventured shyly to return the smile.

"Now, my friends," the Controller said—and by this time Pak had grown used to the sight of him—"you kept watch the first night. Tell me what you saw. I know all about it, so it is no use lying."

"It was cold and later it rained," Krkek said on behalf of both of them, as neither of them opened his mouth. "It was hard to keep a fire going."

"I have been told that a number of men came in the middle of the night and plundered the boat. Perhaps there were so many of them that you were afraid and ran away. There is no need to be ashamed of that, for you are simple folk and no warriors."

"That is so," they all murmured complacently, for this seemed to them a good way of putting it. Sarda then opened his mouth. "I did not see any men," he said, and shut it again.

"And you?" the Controller asked, looking at Pak. This was unpleasant, for his light eyes were like a blind man's, and yet they looked keenly in Pak's face. He felt hot under his head-dress and his hair stood on end. He wrinkled his forehead and thought hard, for he had a poor memory.

"I don't know whether I saw any men or not," he said at last.

"How do you mean, you don't know? Are your eyes bad?" the Controller asked patiently.

"Very bad. They would not keep open, sir, although I strictly commanded them to. But for as long as they were open I saw no men," Pak said.

Now an event happened—the white man began to laugh. He opened his mouth and laughed aloud. At first they all stared at him, and then the laughter caught on over the whole courtyard. They all pointed and cried out, "Look, just look at him—he is laughing!"

Above all the noise Rib's voice could be heard saying, "Pak had a quiet night for once. He had not got to sleep with his wife!"

The punggawa extended his hand and the laughter slowly ceased. The white man got to his feet and his face was now very serious.

"You people, men of the coast of Badung," he said, "when this boat was wrecked it was driven by the storm, but it was a good ship, laden with money and goods. Is that so?"

There was a murmur of assent.

"When you go down to the shore now, what do you see? A few boards—not even good enough for mussels to take possession of. I want to know what has become of the ship. What has become of the goods and the ringits it carried? Who destroyed it and took away its masts and planks?"

The men stirred uneasily on their bare heels at this direct interrogation. Many of them chewed feverishly and not one made any reply. Someone from behind near the wall growled out that the sea and Baruna, the sea-god, had taken what it pleased them to take, but the murmur soon died away.

"You men are responsible for this ship," the Controller said in a loud voice. "I stand here in the name of my master, the lord Resident of Bali and Lombok, who is a just man and loves you as his own children. If you restore what you have stolen, you shall be pardoned. If not, ships will come with cannon and rifles and you will rue the day you plundered that boat."

The Controller sat down again and wiped the sweat from his face with a white cloth. Profound silence ensued and the men's faces went mute and blind. They clenched their teeth and said not a word. They had been insulted and there was nothing they could say. The silence went on and on and lay like a weight on the courtyard. Suddenly, when it had become almost intolerable, a man stepped forward. Every eye was fixed on him. It was Bengek, the husky man, the son of the witch.

"May I speak?" he asked the punggawa, and the punggawa nodded.

"I am a fisherman, sir," Bengek said in his whispered tones that all the same could be heard in the farthest corner of the yard. "I have to go to sea when it is dark and the men in the village are asleep. I went out earlier than the other fishermen on the night of the shipwreck—and I saw some men. Other nights, too, I saw them, when there was no moon. They waded out and boarded the wreck. They were men from Gianjar."

"How do you know that?" the Controller asked quickly.

"I know their boats. They are built rather differently from ours in Badung," he replied huskily. After pausing a moment longer he retreated again into the crowd. The men showed their relief by whispering together. What Bengek had said was good and to the point. The only pity was that they had not had a better spokesman.

The Controller spoke in a low voice to the punggawa—this time in Malay. Krkek pricked his ears.

"You can go to your homes, I need you no more," the Controller said to the people.

They drifted slowly out of the courtyard; they went unwillingly, for at that moment the Chinese, Njo Tok Suey, made his appearance and with him the other one, the one to whom the ship belonged, and whom Raka had carried from the wreck on his own shoulders. There was a third Chinese with them, and the white man looked at the three with an unfriendly eye.

The men hung about the road in knots discussing the situation.

"Are we to be called thieves, and threatened?" many of them asked, shaking their fists. Krkek, always level-headed, went from group to group, calming them down. "The white man was displeased with the punggawa," he told them. "I heard what they said in Malay. He said it was true that copper from the ship had been found in Gianjar. He called the punggawa dishonest and double-tongued. And he does not love the Chinamen."

Some of them collected round the husky man, who as a rule was avoided, and asked him about the men he had seen. Pak had his own reasons for preferring to keep out of his way; also he was as limp and weary as after hard labor in the fields, and wanted to get home as soon as he could to tell the news. He carefully avoided the road, for he saw Dasni there with her wares beckoning to him, and set off for home across the fields as fast as he could go.

But when he got back, bursting with excitement and the news he had to tell, he found they knew it already. Puglug, in her unpleasant way, had heard all about it at the market and as usual knew more than he did.

"... and the gamelan played as he entered the puri, for he is a great friend of the lord of Badung and he must have the truth," she was saying, and Pak found that all his juicy bits about the white man were forestalled. "He only had to give the Chinaman, Tan Suey Hin, a look and he confessed at once that he had been paid two and a half ringits for accusing in a letter the people of Badung of taking copper from the ship. He was promised two hundred ringits for giving false witness, but the white man can see through your bones to the bottom of your heart, where the truth lies—"

"The truth is in the liver, not in the heart," Pak said in ill-humor, for the sake of getting a word in.

"Then I advise you to keep your liver out of sight," Puglug said with ready wit, and everyone laughed. Women, Pak thought sadly, have quick tongues like serpents. And he put on another head-dress and went to the river to bathe. On the way he bought fragrant oil from a woman vendor and smeared it behind his ears and over his shoulders and then waited for Sarna.

The western fields had lain fallow long enough and, next morning, Pak went out and dug in as manure the ashes of the burnt straw and offered up the first offering and let in the water, thus starting afresh on the cycle of ploughing, planting and harvesting. It did him good to be hard at work again and to feel the sun beat on him and the sweat run down his body. Nevertheless, a new care was added to those he had already. He stayed out in the sawah long after the kulkul had called the men home to eat and rest; and he had a particular reason for this.

The field next to his belonged to Bengek, the fisherman, and his ill-famed mother, and ever since hearing the white man's threat Pak had been haunted by the thought of speaking to the husky man about the plates. But Bengek was a lazy cultivator, and though it was high time he got to work on his sawah nothing was to be seen of him.

Pak went to the river and washed his cow and then drove her in the direction of Sanur, for he was resolved to run Bengek to earth in his home. His cow was refractory, for she knew it was time to go home. "Come, my mother, we must go to Sanur," Pak explained to her as he urged her on in the way she had to go. "I am tired too, my sister, and we will not stay there long."

He tied the beast to a tree outside Bengek's yard and went cautiously in. It was the house nearest the sea and a little way outside the village, not far from the Temple of the Dead, where an enchanted and sacred frangipani tree stood in a bright light of its own. The walls were not built of baked mud but of rough gray coral, in which here and there a piece of red coral was embedded and looked like a sore place. The yard was large and clean and had an almost opulent air. Bengek was there mending his nets and his mother, the witch, was busy in the kitchen.

"Peace on your work," Pak said with exaggerated amiability. "Peace on your evening, old lady." For he was afraid of her. She came close up to him, greeting him in a sing-song voice, and when he looked at her eyes he saw that they watered, which is a certain sign of a witch. "Sirih, my son?" she asked in a friendly way, offering him her own basket, but Pak prudently declined in case she cast a spell on him.

"I looked for you on the sawah, but you didn't come," he said to open the conversation, and Bengek glanced inquiringly at him.

"I am a poor peasant but a good fisherman," he said casually. "Has anything gone wrong with the water that I am to blame for?"

"No, nothing at all," Pak said hurriedly. "It's something else. I was quite astonished at what you told the white man about the men from Gianjar . . ."

As the husky man neither answered nor looked up Pak had no choice but to proceed.

"I don't know if you remember our encounter that night—"

"I don't," Bengek said.

Pak's next words stuck in his throat. "It is about the plates you gave me that night—" he stammered. Bengek threw down his net and looked him in the face. "What about them?" he asked.

"They are very beautiful—but if they came from the Chinaman's boat I shall have to hand them up to the punggawa," Pak said uncomfortably.

"They did not come from the boat and you must not hand them up. Nobody has asked about any plates. There was talk only of copper and iron and ringits."

"Where did you get the plates from?" Pak asked straight out.

"Out of the sea. They got into my net instead of fish which I would much rather have caught," the fisherman said. Pak breathed hard. "Why didn't you keep them?" he asked.

"What should I want with plates? I have no wife and want no toys for children."

"But they are valuable—" Pak said shyly.

"No, they are not. Do you think I should be such a fool as to give them to you if they were?" Bengek asked. "They are worth just as much as the little kindnesses you do me as my neighbor on the land, and no more," he added. Pak's heart was at once lighter and heavier.

"I buried them in my field and offered them up to the goddess. But they came new and beautiful out of the ground again in token that the goddess had taken her joy in them and that I might now make use of them—" he said, breathing more freely.

"Well then, that is all right," the husky man replied with indifference.

"I mean—I wanted to ask you—if I now do what I like with the plates, will you tell people that you gave me them?" Pak asked, forcing himself to come to the point.

"Who? I? No," Bengek said tersely. Sometimes his hoarse voice ran on volubly, as he had shown in the presence of the white man, and sometimes his mouth seemed too lazy to open or shut. He laughed abruptly and it sounded like a cough. "Let's leave it at that— the goddess gave you them," he added .

Pak stood irresolute. "I'll gladly give you a hand any time on your sawah when you're behind."

"That's very kind of you," the fisherman replied.

Pak went politely across to the witch and took leave of her. He was afraid of her. "Peace on your way, my son," she said with a titter. Pak took his cow by the rope and went off at a good pace so as to reach the village before dusk. "Sister," he said confidentially, "we can be glad that's over."

But it seemed that peace had departed from Pak's life ever since the plates entered it; for a week later, it was the fifth day of the fourth month, the following incident occurred:

On that day Pak was busy laying straw on his yard wall and there was silence in the yard. Puglug had gone to Badung to the big market, and the aunt to the next village to attend a funeral. The old man was asleep in his balé, wearied with the heat of the day. Pak was happy; he hummed softly to himself as he spread the straw and smoothed it down to give the wall protection and a good thatch. Then at the farthest side of his premises, where the garden ran on into a coconut palm plantation, he heard a peculiar noise. It sounded like someone crying, and after a moment or two he went to see whether his little daughter Rantun had perhaps hurt herself in some way. But there were no children to be seen, and then he remembered that they had all gone with Lantjar when he took the ducks out into the fields. Pak looked round about and felt a little uneasy, for it is not very pleasant to hear inexplicable noises and to see nothing. But suddenly he caught sight of something yellow thrown down or crouching on the ground among the palm trees; his heart stopped and then raced and he bounded to the spot, for he had recognized Sarna's yellow kain with the blue butterflies.

She lay crouching close to the ground with her hands pressed to her left ear, sobbing as though in great pain, while blood welled out between her fingers and trickled down. Pak went cold with distress as she sat up. "What have they done to you?" he asked in horror. But Sarna only pressed her head against his breast and the blood ran warm and sticky down his body, and when he tried to tear her hands from her face she held them there as tight as steel.

"No one has done anything to me," she sobbed. "Oh, Pak, can I hide in your house?"

He looked round about him; he knew that Puglug was not at home and he would not have cared if she had been. So he helped Sarna to her feet, and supporting her firmly with both his arms, led her past the house altar to his house. "What has happened to you? Who has hurt you?" he asked again and again, while at the same time, not wishing to forget the rudiments of good manners, he muttered that his cabin was wretched and dirty and no place to receive so great a beauty as Sarna. As he spoke he could feel how his heart turned over for pity and fear on her account.

It was not until he had pulled her on to the sleeping bench, and was nursing her in his arms as he did little Klepon, that she consented to remove her hands from her face. They were covered in blood and more blood streamed from her ear and down her neck.

Now Pak saw what had happened. The round hole which Sarna's vanity delighted in adorning with pretty earrings was torn right through the lobe, which was in two bleeding fragments and could never serve for adornment again.

"What does it mean?" he whispered in horror, for his throat was parched. Pak could not bear even to kill a fowl and to see Sarna bleed was an agony to him.

"It means that I refuse to lie in the bed of an ugly old man," she said, sitting bolt upright; and her eyes flashed through their tears. "No, never will I do it," she said. "The mere thought sickens me and I will be disfigured for the rest of my days rather than submit to it."

"Come," Pak whispered, "let me stop the bleeding—shall I run to Teragia?—she has medicine. What did you do, my Sarna—did you do it yourself? Who is the old man you won't give yourself to? I don't understand. Tell me all about it."

Sarna took her head-dress and held it to her torn ear, and although she still sobbed she began to smile and the blood ceased to flow by degrees.

"Do not run about like a chicken after its head is cut off, Pak," she said. "Just hold me tight and I will tell you everything. I am glad I did it and you ought to be glad too."

In the nick of time Pak remembered that there was holy water on the premises, and he ran off to his uncle's balé to get the pitcher. He brought it back and sprinkled the wound with it; he took Sarna in his arms, and then he could feel that she stopped trembling, but still he did not understand.

"Don't you know that the raja's people go round the villages looking for girls for his bed?" Sarna said with more composure. "But I have done enough to make it impossible for them to drag me to the puri and hand me over to the raja."

"The raja—" Pak stammered, staring at her. He had heard tales now and then of girls mutilating themselves in this way when they did not want to be taken into the puri, for it was impossible for a raja to have a woman near him who was disfigured in any way. But they were always girls who had done it out of desperation, because they were in love with a man of the village and could not bear to be parted from him. His heart swelled within him until he felt it in his throat.

"Why did you do it? Tell me," he asked her breathlessly. And it seemed to him incredible that a girl of Sarna's radiance and charm had wounded herself with a knife for his sake and rejected a raja. "Did you do it for my sake?" he whispered, feeling that he was uncouth and dirty from labor and reeking like a swine. Sarna looked at him and laughed softly.

"For your sake?" she said. "Yes, for your sake—"

At this moment the old man came from his balé, for his sleep was light and he had heard Sarna's sobbing. Pak said nothing. He only took his arms away from the girl quickly and squatted down at a distance from her, as propriety demanded. And the old man said nothing either, and, although he saw it all, he did not look but just picked up a basket and disappeared again behind the house.

"The raja is as old as the hills and has been sick for years, as you know. Now they are going to put girls in his bed to warm the marrow in his bones, for his inside is going cold and his entrails are slothful within him and his breath stinks with his sickness," Sarna said. "But they will not have me as medicine for a corpse even if it's the lord of Pametjutan a thousand times over. I am young and I will not be buried alive."

Pak began now to understand. If it was not a question of the young lord Alit, but of the old tjokorda of Pametjutan, and if it was as Sarna said, then her crazed action seemed comprehensible. Sarna took the cloth from the wound now that it had stopped bleeding, and Pak shuddered slightly when he saw the limp, torn lobe. Sarna looked closely in his face. "Now I can never wear earrings again," she said, smiling, while her eyes filled again with tears.

"That is nothing, my little bird—" Pak said, clumsily comforting her. "You are beautiful without any adornment."

"There were little rubies set in them, they cost seven ringits," Sarna lamented. But Pak took her in his arms and said, "And when you marry you will in any case have to give up your earrings, sister."

Sarna nestled up to him and said no more, and after a while the cooing in her throat that always made his pulses beat was to be heard again. "My father will beat me when I get home," she said. Pak, too, feared the wealthy Wajan.

"My father thinks it an honor to be chosen out for the raja of Pametjutan, to be a woman of the palace with lovely kains and no more work to do."

"And all that you have thrown away?" Pak said in a transport. He was prouder of what Sarna had done for him than of anything that had ever happened to him in his whole life. He felt dazed as he thought that he had never known her, never known anything about her until that day. Sarna, the pretty Sarna, had destroyed her own beauty with a knife.

"I will not be shut up as a raja's wife," she said, thinking aloud. "They are hidden away and are no better than prisoners. And the raja is old—he will die soon and then his wives will have to be burned—and I don't want that. But my father will beat me—"

"And so you came to me?" Pak said.

"To whom else could I go?" Sarna asked. Never had he heard words like these. To whom else? To whom, indeed? He stretched to his full height and two fingers' breadth more, and his muscles grew tense. "Your father will not beat you—he has me to reckon with," he said proudly. A happy thought came to him and he jumped up. "Wait, I will show you something no one has seen yet," he said, and ran for his spade.

He had buried the plates near the house altar two days before, and now he took Sarna with him and quickly dug them up with a strength in his arms he had never known before. The pig came up and routed in the earth with his snout. Pak kicked him aside. Sarna squatted on the ground and from time to time she was shaken with a sob, but she was inquisitive and did not cry any more. At last the plates were unearthed and the roses were as fresh as on the first day; the soil could not obscure or hurt them. Pak wiped the plates on his kain and they shone at once. "There—they will be yours when you are my wife," he said, rather out of breath, and laid them at Sarna's feet. She gazed at the treasure open-mouthed and then at Pak and then back at the plates. She said nothing. She stroked the flowers tentatively with her finger-tips and then started back as though afraid. Then she looked again at Pak. He laughed aloud, for it was clear that the plates made a great impression; he began to brag and handled the plates carelessly, clapping one over the other, as though a man like him was quite used to such things. "Take them, they are a present," he said, but Sarna shook her head. "I am afraid of my father," she said again. Pak buried the plates and the pig went disappointedly away. Pak, too, began to be afraid, not only of Sarna's father, but also of Puglug and the noise she would make or, what was worse, her silence, when she came home and found Sarna in her own house. A happy thought struck him. "I will take you to Teragia," he said. "She will see to your wound and make it heal quickly and leave no scar. And Teragia will take you home to your father and speak to him. She is good and has power over people and he will do nothing to you." Sarna looked at him once more, searchingly this time, as though she detected the lurking fear in his heart, and at last she nodded. "Do not come with me," she said finally. "I will go to Teragia alone. Everyone in the village knows by now what I have done, and there must not be any gossip about us."

Pak was thankful she was so sensible and relieved she was going before his domestic troubles broke upon him.

"My father," he said later to the old man, "where would be the best place to build a house for a second wife? And how soon could I start on it?"

The old man laughed to himself and replied, "I will ask my friend, the pedanda, what day would be favorable for building the foundations. And don't worry any more. Even though it is a mistake to marry a woman for her looks, you will soon have had your fill of her and she will soon bear you a son and you will have peace."

* * * * *

Although the weeks that followed were the most eventful in Pak's life, there was a strange stillness in the household. Puglug had been mixing magic potions with his food in order to turn him from Sarna, but when she saw how useless it all was she gave in and did not even say anything, although she knew all. Puglug could be silent with the best when it was her policy; and Pak, who was eagerly absorbed in his preparations, actually believed that she was not aware of his plans. On his side he ignored the little troubles that began mysteriously to arise in his daily life. Sometimes there was not enough to eat when he came in from the sawah, or else he had the same remains put before him day after day long after the ants had infested them. When he looked for a clean kain there was none to be found and Puglug informed him that she had forgotten to do the washing. Or else she had an inflamed place on her arm and could not pound the rice for the household. Then she let the large pitcher fall from her head over the dried copra on the very day when he was taking it to Sanur to sell to the Chinaman. But nothing of all this broke in on Pak's dream, for now he would have a second wife and his life would be as ripe and full of flavor as a durian fruit.

It turned out as his father had promised. The third Friday of the fourth month was the appointed day for beginning the building and Pak had brought along the earth and stones. He himself built the foundation walls, ramming the ground hard to receive them. He would have liked to have used red stones, like those of which Wajan's chief house was built, but he could not find any and it would have been too costly to buy them; and so he used coral as everyone else did. Puglug went round the four sides and spat red betel-juice in her consternation, for it did not escape her that Pak had laid out a building rather larger even than his own house. Meru, on his return from the town, whistled in astonishment. "I've heard already that you carried off his chosen beauty from under the raja's nose, brother," he said good-humoredly. Pak was not sure whether this was said in jest or admiration, for Meru had a great reputation for his knowledge of women and his taste in them. "I shall want a garuda bird with Vishnu on its back for the main beam," he said in lordly style.

"What will you give me to carve you one?" Meru asked.

"Nothing, as you are my brother," Pak said in a wounded tone. Meru whistled again. He could carve garuda birds and Vishnus in his sleep by now—he had done so many for the puri at Badung. "A garuda bird and Vishnu an arm's length in height and painted in red and gold, the same as in Bernis's house," Meru said. "Would that be good enough for her Highness, my brother's second wife?"

"Who is Bernis?" Pak asked. But Meru did not answer. Instead he took his knife from his girdle and began playing with a piece of bamboo. "I'll give you my white cock," Pak said at last, and this was not a bad bargain for Meru.

"The men in the family have all lost their wits," Puglug remarked to her aunt, taking care that Pak should overhear. "They say at Badung market that Meru is poaching in the puri preserves. One brother has lost his head in the village street, and the other will lose his head to the raja if he does not keep his hands off the palace women."

Pak felt a touch of anxiety, for if it was true that Meru was making love on the sly to one of the raja's wives he was in very real danger. He had a brief talk as man to man with his young brother. "You must not run after the women of the puri," he said. "No good ever came of that kind of thing."

Meru slapped himself on the thigh and laughed. "I run after the women?" he shouted. "I like that. It's they who run after me, the little hens. The puri is full of slave-girls and they are all crazy as cats after the rainy season. Look after your own women and I'll look after mine."

"And I'll want four carved cross-beams as well. I want the house to look imposing!" said Pak to end the discussion.

He went about looking for the straightest and best-grown trunks in the plantations, for if he could not buy nanka wood timbers, he wanted at least to have the best durian trees he could find. The best durian trees grew in Wajan's plantation on the edge of the village and this suited Pak particularly well. He could bring off a fine stroke of diplomacy as well as a good bargain.

One Thursday morning he presented himself in Wajan's courtyard wearing his silk saput about his loins and a new head-dress. Wajan received him amiably. As politeness enjoined Pak first talked at length about anything rather than his errand.

"My father tells me the great rain will come soon," he said, and, "I hear that you have a srawah among your cocks that ought to be invincible," and, "I have been asked whether I will have my mother burned at the burning on the fifth day of next week. But I have refused because I want her to have a pyre to herself and not have her burned with thirty more—which could not be any pleasure to her soul."

This was sheer bragging, for Pak had not even got the twenty thousand kepengs for the communal burning. A private one, such as only rich people could afford, cost ten times as much, and this was a sum beyond Pak's conception. Wajan, however, was as amiable as before and made lavish offers of sirih. And then Pak came to the object of his visit.

"I am employed in building a house for a second wife and her house has to be a finer one than my main house," he said in one breath, for he had thought out this piece of eloquence beforehand. He could not possibly have hit on a better way of informing Wajan of his designs on Sarna and respecting the proprieties at the same time.

"I heard something about it," the old man remarked. "I wish you joy and peace in your house."

"I have been looking round for trees for the timbers of my new house. Nobody has such fine ones as you and I wanted to ask whether you would sell me six durian trees and four palm trees from your northern plantation."

"Why not?" Wajan said. He would reckon the price and perhaps he would let him have them, although he had really intended them for fruit. Pak in his reply again laid stress on his desire to build a fine house, and repeated that Wajan's trees would suit him better than any in the village. But when Wajan asked six hundred kepengs a tree, Pak's heart sank and he gasped for air. He could not pay this price, and yet he did not wish to appear a poor man in the eyes of his future father-in-law. He offered to pay half down and to work for the rest in Wajan's sawahs. When at last the deal was concluded, Wajan sent his youngest son up a palm tree and offered Pak the milk of a young coconut as an honored guest and Pak walked home on air, swollen with pride and satisfaction.

Next day he went with his axe, accompanied by several of his friends, to fell first the four palms. He did as his father had taught him. He embraced the trunk of each palm. "Palm tree, my mother," he said, "I must fell you not because I wish to kill you, but because I need posts for my house. Forgive me, dear palm, and allow me to cleave your trunk with my axe." And when they felled the trees and their crowns sank to earth with a loud rustling, Pak felt the strength of ten men in him, for he caught sight of Sarna hiding in the plantation watching him at work; and nothing makes a man so happy as when the right woman admires him as he works.

While the trunks were left to dry, he went out to cut bamboo stems for the roof, and he was fortunate in having a bamboo thicket on the edge of his sawahs; so he did not have to buy them. The bamboos grew cool and tall, shading the stream that ran beneath them, and Pak had good weather for cutting them and shortening them to the right length. He also mowed alang-alang grass for the thatch; it grew tall in his uncle's pasture, almost up to his chest. It hissed and whispered as it fell to his sickle and lay in swathes and was dry in two days and ready to be tied in bundles. He spoke to Krkek, who sent him men to help him build the roof, and he paid them with rice from his well-filled barns.

While this went on Puglug had an attack of her former volubility, and shouted a number of unpleasant remarks as she went about the yard, without addressing them to anyone in particular. The women of the household made themselves even more disagreeable when the posts were erected and the time came for an offering to be deposited in the north-east corner of the house; this only a woman could do. Puglug was not to be found on this festal day, and her spiteful disappearance wounded Pak to the heart. And then his aunt, who behaved as a rule as though she was the only woman in the village who understood the right way of making an offering, grumbled and made difficulties about preparing and depositing this one. It was beneath her, she said, to prepare the way for half-grown pullets and she did not care a grain whether the new house was blessed or not. All this was extremely painful to Pak, for Teragia's father, the balian, had come to say the proper prayers and for half an hour all was confusion and dismay. But at last Teragia herself appeared and, putting her hand on Lambon's shoulder, showed her how to prepare the offering. And Pak's little sister, rather awkwardly and yet with the grace of a former dancer, advanced with the offering; and then the balian was able to pray for a blessing on the house and that sickness might pass it by. Also his aunt finally felt able to display her knowledge, and so the eight prescribed offerings were laid at the right spots in order to conciliate the house god, Begawan Suwa-Karma. It was a great day for Pak and also for the poultry and the dogs, who later devoured the rice and the roasted entrails in the offering vessels.

Puglug, however, felt otherwise, and what seared her soul and made her particularly short-tempered with her husband was the splendor emanating from the red-and-gold Garuda bird of Meru's handiwork which hung on the centre post of the house.

Pak's days were fully occupied at this time and he saw very little of Sarna. For now he had the walls to finish and the door to fix, besides working in Wajan's sawahs to pay for the trees. He also spent a lot of time cock-fighting, for he felt happy and successful and could bet with a good courage. His white cock did, in fact, win three times, and in this way Pak procured seven hundred of the three thousand kepengs he owed Wajan. And he went to the beach collecting coral, which contained a lot of chalk, and carried it in baskets to the lime-kiln in Sanur and gave the lime-burner six ripe coconuts for burning him beautiful white lime to wash the walls of his house with. Also he took his copra to the Chinese, Njo Tok Suey, and got two thousand two hundred kepengs for it. It was a poor price, but it helped towards the expenses that still lay before him.

When the walls were finished and the door fixed, Pak took his spade and dug up the plates before Puglug's eyes, and put them in the wall—one over the door and the other two on each side. By this time the house was as good as finished, and it had such an air of wealth and splendor, that the whole village collected to look at it and there was scarcely an hour of the day when there were not a few people in Pak's yard gaping at it and uttering cries of admiration. It took Pak all his time to preserve his modesty and to call his new house a wretched dirty hut, but he did so for the sake of good manners.

In the midst of all this stir it happened that Pak was summoned to the punggawa on a Wednesday on which the omens were unusually favorable. He found the punggawa's servant at his gate when he came home from cutting fodder for the cow, and the message was so urgent that he went straight back with him, only stopping on the way to wash himself in a stream. Pak felt somewhat disconcerted and out of his depth, for neither was his father with him, nor could he ask Krkek what the meaning of this summons might be. He had an uneasy suspicion that his plates, which were now so openly exposed on the walls of his new house, might have something to do with it. Also the topic of the wreck had never quite died away and people from the court of Badung were often in the village, asking questions and searching for wreckage.

And when he entered the punggawa's courtyard the first person who met his eye was a man of great influence in the palace. This was the anak Agung Bima, a relation of the lord of Badung, as Pak well knew. He sat beside the punggawa on a finely woven mat chewing sirih. Pak squatted low with clasped hands and waited.

"My friend," the anak Agung said, "I seem to remember that your family has belonged to the puri for two generations. Did your father hold sawahs under the old lord?"

"That is so, your Highness," Pak said with awe.

"Your brother, too, works in the puri and I have only lately honored him by the order for a kris holder," the anak continued.

Pak inclined himself once more. Puglug's ominous allusion to Meru's love affairs passed through his mind, but he breathed again when it occurred to him that the whole interview seemed to be intended as an honor and distinction.

"Our lord, the Prince Alit, is my brother," Bima went on, though this was a lie. "I am his eye, his mouth and his hand."

Pak accepted this with deference. Are they going to give me another sawah or are they going to take one away from me? he thought in dismay.

"You have a sister; she is called Lambon, is she not? And she is beautiful and a good dancer?" the anak Agung said unexpectedly.

"I have a sister—Lambon," Pak said. "Unfortunately she is much too old to dance and she is ugly and a burden in the house."

He inwardly thanked his father for having taught him his manners so well, that even when addressing high dignitaries of the court he knew the right thing to say. Bima waved his politeness aside and came to the point.

"I have come here to tell you that your sister has been chosen to enter the puri. If she is, as I hope, of a ripe enough age, she can be received on the prince's next birthday as one of his wives," he said without further beating about the bush.

Pak's brain did not work fast enough to take all this in at once. An idiotic expression came into his face, his mouth opened, his eyebrows went up to his head-dress, and he stared at the punggawa.

"My sister Lambon—?"

Naturally a number of people had attached themselves to him as he went to the punggawa's house, and now there were whispers of astonishment and wonder behind him. A crowd of village children renewed their attempts to peer over the wall and Pak expected any moment to hear a scoffing remark from his friend Rib.

"Thank the anak Agung," the punggawa now told him, "and bring your sister to the puri early tomorrow morning. I am glad that your family has received this distinction, for I know that you and your father are good men and loyal subjects of your lord and master."

"I am to bring her tomorrow?" Pak asked. She has not even a new kain, he thought. "She has not even a new kain," he said aloud. He heard laughing behind him.

"She will be provided in the puri with all she requires in the way of dress and adornment," the anak Agung said. "You have only to bring her and to ask for me."

But a happy thought had found its way into Pak's brain, befogged as it was by this great honor. "Do I not receive a little present if I give my sister to the raja—so that I can fit her out and dress her?" he asked.

The punggawa wrinkled his brow and the anak began to laugh.

"You ought rather to offer me a present for proposing your sister's admission to the puri—not ask one from me," he cried out, and Pak remembered that his brother Meru in his impudent way had called the anak a corrupt and avaricious rhinoceros. But something told him that there was money to be made out of it, and as he needed money, a lot of it, for his marriage he plucked up his courage.

"I will speak to my sister," he said. "She is still a child and she may be afraid of entering the puri." As he said this it occurred to him that it might be the truth. He knew little of what Lambon thought and she seldom talked in his presence.

This aspect of the matter was discussed at some length and when Pak took his leave the anak Agung had parted with five ringits— twice as much as Pak had expected and half what Bima had been prepared at the outset to pay. Pak returned home escorted by an excited throng. Puglug, of course, had heard it all already, and he found the women of his establishment collected in a circle with Lambon crouching in the middle like a little inert chrysalis. It annoyed Pak that he could never be first with the news, but he had his ringits in his pocket and a great honor had come to his house.

"Are you not glad to be one of the raja's wives?" he asked Lambon. She looked at him with big eyes and nodded without a word.

"You don't quite understand yet what it means," he said impatiently.

"I am stupid, my brother," Lambon whispered. "Shall I be at liberty in the puri?" she asked a little later. "Or shall I be kept a prisoner?"

Puglug and her aunt broke out into dissertations on the honor and felicity awaiting her. She kept her hands folded in her lap and smiled absently.

"You must be very happy, Lambon my sister," Pak warned her. And Lambon said gently—Yes, she was very happy.

The women had enough to occupy them all that evening, for Puglug ran out to buy fragrant oils and a new kain, while her aunt searched Lambon's head for lice and gave her hair a thorough combing. Also her old kain was washed and her eyebrows shaved, as though she was to dance the legong again. Next morning the excitement flared up afresh. Lambon was sent off early to the river to bathe and Puglug packed her belongings in a square basket. They also got her pisangs and papayas and put them in a red fancy basket, and said that they were intended for an offering. This was not out of a fear that there would not be enough to eat in the puri, but because it would make a better impression not to arrive empty-handed. Pak was already arrayed in his best to take his sister to Badung, and now he loitered waiting at the gate, for it was a long time before she came back from the river.

After bathing she went past the pedanda's house and she longed to say good-bye to Raka before she became a wife of the raja's. But when she came to the gate she did not venture to go in, but crouched down outside in the grass and laid her head on her arms and waited for she knew not what. She was still there when Teragia came home with water from the spring. Teragia bent over the little crouching figure and asked, "Are you sick, Lambon, my little sister?"

"No," Lambon said. "I am very happy. I am going into the puri today to be one of the lord's wives."

Whereupon Teragia looked searchingly in her face for a moment and then led her affectionately into the courtyard and called for Raka. He came up with an armful of young papayas from the plantation. "Lambon!" he said. "How tall you have grown! I haven't seen you for a long time."

Lambon stood with drooping head, unable to speak. Teragia put her hand under her chin and said, "She wants to say good-bye to you, Raka, before going into the puri to be one of the lord's wives."

When Raka heard this he laughed out loud. "Has not Alit more wives than he wants already?" he cried out. "And the anak Agung Bima keeps on combing the villages for more."

Lambon threw back her head and said with energy, "It is a great honor and I am very happy. I have seen the lord Alit and he is handsome and has a fair skin, and he is going to make me his wife."

Raka said nothing. He looked at Lambon at first with surprise and then reflectively. "Alit is good and a true friend to those whom he likes," he said earnestly. Lambon stood a moment longer with her arms hanging at her sides and an expectant look in her face. Then she said, "I only wanted to say good-bye. Peace remain with you," and she turned to go. Teragia quickly put a few large blue flowers, such as grew only in the pedanda's garden, in her hair and stood beside Raka in the gateway—waving to her as she went down the village street until she had turned the corner.

At the last moment when all Lambon's preparations were made, and she had said good-bye to everyone, and was setting out with her basket on her head escorted by Pak, his little daughters came running out of the house weeping loudly. They ran the whole length of the village beside Lambon, Rantun with little Klepon on her hip and Madé with nothing on. But Lambon did not weep as she left the village but had still the same dazed, gentle smile and lowered eyes.

It took them an hour to reach Badung and Pak was perspiring when he handed his sister up to the gate-keeper. He laid his hands on her shoulders and at last pushed her from him. But he did not know what to say to her in farewell and he was sorry that his mother and hers was not alive.

"Can I come and see her?" he asked the gate-keeper.

"It is not usual," the man said, and a glimpse of Lambon's green kain as she vanished was the last Pak saw of her.

＊   ＊   ＊   ＊   ＊

Pak quickly forgot his sister, for now all his thoughts were taken up by his second wife. When the house was finished, the pedanda himself came to put life into it. Nine offerings were made, as well for the gods as for the demons below. The pedanda addressed each one of them, so that no misfortune should befall the house, no fire break out and no sickness enter. The timbers of the house were smeared with lime, charcoal, the blood of a fowl, coconut oil and powdered sandalwood. The plates shone over the door and new mats were spread on the two sleeping benches. Puglug and his aunt behaved this time with propriety, and it was only Pak who ran about in a fluster of agitation as though he would burst with excitement. For there was nothing left to do now but carry Sarna off.

The whole village knew about it and the pedanda had ascertained the auspicious day and told Pak's father. But of course no one in the village spoke of it and all went about their work as usual. But Pak had spoken to his friends, Rib, the jester, and Sarda, the fisherman, and they were ready to help in the rape, as the custom was.

That afternoon Sarna did not go to the river for water but to the spring, and she told Pak the exact time when she would be there. So he and his two friends hid themselves among the roots of the old wairingin tree, and when Sarna had put her jar down they rushed out and carried her off. She defended herself with a branch but they only laughed; and afterwards, rather breathless with the fun, they sat down and rubbed her arms and legs with cold water. Then they set off over the sawahs, Sarna in front and Pak some distance behind her and then his two friends. Rib's sawahs were some way out and they were bound for a deserted watch-house which stood in his fields. The sun had nearly set when they reached it; all the birds were singing and the chirping of grasshoppers and the jarring throb of cicadas was to be heard all over the rice-fields. Then darkness came quickly down and a thousand frogs began to croak. The night wind stirred the clappers in the ripening fields and great fireflies flickered through the air and settled on Sarna's hair. Pak's heart throbbed with all these night sounds after the excitement of the day.

Rib, in spite of his jocularity, was the very pattern of tact and good behaviour and made not a single ribald remark when he and Sarda left the two by themselves in the little cabin. They had brought food and two oil lamps with them. The trickle of water running into the fields could be heard nearby and the moist rich earth smelt of fruit-fulness. From the other side the green scent of the ripening sawahs was borne on the wind. All this was so familiar and homely to Pak that his heart came to rest after all his agitation. He stood in the doorway of the hut with his arm round Sarna's shoulders looking after his friends as they vanished in the dusk across the fields. He could still hear them laughing and then far away the kulkul beating in Taman Sari to summon the men. For now the rape had been detected and they had been given time to hide themselves and the next thing was to make a great uproar about it.

"Sarna," Pak said softly, "I am content." He looked once more over the sawahs and then he pulled her inside the hut and shut the door and slept with her and made her his wife.

Meanwhile the village was bright with torches and loud with the beating of the kulkul and the shouts of the men. They ran hither and thither searching everywhere for the raped girl except where the runaway couple were hidden. Wajan tore his hair and lamented loudly, and after a time Rib and Sarda arrived and endeavoured politely to soothe and console him.

Then it became known that Wajan, in spite of all Pak's diplomatic moves, was seriously annoyed by the carrying off of his daughter. Even when Krkek himself put it to him that, with her disfigured ear, she could not expect a better husband than the honest and hardworking Pak, even then he stuck to his grievance and raged and demanded damages for his pained feelings and the deep insult he had suffered.

After three days Pak returned to the village with his new wife and begged forgiveness of his father-in-law. It was then settled that he had to pay eight ringits for the abduction, and the whole village considered this hard and unjust. But Pak was too happy to care. He dug up the eight ringits and now he had only twenty-four left of his savings beneath the floor of his house, and there was no more talk of the burning of his mother's bones.

"How does your house please you?" Pak asked his second wife.

"Quite pretty," Sarna said, and it did not sound very enthusiastic considering the plates and the splendid garuda bird. "If I had married the raja I should have had a roof of Chinese tiles." Since her ear had healed she had talked of nothing but her rejection of a raja, and of the great sacrifice she had made in order to marry a common man like Pak. But Pak only laughed for, in the first place, it flattered him and, besides, he knew Sarna in the intimacy of the night and she was his wife, and he knew the sweetness of her and her continual hunger for his embraces.

The wedding was celebrated at the same time as the consecration of the new house, and Pak spoiled all the festal ceremonies by his excitement and forgetfulness. His uncle and aunt, his father and brother all pushed him this way and that and helped him to get through it properly. Sarna, however, never lost her head for a moment; she sold him rice in the courtyard and she let him beat her, and broke the string and walked through the fire at the ceremony of union. And she bathed in the river and came back and laid herself down on the floor of the house with a lighted torch beside her at the ceremony of cleansing. And finally she sat down opposite the pedanda with her face to the east. He spoke to the souls of their forefathers and offered up the prescribed offerings, sprinkled the pair of them with holy water, and did a lot more things which Pak could never afterwards remember. But it all signified the dedication of the marriage and after that they were man and wife.

For Pak, the whole day was enveloped in a droning mist, and he marvelled at Sarna's gracious way of attending to the guests as though she had long been used to living in his house. Now and then he took a sly look at Puglug and saw that she was dressed in her best with flowers in her hair, just as though the marriage was of her own making. Also she had cooked a splendid and sumptuous meal and called Sarna young sister and friend in a loud voice. And Sarna, like a kitten, thanked her loudly and often. She wore a large hibiscus flower over her ear and this concealed the mutilated lobe. The gamelan arrived too, for Pak was a member of it, and it took up a position near the gateway and Pak's father beat the gong instead of him, since he was being honored that day and had to listen. When night came on the whole courtyard smelt of spilt palm wine and the guests were still drinking when Pak, wearied out with a surfeit of honor and happiness, had fallen asleep with his head against a post of his new house.

By the time all the dissipation and excitement of these weeks were over it was time to reap the eastern fields. The sawah absorbed

Pak once more and it was there he lived the life he loved best. He was happier at home than before, but things were not so simple as they had been. Puglug put a great deal of work on the new wife; and Sarna, with an amiable smile, put it back on Puglug again. "If I had married the raja—" she was very often heard to say.

After a time Pak ceased to laugh good-naturedly over this. Sarna was his wife, and though in the ardour of his love he had built her a house on which three plates were displayed, she would have to be put in her place all the same. It was still as sweet as ever to fondle her and sleep with her, and he still called her sometimes by the names of fruits and birds. But he got used to her and it happened as his father had said: the hunger and the fever and the restlessness passed out of his blood like a sickness that was over.

Not that Sarna was of no use in the household. She could catch dragonflies and roast them to a turn, and she had a cunning hand at cutting out palm-leaf decorations for the offerings. Things did not go equally well in the months when it was her task to see to his meals. But he forgave her that, for in the very first month after the marriage her kain remained clean and Pak had hopes of a son.

"She must not pound rice or carry water, for she promises to bear a son to our house," he said confidentially to Puglug. His first wife pulled a face. "You would think she was a raw egg," she said. "How shall the son be strong if the mother does not work?"

In spite of this Pak observed that Puglug spared his second wife the heavier labors when her womb began to grow big, and he was grateful to her. He never let a week go by without spending a night with Puglug in the chief house, and he praised her cooking and her children. Moreover, at about this time he was allotted another sawah by the lord of Badung, probably because Lambon had been taken into the puri. More rice for the household and more work for Pak. He was glad to do it. He gave the eastern fields a rest and pressed on with the western ones and began ploughing again and breaking down the soil, three times, with aching back and thighs. He talked to the earth and took offerings to the rice goddess and explained to his cow what they had to do. The tjrorot sang and it sounded like a tiny kulkul, and his father came and surveyed the growing crops. And all the time Pak waited for the birth of his son, dreaming great things of him. I will teach him to plough and sow and plant, he thought. I will take him between my knees and show him how to beat the gong, he thought on other days. At other times he thought how he would impart all he knew and had experienced, as his father had done with him.

Soon after the New Year had been celebrated came the day when the child was born. Pak was out on the sawah mowing weeds when Rantun came running to him. "Your wife is taken with great pains," she called out from far off. "The little brother is going to be born." At this Pak was seized with fear and joy at once, as though a hand was at his throat. He did not pause to wash off the mud in the stream, but ran home, perspiring all over his body, and reached the yard breathless. From the gate he could hear Sarna crying out, and this seemed to him strange, for Puglug had given birth to three children in complete silence and with tight lips. The yard was full of women. It seemed to Pak that all the women of the village had collected; some ran inanely to and fro like fowls and some sat motionless, some gave advice and some prepared the offerings.

Rantun clung to his hand when he went into Sarna's house, and crouched beside him as he sat down behind Sarna and supported her body. "Take good heed, Rantun," he said, "for you, too, will have to bear children."

He felt very sorry for Sarna; her body streamed with sweat and her kain was soaked and her eyes were shut and she threw herself about and cried aloud. But if she had not cried out he would have been even sorrier for her. "Puglug never cried out," he said out loud. But Puglug signed to him to be quiet and Sarna cried out more loudly than ever. After a while Pak was soaked with sweat, too, and the cries rang in his ears. He would have liked to ask his father whether his mother had cried out in this way, but his father kept out of the way on this occasion. So Pak stayed sitting behind Sarna on the floor and the time passed endlessly and yet never moved. "Why is it taking so long?" he asked the women.

"The child will be born at the appointed time," the old midwife said. She massaged Sarna's body and put a rope in her hands which was fastened to the door and was meant to help her in her labor. Pak looked at Puglug's face; it was composed and in its ugliness he now detected great goodness and strength. He would gladly have laid his head in her capacious lap and rested, for he was wearied out with Sarna's labor. But she only nodded to him to put his hands on Sarna's body and said, "You must help her so, for you are the husband."

The sun already slanted down the sky and Sarna's cries went on and on.

"I have had enough," Pak said, getting up and going out into the yard. Is she made of other stuff than other women? he thought, feeling impatient with Sarna. She cannot pound rice and she will not help Puglug with the work, and when she ought to bring forth a child she breaks down. But as he thought this he gave a start, for he had forgotten that there might be danger. He went back into the house; the women had hung two oil lamps beside the plates. Pak looked round for his first wife. "Puglug," he said, and was surprised to find his throat and lips as dry as dust. "It cannot last much longer," Puglug said consolingly as she went up to him. "Sarna is young and slender and the child has first to make a way for itself."

"Is there danger?" Pak asked, feeling grateful to Puglug. She laughed at him and took his hands between hers and rubbed them. "No, there is no danger," she said as if he were a child.

Pak went back and sat down again behind Sarna. He wondered at her. The bare earth was beneath her so that its strength could pass into her and the child, but Sarna had no strength. Her head hung limp like the flower on a broken stem and she whimpered on and on. Even in her womb there was no movement now. The sun set. Pak looked from one to the other of the many women who filled the room. Is it dangerous? Is she dying? Will she bear me a dead child? he wanted to ask. But the women appeared to be indifferent. They chewed sirih and some of them had leaves in their hands, from which they ate the cooked rice Puglug brought them. Then he saw his aunt come up the steps with a sharp bamboo knife in her hand to cut the umbilical cord. Sarna began to cry out more loudly and Puglug wiped the sweat from her forehead. He had taken her as his wife in the watch-house among the sawahs and she had been sweet, but now she looked ugly—broken. She was no good at bearing children or at anything else. She turned her eyes to him and whispered, "Oh Pak, help me. Oh Pak, help me." Then she cried out aloud, "Oh Pak, help me!" Pak began supporting her back again and pressing down on her womb as Puglug had shown him. The earth round Sarna was wet with sweat in large dark patches and he thought: This child will never be born.

Suddenly Sarna gave a long and piercing cry. Puglug and his aunt bent over to help her. And then Pak saw that his child lay on the earth; it had tiny sprawling limbs, and it was a son.

Sarna fell back in his arms and smiled the very moment her pains were over. "Is it a son, Pak?" she asked. "Yes it is a son," he answered, breathless for joy. He stroked her forehead and her wet hair and her shoulders and held her on his knees, until Puglug had parted the child from the umbilical cord. All the women now talked at once and pushed him out of the house and showered congratulations on him. Pak suddenly found himself alone, while an immense stir began in the house. He ran to his father and shouted: "It's a son and he's fine and big." The old man came down from his balé. "Offerings must be brought," he said, "and you must build him an altar, on the right of the house, where they bury the afterbirth, the little brother of your son."

The yard was full of torches and women and shouting, and women crossed from the kitchen carrying large vessels of water to wash the mother and the child.

Puglug had always cleansed the house herself after the birth of her children, but it appeared that Sarna was too weak and the other women did it for her. Even the next day when she went to the river to bathe Puglug had to help her; and she supported her younger sister down the steep bank without complaining. She did not say: "I bore my children without crying out and I needed no help." All the same Sarna held her head high and said: "I have borne a son to a house where before there were only daughters."

As for Pak, he sat at home holding in his arms the little bundle wrapped in white linen, that was his son, and he forgot everything else in the fulfilment of his dearest wish.

And he named him Siang, the light and the day.

The Birthday

"H AVE you packed?" the Resident Berginck asked as he put down the pen with which he had just signed a letter.

"Yes, I'm ready to start, Resident," Boomsmer said, coming to a stop near the door, pith helmet in hand, with a click of the heels.

"Then this is our last cigar together," the Resident said with a smile as he pushed a chair forward. Boomsmer bowed and sat down stiffly, for his uniform creaked with starch and his collar was extremely high. They bit the end off their cigars. "Allow me, Resident," Boomsmer said, offering his superior a match, and then left the next remark to him.

"Sorry we're losing you, Boomsmer," Berginck said, unbuttoning his tunic. "Honestly, I'm sorry. But of course I'm glad you are getting a step up. You'll like Palembang. It's a decent place and less worry than we have here. I was stationed there for a few months in my young days. The planters have a nice club. The climate certainly is a bit warmer—"

"I should like to thank the Resident most heartily for his interest—there was little I could do here—my post gave too little scope. As Assistant Resident of Palembang I shall naturally be able to do more—"

Berginck was no longer listening. He was reading through the letter he had just signed. The last sentence did not satisfy him. "When does the *Zwaluw* sail for Banjoewangi?" he asked distractedly.

"At two o'clock," Boomsmer answered.

Berginck pushed the letter aside. He had no love for documents and sweated blood over the writing of his reports. He was a seaman by temperament and upbringing and he liked the colonial service, where not everything as yet was cut and dried. But he loathed office work.

"I hope you won't be eaten alive by ants—the *Zwaluw* is creeping with them," he said. "Not those gentlemanly big fellows but the little ones. They can make life an agony."

"I've sailed on the *Zwaluw* many a time, Resident," Boomsmer said. She was the old Government boat whose job it was to carry officials up and down the coasts of Bali and Lombok whenever there was trouble.

"Now listen, Boomsmer," Berginck said, coming to the point. "I want you to give this note to the Government with your own hands. You are sure to stop a day or two in Batavia."

"Two weeks to be exact, Resident."

"Yes—well, this *précis* I've drawn up is pretty full, but all the same it might be as well if you were in a position to tell the Governor by word of mouth anything he may want to know."

"Of course, Resident."

"Best if I could have gone myself. This business has taken on a certain importance—but I can't leave just now. Well, you know what it's all about."

"Not in detail, Resident," Boomsmer said with an injured air. "My colleague Visser was entrusted with the inquiry."

"You don't need to envy him for that," the Resident said genially. "There was little pleasure or profit in it. Here are the facts in a nutshell. This fellow Kwe Tik Tjiang finally piled up a claim a mile long and swore to the plundering of his ship. We know what a Chinaman's oath is worth among themselves. He also bribed another Chink to give lying evidence, and a few more tricks of the sort. No one has ever got out of him how much in money and goods there actually was in the *Sri Kumala*. Not so much as he says, anyway." The Resident described a circle in the air with his cigar. "But...." and then he forgot to continue the sentence.

"But it is not disputed that there was pilfering and plundering, Resident," Boomsmer put in, sitting right at the edge of his chair, a habit he had contracted during long years of subordinate positions and not easily got out of even though he had made a big stride forward in his career.

"Yes, there was pilfering and plundering. No doubt about that," the Resident said. "Cleaned out, in fact. It seems to me that the people of the coast went out with a real good will and reduced the ship to matchwood. The copper plates alone were worth five hundred guilders. It's true I can't get to the bottom of how much was carried off and how much simply went overboard when the ship struck, but it seems clear that at least one thousand nine hundred and twenty-six guilders in money and goods have been stolen."

"In Badung," Boomsmer said. It sounded like the banging of a door. The Resident looked at him for a moment in silence and thought of something else.

"In Badung and Gianjar. To be accurate, more of the plunder was found on Gianjar territory than in Badung."

"The Government will not take much account of that," Boomsmer said with a smile.

"You may be sure of that. There would be no object in picking a quarrel with a province which is Dutch in any case. The Government will only want to establish one fact, and that is established already—Badung has violated Clause 11 of the Treaty of the 11th of July, 1849."

"It seems hardly credible that the authorities have shut their eyes to all this for over fifty years."

"Possibly, Boomsmer. No doubt. That is for the Government to consider. I hold an inquiry and make a report. That's all."

"These people could be brought to heel for good with two companies of soldiers," Boomsmer snapped.

"Two companies? I'm not so sure about that," the Resident replied.

"We are not defeatists, I hope, Resident?" Boomsmer observed, and Berginck shot a quick, short-sighted glance at him.

"Defeatists—good God, no, Boomsmer. But I have been longer on the island than you have. I can remember the retreat from Lombok. How many men did that cost us?"

The Resident got up and stood at the edge of the stoep looking out on the lawn with its Dutch borders and Balinese statues. But he did not see them. God knows what met his distracted gaze at that moment.

"More than two companies, then," Boomsmer said behind him.

The Resident recalled his wandering thoughts. "I am a nervous old man," he said smiling. "I don't care for the noise of guns and particularly when they open out on defenceless people armed with spears."

"According to our agent's report," Boomsmer said sharply, "these defenceless people of Badung have more than six hundred breech-loaders and four guns in the Puri. My unalterable opinion is that we have looked on long enough while they armed themselves to the teeth. Action must be taken, energetically, and quickly—that is my conviction, if I may express an opinion, Resident."

"Oh, of course, yes," Berginck said. "You are quite right. Take this to the Governor. If we are to make war, better do it thoroughly. I have no use for half measures."

"Then, with your permission, I will now take my leave, Resident," Boomsmer said, standing up. But the Resident remained seated and still lost in thought.

"I wish we could have settled the matter in a friendly way. I wish the lords of Badung and Tahanan showed as much sense as our Gusti Nyoman here. They can only be beaten and they know it. Why in the devil's name are they as obstinate as buffaloes?" he said to himself.

"The tjokorda Sri Paduka Gde Ngu Alit of Badung promised a strict inquiry," Boomsmer said, ironically stressing the long array of titles. "Has anything come of it?"

"No, of course not. What do you suppose! I never expected he would admit the robbery. The Balinese are touchy, they have a tremendous sense of honor and a sort of pride we don't understand. God knows what's at the back of their minds to make them so foolishly, really idiotically, stubborn. I'll tell you something, Boomsmer: I've been many years in the service here but I don't understand these people; even yet, I don't understand the first thing about them. If I did, then probably no punitive expedition would be necessary."

With that he went to the table and quickly put the letter in an official envelope without reading it again. The Resident is trying his hand at psychology, Boomsmer thought contemptuously. He himself had had a better education than all these old-time officials and thought a good deal of himself in consequence. He was glad to be leaving Bali and it was a stroke of luck that he had this particular letter to deliver. He had friends in every one of the Government offices and an extensive correspondence. He knew how the wind blew. He knew that the Governor-General would be glad to have an excuse at last for proceeding against the southern territories with a clear case and a good conscience.

"May I thank you once more, Resident, for the confidence you repose in me—I shall endeavour to conduct the matter in exact accordance with your views," he said and bowed.

"Yes, that's right," Berginck said, buttoning up his tunic again. "Best of luck in your new job. And when you get to Batavia, remember me to all the fellows at the Club...."

He gave a last look at the bulky envelope as it vanished into Boomsmer's attaché case. "We're sure to come across each other again," he said, holding out his hand to the new Assistant-Resident. "And send Visser over to me at once, will you?" he added as Boomsmer bowed himself out.

A large red-spotted gekko, which was clinging to the roof, uttered its cry seven times in succession. The Resident waited—but it did not come again. He sighed. Bad luck, he thought to himself. Superstition got a hold on one out there by degrees. He knocked off the long ash of his cigar and sent his servant for a gin.

✳   ✳   ✳   ✳   ✳

In the puri of Badung three large turtles had been killed and men had been busy since early morning stripping the rich flesh from them, cutting it up, seasoning it and impaling it on little wooden skewers. The smell of the preparations for the feast pervaded the courtyard where the cooking balés were. The satees with the turtle meat rested on two long bamboo poles and the men squatted alongside, turning them over the fire, hundreds and thousands of spits of roasting flesh.

Suddenly there was a downpour which extinguished the fire. The rainy season had begun two weeks before; the sky was massed with heavy black clouds and looked like a meadow full of pregnant cows. The satees were rushed to safety in a balé with shouts of laughter. The rain poured down on the grass-thatched roofs and flowed off in streams. Fresh fires were kindled under shelter and the smoke curled up into the bamboo timbers and found no outlet, for the rain came down round the balés like a blanket. The smoke hung blue and acrid between the roof posts and stung the men's eyes and made them water. Slave-girls came running with shrill cries to urge greater speed. From the next courtyard came the squealing of wild boars that were being slaughtered, and the quacking of ducks that were being caught. Naked children splashed through the broad puddles with hats as big as baskets on their heads or huge kladi leaves to protect them from the rain, carrying eggs, rice and vegetables of all kinds.

Old women, famed for their skill at cooking, argued with young ones, who thought they knew better. Two slaves came along who were already drunk, and two others, who had also had something to do with preparing the palm wine, were having words and at last started fighting with their fists in the drenching, almost deafening torrent of rain. One of them ended in a puddle and the other went on victorious, with two large glass bottles attached to a pole on his shoulders, bottles such as had never been seen in the puri before.

Three Chinese and an Arab were here, there and everywhere and in all the courtyards at once, giving orders and putting things right and wringing their hands—for they knew the ways of the white men and were therefore charged with superintending all the preparations. It was the birthday of the lord Alit, and the Resident of Bali and Lombok, the tuan Besar Mynheer Berginck was expected as guest.

The wives' quarters were in a turmoil that morning. Many of them had never seen a Dutchman and they were trembling with curiosity and excitement. The prince had commanded them to put on all their finery. Boxes and chests disgorged silver and gold stuffs, crowns of gold-foil, breast-bands of bright silks. Slave-girls were beaten and slave-girls were sent to the gardens for flowers for the hair. Slave-girls laughed and slave-girls cried. Wives came to blows and wives were reconciled and embraced each other. Wet, dripping, fragrant flowers were heaped in baskets on every side and were shared out with trembling hands. Rivers of oil were poured on heads of hair, nails and teeth were cleaned, a last search for lice set on foot. And all the while the rain hissed and pattered and rose up in little circular fountains from the puddles.

Ida Katut, the little story-teller, was to be seen in the farther court-yard, rubbing his hands, looking, listening, eyes and ears everywhere at once. The men who brought the Badung gamelan came along under Chinese umbrellas of waxed paper. The celebrated gamelan of Kesiman was expected too, and nobly born guests from all the puris of the surrounding country. Guards in warlike array were posted on the two towers flanking the entrance, some armed with lances, some with long firearms. Within the wall, on a raised platform, were two guns. Dewa Gdé Molog, the commander-in-chief himself, had stationed himself there to keep an eye on the men entrusted with the important and dangerous duty of firing the salute. They were Ksatrias, men of the warrior caste and without fear, and it was to be hoped the guns would be fired with success and not kill anybody. Kulkuls were beating everywhere—between the wairingin trees before the entrance, in the town of Badung, in the puri of the old lord of Pametjutan and in all villages from far inland to the roast of Sanur.

The Government boat, the *Zwaluw*, had been sighted an hour ago and was now beating about behind the wall of rain in a heavy sea trying to make land. The gamelan was playing lively and festal airs on the beach without ceasing. Owing to the rain a sort of balé was quickly run up to shelter the musicians. Garlands on tall bamboo poles, decorated in every imaginable way, extended all along the village streets and in the niches for offerings at every gateway were woven streamers of palm-leaves in two colors, as at the New Year festival A group of court dignitaries, many pungga was and many relations of the prince were assembled in the courtyard of the pung-gawa of Sanur waiting for the signal which would tell them that the Resident had landed. The pedanda, Ida Bagus Rai, could be seen in full regalia, with the tall crown on his head and the bearer of his umbrella behind him, being carried in a chair down the street.

Everyone was in the streets, rain or no rain, and the village priests had lighted fires in the court of the Coral Temple and brought offerings to stay the downpour. Volumes of thick white smoke rose from these sacrificial fires and all the people watched hopefully and waited for the rain to cease.

When the fires had been alight long enough for a man to chew a plug of sirih, it did in fact stop raining and the sun suddenly shone out in a sky which became bluer every moment. The palm trees, washed and refreshed, sparkled and the moist air was heavy with the scent of flowering bushes. The gamelan played louder, as though it had got its second wind.

Now the men on the beach could see a small boat leave the *Zwaluw* and make quickly for the shore, dancing like a cork. The dignitaries emerged from the courtyard, some carried in chairs, some riding on white horses. A squadron of mounted lancers dashed from the palm grove where they had been sheltering from the rain and trotted to the shore. Little fountains splashed up under their horses' small hooves. Girls in beautiful dresses and breast-bands came out of the houses and stationed themselves on either side of the road, holding up offering plates in their left hands. White and red flags were flying, fringing the beach. And now the Resident could be seen, neither very tall nor very young, clothed in white, with many gold buttons and decorations on his coat, getting out of the boat and waving aside the two bearers, who offered to lift him on their shoulders and carry him across the wet sand.

There was only one place on this morning of noise and excitement where silence reigned, and that was the house of the old lord of Pametjutan. The old man had passed the night in great pain and now lay exhausted on his couch, propped up with many kapok cushions at his back. The two balians of Badung and Taman Sari had been in attendance. They had massaged him and given him narcotics and now the prince felt easier. He pulled at his opium pipe and his head grew clearer and threw off the fevered haze of the night. Alit, the young lord, his nephew, whom he had adopted, squatted beside him and his usually limp face had a remarkable expression of concentration, of exertion, or perhaps preoccupation. He, too, was smoking opium to clear his head for the hard dunking this critical hour required. Unconsciously he let his fingers run up and down the vertebræ of Oka's spine. The boy crouched at his feet and his warm smooth skin had a calming effect on his master.

"We are agreed then, father," Alit said. "We cannot submit to the shameless demands of the Dutch. They are only seeking an excuse to humble us. If we give way to them this time, they will find some new reason for oppressing us. They are proud, although they have no caste, and they have no manners. They do not seem to understand with whom they are dealing. Because a few lords have turned renegades and traitors they think they can cow us all. They will see that they are deceived about Badung."

The old lord looked long at the younger one before he spoke. "I am glad to hear you speak as you do, my son," he said. "I am old and tired and sickness has made the fighting blood in me slothful and often clouds my thoughts. But you are young and you must oppose your heart and your forehead to the white men. I have watched you grow up, and I was not sure that you would hold to the way of our fathers. Sometimes you seemed to me to think more as a Brahman than as a Ksatria. I am glad that you have not forgotten your kris for your books."

"I have discoursed," Alit replied, "in long prayers with our forefathers. My friend, the pedanda of Taman Sari, has spent many days and nights with me and helped me to find the way. The old books, my father, are as strong as the kris, and even stronger, when they are understood rightly. I have learnt one thing from them—that I am nothing, I, Alit, the lord of Badung. I am only a link in the chain, one single bamboo pole in the whole bridge. I must hand on what I have received from my mighty forefathers. I am not free and it is not permitted me to act by my own choice. I cannot give away or throw away or sell my inheritance and I must stand firm there where my birth has set me. That is what I have read in the books."

The old tjokorda smiled as Alit said this. It seemed to him that there was no need to labor in so many abstruse words a point so simple as this, that pride and honor could not be surrendered. "It does not matter by what roads we arrive at our resolve," he said gently. "You come from one side, I from the other. The main thing is that we meet in the middle and are of the same mind."

Alit got up and opened the door on to the portico, for the opium smoke made breathing difficult. "It has stopped raining," he said, looking out into the courtyards, thronged with people passing to and fro, where the sun shone in the pools of rain. The sound of a gamelan was wafted over the moist air. "I wish I knew how old I was," he said turning back meditatively to his uncle's couch. "No one has kept count of the years for me. They make a great noise over my birthday, and six girls, I am told, are going to be married to me to complete the festivities. But when I look within myself, I do not know whether I am old or young."

"You are young, for you were a child when the Batur Mountain burst and hurled great stones on to the beach," the old man said. "And you have not even begotten your first son."

Two messengers came running through the court and fell on their knees at the foot of the steps, making a great show of their exhaustion and breathlessness. "It appears that the Resident has landed," Alit said, turning back into the room. "I must get ready to receive him." He beckoned to Oka and supported himself on his slender shoulders.

"Beg the Resident to excuse me. Show him all the hospitality Badung has to offer. You can give way on small points—but stand fast on the main one," the old lord said. Alit took his leave with tender devotion, and as soon as the door closed behind him, Madé let his head sink back on the cushions, shut his eyes for weariness and once more his brain was clouded with pain.

Alit motioned away the chair-bearers and umbrella carriers who awaited him on the steps. He wanted to take deep breaths of the fresh moist air before receiving the Resident. The day, with all its festivities and demands, rose before him like a mountain. He walked quickly through the courts, greeted on all sides, but his eyes saw nothing. His bare feet trod through the puddles and over stones. Once he grasped behind his shoulder for his kris and pushed it more firmly into his belt.

A shadow fell across his path and when he looked up he saw Bijang before him. She was a tall, white-haired woman and the mother of the old tjokorda. She was as old as a stone or a wairingin tree and the skin was stretched so tightly over her skull that her head had grown as small as a child's. Bijang was held in great honor in the puri and she kept a firm hand over the wives and slave-girls without fear or favor. Though she leant on the gold handle of her stick she walked without difficulty and her sight was keen. It was remarkable that in Bijang's hundred-year-old face the young girl was still to be detected in a smile or a glance under her eyelashes.

"Where are you going, child?" she asked, with her arm round Alit's hips.

"I must greet my guests, mother."

"I know," she said, looking keenly at him. "You have offered the white man a lodging for the night. Is he your friend?"

"He calls himself so," Alit said. "Perhaps he may be. I shall soon know."

"Be careful," the old lady said, "Think thrice before you speak once. And, if you want the advice of a stupid old woman," she added, smiling confidentially, "stop Molog's mouth. He talks too loudly and too much and he has more courage than sense."

Alit looked confidingly in her face and she blinked her eyes in a way that made him laugh. He conducted her as far as the steps of her balé and then proceeded on his way through lanes full of fowls, pigs and ducks. He had scarcely reached the puri and entered his own house when there was a roar and the glass panes shook in his windows.

The guns had been fired to salute the Resident and the critical day had begun.

✳   ✳   ✳   ✳   ✳

Muna, the slave-girl, crouched in front of Lambon, carefully shaving her eyebrows. She squinted in her eagerness and her tongue went without ceasing like a clapper in a rice-field. "I thought the earth had burst or the Batur Mountain broken out and was hurling stones out of itself into Batur Lake, as the old people say happened once. But it was that thing they call a cannon. Bernis fainted even though she stopped her ears with her fingers and we had to throw a lot of cold water over her to bring her round. Were you frightened too, Lambon? You look as though you'd been crying."

"So do you," Lambon said without moving her head in case of interfering with the ticklish business of her eyebrows.

"I? That means nothing. Bernis beat me, and I know her. She never stops till she sees tears. She gets more difficult every week and I know why, but I don't say. I'll tell you because you have always been kind to me. She has her eyes on a young man whom you know too. But he won't take any notice and it's only right. He must not see the wife of a raja even if she puts herself right in his path. He keeps to slave-girls who are free and can give love where they please. He is a very young man and you know him, too."

"I know no men," Lambon said. Muna had finished the shaving and now she pulled a basket containing powder and lamp-black towards her with her foot and after she had blown on Lambon's eyebrows the task of beautifying began.

"Yes, you do. Just think," she said.

Lambon thought. "Raka," she said.

Muna fell backwards for laughing. "Raka," she screamed. "What makes you think of Raka? Of all the men you could think of he's the very last! No, if you want to know, it is Meru, the sculptor, your brother. You are like him and that is why I am fond of you," she added rather more soberly. Lambon nestled up to the little slave-girl for a moment, for she felt very lonely in the puri and hungered for a little warmth.

"What has my little sister been crying about?" Muna asked gently, rocking her to and fro.

"I am afraid," Lambon said.

"You need have no fear. You are the youngest and most beautiful of the six wives to be married to the lord today. Old Ranis told me he asked after you twice. You will see, he'll send for you tonight and nobody else. And tomorrow I shall not be able to come and play with you. I shall have to call you mistress and use many fine words when I address you."

Lambon smiled sadly. "That is what I am afraid of," she said, "that he will send for me."

Muna pushed her away and looked at her, shaking her head.

"I don't know how to behave," Lambon whispered.

"What have you been doing all the six months you've shared a home with Tumun, that's what I'd like to know," Muna said with a certain severity. "If you did not learn from her, you will never learn. They say she was a whore in Kesiman for five years and there is not a woman in the puri who is so experienced as she. That is why the youngest girl always lives with her so that she can teach them. But you are none the wiser, apparently."

"Tumun was always kind to me," Lambon said.

Muna looked at her friend and still shook her head. "You have no more will of your own than a papaya hanging on the tree. It is all the same to you whether you are picked or not," she said reproachfully. At that moment she heard a noise and slipping noiselessly away she climbed on to a wall and looked over with rapt attention into the next courtyard. Lambon put her hands to her hair without daring to touch it, for it was already fluffed out and piled artistically on the crown of her head; so after letting her hands hover about it she put them in her lap again. Muna came back and her kain was wet where she had sat on it.

"Now they have conducted the white man to the large balé," she whispered excitedly. "That's where the great council is to be held. Ida Katut says the white man is very pleased with the special house built for him. But Ida Katut says he is no raja, though he expects and receives such great honors. Ida Katut says he has brought the prince a wonderful present. It is a little house of tortoise-shell and on the roof lie two figures of heavy yellow metal, a man and a woman, and the man holds a sickle in his hand. Underneath them is a large face with many figures on it and it shows the time. Inside the house there is a heart beating and as soon as an hour has gone by, a bell sounds and music plays. The music, however, is not beautiful, Ida Katut says, and he has heard it, and the hours are shorter than ours, for the white men have greater haste and less patience. The Master, our Lord, greeted the white man in the speech of Java, Ida Katut says, and called him Brother. But I must say I call it bad manners to shoot off cannon and frighten a guest when he arrives. Now let me have your legs and I'll rub them with oil, for today your whole body must be smooth. And if you would like to see your brother Meru let me know and I'll bring him to you secretly. But you mustn't think because of that…"

"Muna, what are you doing here?" Tumun called out. She was coming up the steps. "Your mistress Bernis is shouting for you so loud that the very monkeys are frightened and breaking their chains. She has got a wet cord ready to give you a good beating with because you have kept her waiting with her hair all uncombed. Run, run quick —I'll get Lambon ready."

Muna pulled a face and ran off like a little monkey. It began to pelt with rain and she flung her kain over her head to protect her hair and splashed bravely on through the rain puddles with naked legs gleaming.

✳   ✳   ✳   ✳   ✳

The conference took place in the large open balé. It was shut off from the outer world by the sheets of rain that ran down off the roof, which was constructed in two tiers. Sometimes this rush of water made such a noise that it drowned the speeches and its monotone had such a drowsing effect that a few old dignitaries in the back rows nodded. The Resident and his staff sat on chairs at a long table. Both chairs and table had been provided by the Chinese for the occasion. The prince, too, had a chair on which he sat very uncomfortably with his legs folded beneath him. Although he wore a short black coat with long sleeves he shivered with cold every now and then, and also with the strain and mortification of the proceedings. The Resident, on the other hand, felt hot in his starched tunic and its collar begin to wilt beneath his fleshy chin. Visser, who sat beside him, helped him out with a few murmured words in Balinese, for though the Resident spoke Javanese fluently, there were nevertheless moments when the raja was perplexed by the stilted and involved expressions of one who had learnt the language only from books and was endeavouring to put his meaning into polished and high-sounding phrases.

It was nearly dusk when the session drew to a close. The Resident rose to his feet and, casting his eyes over the counsellors and court dignitaries squatting in row after row on their mats, said in conclusion:

"The Government of my country has shown great forbearance and patience. It has been reluctant to send soldiers and guns to Badung and to take by force the sum of money we have the right to demand. I have come here as your friend and elder brother and as such I have been received, for which I thank you from my heart. And as friend and elder brother I counsel you here and now for the last time: Let Badung pay the sum of three thousand rix-dollars as compensation for the ship which was plundered and destroyed on the coast of Sanur. With that the whole matter is at an end and the independence of Badung remains unimpaired."

The Resident surveyed the dour faces of the assembled Balinese—large oblique eyes, lowered eyelashes, compressed lips, and on every forehead a look of drowsed insensibility. He felt the blood rush to his head.

"If the Counsellors of the Lord of Badung care for the peace and security of their country and their lord they will give their voice for paying the money, just as I have again and again counselled my Government to abstain from taking the field against Badung. But as friend and brother I must warn you that the patience of my Government is at an end. This is my last word and I have no further proposal to make."

The Resident had raised his voice at the end to be heard above the rain. When he sat down Visser stood up and repeated what he had said in Balinese so that all should understand. Nevertheless the faces of the men remained completely impassive. The silence was broken only by the rain. Then Molog, the captain, leant forward and said, "And what happens if Badung declines to pay?"

The Resident jumped up and his forehead went crimson. "That is a question I do not wish to answer," he shouted. "But whatever happens will be Badung's responsibility."

Lord Alit had scarcely spoken during the whole discussion. He had left it to his counsellors and dignitaries to speak for him. Now they all looked at him as though they awaited a final answer. He raised his clasped hands to his brow and remained thus for several moments in mute concentration. When he began to speak, Ida Katut, who as usual sat at his feet, observed that his lips had gone white.

"I have heard the words of my friend and brother, the Resident of Bali and Lombok," he said, and his voice was so low that the men in the back rows put their hands to their ears, "and I thank my friend and brother for his advice and also for his wish to keep war and subjection from our borders. I, too, desire peace. In proof of this I have today come to new agreements and put my name to new documents, by which I have promised to give up old and sacred rights and usages of this country. It is true that for a long time no widow has been compelled to suffer herself to be burnt with her dead husband; but from now onwards widows are strictly forbidden to seek even a voluntary death. I have agreed also to a limitation of the death sentence, not because I consider it right but because I wish to give the Dutch Government a proof of my goodwill. As for the payment of three thousand rix-dollars I cannot myself alone decide this question. It is unfortunate that my co-regent and father, the lord of

Pametjutan, is stricken down with sickness and incapable of taking part in this conference. I will consult with him about it as soon as he is strong enough and I will then send my answer to Buleleng."

"The lord of Pametjutan was not too weak only the other day to enter personally into a sworn alliance with the lord of Tabanan," the Resident shouted angrily. The courtiers stirred uneasily, and the light skin of the young lord went almost white, but he controlled himself. "The Dutch Government," he said gently, "have frequently expected us to keep the peace with our neighbors. The alliance with Tabanan carries out this wish of theirs."

Suddenly the rain stopped and the abrupt silence was like a void in which the voices lost themselves. The Resident collected himself and mastered his temper.

"My friend, the lord of Badung, has two weeks in which to give his answer," he said tersely. "If the three thousand rix-dollars are not paid by the sixth day of next month, my Government will blockade the territory of Badung and send warships. I thank the raja and his counsellors for this discussion. I have no more to say."

He stood up and pushed back his chair before Visser had finished translating this ultimatum into Balinese. The assembly then broke up with a murmur of voices and a stretching of limbs. "These Dutch have little patience but much tenacity," the anak Agung Bima said to the anak Agung Wana. The roof now only dripped and the court yard was pink with the reflection of the clouds sailing overhead. The prince overtook the Resident on the steps and laid his hand on his shoulder.

"My friend is tired out with so much talking," he said friendlily. "We all need a little rest. The evening promises to be fine and my dancers are eager to show what they can do. Our little festivity begins with the rising of the moon—we will enjoy it together as brothers."

The Asiatic smoothness of this exasperated the Resident, who was already harassed by the exhausting and fruitless sitting. He could control himself no longer and his only response was to shake the prince's hand brusquely from his shoulder and to go on without a word. Alit stopped dead on the steps, white with mortification. His courtiers now all spoke to him at once, but he did not hear them. He looked with frowning eyes after the short white form as it quickly crossed the court and his breath came and went in short sharp gasps between his clenched teeth.

The house in which Berginck was lodged had been built specially for his visit. As a further mark of hospitality an attempt had been made to build it in the style of the Dutch houses of Buleleng, with a stoep and walls painted yellow and many hanging lamps with silk shades. Even the portrait of the Queen of Holland was not wanting: it had been cut out of a newspaper and tacked up on the wall. A few lancers crouched at the entrance as a guard of honor, but the Resident had as well a guard of his own, four Dutch soldiers with beards and barrel-chests and the slouch hats worn by the colonial troops.

"Can't say the palaver was a great success, eh, Visser?" Berginck said as he mounted the steps and lit a cigar. He pulled hard at it in the hope of calming his nerves, but for some reason he found it tasted of nothing and taking it out of his mouth again he looked disapprovingly at it.

"They've taken offence," Visser said. "We must have trodden on one of their Balinese corns again without knowing it."

"I'm fed up with these everlasting talky-talkies which lead to nothing, that's all I have to say," the Resident said testily. "We go round in circles and get nowhere. I feel sometimes that they're simply making fools of us." He took another look at his cigar, cursed under his breath and threw it into the courtyard. "Well, see you later," he said, and went on up the steps.

"Is it the Resident's wish that I should draw up a report at once?" Visser asked from below.

"Do what you like. We shall have to talk to these people again tomorrow. Wait a bit—you know the young lord better than I do. What sort of a fellow is he? I can't make him out. He seems soft and yet he's as obstinate as a mule, pig-headed to the pitch of absurdity..."

"I have always taken him for something of a visionary, Resident. More of a student than a raja. It's easier to know your way about with a realist like our Gusti."

"The Lord only knows," the Resident sighed as he vanished indoors. Visser sighed, too, and withdrew to his own quarters. The Resident stood irresolute in his room: twelve chairs stood in a row against the wall in a way that looked to him positively feeble-mind-

ed. He was in a temper and his head throbbed. But at the same time
he felt a familiar tingling in his veins, like the pricking of millions of
needlepoints. So that is it, he thought. Malaria. In a state of exasperation, he threw himself on his bed, which was provided with clean
lace curtains and a new mosquito net. He reached for a tin box,
which served to protect his personal belongings from ants, and took
out two quinine tablets. "Idiotic—a pack of children. They want a
good whacking, with those guns of theirs." He held his breath and
shut his eyes. Now his head began to ache. "That Molog with his
great snout," he said aloud. "It's people like that who are to blame if
things get serious." Suddenly a cheering thought occurred to him.
They have their Molog, he thought, and we have our Boomsmer. In
the first onset of fever he saw the two of them letting loose at each
other with peas out of toy cannon. He pulled his travelling rug over
him, as the first feverish shudder ran down his spine. Taking a look
round at his bed he found that Badung hospitality had provided
even a Dutch wife and pulling the customary kapok quilt in its
white cover over him, waited for the quinine to lull him to sleep.

✳   ✳   ✳   ✳   ✳

"I want to be told as soon as Raka comes," Alit said to the boy Oka.
"Stay here and wait for him." He had taken off all his clothing except a thin kain, and walked quickly away followed by a servant.
The sun was setting and the sky was unusually clear after the rain.
Alit distended his chest and took a deep breath. He was pleased with
himself and his heart was light. With his jacket and kris he had cast
aside the day's anxieties and everything now was good.

The way to the bath led past the pond and he paused a moment
to watch two marabus, male and female, which were playing together in a grave and dignified fashion. He looked forward to the
night and its festivities. Even before he reached the bath the kain
slipped down over his hips.

The bathing-pool, crowned by a small temple, was of remarkable
beauty. The water flowed into a deep stone basin from the mouths
of seven bronze serpents and as it was brought to the puri from far
away in the mountains it was cool and clear. It also had a peculiar
power in it of which Alit was often aware when weary or sad. He

stood naked under the falling water and let the coolness flow over him long and luxuriously. It washed from him those last hours and the insult he had suffered at the hands of the white man.

A strong smell of flowers hovered over the pool, for lavish offerings had been placed in the little temple in honor of the day. High above, the pigeons wheeled with a tinkle of their silver bells, and though the dusk already enfolded the puri their white plumage reflected the sun.

The prince wrung the water from his long hair and put on the clean kain which a servant held out for him. As he left the bathing pool he saw Oka running towards him. He did not wait to hear the message but hastened back to the house. Raka was waiting at the foot of the steps. He bowed himself with clasped hands and Alit put his arm round his shoulders and led him into the, portico.

"I have brought you a present," Raka said as they went up the steps together. It was a sign of the sympathy between them that neither said a word of the Resident's visit. Oka squatted beside a finely woven hamper out of which from time to time a cock's head with a valiant red rose-comb bobbed up and disappeared again.

"He's a djambul and he will win you many a fight," Raka said, holding the present out to his friend; with the full sense of its worth Alit let out a shout of joy. "You knew how I envied you him, Brother," he said enchanted. Raka laughed as he took the bird out and held it up tenderly in his hands. "It is a djambul, as you say—and he comes from Bedulua," Alit said with his whole mind absorbed in examining its plumage and feeling the muscles of its thighs. The cock extended its neck and crowed a challenge. The two friends laughed.

"In seven days you shall fight, my friend," the lord said to console him. He stroked the bird's neck feathers and swayed it up and down in the air to excite it. A bevy of wives passed by, twittering like birds and arrayed in all their finery. Raka dropped his eyes, for it was not permitted to look at the prince's wives. Alit called out to them, "Mercy—your beauty blinds me!" and they giggled as they vanished round the corner.

"You are happy, my brother?" Raka said when their gleaming hair, naked shoulders and glimmering trains had gone by.

"Yes, I am glad," the prince replied. "I have some dark and unpleasant hours behind me, but now I know the path I shall tread and I am happy." He signed to Oka and the boy took the cock and put it back in the hamper.

"We will take him ourselves to the other cocks," Alit said. "I want to see what he has to say to my Buvik." He picked the cock up again with the firm and gentle grasp of the fancier, feeling as he did so the hard and taut thigh-muscles beneath his fingers. It was a moment of complete contentment, warmed by Raka's presence and cooled by the light breeze of approaching night.

Just as they were leaving the house to go to the cocks, one or two persons made their appearance, bending low as they came. "What is it?" Alit asked, recognizing his cousin, the anak Agung Bima among them.

"The women have been awaiting you for a long time in the eastern balé, my brother," Bima announced. "It would be as well if you would allow yourself to be married to them before the moon rises and the feast begins. The pedanda, too, has been waiting for a long time."

Alit looked at Raka in dismay. "I had quite forgotten the women, I had indeed," he said, laughing at himself.

"What women?" Raka asked.

"The ones I am to marry," the prince replied. He stood irresolute for a moment on the steps with the cock clasped to him. The bird stretched out its neck and crowed impatiently. Alit give him to Raka and went quickly up the steps and into the house to the kris-holder in the corner of his room. He took the kris in its scabbard from the grasp of the wooden figure and put it into Bima's hand.

"Here," he said. "It will do if the women are married to my kris."

Without another glance he took the cock from Raka, delighted to feel its warmth and strength and buoyancy within his grasp again, and hurried Raka along with him to the balé where the cocks were kept. Servants with torches and lamps passed through the court-yard, for night had fallen.

The anak Agung Bima carried the kris in his arms as if it were a child. The pedanda, Ida Bagus Rai, sat in the eastern balé on his cushions, with his tall crown on his gray head, and prayed. The balé was draped with rich hangings and filled with all the special offerings that are proper to the marriage ceremony of a raja. Behind the pedanda the six girls who were to wed the prince knelt in a row. Lambon was the youngest of them and they all looked at once excited and weary, for they had been waiting since noon. The other wives sat in a circle and the slave-girls crowded inquisitively behind them. The six girls were magnificently dressed and adorned and scarcely dared to move in their gilded robes.

Bima bent his head to the priest's ear and he in turn nodded without interrupting his prayer. Now the anak Agung drew the kris from its scabbard and held it for a moment upright before him— the sacred kris Singa Braga on which were the Lion and the Snake, The girls' heads stirred like flowers swept by a wind. Bernis, who sat with the rest, said aloud, "It is too boring for our lord to come himself." Someone laughed and an old woman enjoined silence. Bima stuck the kris in the wickered bamboo of the wall and that was all. The weapon stood for the man who meanwhile amused himself with the cocks.

The six girls, pushed forward by a few experienced old women of the palace, took their places before the priest and the ceremony began. The pedanda called on the gods, sprinkled the backs and palms of the girls' hands with holy water, strewed shavings of sandalwood on their bent heads, blessed them and—with his eyes on the kris—gave them to the Lord Alit of Badung.

When it was all over they still waited, uncertain what else to do, until the pedanda rose and left the balé. Whereupon all the women began talking at once and filled the court with their cries and laughter. The anak Agung Bima took the kris from the wall, returned it to the scabbard and bore it away. Lambon was the last to be left standing there, stiff and motionless as a gilded statue. "What happens next?" she asked in astonishment. "Now there are lovely things to eat. Come quickly to the big house and Ida Katut will tell us stories," Tumun called to her. Lambon was still at a loss. "Am I the raja's wife now?" she asked the vacant air. But no one answered. The slave-girl Muna flitted past and after her came Bernis crying out, "The moon will be up in a moment."

Lambon sighed and, picking up her trailing kain in her fingertips, followed the other women.

❊   ❊   ❊   ❊   ❊

It happened that evening that Raka and Lambon saw each other again for the first time since she had been taken into the puri, and the sight changed both their lives, and everything grew radiant and yet overcast as though by an evil enchantment.

Just before Raka began to dance his eyes fell on Lambon; or, rather, Lambon unknowingly had been gazing at him for a long while without once turning her eyes aside or the least concealment.

She sat with the other wives of the lord on the mats of a low balé and Raka did not at first recognize her. He only knew that he had never seen a woman so beautiful as she. His breath failed him and his heart stopped and then sprang up like a wild beast and carried him away. He forgot where he was and what was going on around him; he merely stared at the raja's wife, seeing only her among them all. She wore her hair dressed with art and entwined with orchids. Her face was lightly tinted with yellow powder and a deep pool of dark sweetness stood in her eyes. Her head was gracefully poised and erect on the stem of her neck. Her parted lips were arched and expectant and seemed to breathe a promise. She was closely enveloped in a purple kain, painted with very large gold flowers and an ivory-colored zone, interwoven with gold, encircled her. The lines of her shoulders, her arms, the tender rise and fall of her breast as she breathed—all this seemed to Raka utterly and incomprehensibly beautiful. She shone out among the other women, who were also beautiful, as a ruby among pebbles. Her eyes met Raka's eyes with a strange and undeviating earnestness. And it was only now he realized that this beauty was Lambon, the child of Taman Sari, the little dancer with the girlish legs and arms who wore a dirty sarong, the hard green unopened bud of which he had thought so little. The bud is in flower, he thought, and the thought inspired a wild excitement that rent his being. He stared at Lambon and never had he known such tempest in his feelings. His muscles contracted, his breath came in gasps and his mouth was filled with saliva as though he had been chewing sirih. Someone gave him a nudge and he pulled himself together. The gamelan called.

He walked out from the bamboo roof beneath which he had been awaiting his dance and, tearing his eyes from Lambon, began to dance. It seemed to him that he had never danced before. He felt strong and young and beautiful in every limb because he knew that

Lambon's eyes were on him. He had never been so happy before, so torn and tense with excitement as during these moments while he danced. He saw Lambon and saw nothing but her, even when his eyelids drooped and his eyes closed.

Teragia, who sat among the spectators, bent forward as Raka stepped out into the light. She held her sleeping infant son in her arms, born three months before. Since his birth she had grown even more lean than before, and two fine wrinkles had appeared at the corners of her mouth. She looked at her husband with a searching, almost anxious look. He is not himself, she thought. The child felt for her breast in his sleep and she smiled. Raka seemed to dance endlessly on and on with the reflection of the lamps in his lost and dreaming face, and the gamelan repeated again and again the music of his dance. Teragia looked about to see if no one else marked the alteration in her husband. But though many followed the movements of the dancer with delighted and even enchanted eyes, everything went on about her as it always did. People chewed and drank and talked during the performance as usual. The stranger, the White Man, sat as guest of honor on his uncomfortable chair and looked down with heavy eyes. Teragia observed that he was suffering from the heat sickness and felt a fleeting pity for him. She could tell people's thoughts and was aware of all they felt. His high collar constricted the stranger's blood, his head ached and he would gladly have closed his eyes, but politeness compelled him to sit erect and smile. Her glance travelled on over the courtiers, many of whom had fallen asleep, for it was long past midnight. She looked at the lord and her glance rested on him. Alit, too, had bent forward—he, alone of them all—and he was gazing at Raka who still occupied the stage, now gliding, now retreating, now poised with tremulous hands stretched out above his head.

At this moment a murmur ran through the palm tops that hung down over the walls of the court and the first drops of a downpour came pelting from the sky. There was consternation and laughter. Teragia drew her little son under a fold of the cloth wound about her breast to protect him from the colder air. Those who were in balés or under cover could laugh as they looked out at the rain, which now came down in a torrent, but the simple folk from Badung who had been squatting in a circle round the arena with their children about them began talking and shouting; they took the cloths from their heads and wrapped them round their shoulders, crowding together and at last running for shelter to the watch-towers and any cover they could find. The gamelan, too, stopped playing and the men carried their precious instruments into the shelter of a balé. Raka alone, with visionary, unseeing eyes danced on, as though all things had already dissolved away—until, suddenly stopping, he looked about him in astonishment and down at his rain-drenched limbs, and then in a leap or two left the stage.

The rain now came down in such torrents that the lamps were extinguished. Everyone talked and laughed at once, taking it all as a huge joke. The anak Agung Bima summoned servants and sent them off in all directions. Torches appeared and slaves brought great vessels full of palm wine. The dancers were offered young coconuts to quench their thirst after their exertions.

"I suppose we can go to bed at last," the Resident said to Visser. "I scarcely know where I am with this damned malaria in my bones."

"It will go on a long time yet, I'm afraid," Visser said. "This is only a little interlude and the show will go on for hours."

"They have a remarkable notion of time, these Balinese," Berginck sighed and leant back in his chair again. Visser drank his palm wine. The rain beat its ceaseless tattoo on the grass-thatched roofs.

Lord Alit would have liked to go and join the dancers, but he could not desert his guests. He sat on for the sake of politeness, keeping an eye out in the hope that Raka would see him. He beckoned twice to him, but Raka was standing under the bamboo shelter, from which the dancers came on, and he did not appear to see. Alit signed to Ida Katut and the old story-teller trotted away through the rain and brought Raka back with him. The prince introduced him to his guests and Raka politely sat on his heels and smiled as though in a trance at the white tuan Besar's compliments. Then he remained squatting there a little below the prince and with his face averted. The rain kept on. The lord, seeing his guests talking together, gently touched Raka's shoulder. Raka turned and looked at him. "Oh, it's you," he said. "It seems to be raining."

Alit could not help laughing. "It has that appearance," he said. "But your father says it will soon be over and then the dance must go on."

Raka continued to look at him but with eyes that took nothing in. Alit shook him gently by the shoulder. "What is the matter, Raka?"

"What is the matter? Nothing," Raka said. He had only just realized that Lambon had become the wife of his closest friend, unapproachable and forbidden even to his sight.

"Are you sick?" Alit asked with a more vigorous shake.

"Sick? I? No, I am not sick, my friend," Raka said in the same absent-minded way.

The rain came down more violently than ever and the leaves of the palms bent before the wind.

"Will the festivities be continued?" the Resident asked the prince in Javanese. He felt wretched and was afraid he might even become delirious. His mind was dazed and he could not imagine how he should get through a conference in the morning.

"The rain will soon be over and the dancing will go on. I beg your forgiveness for the interruption. North Bali is dry and has better weather, I have been told," the prince said politely.

"No earthly hope," the Resident said to Visser. The Controller shrugged his shoulders in sympathetic resignation. Alit bent again to Raka.

"Would you like to spend the night in the puri?" he asked. "You will be tired and the roads are wet. There is a lot I want to discuss with you. Tomorrow is a decisive day."

"I will stay with pleasure," Raka replied. "But I shall not be tired …"

The lord turned to his guests again, and Raka's eyes wandered to the balé where the wives were seated. He could not see Lambon, for the rain had put out the lamps and the torches gave only a fitful light. Raka heard someone address him, but he could not understand what was said, and the Resident gave up his attempt at amiability when he observed the deaf and dumb expression in the dancer's face.

Raka wanted to go to Lambon. He wanted to go to Lambon. There she sat in the darkness within ear-shot, yet he might not call or speak to her—he might not even look at her, for she was the raja's wife. His longing for her was something such as he had never felt for anyone or anything in his whole life before. The rain murmured on. The balé in which were the prince's wives was dark and echoing with laughter. He could not go and pull Lambon out and carry her off.

He did not understand what had come to him. He had often heard that this kind of madness existed, and that men went out of their senses from the longing for a woman. You could read of it, too, in the old books. But he did not understand how it could happen to him—to him for whom life was all play, and whose lightest wishes had always found fulfilment.

Lambon sat in the dark and looked across at Raka. That is Raka, she thought. Raka, the beautiful, and he noticed me. Forgetful as she was, she had never been able to stop thinking of Raka all the time she had been in the puri. She had been docile and Tumun had found it easy to teach her how a wife of the lord should walk, and how she ought to lower her eyes and how answer her lord. She had learnt to dress herself with taste and to be pleasing to men. Nevertheless she had felt like a prisoner all through the time of probation. In her dreams she was often coming over the sawahs from Kesiman and bathing with Raka in the river. Now she was the wife of the lord. Every door was walled up. I am the raja's wife, Lambon told herself. There sat Raka longing for her and she was the wife of the raja. Old Ranis had been put in charge of her and she sat behind in the darkness and let nothing escape her. Lambon put her hands to her hair. It was no longer hers but the prince's. Her limbs were his, her face, her smile.

Servants came with freshly filled and lighted lamps—now it was light again. Lambon did not venture any longer to look at Raka. Raka, too, turned his head aside after he had filled his eyes for one moment with the sight of her. The rain left off and the patter on the palm tops died away. Only the eaves dripped and the dancing arena was dark and wet.

"The rain has stopped," the raja said to his guests. "The dancing will begin again at once."

"Splendid," the Resident replied with a great effort. The gamelan players set up their instruments once more. Ida Katut gave Raka a gentle nudge. "What's that ?" Raka asked abstractedly. "You must join the other dancers," the little man whispered. "Has it stopped raining?" Raka asked in surprise. "Where are your eyes, my son?" Ida Katut jeered, but then he bit his tongue as though he had guessed Raka's perilous desire.

"Have I leave to join the other dancers?" Raka asked with ceremony, facing Alit and his white guest with clasped hands. He tried to rouse himself from his trance. Alit smiled at him. "But I will see you after the dancing is over?" he said in a kind though distant tone. Raka rose to his feet and went across to the small bamboo-roofed balé where the dancers were assembled. The gamelan began playing. The narrator and his comic servant stepped on to the scene and made a few jokes about the rain and the wet ground. The spectators, who had now collected again, laughed loudly. Raka waited his turn. He waited for the blue veil to rise before his eyes and enclose him as it used to do. But that other world of thought would not take shape and he remained alert and wakeful. I must see Lambon, he thought, I must speak to her. I must have her. The gamelan called and with tightened sinews he stepped out from the balé. He drew himself up with head thrown back in an attitude of pride and virility as the Baris dance required, but he did not know he was dancing. He thought only of Lambon. It is dangerous, he thought, to love the wife of a raja. The penalty is death. I cannot help it, he thought again. Even though my life is at stake, I must see her and have her. It was to these thoughts that he danced.

He was breathless when the dance was over and he began taking off his robes. "You are bleeding, Raka," the narrator said, pointing to his cheek. Raka felt his cheek and looked at his fingers with astonishment. "Forgive me," the other Baris dancer said. "It must have happened in the fight."—"I don't feel it at all," Raka said with a laugh.

Everyone left the balés. Of Lambon nothing was to be seen. Raka stood irresolute in his gleaming dress, for it had just occurred to him that his other clothes were in the prince's house, and he did not know how he could meet the eyes of his friend with this new and perilous tempest in his heart. He wiped his cheek again and saw that his fingers were covered in blood. Suddenly he left the balé and pushed his way through the dispersing crowd. He had made up his mind to waylay the prince's wives on their way back to their own quarters. He wanted to see Lambon again and make a sign to her. The balé where the prince's wives had been sitting was already deserted.

A small dim figure in a rain-soaked kain barred his way. "Highness," she said politely, "my mistress sent me to you."

"Who is your mistress?" Raka asked quickly.

"It is better to name no names," the slave-girl Muna replied in a low voice. "She comes from your village and that is why she sends me to you. She begs you to tell her family that all is well with her. And that she has not forgotten those in Taman Sari who were dear to her."

Raka received the message in silence. Then he replied, "Tell your mistress that she is missed in Taman Sari. And tell her—"

"What shall I tell her?" Muna asked when Raka paused.

"Nothing else," he said. "Tell her that I have received her message. And tell her this too: The bud has become a flower. Will the flower be plucked or will it fade?"

Muna laughed softly from delight at sharing the secret. "The flower will be plucked, Raka, if I know anything of flowers," she sang. Suddenly she held out her open hand with a flower in the palm. Raka recognized it. It was one of the orchids entwined with Lambon's hair. He seized it. It had a sweet and secret scent. Raka closed his eyes and drank in the perfume as though it were Lambon herself. When he opened his eyes the little slave-girl had vanished. He stood dazed a moment and then laughed aloud for joy and excitement. Beckoning to a servant as he returned to the outer court he told him to fetch his clothes from the raja's house. By the time he had rejoined the other dancers and changed his clothes it was beginning to rain again. But Raka did not wish to see the raja again that night. He took the road for Taman Sari, feeling as though drunk with palm wine. He had stuck the orchid under his head-dress and its smell was laden with a secret and a promise and a threat.

That night Teragia woke to hear her husband crying out in his sleep, and when she held the oil lamp above him she saw that his cheek rested on a crumpled flower.

That night the old lord of Pametjutan was in such pain that he had a mind to die. But his mother, who was a hundred years old, watched by his bed and held him as if he were a child and forced him to live.

That night the captain, the warrior Dewa Gdé Molog, dreamt he had twelve cannon and that he discharged them all at once, and that the white man was shot to pieces, but so were he himself and all his warriors.

And the Resident, half-delirious with malaria, sat for his examination in navigation and was ploughed because he could not solve an elementary nautical problem, for the gamelan never stopped playing and distracted his mind.

That night the young lord waited long for Raka to come to him after the dancing ended, and his opium pipe was ready and his heart open for an intimate talk. But Raka did not come. And as the raja was lonely and disappointed, he sent his boy, Oka, to fetch the youngest and loveliest of his wives to beguile the sleepless hours,— Lambon, the dancer, with faded orchids in her smooth hair, in the hour before the first cock crowed.

✳   ✳   ✳   ✳   ✳

The Bad Time

THE misfortune that came to Pak's house began almost unnoticeably with sickness among his fowls. At first it was only two or three of the young black ones and then it spread to his whole flock. They sat with open beaks and would neither eat nor drink. His old father blew down their throats and pulled at their tongues, and his aunt compounded a medicine of poultry droppings and powdered chalk. But the fowls refused to swallow it, and after a few days their limp, dead bodies were found here and there in the corners of the yard.

Pak skinned one of the dead fowls and nailed it up with wings outspread on the outside of the wall in order to keep the spirits from further mischief. But the sickness spread, and at last attacked even his lusty fighting-cocks in their bamboo basketwork cages, and this was indeed a cause for sorrow and alarm.

Pak's head hung down and even Meru was grievously afflicted, for he had set his heart on the white short-tailed cock which his brother had given him when he executed the carving for the new house. But Sarna, who did not like to see long, sorrowful faces around her, did her best to cheer her husband up, and she only needed to put her little son on Pak's hip to see him laugh again. Also she begged three young cockerels of her father and brought them home with her, and when Pak came in from his labor there was crowing to be heard once more from the baskets in front of his wall and he was happy. And Meru carved a beautiful little cock as a toy for Siang, and the child carried it about with him wherever he went and bit at it, for his first teeth made a very early appearance.

But this tribulation was scarcely over before the cow calved and died. She was a young beast and very good on the sawah and with the plough. Pak heard her mooing in the night; it was so loud and long-drawn-out that it waked him, though he was in a sound sleep. When he got to the shed he found his father already there, trying to help her. He had a torch stuck in one of the posts and by the light of it he was doing his best for the animal, who stood with trembling flanks in the litter of dried leaves. The old man was stroking and pressing her sides with all his strength and the sweat ran down his face. "Her calf lies wrong in her," he said, for he knew everything. "It will come with its hind legs first and will tear the mother if we can't manage to turn it round."

Pak's uncle came, too, on thin crooked shanks, with his kain girt up, and gave much agitated advice. The women kept at a distance, for this was the men's business; but the aunt, as always, was very sure she knew best. "You had better go to the sawah and catch an eel and give it her to eat as they do with women to lighten their travail," she said. "I never heard such nonsense," Puglug replied; she had got up in the middle of the night to pound leaves so that the cow could gain strength for the labor of calving. Whereupon a brief battle of words raged round the pots and pans in the kitchen.

The three men worked hard to help the beast. "Have patience, mother," they said to her, "you will have a fine child; you are young and strong and you must help your calf now that it wants to come out of you, dear mother." The cow looked at the men with her large brown eyes; they were her friends with whom she worked on the sawah, and her breath came fast and sometimes she stretched out her head and bellowed. The uncle's old buffalo grew restless and answered with strange sounds as he rubbed his sides against one of the posts of the shed. The women, Puglug and the aunt, lit a fire in the yard to ward off evil spirits, but Sarna slept through all the commotion within the walls of her house, her little son in her arms. In the sixth hour of the night the calf, with the old man's assistance, came from the cow and he dried it with leaves. But the cow rested her head on Pak's arm, who was squatting beside her in the litter to support her, and died without uttering another sound.

For two days the women tried to keep the calf alive with the milk of young coconuts and a brew made from pisangs, as they did with babies when their mothers died in giving birth to them, but by the third day the calf was dead too.

Pak went about in deep despondence, for he had ploughed the western sawahs once, and it was time to plough them a second time and the cow was dead. His uncle's old buffalo had no longer the strength to do the work on all the sawahs belonging to the family.

Once more it was Sarna who bestirred herself to seek help. She spoke to her father. "Our cow has died," she said, "but I am sure my father would lend my husband his buffaloes, so that we shall not get behindhand with the work on the sawahs."

The rich Wajan, however, who had become rich by never putting himself out for others without some return, replied by asking, "How much rice will Siang's father pay me if I let my buffaloes work on his fields?" Although he paid his son-in-law a compliment in calling him Siang's father, his answer was churlish enough to put Sarna in a rage. "The father of Siang is now your son," she said in a loud voice, "and I would be ashamed to take him back such an answer. If you won't help him, his friends will."

"I will lend him the buffaloes," the rich Wajan replied to this, "if, for every day they are at work on his sawah, he works for two in mine. That is a good bargain for him, for two buffaloes are not twice but eight times as strong as a man." Sarna indignantly put her little son on her hip and took him away with her, for she knew that Wajan would have liked to play with him. She delivered this churlish message when she got home and Pak sighed deeply at hearing it. "The gods did not make men that they might work till they dropped, but that they might enjoy life and have time to keep the feast days and have enough rest."

"That is so," his father agreed. Puglug received Sarna's report with a mocking smile and went on with her work in silence. She was consumed with jealousy because the younger wife, useless though she was in the house, assumed great importance on the score of the help to be derived from her rich father. And when next Pak spent the night with her, as he did from politeness and for the sake of peace every week, she went to the back wall of the house and produced two strings of kepengs which she held out to him in the palms of her hands, a thousand pierced coins to each string, without a word issuing from her tightly closed lips.

"What is that for? Where did you get all that money?" Pak asked, taken aback.

"Earned and saved—not stolen," Puglug said. "You can buy buffaloes with it, father of Siang, instead of depending on the churlishness of the rich Wajan. You do not eat his rice and he has no say in what you do. But do not buy any cows, buy young buffaloes. Rib, I know, has two strong two-year-old animals to sell, and he will sell you them cheap as he is a friend of yours."

Pak marvelled at his first wife, as he did at women all his life, for the way they always did and said the unexpected thing. But two days later when Puglug had gone to market with her produce he dug about in the wall to find more of her savings. He did find the hollow in the wall, but there was nothing there but the little linen bag containing the dried navel strings of his two elder daughters, which Puglug had kept, as was only right, as mascots to ward off evil.

Pak was overdone with work at this time. There were not only his own five sawahs, and his uncle's two fields, with which he had to help. He was also a member of two guilds, one for the rice harvest and one for the care of the village coconut plantations, and the members had to give mutual help. He had besides to attend the meetings of the village council, on pain of a penalty for absence, and the gamelan runner was scouring the village almost daily to summon him and the other players for rehearsals and performances. Moreover, the rainy season had brought down the outer wall of the Temple of the Dead and the village had decided to rebuild it from the foundations. Two new gateways rose behind bamboo scaffoldings and skilled carvers and stone masons were to be seen at all hours of the day busily employed on the work. Pak, who was no hand at the fine arts of decoration, was told off, with many others, to collect fresh coral stone, carry it to the site, dress and put it in position. He did this gladly. But he resented it, for it deprived him of his last remaining hours of leisure, when the punggawas and officers of the court rounded up all the men to whom the prince had given sawahs and enlisted them for work in the puri of Badung.

New outer walls were being erected round the puri too; and trenches were being dug and water being conducted to the palace in a complicated manner, so that the trenches could be filled at a few hours' notice. An extraordinary activity and excitement reigned throughout the territory of Badung. At all hours, Molog, the captain of the warriors, could be seen drilling his men and the rattle of musketry practice often alarmed the peasants, until they got accustomed to it and even delighted in the noise, as though it had been Chinese crackers.

The job that more than once fell to the lot of Pak and several more men was to load the wooden pack-saddles of the lord's little horses with rice and coconuts and conduct the whole train by side-tracks to Tabanan. Each journey took several days, during which work on his sawahs was at a standstill. But there was no help for it, for Pak was a subject and servant of the lord, as his father and grandfather had been before him.

At the same period a fresh disaster befell. Pak's twelve coconut palms, and all the plantations of the village, were so overrun with squirrels that there was no getting the upper hand of them. They ate their way into the ripening nuts until these fell to the ground and were nothing but empty shells. The children collected them for firing and Meru found some in which the squirrels had gnawed two deep eye-sockets and carved funny masks of them. But Pak was annoyed: it did not seem to him an occasion for joking. He was up all night with the other members of the guild, trying to drive the animals away with torches and shouting and the clatter of bamboo sticks. But they did not have much success. As soon as the squirrels were chased away from the Taman Sari gardens they made off for the palms of Sanocr and the men there drove them back again. This led to bad feeling between the villages, and even between different parts of one village, and the young men got quarrelsome and the children fought in the streets. The pedanda, Ida Bagus Rai, intervened in person and begged the people to make up their differences; it was no time for disunion. Not only had a comet appeared in the sky, which from the earliest times had always signified war, as the older men observed every night as they gazed at its dull red trailing glow among the other stars; but, what was worse, the two Dutch ships, which had been seen one day off Sanur, had cast anchor and looked like remaining there for ever. The fishermen, Sarda and Bengek, and others who had keen sight, could see guns mounted on their decks with their round black muzzles trained on the shore. And then a little later three large, flat-bottomed boats put off, with a gun in each. Soldiers in blue uniforms and with scowling faces mounted them on the beach after making an emplacement of stones for each, and left them there as a threat and a warning. The people of the coast found it hard to get used to the sight of them—many avoided looking out to sea where the two great ships were to be seen day and night at anchor.

Puglug came from the big market at Badung and regaled the listening family with all the news she had gathered.

". . . and they say the white men's raja has demanded a tremendous sum from the lords of Badung, for that stinking Chinese boat that was wrecked at Sanocr. Why, we've all forgotten all about it! But the rajas of the white men have written letters and sent ambassadors and they say in the market that they demand nine hundred thousand kepengs"

"How many kepengs?" the old father asked, putting his hand to his ear.

"Nine hundred thousand kepengs or even more," Puglug repeated, holding up nine fingers.

"Mbe!" Pak cried out, quite overcome, but his uncle shook his head and said, "That is the sort of rubbish the women talk when they get gossiping at market. Nine hundred thousand kepengs—there is not so much money as that in the whole world."

"That is what the white men ask, and my uncle is right—so much money does not exist, at least in Badung. That is why the ships of the white soldiers lie off the coast and the order has come to shut off the frontiers of Tabanan and Gianjar, so that the people of Badung can sell nothing any longer, and that, too, is why the father of my children has to take rice by side roads to other countries, in case the soldiers of the white men should know anything about it."

"You are talking a lot of nonsense," Pak said crossly. "If we don't have a better harvest than we have had lately, no one in Badung will want to sell rice to Gianjar and Tabanan; we shall have to go to their markets and buy from there, unless we mean to starve."

"That is forbidden too. They want us to starve. And if the white rajas hear of rice coming in from elsewhere, they will shoot their guns and destroy our villages. That is why there is a comet in the sky."

"How could they destroy our villages?" Pak's father exclaimed. "Are we soldiers? It has never yet happened that soldiers fought with peasants. If the comet means war, it has nothing to do with us Sudras. The white men's soldiers will have to fight it out with the

Ksatrias, who are making such a noise with their rifles under Molog's orders."

"That is so," said all who had been listening.

Yet an uncomfortable feeling hung over the villages, for these rumours and others like them kept on cropping up. And even if Puglug was only a foolish market woman, there were intelligent and experienced people such as Krkek who were of the same opinion.

The next time Pak slept in his chief house with Puglug, she sprang a new cause for anxiety on him in the intimacy of the night. "I am only a foolish woman and it is not for me to give you advice, father of Siang," she said, and Pak pricked up his ears when he heard himself addressed so ceremoniously. "But if I had a younger brother like Meru, I should not let him keep on going to Badung. I should make him work on the sawahs. I would rather tie him fast like a buffalo, and put a yoke round his neck like an unruly boar, than let him spend his time as he does in the puri. I am only a foolish woman, but that is what I should do if I had a younger brother."

"What are you talking about, wife?" Pak asked, but all the same he had a strange feeling of uneasiness, for he knew that Puglug was no fool, talk as she might, and she had made the money for him to buy the buffaloes with. "You know as well as I do that Meru is employed in the puri to carve the doors of the new temple tower."

"The doors have been finished long ago and Meru has no longer any business in the puri," Puglug said to this. Pak thought it over for a moment. "It's the women in the puri. It's them he's running after," Puglug added, and said no more.

"It will be time enough to worry when Meru comes and tells me that he wants to bring a slave into the family as his wife," Pak said.

"I was not talking about slaves," Puglug said, and with this the disquieting talk was at an end.

Pak decided to speak to his young brother. "Meru, my younger brother," he said when Meru came home at the end of the week, "I want you to help me with the planting instead of going to Badung. You eat my rice and I have the right to your help on our sawahs."

Meru pulled a face, but as he was a good-natured and amiable fellow he stayed at home for the next few days, got up at cock-crow, girt up his kain and helped his brother with the planting of the new sawahs. But he was not so cheerful as usual; he spent his leisure time sitting in a corner of the yard carving a piece of light-colored wood without saying a word to anybody. His old father squatted beside him now and again and looked on as the work took shape beneath the deft strokes of the knife, but he could not make much of it.

"Do you see what your brother is carving there in the corner?" Puglug asked, as she sat down near her husband.

"No—is it something good?" Pak asked. He was feeding his cocks and giving them water.

"It is a stag leaping a doe," Puglug replied, compressing her lips as her habit was ever since Sarna had joined the household.

Pak went and watched Meru at his carving. It was a stag and a doe and the male animal was mating with the female. The carving was still in the rough, but it was easy to see what it was going to be. Nothing of the sort had ever been seen before. Pak could not help laughing at it—it made his blood tingle.

"For whom are you carving that, brother?" he asked.

"For myself—just to pass the time," Meru replied. Pak went back to the women.

"It's a stag leaping a doe," he said. "I like it, though I have never seen such a piece of carving before. What is wrong with it?"

"It shows where your brother's thoughts are," Puglug said as she picked up little Klepon and went away. Pak looked at his second wife in astonishment and Sarna burst out laughing at the bewildered look in his face. "What did she mean by that?" he asked in perplexity.

"Your young brother seems to have warm dreams. He has a woman in his thoughts," Sarna said, for she understood such matters. Pak forgot her strange smile as she said this, but it came back to him later when the disaster had already befallen Meru.

They finished the planting of the new sawah and Meru helped also with the cutting of the alang-alang grass. On the third day he made off to Badung again and stayed there for two weeks.

Then a message came from the punggawa of Sanur with the request that Pak and his father would go to him. "What can be the meaning of it?" Pak asked the old man on the way, as he helped him along the banks between the sawahs, which were slippery with the rain. But his father, who was never at a loss, could only shrug his shoulders in silence.

"Perhaps the prince means to give us another field. Puglug tells me that he is very pleased with Lambon and has her with him oftener than any other of his wives," Pak said optimistically. But his father shook his head. "It is Monday today and an unlucky day for all dealings with the authorities," he replied curtly.

The punggawa received them with unusual kindness and they squatted down before him and there was long talk over one thing and another. He signed to his servants to offer these two simple men sirih, and even then it took him a long time to come to the point, for it was not a pleasant task to have to tell the old man what had to be told.

"Grandfather of Siang," he said at last, and the old man smiled with pleasure, for it warmed his heart to hear himself addressed thus, "your son, Meru, the carver, has done wrong and must be punished."

The punggawa did not address Pak, the brother, but only the father, and the old man lowered his eyes as he had learnt to do when as a young man he was in the service of the lord.

"He has lifted his eyes in unseemly fashion to a wife of the lord Alit, our master," the punggawa went on, "and you know what that means."

The old man opened his mouth twice before he spoke. His lips had gone dry and he had to moisten them with his betel-stained tongue before he could utter a word.

"Must he die?" he asked submissively.

"Our lord and master is of great goodness," the punggawa said. "He has turned his eyes away from the crime and grants your son his life."

Pak sat in a daze as though someone had struck him a blow on the head. "Must he be banished—to Lombok or the island Nusa Penida?" he asked hoarsely.

"Banishment is only for men of high caste. You ought to know that," the punggawa said, without so much as looking at him. Silence followed. My brother Meru, Pak thought. Suddenly he remembered how he used to carry his younger brother on his hip. They had herded the ducks and their father's two cows. Meru's kite had always flown higher than any other boy's. The singing in his head and all round him went on and on.

"I sent for you to tell you that the punishment will be carried out tomorrow when the sun is in the first quarter. Go to the puri of Badung to take your son and brother away, for he will need your help," the punggawa said. He looked at the two men—dumb with fright and grief—and added, "It pains me that your family should suffer thus. Meru has done nothing base: his crime is one that any man can understand. Bernis is a beautiful woman and men are weak and it is easy to fall. But even though the prince in his goodness spares his life, yet honor demands that Meru shall pay with his eyes the penalty of having looked upon a wife of the raja."

Pak cleared his throat and asked, "And what happens to the woman?"

"She is of high caste. The prince casts her off and she is banished for ever," the punggawa said.

Pak and his father sat for a moment longer mute on the ground, and it was some small comfort and appeasement to have sirih to chew. Then the punggawa helped the old man to his feet and laid his hand on his shoulder. When Pak looked at his father he saw big tears rolling down the old man's cheeks and his own throat pained him and there was a bad taste in his mouth.

They did not say a word as they went back across the sawahs to Taman Sari. In the village Pak's father parted from him. "I will go and speak with my friend, the pedanda," he said, stopping at the gate of his friend's house. Pak went home alone, blinded with grief. The people he met looked after him when he made no answer to the greeting they called out to him.

He sat down in his yard on the steps of Sarna's house and took his little son on his knee to comfort him. The women gathered round and his little daughters too, looking at him anxiously.

"My brother Meru will come home tomorrow and he will be sick with his eyes," he said after a time. "Get the eastern balé ready and put cushions on the couch. You can also take the curtains from Sarna's house and wash them and hang them round his bed." As soon as he said this he realized that Meru would no longer be able to see the curtains and he laid his head on the shoulder of his little son and began to weep. His three little daughters leant up against him and Klepon, who was just beginning to talk, said, "Father, father, father . . ."

The women talked together in low voices in the kitchen. "I could have told you what was coming," Puglug whispered. "Old Ranis was talking about it at market. Meru used to sleep with a young slave-girl, called Muna, until her mistress, the beautiful Bernis, noticed him and took him away from her. So Muna went and told the anak Agung Bima all about it, and it's he who is in charge of the wives. She was sorry afterwards and took it all back and said she had been telling lies out of anger against her mistress, who often beat her. But the anak Agung Bima kept his eyes open and watched them, and he observed that Bernis and Meru exchanged secret signs and were meeting each other. After that there was no help for it and it must be borne."

The aunt had already begun preparing special offerings for the house altar, and the women resolved in whispers to take offerings to the village temple as well and to have prayers offered up to the gods that they might lighten Meru's affliction. The task of preparing and decorating the offerings helped them through the long hours of the night; and the men did not sleep either. The old man came home late and went straight to the house altar and squatted in silence before it hour after hour.

In the morning he was dressed and ready before Pak had wound his loin-cloth about him. They did not go down to the river to bathe that day, for they shuddered with dread. The uncle went with them too, and they were joined on the way by a few friends of the family who had heard of their sorrow. Pak was afraid lest the journey would be too much for his father, but the old man had cut himself a staff and led the way with the even stride of a peasant. Not a word was said as they went along, and as they reached the puri of Badung the sun was still below the trees.

The gate-keeper let them in and pointed to the courtyard in which judgments were given. There was a lofty open building there, built in the same style as the watch-tower and painted in white and red, to show up the pains of hell depicted on the walls. Some officials of the court sat aloft there, and there were other men squatting on the walls that surrounded the courtyard, waiting for the proceedings to begin. There were no women to be seen and Pak gave a fleeting thought to Lambon and wondered whether she had heard of her brother's fate, and whether she might possibly be able to beg the lord to pardon him. But at the same time he knew that pardon was out of the question in a case where the raja's honor was involved, and he resigned himself.

After what seemed an endless time there was a movement in the courtyard, and men armed with spears advanced with Meru in their midst. He was in his best kain and wore his kris in his girdle. There was a hibiscus flower in his headdress over his forehead. But what horrified Pak was that he wore a loin-cloth of the cloth in which the dead were wound.

The sun was shining. Meru stood in the middle of the courtyard with a fixed and unconscious smile as though asleep. One of the officials stepped down from the court of justice and, standing before Meru, read his sentence from a lontar book. Meru did not stir and gave no sign of having heard it.

After this another man of high caste stepped up to the little group of relations and friends and said, "If you wish to greet your brother and speak with him, you may do so now."

Pak looked questioningly at his father. But the old man shook his head. "Better not disturb him," he said softly without taking his eyes from his son. "As he is now he will feel the pain less."

As no one spoke to the condemned man, another man came down from the court-house and approached Meru. He, too, was in ceremonial dress and wore a white cloth.

Putting both hands on Meru's shoulders he addressed him in a loud voice.

"Brother," he said, and his voice reached the farthest corner of the courtyard. "It falls on me to execute the sentence. I do not do it because I wish you ill. Forgive me in that I must cause you pain and allow me to carry out my office."

In as loud a voice Meru answered, "Do your duty."

The man put his hand to his girdle and took out a bamboo knife. Two other men stepped behind Meru and held him fast. Pak turned his eyes away. There was a little altar of bamboo, adorned with flowers. There were a few hens searching here and there for grains of rice. There was a funny-looking little white dog.

The man who stood there in the middle of the courtyard flourished his knife twice and plunged it into Meru's eyes.

Not a sound was to be heard. Then he let the instrument fall to the ground and received Meru in his arms as he fell forward in a dead faint.

Pak carried his brother out of the puri over his shoulder and he seemed to him strangely light, no heavier than a child. His friends quickly brought a bamboo stretcher and laid the unconscious man on it. Blood trickled in two thin streams from the sockets of his eyes and the closed lids fluttered like the wings of a captured butterfly. One limp arm hung down from the stretcher as the men raised it to their shoulders and moved off, and his father walked beside them holding his son's hand. It was a long way to Taman Sari. No one spoke a word.

When they got home, the pedanda was there waiting and also Teragia with her father, the balian. They laid Meru down on the cushions with the freshly washed curtains and stood beside him. Towards evening his consciousness returned, and the gamelan, of which Pak was a member, came and played in the yard for many hours, for nothing helps to lighten pain so well as music.

Yet for many days Meru groaned and cried out and threw himself about in his intolerable agony and for a week it seemed that he would die. But he was young and strong and by degrees he recovered. At first he tried to walk with his hands on Rantun's shoulders, and they all helped him as he groped his way about. He asked for his knife and cut himself a stick and with its help he ventured out into the village street. Pak often gave him his little son to hold, in the belief that the warm touch of the child would console his brother as it always did him.

One day when Meru was groping his way about the yard he came upon the piece of carving he had begun before his disaster befell him. Squatting upon the ground he held the block of wood in his hands and ran his fingers over the surface of it. Another day they saw him with the carving on his knees, working at it with his knife, while with his fingers he touched and felt it since he could not see it. "What are you carving at there, brother?" Pak asked with a smile. "Nothing," Meru replied, raising his sightless face from his work. But Pak had seen what it was. A clumsy arrow now pierced the flank of the stag who leaped his doe: the creatures were slain in the very moment of their greatest happiness. Pak did not know what to say for grief at the sight of it and after a while Meru put his unfinished work away and never touched it again. "I cannot see what I am doing," he said, and looked with empty eye-sockets into the darkness that enclosed him.

Pak's father was a great deal with the pedanda during these weeks and had long talks with him. One day he came home and called the whole family together—the uncle and aunt and Lantjar, too. "My friend the pedanda tells me that there is only one means of warding off further misfortune from our house," he said, "and you all know what it is."

They hung their heads, for they did in fact know. The body of their dead mother had not yet been burned and this neglect had continued for too long. It was no wonder that her soul, seeking rest and finding none, had given marks of displeasure in order to insist on the peace which was her due.

"Fortunately there is to be a large burning at Taman Sari on the fourth day of next month. I have spoken with the council," the old man went on, "and it seems it will not cost more than twenty-two thousand kepengs to have the corpse burnt. This sum must be found."

"It shall be found, father," Pak said shortly. His conscience had long been troubled and burdened, because in the pursuit of his desire he had almost forgotten his dead mother. A feeling of great relief came over him now that the cause of all their misfortunes had been ascertained and openly avowed, and the means of avoiding even worse disasters made clear. He dug up his ringits and found there were no more than seventeen, for he had spent a great deal since he married Sarna; Puglug rifled all the mouseholes where she stored up her savings and collected all the money she possessed. It came to three hundred and seventy-six kepengs. Pak talked seriously to his uncle and he produced three strange silver coins, which looked as if they might be Dutch. Pak puzzled and scratched his head, for they were still far short of the sum required, and then he sold Meru's kris to the rich Wajan, who wanted one for his son. Wajan bargained and made difficulties and then gave him six hundred kepengs for it, which was too little. Meru, however, knew nothing of the deal, for he could not see, and what could a blind man want with a kris?

And so, as the day of the burning was approaching and the cremation beast had to be fashioned and the cremation tower built, not
to speak of the cost of offerings and dues, Pak set off once more for
Sanur to speak with the Chinese, Njo Tok Suey.

When he came back he was almost cheerful and he said to his
father, "I have mortgaged the two western sawahs to the Chinaman
and he has given me thirty ringits for them, so now we can have
a very fine cremation indeed and there will be money over for un-
foreseen expenses."

"That is right, son," the old man said. "But how will you pay off
the debt, for the sawahs do not belong to us but were only given to
us by the lords of Badung."

But Pak could not bear to hear the lord of Badung mentioned
without having a bitter taste in his mouth as he had had on the day
when the sentence was carried out on his brother. And so he only
shrugged his shoulders and a moment later said, "I will sell half the
crop and pay the Chinaman. It is not the raja's business how we
meet our private troubles."

Puglug made an outcry, "And what shall we live on and what shall
we eat if you sell the rice crop? Anyone would think that you could
see no farther than your nose."

"You mind the kitchen and feed the pigs instead of interfering
in what is the men's business," Pak said, observing once again how
ugly his first wife was with her untidy hair and hanging breasts. "I
will put the new sawah under yams and maize as soon as it is harvested, so that we can get through until next harvest," he said to his
father, hoping for his approval. But Sarna made a face. "Did I marry
you," she said, "to live on yam and maize like any beggar's wife?
Our son will fall sick on such stuff."

Pak, however, shook off his cares, and the whole household and
the whole village threw themselves joyfully into the preparations
for the great cremation. A creature in the shape of a fish was constructed to receive the bones of their deceased mother, and a high
tower of bamboo, covered in cloth and gilt paper. Offerings were
prepared, and the presents to be burnt with the body, and Puglug
brought a number of small earthenware vessels from the market.
Kepengs were stitched on to tenter-frames in the likeness of a wom-

an. Priests were paid, quantities of palm wine bought for the guests and bearers, food was cooked for days together.

The joy and excitement increased as the day of the cremation drew nearer. The women were the best of friends over the preparations and the children jumped for joy. Even Meru seemed to share in the general happiness and a shadow of his old high-spirited laughter was to be seen again in his blind face.

Three days before the cremation the whole family went to the cemetery, where many more had already assembled. Graves were being opened on all sides and the remains of the dead brought to light. Pak's family soon found their mother's grave, although she had lain there so long that the mound in the course of years had got flattened. They opened the grave and allowed Rantun to be first to search it; with zeal and an air of great importance she grubbed in the soil with her small hands. They all cried out with joy when a small bone was discovered, for they had begun to fear that nothing at all would be found. And now they all took part in the search and unearthed the skull next from the moist ground and a good large piece of the back-bone; they pulled the bones this way and that and spent a long time in showing the soul of the deceased how dear she had never ceased to be to her family. Then they enveloped the bones in the piece of white linen they had brought for the purpose and carried the light bundle home.

For the next three days the whole village was in a state of wild joy and excitement, for there were forty-two funeral towers ready and over seventy souls were to be set free in the fire, so that they could rise to heaven and return again to earth in a new incarnation. On the day of the cremation itself the gamelan played from early morning, and the posts of the towers were wrapped round with bright-colored cloth, and the Temple of the Dead received rich offerings. The pedanda came to offer up prayers and give blessings, and lamps were lighted at many gateways to show that the house harbored one of the dead.

The tower stood ready in front of Pak's yard, a gorgeous affair, gleaming with all its decorations. And at the cemetery the cremation beasts were set up, white bulls and cows for the Brahmans, lions for the nobles, and fishes or elephants for the corpses of lower caste.

Some of the poorer people had no beasts at all, but only decorated boxes, and Pak was glad to be able to do better than that for his mother's soul. In all this excitement Pak had utterly forgotten having mortgaged his sawahs, and he enjoyed the festivity and all the joys of the cremation without a cloud on his mind.

When the moment came to carry the handful of bones, wrapped in white linen, to the tower, it appeared that there were still many in Taman Sari who wished to pay honor to Pak's mother and to show that she had not been forgotten. Indeed, the crowd of those who wished to lay a hand on her remains and to help carry the tower grew larger and larger and two groups fought for the privilege as though she had been a noted figure in the village. It took a long time, too, before they joined the other towers, for the bearers, with laughter and shouts and every sign of enthusiasm, took many roundabout ways and even went as far as the market-place under the large wairingin tree. All this, however, served to confuse the evil spirits and to prevent them following after the soul of the deceased. Pak himself carried the bones up a bamboo ladder on to the tower and his father followed him. They stayed there while it went swaying on its way to the cemetery, for they were the next of kin to the dead, and Pak was glad that the old man had lived to take part in the ceremony.

The white and gaily decorated glittering towers formed a long procession as they moved along the street, borne on the bare shoulders of hundreds of perspiring and laughing bearers and headed by the gamelan. It took over an hour to reach their destination behind the Temple of the Dead. The cemetery was still rough with the recently opened graves and the bearers by this time were merry with palm wine. Strong men of the village who knew how to make the fire burn well stood by the heaped piles of wood. Each family took its dead from the tower and the women sang and passed along, bearing offerings on their heads.

The bones of Pak's mother made only a small packet and the smell of moist earth rose from them and reminded Pak of the smell of the sawahs. He himself deposited the bones in the belly of the wooden fish and the rest of the relations and friends crowded round to show their love. They laid pieces of cloth on them as well, and poured much holy water, and then broke the jars and threw them away. The pedanda went from beast to beast, blessing the dead and ordering the ceremony.

Flames now shot up on all sides from the heaps of wood laid under the beasts, and men damped down the fire with sods to make it burn in the right direction. There was a crackling and roaring of flames, and skulls and bones began to catch alight. Pak, too, pushed in a burning bamboo stem into his mother's pyre and the women remained standing round it, silent and a little sad as they thought of the deceased. The volumes of smoke were so dense that it took away the breath and made the eyes smart. When they were sure that the pyre was burning well and the cremation beast was black and charred by the flames, the family, as was right and proper, returned home.

They entertained their guests, ate and drank and talked their fill and the children told Meru all they had seen.

It was not until late at night, when news came from the cemetery that the fire had burnt out and the ashes had cooled, that they went back there. And now torches could be seen flitting about on all sides in the drifting smoke as each family collected the white ashes of the bones from the darker ashes of the burnt-out pyres. Pak gathered all he could find and the women put them in an earthenware jar to take home.

It was now time to cheer the souls of the dead in their loneliness as they hovered homeless, and unused as yet to their new state, over the ashes they had just left. Fireworks were let off and the streets were in an uproar with the noise of rockets and shouting and singing. The smoke of the torches mingled with the smell of the cremation pyres. The children were wrought up to a high pitch of excitement by all the festivities of the day and did not want to go to sleep. Pak looked anxiously at his father to see if he was tired out, but he was happy and full of life as he told story after story to his guests.

The women powdered the ashes and put them in a coconut and later the pedanda came to pray and bless them. The village echoed with the letting off of fireworks and the bearers paraded the village singing at the top of their voices, for they were by now very drunk with palm wine. The fourth hour of the night had passed by the time the procession left Pak's house to carry the ashes to the sea and consign them to the waves for the final purification. The chil-

dren insisted on going too, and as the family set off slowly down
the street with their light load they were joined by other torchlight
processions whose destination was the same as theirs. There was a
smell of torches, of the sea and of thousands of faded flowers. The
dark beach was alive with lights and crowded with people and every
face had a look of tense excitement. The tide was high, and as soon
as they consigned the coconut to the sea the waves snatched it up
on their foaming crests and carried it rapidly away.

Pak softly touched his father's shoulder as he stood looking after
the shell as it danced in the water. "Are you not tired, my father?"
he asked, and the old man nodded back.

"Your mother was a good wife," he said as though the vanished
years had passed before his eyes as he looked out on the sea. "She
was a good wife and now her soul is glad to be released. She will
return to us soon in a new child and be with us again."

Pak's head was whirling with fatigue and all the honors done and
received and all the palm wine. Sarna carried little Siang, and Rantun staggered under the weight of Klepon, who was fat and heavy.
But at last she fell asleep as she walked and Pak took his two elder
daughters in his arms and left the youngest to Puglug. Thus they got
home at last and slept soundly without a care. And, sure enough,
Sarna told her husband soon after that that she was expecting a
baby, a second son for the house.

And then, just as Pak congratulated himself on having warded
off all misfortune and purchased security for the family, just at that
very moment rats began to infest the sawahs.

He had let in the water on an auspicious day and ploughed the
first time and broken down the soil and brought the prescribed offerings and prayed to the goddess Sri for a good harvest. He had
put out the seedlings in a corner of the field and strewn cooked rice
over the field and sprinkled it with holy water and prayed again.
His back ached from his labors. When the seedlings grew tall and
showed their dark green tips, the sight gladdened his eyes and he
ploughed and prepared the ground a second time. It was heavy
work, for the young buffaloes were stupid beasts and slow to learn
what was required of them. Pak had levelled the edges of the field
with the spade and dug the corners, where the plough could not go,
by hand, and he had kept the water at the right height and neglected

nothing. He waited ten days and ploughed a third time and gave the fields three days' rest and then he went over it twice with the lampit and levelled it until his sawah was like silk under its covering of water. And he got the loan of cows and asked his friend Rib to help and went over the ground again with the largest lampit and three teams. Before this he had mown the edges and buried all the grass and weeds deep in the mud so as to make the ground even more fruitful and he allowed no woman on the field but gave it all the strength that was in him.

Then he took up the little plants and trimmed and bundled them. And he planted them all by himself, for Meru could not help him now and his uncle lay at home with pains in his joints and was of no more use, and it was one of the hardest days of Pak's life. And he waited for the auspicious day and watched for the constellation of the Plough and set up an altar on the left of the water inlet and made more offerings and prayed. And so the days passed and all was done with care and in proper order, and when the right time came the women were allowed on the sawah to weed and the children caught caterpillars and dragonflies for their meal times and Lantjar drove the ducks out to seek their food in the mud. Puglug worked hard and the sweat ran down her fading breasts, but Sarna said that it made her back ache to bend, because she had the child within her. She left off working and picked unripe green fruit, for which she had a great longing. Pak only laughed; he rejoiced at the prospect of having another son and he spoilt Sarna a little at this time.

The stalks grew longer and in four and a half months the ears began to show. A festival was held in the rice temple and a new altar was built on the fields. The ears hung heavy and were already a silvery green and Pak sniffed up the moist green smell of the grain into his nostrils and began making the clappers to scare the birds and his heart was glad. He was going to have a fine harvest, the best for many years, and pay off his debts with enough over to feed all who lived on his rice.

One morning he went out on to the sawah, not to work but to see how things were going and to gladden his eyes with the sight.

All he saw was the stalks—the ears had vanished as though evil spirits had made off with them.

Pak felt as though the edges of the sawah rose under his feet; the sight turned his stomach and he vomited. He looked a second time, but there was nothing to be seen but the bare stalks and no ears at all. He crouched down before the altar, which he had built to Sri, and he felt a cold sweat run down his temples, and down his sides, too, ran a cold sweat. He shuddered violently and felt sick as he looked at his fields with all the grain gone after all his labor. He sat down by the edge of the field with his feet in the muddy earth, for his legs gave beneath him, and held his head in his hands. Then he noticed a strange movement among the haulms and saw a large rat disappear into the mud and then another and another. And then he saw that all the ground was heaving with rats. The stalks rustled and stirred with them and now and then he could hear the nibbling of their teeth.

After some time Pak stood up and looked about him. He found that the fields of his neighbor, Bengek the fisherman, were eaten bare and so were the crops on all the fields around. It is as well I planted yams on the new sawah, he thought gloomily. The rats have come to my fields, he thought. Why do the gods punish me, he thought, now that I have done all I ought and had my mother burned and offered up every offering to the Lady Sri? We shall die, he thought, for when there is no rice people must die. What shall I do now? he thought. He bent down to pick up a clod of earth and threw it at a rat and it scuttled away. There are the souls of evil men in them and they will leave nothing. Darkness had fallen before he thought of returning home.

The men of the village were sitting outside the town hall talking in undertones as Pak went gloomily by. They called out to him, but he did not hear. When he got home he found they had heard the news. Puglug brought him his food, looked at him with pity and said nothing. Her look annoyed him; he longed for consolation. "Is it not Sarna's month to give me my food? Why do you push yourself in?" he said.

"Sarna is sick and cannot wait on you," Puglug replied, "and Siang, too, is feverish. We sent for the balian and he has given him medicine. Now eat, father of my children."

It went against Pak's stomach to take food; he still felt bad from the blow he had had. He got up and went to the fine house he had built for his second wife and stepped in. Sarna was crouching on the couch, holding her little son on her lap. Her eyes were hollow and when he touched her he could feel that she was hot.

"Have you got the heat sickness?" Sarna was smeared on the breast and shoulders with a yellow ointment and the child, too, had a whole lump of it on his forehead.

"It hurts me to breathe," Sarna whispered, "and I feel I shall die."

Pak let his hands fall and did not know what to say. Why does all this happen to me? he thought in a daze. He went out to find his father. The old man was asleep in the kitchen. "He was shivering for cold and came to lie down by the fire," his aunt whispered, making room for Pak. His father had heard him come in in his sleep and sat up. He drew Pak to him as though he was still a child and put his hand on Pak's knee.

"Many years ago we had rats in the fields and nobody knew why the gods punished us," he said. "Then the priests found that an old temple had sunk from neglect into the earth of the sawahs. The men dug it out and built it up afresh and the rats were caught and killed. We made little towers and burnt them so that the souls imprisoned in the animals were set free, and we carried the ashes to the sea. Next year we had a fine harvest and no more was seen of the rats."

Pak cheered up; it sounded consoling and he could fancy to himself the rats' little funeral towers.

"Many people say that the souls of children who were not burnt because they died before they teethed inhabit rats and mice," he said thoughtfully, "but why should the souls of children do us such mischief?"

"That is rubbish," the old man said. "The souls of children fall on the earth as dew; that is not disputed, and they are kindly and freshen the sawahs with their moisture."

Puglug now came into the light of the kitchen fire. "A runner of the subak has come to say that the men are summoned to a meeting to discuss the disaster," she announced. The kulkul sounded through the village in short quick beats. Pak sighed heavily, wound his head-dress about his head and set forth.

As the whole village this time was involved in the misfortune and no one knew what the reason for it could be, although many connected it with the comet and the presence of the two Dutch ships, the council decided that the gods ought to be asked about it.

They waited for a day that was favorable for matters of magic and this chanced to be the fourth day of the next week. Meanwhile offerings were offered up somewhat at random and the rats devoured what was left of the ripening crops. When the day came they all waited impatiently for the evening and then assembled in the village temple. The gamelan played and the unmarried men and girls went in procession to the pedanda's house to fetch Teragia, for it was through her mouth that the gods were to speak.

Teragia looked serious and composed and she had put on a black kain and a white breast-cloth. Two servants followed her, one carrying a basket of offerings and the other holding her sleeping child. Ida Bagus Rai did not join the procession, since it is better for the pedanda not to have anything to do with affairs of magic; but the village priest and Teragia's father were already waiting in the temple. Two umbrellas were held over Teragia and the gamelan preceded her as she advanced along the street, for she was holy.

"Where is Raka?" some of the men asked, and the women looked about for him in the crowd. But Raka was nowhere to be seen and someone said he was at Badung with his friend, the lord.

Teragia was conducted up into the balé Her father had already filled the water jar and got the smoke started, and Teragia sat down cross-legged before it. No one spoke to her, but two women supported her on each side and held her when, soon after, her head fell forward. The gamelan played on and then ceased, and in the silence that followed the crowd began to sing, the women at first, and then a few men joined in in the guttural tones of the old chants.

Teragia had fasted for half the day, for she knew from experience that this made it easier to fall into a trance. She shut her eyes and inhaled the smoke of resin and sandalwood, which rose up at her feet, and extinguished herself as she might put out a fire. She could feel how she lost and forgot herself, and how a vacancy spread within her as though she were not a person but a barrel. She knew nothing of time and place; she soared and hovered and there was nothing around her but the singing. Her eyes were shut and she would have been unable to open them if she had tried; her limbs were heavy at first, then light, and then they disappeared, as though her body, too, had left her as soon as her soul had made room to receive the divinity.

She did not know how long it took to reach this stage; but everything was then yellow on every side of her, a yellow that did not exist in the real world but only in her trance; and then she knew nothing more.

As soon as her eyes became fixed and her head fell forward, they knew that she was ready to take the divinity into herself, and the old women crouching behind her supported her. Her hair lay so close to her finely shaped head that she might have been a priestess and her face was beaded with sweat as with a lustreless dew. When her limbs began to quiver and she sank into the old women's arms, the singing ceased and everyone kept completely still and waited for the message of the god. In the stillness a bird could be heard singing in the cambodia tree in the temple court, and this made the stillness all the more profound.

Suddenly Teragia's lips received the afflatus and she began to speak. A murmur ran through the crowd when a strange, deep, ringing voice issued from her mouth in a speech they could not understand—Kavi, the old Javanese tongue, which only pedandas and scholars knew. Although they could understand nothing, the people of Taman Sari listened breathlessly, for this was the critical moment which was to bring them the sole remedy for the misfortune that had overtaken their sawahs. The god spoke slowly and for a long time out of Teragia's mouth. The old women supported her rigid body and her father sat close to her in the balé, listening with rapt attention, for he had to report the message later in the common tongue. Here and there in the crowd others fell into a trance, men and women and even two half-grown children. They, too, began to talk all at once. While the burble of voices grew louder and the excitement increased, Teragia's message seemed to have come to an end. She lay back silent in the women's arms, but her soul had not yet come back to her. Her father sat opposite her and waited, since it is not good to break a trance. When some time had gone by and she still did not come to herself, he dipped his finger-tips in the holy water and sprinkled her with it. Slowly the fixed look in her face relaxed and she opened her eyes and smiled at her father. She was very tired and somewhere in the crowd she could hear her baby crying in the arms of the servant; it had woken up and was hungry. She struggled to her feet with an air almost of embarrassment and vanished in the crowd. There she unloosed her breast-cloth and gave her child the breast.

Meanwhile her father gave the chief men of the village the message which the god had spoken through her mouth and everyone crowded round him, not to miss a word. This was what the balian said:

There were in the hands of the people of the village certain precious objects which belonged to the gods and were wrongfully withheld from them. The gods would not be reconciled until these objects were restored to them. Moreover, a new shrine was to be built in the rice temple at the confluence of the two streams north-east of Taman Sari and every man must contribute labor, money and taxes; also everything that had been stolen must go towards the building of the shrine. Thus had the god spoken and enjoined, threatening them with misfortune if the command was not obeyed and promising good fortune and good harvests if they did as he said.

A murmur of dismay ran through the people, for this was a hard message, as hard as the fate that had befallen the sawahs. Most of the men crowded round Krkek, for he was head of the Subak and the building of a new shrine in the rice temple concerned him first of all. But after a few minutes their depression gave way and some even began to laugh; after all, it was good to know at least what the gods required of them. The wag, Rib, chaffed the men nearest him and asked them, one after another, whether they had any of the stolen valuables, imitating as he did so the self-importance and inflated dignity of the punggawa of Sanur. And the men all laughed and said they had nothing they ought not to have and had always paid the gods and the temples their dues in offerings and taxes. Yet they eyed one another covertly for any sign of conscious guilt.

By degrees the crowd dispersed, keeping together in knots with torches alight to ward off lejaks and evil spirits. But Krkek resolved that the building of the temple should be begun on the next auspicious day and that it should be built of free-will offerings; and he told the other men to bring their contributions to the large townhall before the next full moon. A number of men went back with Wajan, who had invited them to his house to drink palm wine and discuss the new situation.

Pak and Sarda, the fisherman, carried the heavy gong between them behind the rest of the gamelan players to the building where the instruments were kept. He had been in a strange state all the evening, with cold hands and feet and a fevered buzzing in his head and his ears. It seemed to him that the divinity had unmistakably spoken to him personally and that he alone was the guilty cause, not only of his own misfortunes, but of the disaster that had befallen the whole village. He was the man who had wrongfully withheld stolen treasure from the gods, it was he on whom the penalty fell. In his vanity and blindness and conceit he had taken the plates away from the goddess Sri; he had dug them up out of the earth of his sawah in order to give his house the splendors of a palace and to win a smile from Sarna. He slunk along with the bamboo pole, from which the large heavy gong was suspended, eating into his shoulder and his whole body burned with shame. His fields were laid waste and at home Sarna with his only son lay sick and near to death. But the guilt was his; it was his folly and wrongdoing that were the cause of it all; he had lied to himself for the sake of the plates which were not really his.

He refused Wajan's invitation to drink palm wine, for it was no time for palm wine, and he did not hear what Rib said to him when he put away his gong with the other instruments. He was afraid of going on home alone, although he had a torch and had prudently put a piece of garlic in his ear before starting. However, he got home without any untoward encounter and saw that the offerings to the demons were in their place at his gate and that Rantun had also put glowing coconut shells beside them to show him the way. The sign of there being sickness in the house hung from the offering niche beside the gate and reminded him of the danger that threatened Sarna and Siang. He stepped over the bamboo grating in the gateway and started at the sight of his own shadow as it fell on the piece of wall beyond that served to confuse the spirits. Holding his torch high in the air he went to Sarna's house. The door was shut and Rantun lay asleep on a mat in front of it, a trusty little guardian of the sick. Pak's heart warmed at the sight of her, and bending down he covered the child with his loin-cloth, for the night air was chill and misty. Then he raised the torch to the plates in the wall and looked long at them.

They were as beautiful and precious as on the first day and the roses looked like real ones. The porcelain was white and smooth and there was not a crack to be seen. And yet these plates had brought dire misfortunes to Pak and his household. He sighed heavily and opened the door and went in.

Sarna lay on the couch with her child beside her, but her eyes were open. Pak held the torch over them both and looked closely at them. Sarna muttered feverishly and he could not understand what she said. He crouched down beside her and touched his son's body and found it burning with a dry heat. A wooden bird was suspended over his crib and on it were offerings to Kumara, the goddess of children, and more offerings lay on the roof-beam.

"How are you, mother?" Pak asked, putting his hand on Sarna's brow. But she only went on muttering and did not know him. He took the child from her side and laid him in the cradle. It frightened him to feel how limply he lay in his arms, almost as if he were already dead. The smoke of the torch filled the room and Sarna coughed painfully without ceasing to mutter feverishly. He opened the door to air the room, but then it occurred to him that the damp night air might be the death of Siang; so he shut it quickly behind him and stood in the portico beneath the plates. He sighed deeply as he reflected that he had never in his whole life been so overwhelmed with grief and care as at this hour. His heart in his breast was as tight and small as a clenched fist. He put out the torch and found his way to his father in the dark. The old man had taken to sleeping in the kitchen near the embers in the hearth, for his blood grew chilly with advancing years. Pak lay down close to the old man without venturing to wake him. But after a short time his father knew he was there and stroked his face with his hand. "Son, why do you cry?" he asked. "My misfortunes are more than I can bear," Pak said, and sobbed without shame, for when he was with his father he always felt that he was still a little child. "My wife and my son are going to die, and what will become of me then?" He secretly hoped that his father, who always had comfort to give, would contradict him. But the old man only went on stroking his face and said after a long pause, "It must be as the gods will."

He took a corner of his kain and wiped the tears from Pak's face. Pak sobbed a little more and then, creeping closer to his father, he nestled against his old hide which was as dry and rough as the bark of a tree, and finally fell asleep and dreamt of his sawahs.

It was no easy job chipping the plates out of the wall. Pak got to work early next day and tried one tool after another. But the plates were firmly bedded into the wall and he was afraid of breaking them. It might only anger the gods further if he offered damaged and broken plates for the building of the temple and he could not go too carefully. When all his attempts failed, he decided to pull the wall down in order to get at the plates without damaging them. Nearly the whole day was spent over this task and the family stood round in astonishment watching Pak at his incomprehensible labors. As Sarna shrank in pain every time a fragment of the wall crashed to the ground, Puglug offered to take her young sister and the child into her own house. Puglug was glad to do it and she nursed them with the greatest care. She is a good wife, Pak thought, not for the first time. However unpleasant Puglug might be when things were going well, she was a tower of strength whenever disaster threatened the household.

Pak wiped the plates clean on his own kain and took them to the town hall. He left the wall in ruins, promising himself to make it good next day. He was in haste to hand the plates over for fear they might bring further misfortunes.

Krkek was not very much surprised when Pak handed over the plates to him, for everyone in the village knew of the treasure with which Pak had adorned the house of his second wife. "The pedanda has helped us with the plans for rebuilding the temple," he said. "We shall build three new shrines, one for our forefathers, one for Vishnu, Brahma and Shiva and a throne of stone for Suria. Every man in the place must contribute one ringit and work two days of the week. The pedanda has promised to carve the stone figures for the gateway himself. I will ask him where your plates shall go. They are very beautiful and perhaps they might do well for the base of Suria's throne."

Pak's heart was lightened once he had handed over the plates. There were a number of men sitting round; some had brought their cocks along with them so that they, too, might enjoy what was going forward, and others played a gambling game on a mat. The rebuilding of the temple was a source of pleasure and soon they were all ready to forget that the rats had eaten all the rice off the sawahs. Pak inspected the heap of things which the first day had produced and marvelled in silence. There were boards and small bits of iron and even smaller pieces of a reddish metal he was not acquainted with, which had gone green in places. There were several paper parcels of rusty nails and some pieces of sailcloth which might do for a skilful hand to paint pictures on. There was also a small heap of money, coins of all sorts, ringits from Singapore, a good number of kepengs, and Dutch money as well, stamped with the young, high-bosomed, long-nosed goddess of the white man.

Pak was not very quick in the uptake, but as he stood there inspecting the first results of the requisition, it dawned on him to his great astonishment that he was not the only one in the village whom the sea had enriched with the property of the gods. Even though they had all, when interrogated by the punggawa, indignantly disclaimed any part in the plundering of the Chinese ship, it was clear all the same that many of them had somehow come into the possession of stolen goods. When Pak had finally arrived at this conclusion his conscience was appeased and a broad grin of relieved surprise spread from ear to ear.

Now that he had delivered up the plates, he went so far as to expect that Sarna would be well again by the time he got home, and he made haste to get back. But Sarna and the child were still unconscious and their souls were not with them. Teragia was sitting beside them looking anxious. Her father had sent her with an ointment which she was rubbing over Sarna's and Siang's limbs. "Will it help?" Pak asked.

Teragia smiled to console him. "I will pray to the gods that it may," she said. Pak sent Lantjar to the garden for three papayas as a present in return for her trouble.

Next he went to offer his help in the levelling of the ground for the new temple. It was hard work and he wanted to do it. He carried some young trees along over his shoulder and helped to plant them. While the work was going forward, Meru, with the help of his stick, came to the site where the streams joined and sat there with his new-found smile on his blind face. The men asked his advice about the decorative work to give him pleasure and held out pieces of wood and stone for him to feel and say how they could best be used. Meru ran his fingers over them and the pedanda told the men what gods and demons and beasts they were to carve or chisel out of them.

"By the way, has the fisherman, Bengek, the husky man, handed anything up?" Pak asked desperately. Krkek, who was always wide awake, looked keenly at him. "Why do you ask that?" he said slowly.

"It seems to me that Bengek, whose mother is a witch ought to contribute something to the building too," Pak said, and said no more.

"I will inquire in Sanur," Krkek said.

Three days went by; Pak knew that Krkek had been to Sanur, and when he saw him again at the site, he came to a stop beside him after unloading his planks from his shoulder and wiped the sweat from his face and waited. As Krkek made no remark, he asked when he had recovered his breath, "Has the fisherman Bangek handed up anything for the building of the tower?"

"No," Krkek said. "And what has it to do with you?"

When he got home Pak sat down to think. What was the good of building a temple with the sweat of their brows and giving up all they possessed? he thought. As long as the husky man kept what was not his, the gods would continue to punish them. It is not my place to speak, he thought, but sooner or later Bengek must give up what he fished out of the sea.

Hours went by while he thought this over and at night he went to see Krkek and talk to him again. "There are people," he said, "who believe that all the trouble comes from the house of Bengek and his mother, the witch. If the people of Sanur would ask the gods properly, they would be bound to find out what had to be done about it."

For the first time Krkek allowed it to be seen that he understood. "It is possible," he said, "that Bengek ought to hand over more than many others, since he lives close to the sea and is a fisherman and all is fish that comes to his net, and his mother takes the left-hand path."

Pak went home and waited. He sat beside Sama, who was delirious and so weak and worn out that she could not speak. Also rice was now getting short and the yams on the new sawah were not ready yet; and besides, it was possible that a diet of yams might be fatal to his sick wife and child. Puglug grated coconuts and mixed them with the milk of the young nuts and tried to make Sarna eat, but she only turned her head away. The flow of her milk was stopped and Puglug had great difficulty in keeping little Siang alive from one day to the next by giving him mashed pisangs to suck on her fingers.

"Why do you keep on calling out after Bengek the husky in your sleep?" Puglug asked her husband.

"Do I?" Pak said in alarm. "It must be because his fields are next mine and he neglects them. I am afraid that more vermin will infest the sawahs. If his fields are sick, how shall mine flourish?"

Puglug shut her lips tight and stared him in the face until he felt quite uncomfortable and turned away to go to his buffaloes.

No one knew who started the rumour nor how it spread, but within a week all the villages round about—and all suffered from the plague of rats—were saying that Bengek's mother must have something to do with the disaster. Many who had always feared her up to now took courage and told fearsome tales of her. She had been seen at night in the cemetery, offering up the blood of slaughtered fowls. Her eyes watered and children to whom she had given presents of food fell sick. The watchers who spent the nights in the watch-huts in the sawahs brought strange and dread things to mind. Fireballs had hovered like living things over the rice and one-legged lejaks with pigs' heads had rushed with peals of laughter through the sawahs.

Bengek the husky was now mentioned only in a whisper. He had never put in an appearance at the building of the temple tower and Pak never saw him on his sawah. He had made no contribution and he had not been present at the last cock-fight. Sarda the fisherman said he had not seen Bengek on the sea for a long time; his boat lay high and dry on the beach and the planks were starting in the heat of the sun. The men thought it over and reckoned it out and made inquiries in one place and another; finally it was ascertained that no one had seen Bengek for three weeks—not, in fact, since the rats began to lay waste the fields. The last person, it appeared, who had spoken to Bengek was Meru. He had come across him in Pak's bamboo thicket by the stream. Meru had made his way there to bathe and also to cut himself a new stick.

"Who's there?" he had asked when he heard someone rustling through the branches. And he had heard Bengek's husky voice reply, "It's me." Meru had felt his way towards him as he wanted to know whether the husky fellow was stealing his brother's bamboos. But Bengek had had no bamboo poles in his hands but only two of the worthless bracts that grow at the joints of every bamboo shoot. He remembered it particularly because, as he blindly felt the leaves, the tiny hairs that grew on them ran into his fingertips and made them inflamed for days afterwards.

It could not be said that Meru was the last to have seen Bengek since he could not see at all. But he was certainly the last to have known anything of him. Pak heard his brother's story with astonishment and a vague shudder. He could not get the picture out of his head—the fisherman stealing out of his bamboo thicket with the two large leaves which there was only one use for: to kill someone by mixing the fine prickly hairs with his food. This tallied in a remarkable way with the memory of the swarm of rats in the mud of his sawah and the feeble whimpering of little Siang who was starving for lack of milk.

The whispering in the five villages became a murmur and the murmur became an outcry.

"Where are you going, son?" Pak's father asked when he saw Pak putting his knife into his girdle on the day before the new moon and shouldering a long sharpened bamboo pole, though he had no load to carry.

"I am going to Sanur to look for Bengek the husky," Pak replied briefly.

"Peace on your way," the old man said with ceremony. "And may no evil come to you."

Every road was thronged with men carrying bamboo poles; they came even from Intaran and Renon, although no kulkul had summoned them. More and more joined them, but the fathers sent back their children who ran inquisitively along beside them and no woman thought of following them. When they reached Sanur they turned aside and followed the course of the river behind the village. They forced their way through the bamboo hedge and waded the marsh, both of which served to protect the village against evil spirits, and approached the witch's homestead.

The walls shone with bits of red coral and three dogs bounded from the gate barking furiously. There was no sign of sickness or death posted up outside, but the knowing Krkek stopped and sniffed the air. The homestead was close to the sea and there was a smell of seaweed and salt and fish. They saw, too, the Dutch ships out at sea, and they had been joined by two more, so that there were now four in all. The men stopped and sniffed the air. Mingled with the tang of the sea there was another smell they all recognized—it was the smell of death.

They kicked the dogs aside as they flew at their legs and crossed the bamboo grating and entered the yard. The smell grew stronger.

What first met their eyes was a number of holes dug in the yard, some quite fresh and moist and others already beginning to dry in the sun. In several places the outer wall had given way owing to the ground having been excavated beneath it and two bread-fruit trees lay uprooted; they, too, had had their roots loosened by the digging. The whole aspect of the place was incomprehensible and senseless, as though some unknown beast had made its lair there, or a madman.

The men stood and stared without moving and many of them felt afraid. Pak felt afraid. Krkek stooped to pick something up and threw it down again. It was the head of a chicken; and when they looked around they saw several more lying about. Of Bengek nothing was to be seen.

Krkek went forward alone to the main house. Apart from all the diggings the yard was in order—the implements were in their proper places, the fishing nets were stretched between two trees and the large water barrel was full. And now a fighting-cock crowed from his bamboo cage and that took the eerie feeling from the place.

"How are you, brother?" Rib said aloud to break the silence, as he squatted down beside the cock. The halves of coconut shells were supplied with maize, and water, too, had not been forgotten. Nevertheless, Pak did not venture to budge. He was expecting to see in one of the holes that strange chest which Bengek had fished out of the sea on the night of the wreck.

Krkek sniffed the air again and went round the house to the eastern balé. They found there what they had dimly suspected. Wound in linen and enclosed in a framework of bamboo poles lay a corpse, ready for burial. A few clumsily prepared offerings were beside it; the awkward attempt to decorate them with leaves showed that there was no woman in the house.

The men crowded round the balé and Krkek, who showed great courage that day, pulled the linen winding-sheet aside to see who the dead person was. They bent forward and saw the face of Bengek's mother, the witch, and it seemed to them that she laughed. Krkek covered her face again and hurriedly wiped his hands on his kain.

"Now we're unclean for three days and can't go on with the building of the temple," Rib whispered in Pak's ear. The men stood there, wondering what to do next. "It's high time Bengek buried his mother," Rib went on in a whisper, for he could not resist a joke, and screwed up his nose. The smell was almost unendurable.

"Bengek, where are you?" Krkek shouted across the yard. But there was no reply. The cocks began crowing again and a little tit-jak lizard cried out from the bamboo wall of the house. Suddenly the three dogs ran past the men, all in the same direction, wagging their tails. Krkek hesitated for a moment and then followed them. He looked round at the rest and they came on behind him, carrying the sharpened poles as spears.

They passed the pigsty and the granary, which was empty and looked utterly desolate, and came to the plantation of palms behind the house altar. A tjrorot uttered its note; otherwise there was no sound. The stillness was intolerable and took away the breath.

Suddenly Krkek came to a standstill. "There he is," he said softly, pointing in front of him. The men pressed round him. They had set out full of courage and enthusiasm, eager to bring peace to the villages and to kill the witch and her son, if it had to be. But at the weird look of the yard all dug up, at the smell and the sight of the corpse and the emptiness and silence and eeriness of it all, their courage had oozed out at their heels. Some—and Pak was one of them—thought it possible they were bewitched and attributed to this the lethargy in their limbs and the leadenness of their feet.

They could all see Bengek now. He was digging at the far edge of the plot of ground where the palm suckers grew right up to the wall. The dogs jumped up at him.

"Bengek!" Krkek called out again, and the husky man looked up and saw them.

They were still a good distance from him, and they did not stir from the spot. They merely held fast to their bamboo poles and breathed hard. Bengek stood motionless for a moment, spade in hand.

"Get out," he shouted as loudly as his husky voice could. "Leave me alone. I did not ask you to come here. I want nobody's help. You can go. I won't speak to you. Go."

The men were now crowded so closely together that they formed a small compact knot, although there were nearly a hundred of them. Suddenly some of them broke loose and started running for Bengek; they covered the expanse of ground in great bounds, tailing out their knives as they ran. The rest followed, scarcely knowing what they were about. Pak ran, too, and found himself among the foremost with Krkek close at his side.

Bengek leapt on to the wall and swung his spade. "Go," he shouted, and this time his voice was husky no longer but a loud deep roar. "Go, and leave me alone. This is my place—get out!"

Krkek stopped dead as he ran. He caught hold of the man nearest him and gripped him fast. Those behind charged on and nearly fell over those in front, who stood rooted to the spot and stared at the fisherman.

"Don't touch him," Krkek said in a low, breathless voice. "He has the great sickness."

They stood with their eyes fixed on Bengek, who crouched on the wall ready to defend himself with his spade. Slowly they retreated, for now they could all see it: he had the great sickness—the frightful sickness whose name might never be uttered. They stared at him and they saw his face. It was without eyebrows and bloated, and his thick, swollen ears started from his head; and more terrible than all, he had stuck two large red hibiscus flowers behind those leprous ears.

The men slowly retreated. "The great sickness?" Pak whispered incredulously. "The great sickness, the great sickness, the husky one has the great sickness and the witch is dead," they all whispered. Krkek looked round and saw a heap of stones, which had broken away from the coral-stone wall. He stooped and picked one up and threw it at the leper. Pak, too, picked up a stone—it was rough and heavy to his hand—and threw it. All the men flung themselves on the stones and hurled them at the wretch on the wall. The dogs jumped and howled when they were hit.

Bengek gazed at the men for a moment as though he did not realize what they were doing. Then he threw away his spade and jumping off the wall ran in great bounds to the beach. They did not follow him and he was soon out of range of their stones, His figure grew smaller and smaller and vanished at last in the prickly scrub which bounded the beach. The tjrorot still uttered its cry and a gust stirred the palm-tops and died away.

"The gods know whom they punish," Krkek said softly. "We will go to the pedanda and be cleansed."

Raka

BEYOND the western courtyards, where most of the slaves lived and kept their poultry and pigs, rose a wall, and beyond this wall the stir and noise of the puri suddenly ceased. It bounded a ruinous part of it where no one lived and no one ever went. Creepers and shrubs had overgrown the tumble-down buildings and dragged them to the ground in their embrace. The chief building of this forgotten courtyard was surrounded by a ditch, but the bridge had given way and sunk into the water. The demons who guarded the entrance were nothing now but moss-covered blocks of stone. Wild bees made their homes in the trees and huge butterflies hovered undisturbed above the flowers. Mosquitoes hung in dense clouds over the stagnant water and the smell of decay mingled with the penetrating scent of salicanta flowers.

It was here that Lambon had her secret encounters with Raka. The lovers met there almost daily, for their passion consumed them with such a devouring flame that desire began to torture them again even though they had parted only an hour before. Raka made his way there by a forgotten and crumbling gateway on the west side of the palace wall and Lambon had discovered a path that led by a round-about way from the temple to the spot where Raka awaited her. They had to jump across the wide ditch, and then they were safe in the ruined house on the forgotten island, where perhaps in other days the favorite wife of one of the lords had been housed. The steps had given way and the couches too, but there was a door they could shut behind them and Lambon with Muna's help had brought mats there to rest on. Even before the night on which she and Raka saw each other again Lambon had made this place her refuge. She had sat there hour after hour with parted lips, tranced as the water-lilies were in the standing water. Sometimes she cried; sometimes she fell asleep until Muna came to fetch her. Thus she was led to believe that Muna thought nothing of her spending every hour there that her lord did not require of her. But the eyes of the slave-girl, in which there was just the trace of a squint, saw more than Lambon thought. Her little brain was sharp and well versed in the intrigues of the raja's wives and nothing that concerned the secret crimes of love escaped her. But Muna's liking for her new mistress equalled her hatred of Bernis, and so she loyally and silently protected her from the inquisitive eyes and ears of the puri.

Few words were wasted when Raka and Lambon met. Their love was too great and their longing too strong. They rushed together like two animals, and had no more power to separate than a pair of dragonflies that eddied linked together over the sawahs. It was only when fatigue came to loosen their embrace that the tide of tenderness reached their hands. Then they sat, temple touching temple, on the mats and talked in whispers. They opened the door by a chink and watched the tall bulrushes swaying in the water and listened to the frogs sitting on the leaves of the lotus flowers.

"Are you happy?" Lambon would ask.

"I am happy," Raka would reply. The eternal talk of lovers.

"Will it always be so?"

"Always, my little sister."

"If we are discovered, shall we have to die?"

"If we are, we shall die together," Raka said.

"Yes, then we shall die together," Lambon said, well content.

It seemed a simple thing to die together. Great love is always close to death and parting. It was this constant peril that raised their feelings and their embraces and their happiness to such a pitch The puri had a thousand eyes. Twenty women envied Lambon and, although they flattered her as the favored wife, they would gladly have poisoned her. She was guarded by innumerable spies, young and old. It did not escape them that Lambon's beauty bloomed as a flower, and that her throat and shoulders often showed the tender wounds of love. Muna made an ointment of kunit and a yellow powder to put over the little bruises for fear the prince might notice them. But the other women envied Lambon these marks of love, as old warriors envy one another the scars of battle.

When it was time for the lovers to part, Muna appeared on the wall that separated this waste place from the rest of the puri and whistled three times in imitation of a betitja bird. Lambon tore herself away and Raka remained hidden in the building. It was only long after Lambon had gone that Raka crept out, leaped the ditch and made his way to the overgrown and crumbling gateway, eyes and nostrils on the alert as though he was a beast in the jungle.

It was fortunate that Alit spent his days in a regular manner. There were the hours he spent in the temple, or when the pedandas of the neighborhood visited him, bringing old lontar writings with them; or else he was detained by consultations with his advisers, or the punggawas of the various districts of his realm came to make their reports; or a letter arrived from the Dutch, which had to be weighed and answered. And, as a diversion after so many serious occupations, there were the cock-fights on the open space in front of the puri, which lasted many hours. All this was the concern of men and it gave Lambon time to go her own way in secret. But it was odd that Raka should be absent on all these occasions and particularly that he should neglect cock-fighting; for no one took part in it with more excitement or gambled more recklessly than he.

Whenever Alit had Raka with him—and this was seldom now—it was very obvious to him that his friend had altered. Raka was at one moment buoyed up by the wildest high spirits, and at the next sunk in deep depression. He put out his hand eagerly for the opium pipe and then withdrew it again in alarm, as though afraid that the drug would make him talk. He brought Alit a great many presents, and this had never been his custom before. It had been Alit who had overwhelmed the handsome Raka with gifts and kindnesses. Now it was the other way round. "Are you sick? Have you fever?" Alit asked when Raka fell silent and stared into a corner of the room. Raka merely laughed. "I have never been sick in my life, you know that," he said with a flickering up of his old arrogance.

"You are not the same as you were. What is it? Has someone bewitched you?"

"Perhaps," Raka replied, turning serious.

"I have spoken to your father. He tells me that you have no eyes for Teragia and your little son. Is it a woman?"

Raka hesitated. "Yes," he then said, drawing a deep breath. "It is a woman."

"Why do you not take her into your house? I know of no woman in Badung who would not gladly be carried off by you," Alit urged. Again Raka hesitated before he replied.

"She is married," he said, looking Alit straight in the eyes. Alit blinked his inflamed eyelids. Silence fell between them. Alit's dearest wish was to make Raka again the man he had been before. "Shall I take her from her husband and give her to you?" he asked. Raka jumped to his feet. "Don't torture me, Alit, I implore you," he cried. "And do not let us ever mention this again." Alit looked narrowly at him as he went out and down the steps without having asked his lord's permission to leave him. But Raka was cut to the heart at having to deceive his dearest friend and at there being no help for it.

Lambon, as women do, teased her mind with "ifs" and "ands" when she and Raka were together. "If you had taken me into your house as your second wife before they took me into the puri," she said, "then all would have been well. I should have loved to serve Teragia. I would have been her slave. I think she likes me."

Raka put his hand over her mouth. He could not bear to hear her say this.

"If you had asked the prince to give me to you before his eyes had taken pleasure in me," she said another time, and Raka burned with seven fevers.

"It is too late and he has found pleasure in you. Do not go on saying things like that," he said sternly.

"Muna told me that the lord had given you his favorite horse—and I cannot possibly mean as much to him as his favorite horse," Lambon persisted.

"You talk as though you had never heard of a man's honor," Raka said.

"What should I know of a man's honor?" Lambon said innocently. "I know that the lord is good." She took the crushed flowers from her hair and threw them into the rank growth that choked the ditch.

"I remember one day," Raka suddenly began, "when he and I were children going to bathe in the river together. We were too big by then to bathe with our mothers, and not grown up enough to join the men. And so we went together accompanied by a few slaves of my father's. They were most of them young slaves, only a year or two older than ourselves. They rubbed us down with stones and played about with us in the water. We were all in great spirits that day, I remember; we splashed one another and wrestled and fought in the water, which only came up to our knees. But as we were playing about in this way it happened that the youngest slave accidentally got hold of Alit's head and threw him down. He was a slave, you understand, and not merely a boy of no caste, and he had touched Alit's head. He had no thought of insulting him; it just happened in fun. But Alit went as rigid as a rock. He did not speak a word on the way home. I felt that he would fly into splinters if he was touched—he was so brittle. He went to his father and demanded that the slave's hands should be cut off because he had touched his head and thus insulted him."

"Were the slave's hands cut off?" Lambon asked when Raka did not go on.

"Yes, they were cut off. I happened to see the man only the other day in one of the courtyards. He looks like a leper, with stumps instead of hands."

Lambon shuddered. "Why do you tell me about it?" she asked in a low voice.

"Don't you understand? In Alit's eyes one thing is supreme above all else—his pride, his honor. I believe I know Alit better than most people in the puri do. They think he is good and rather weak, and that he dreams his life away over his books, and that his wives mean nothing in his life. But I can tell you what it is that holds the first place in his inmost soul: pride. There he is as hard as that transparent jewel which can cut all others."

Lambon thought this over for a long while, for it was seldom that anyone spoke to her so seriously. "If that is so, you ought never to come here again, Raka," she said at last. Raka took her in his arms and laughed. "No, I ought not," he said. "And how long could you bear to be without me, my little flower?" he asked, laughing still. "Scarcely an hour," Lambon whispered, and hid her face on his breast. She could hear his heart beating. It sounded like the summons of a muffled kulkul.

❋   ❋   ❋   ❋   ❋

It was not true, as many in the puri whispered, that the prince, who had lived so long among his books, now loved a woman—Lambon, the dancer. He did not love Lambon. It is possible he loved Raka—if love is the right word for a feeling made up in equal parts of sweetness and bitterness, in which pain and delight alternated—with a preponderance of pain owing to Alit's peculiar circumstances. For Alit was ugly and Raka was beautiful. The lids of Alit's eyes were inflamed and Raka's eyes were like the sun. Alit waited for Raka and Raka let him wait.

But as for Lambon, she was the first of his wives in whose society Alit had taken pleasure, the first to be frequently commanded to appear in his presence. He liked to have her with him in his room, silent and pliant as a flowering spray. She seldom spoke and Alit could follow his thoughts undisturbed, while his hand stroked her hair and her skin. She was beautiful and the prince loved beauty above everything. Beauty made him weak and soft. Lambon seemed in his eyes like the women in the old books and poems. When he read them, her picture accompanied him in his dreams of old times and battles long ago. For the lord of Badung was a dreamer, whom birth and fate had set in the place of a man of action.

He hung Lambon with jewels and gave her names from the poems in which he found her likeness. He loved to dress and undress her slender body with his own hands. For this reason he gave her many dresses, and the slave-girls could not weave and dye quickly enough, running gold and silver thread through the weave and painting the cloth with great gold flowers. Alit clothed and unclothed his youngest wife, wishing to see her always in new colors; he played with her hair and let it flow over his arms, and he talked long and earnestly with her about the choice of a color, or the kind of flower she should wear to adorn her head. Also Lambon had to dance for him sometimes, for him alone, crowned with a golden crown. She loved that. She had not forgotten one of the steps she had learnt with her old master at Kesiman, not a single quiver of the hands, not a glance of the eyes nor a movement of the head.

Oka taught Lambon how to knead and roast opium and make ready the prince's pipe. She sat at her husband's feet when the pedanda, Ida Bagus Rai, came and the two men engaged in endless discussions about matters she did not understand. When Alit discovered that she took a childish pleasure in shadow-plays, he often had the linen screen put up and the oddly shaped lamp lighted behind it and then Ida Katut, the story-teller, moved the figures about with dexterous hands and spoke in thirty different voices and made jokes that threw the whole puri into fits of laughter. Alit looked at Lambon—yes, she, too, laughed. It was a rare sight to see Lambon laugh, and therefore he was glad of any opportunity of summoning laughter to her face. As a rule she sat with neck erect and supple limbs and lips just parted, as though a state of wonder never left her.

The prince was beset with cares, for the Dutch blockade did great harm to the country. Coastal trade was crippled and it was only owing to the friendship of the lord of Tabanan that it was possible to keep a chink open on the landward side. But the menace of the ships and cannon in Badung waters was a constant oppression and the raja's pride was galled. He was shut off altogether from Gianjar, and the Dutch had established what amounted to headquarters at Ketewel. The gusti Nyoman from Buleleng was there—the friend of the Dutch, a traitor and a spy.

At that time many preparations were in progress for a journey the raja was to make to the great shrine of Batukau. People and lords with their retinues from many provinces of the island proceeded to the great forest of Batukau to make offerings and pray at the sacred spring. It was not altogether a secret that piety was not the sole motive of the pilgrimage. The lord of Badung wished to have an occasion for meeting his friends the lords of Tabanan and Kloengkoeng, for a final decision had to be made whether to meet the demands of the Dutch or whether the three territories, the last in all Bali to keep their independence, were to continue to offer a resolute resistance. The gusti Wana made it his care that his lord should appear with befitting splendor and the anak Agung Bima put on airs of great importance. Molog, the soldier, grumbled at having to part with many of his lancers whom he would rather have been drilling every day and every hour. Rifles and guns were still being smuggled into the country and Molog informed the lord that his army was a match for the Dutch. It was another matter, however, to acquaint his warriors with the use of firearms. He had appointed a few Arabs as instructors, and they handled the long-barrelled breech loaders with disconcerting ease. His own soldiers fired them with the utmost enthusiasm. The noise of the reports delighted them beyond measure. They would have liked nothing better than to shoot all the powder away in blank cartridges as they might Chinese rockets at a festival. But it was not an easy matter to introduce order and discipline into the army, for all the soldiers had sawahs, which they were always running off to attend to, saying that this was of more importance than preparing for a war.

The lord gave orders that all his wives were to accompany him to Batukau; they were beautiful and he wished to impress the other lords. Also he wanted Lambon with him to prepare his opium pipe before the anxious discussion that awaited him. Heavy buffalo waggons stood ready in the puri and also small two-wheeled carts, drawn by horses. Curtains were fixed to conceal the raja's wives from the gaze of passers-by. The lancers were given new tunics, black and white with red sleeves, of which they were very vain and proud. Anak Agung Bima went about in the villages collecting horses. "Our lord and master does you the honor to make use of your horse for the journey to Batukau," he said as he took the animals from the stable. Their hoofs were polished and shod, and baskets of the wives' clothing and the paraphernalia for offerings were loaded on the buffalo waggons. Umbrellas and chairs were also taken for the solemn ceremonies in the temple at Batukau, also the raja's gamelan with all its richly carved instruments. Ida Katut was almost delirious with joy and excitement. And the best dancers and players of Badung assembled for rehearsals, and worked themselves to death for fear of being outdone by the dancers from other districts when they got to Batukau.

"Will you come with me, my brother?" the prince asked Raka. He did not command him to come; he merely asked and awaited his reply. And Raka said, yes he would gladly come and he looked forward to dancing in Batukau. The truth was that Raka could not bear being parted for days from Lambon and hoped to be able to exchange a word with her somewhere on the way and press her hand unobserved. Also he loved, as the lord did too, to see Lambon dressed in her loveliest robes as she walked to the temple with her basket of offerings and put all the other wives in the shade. And so at last, on the fifth day of the third month, the long train set forth and the grass of the wide road that led first to Tabanan was left trodden bare by hundreds of naked feet.

They reached Tabanan on the first day and were very hospitably received. There was a cock-fight—for of course the cocks had not been left behind—and the cock that Raka gave him won Alit a hundred and twenty ringits and much glory. At night there was dancing, by the dancers of Badung as well as of Tabanan, and Raka outshone them all. The wives of the lord of Tabanan took the wives of the lord of Badung into their dwellings, and they exchanged kains and told stories and their balés echoed with talk and laughter. As for the slave-girls, they got beyond all bounds and some of the lancers had to be beaten because they were so drunk that all discipline went by the board.

Next day the journey was resumed; it grew rather cooler and they came to regions many of them had never seen before. In the villages all the people stood open-mouthed by the road-sides, bending down with clasped hands, and the children ran alongside shouting until they were tired out. Lambon sat in the curtained waggon and when she was not asleep she looked through a slit in the curtains. She hoped to catch sight of Raka and see him give her a secret signal, but all she saw was the backs of the buffaloes and the lancers at the sides of the road. Yet she was content to know that Raka was there. She would watch him dance at Batukau and he would smile at her in secret as she sat in her new purple kain among the rest of the wives.

Raka rode on his light bay horse at Alit's side in the forefront of the train, just behind the first company of lancers. The waggons and baggage carts moved more slowly than the mounted men and the distance between them increased as the day went on. Raka's father, too, rode in the lord's immediate following, sitting his white horse erectly and looking very handsome in his close-fitting black jacket, and he, too, wore a kris as all the other men did.

When they reached the hill villages, where the houses were not thatched with grass but with pointed shingles, the prince said to Raka, "Let us leave the main road and ride by Mengesta. I want to be alone. I have much to think over, and it is not very pleasant to swallow the dust of my entire court."

Raka shrank in dismay, for it was becoming more and more painful to be alone with the friend whom he betrayed and deceived, but
he could not refuse. Alit told the anak Agung Bima of his intention
and at the next turning they went off on their own, followed only
by two servants on foot, each leading a spare horse.

As soon as they had left the main road where the villagers sank
to their knees with clasped hands as the lord rode past, everything
became cool and silent. No one recognized them once they were on
the side roads; and possibly the people of these hill villages did not
even know that a lord and his train were journeying that way. Alit
smiled and hummed to himself as they rode. He was reminded of
his childhood when he and Raka used to set off on their adventures,
alone and without even servants to accompany them.

The life of Bali was unfolded before their eyes as they rode along.
Rice-fields in rounded terraces opened out and then contracted
again and descended step by step to the deep gorges where rivers
foamed over the rocks. Palm groves crowned the ridges of the hills,
which rose one above another up to the Great Mountain, whose
summit was veiled in two long, sparse, white clouds. The huge dark
domes of wairingin trees contrasted with the jewel-like green of the
fields and the tawny temple gateways stood beneath them. Springs
bubbled from the ground and the water was led in bamboo pipes
to irrigate the sawahs. Bamboo thickets met in graceful arches over
narrow brooks, making a cool and secret shade. Gray buffaloes were
asleep in the ditches behind the villages. Naked children wearing
large hats drove flocks of ducks along the dykes. Great bundles of
hay moved along, for they hid the men who carried them. Old men
with faces like dancers' masks walked along with sticks to help
them and sirih pouches at their girdles. Women came from field or
market, carrying baskets or sheaves of rice or towers of coconuts
or great pyramids of earthenware vessels on their heads. The habit
of carrying loads on their heads gave them an erect carriage and a
rhythmic step, and their breasts and shoulders were at once soft
and muscular. Their daughters followed them with smaller loads
on their heads and the six-year-olds balanced only half a coconut
shell above their small, serious foreheads, so as to learn the art in
good time. Peasants squatted at the edges of the fields, resting from

their labors, and in the brooks others stood washing themselves and their cows. And all these people were beautiful and their faces had an expression of softness and trustfulness and good-nature.

The landscape grew more beautiful the higher they went; in the valleys the standing water in the rice-fields was like a thousand mirrors, and the silken slopes of alang-alang grass rippled like water when the wind passed over them. The lovely lines of hill and mountain were interrupted here and there by little islands that stood out from the uplands, each crowned with its temple beneath a wairingin tree. Countless birds sang and red-breasted mountain parrots flitted across the path. White falcons with brown wings hung large and motionless in the air and the darkness of the forest, curtained with lianas and resounding with the cooing of large wild pigeons, was exchanged again for villages where the people sat at their gates, gazing wide-eyed at the strangers riding by. The fruit trees and palms in the courtyards of the houses made tunnels of the village streets, and at the cross-roads stood stone statues of demons to protect the travellers on their way. And everywhere there was the sound of running water, that blessed sound of the island's teeming fertility. From field to field it trickled and rippled and gurgled in its unceasing flow; it ran down from the mountains and poured into the deep valleys, making rice grow in plenty for all, until as a winding river it found its way to the sea. For thus the gods had ordained—the island was theirs and only given to men in loan, so that they should make the ground fruitful and the land rich enough to nourish all, with leisure to keep the festivals and rejoice in the gift of life.

Alit was so engrossed as he rode along that his face had an almost drowsy expression, and Raka looked about him and was lighter of heart than he had been for many a day. The beauty of the country drove even Lambon from his mind for a few hours.

"I have had another letter from the Dutch," the raja said when at last he broke his long silence, and it sounded like the final link in a long chain of reflections. "They are now sending one of their greatest dignitaries to me. He comes from far away, from Batavia, which is a large town in Java. He is a man of high caste and great knowledge and, as I hear, they trust to his persuading me to pay the sum they demand of me." Alit reined in his horse and rode at Raka's side. He talked more to himself than to Raka and Raka had in any case no reply to make.

"How much more they want now, they scarcely know themselves. The Chinese, who would have been content at first with two hundred ringits, now talks of seven thousand five hundred Dutch guilders." Alit laughed in passing, for this was the sort of joke that appealed to his peculiar sense of humor. "Besides this I am to pay a great sum for every day the Dutch ships lie at anchor in my waters—thousands of ringits for the cost of the blockade. They understand figures, these white men. They say the Dutch are better merchants even than the Chinese. If I pay all this money, then—so they say—our differences can be forgotten and Badung be left its freedom as before."

As Alit said no more and merely looked at the landscape with the same drowsily absorbed expression, Raka asked, "And what has my brother resolved?"

"I rode on alone with you away from the rest because I had to be clear in my own mind. I must meet my friends of Tabanan and Kloengkoeng with my mind made up and I must tell the Dutch envoy what I have decided. I shall pay nothing."

"Does that mean war?" Raka asked after a moment's silence.

"Probably," Alit replied. "Yes, probably it means war. War and our overthrow is what the Dutch want and therefore it means war. I cannot pay. They know that. If I paid, it would amount to the confession that we were thieves and wreckers, that we begged for pardon and consented to make retribution. Ask yourself whether you find that possible. Money—" he said contemptuously, and his eyes darkened, "if it were a matter only of money, it would be nothing to pay it. I am rich enough and my family would gladly help me. My uncle has offered to contribute half the sum and Bijang, his revered mother, is willing to give me all the money I could need to satisfy the Dutch. But it is not a question of money. Our honor and dignity and pride are at stake. How can they expect me to pay when by paying I brand myself as thief, a liar and a robber?"

Raka took a sidelong look at his friend's face. "I shall be glad if it is war," he said.

Alit threw back his head and laughed aloud. "You great Molog," he said with affectionate mockery.

"It even has its amusing side," he said, resuming his monologue. "The Chinese merchants on the coast have offered to pay this levy for me, as a gift more or less. Did you know that these Chinese traders in swine and buffaloes had such generous souls? Probably they have reckoned it out and find it cheaper to pay the Dutch than to have their trade ruined by the blockade."

"And what have you replied?" Raka asked, marvelling at the foreign word—blockade.

"Declined, naturally. Am I not only to swallow this insult the Dutch offer me, but to let these Chinese traders pay the cost of it for me?" Alit laughed again at the thought of it. A procession of women, coming from a spring with water-jars on their heads, stopped to look at the strangers on horseback.

"Nyoman of Buleleng and Ngurah of Gianjar, who have come to terms with the Dutch, call me pig-headed and obstinate. They consider me a fool. But, Raka, I tell you I know what I am doing and that I have taken the right path. The Dutch do not in the least want me to give way. They want an excuse for war. Their demands mount up as a papaya tree shoots up in the rainy season. If tomorrow I pay what they ask, next week they will find some new cause of annoyance and make fresh demands. I have had some Dutch writings translated for me, because I wanted to try to penetrate into their thoughts. There can be no peace between them and me. I have no choice. There is only one path for me if I am to listen to the gods and my forefathers and the voice within me. Do you understand that, Raka?"

Raka was overwhelmed with shame at these words. No woman in all Bali was worth the betrayal of a friend like Alit. He, too, had a voice within him, deep within him and he had drowned it and talked it down; he had been as a drunken man for many months, not knowing what he did. He could not speak, but he reined his horse in nearer Alit's and laid his hand on Alit's hand. Alit looked in his face with a smile.

"It is good that we are riding through the country together," he said kindly. "It has made much clear to me. I have looked about me and I cannot believe there is a country on earth as beautiful as Bali. I cannot give it away to foreigners or sell it. I cannot and I may not. What would they make of it once it was in their hands? They do not know our gods and they do not understand the laws by which mankind must live. They would pull down the temples, and the gods would forsake our island, and soon it would become as barren and ugly as the deserts of China. They would grow sugar-cane, not as our peasants do, just enough to sweeten their food and for their children to enjoy; they would cover the whole country with sugar-cane and boil it down into sugar in large buildings, until the villages stank of it, and they would take the sugar away in great steamers to change it into money. They would plant ugly trees in rows and draw rubber from them; they would lay the sawahs waste and cut down the beautiful palms and fruit trees to make room for their towns. They would turn our peasants into slaves and brutes, and leave them no time for cockfights and festivals and music and dancing. And our women would have to cover their breasts as if they were whores, and no one would wear flowers in their hair any more or bring offerings to the temples. And they would squeeze the joy from the hearts of our children, and tear the patience and tolerance and gentleness from their natures, and make them bitter and unkind and discontented, as the white men are themselves. And here am I, the lord over a land which the gods gave to my forefathers, and if no one else will stand in the white man's path, then I must do so, if it is only I in the whole island. I am weak and incompetent and no hero as the great lords of Majapahit were from whom we are all descended." Alit stopped a moment and then asked almost shyly, "Tell me, am I right, brother?"

"I am too stupid to decide such matters," Raka said. "But it seems to me there is nothing else you can do." He paused for the flicker of an eyelid and then added, "It is well for you that you can follow the voice within you knowing that you cannot go wrong."

Alit stretched out his arm and pointed to the Great Mountain. With one accord the two clouds had lifted and now the peak rose high and clear, showing its softly streaked precipices and bearing on its flank the great sanctuary of Besaki and the dense primeval forests in which the rivers of the island took their source,—the Great Mountain, the dwellingplace of the Great God.

"Tomorrow your father will help me to speak with the gods; I know that they will consent to what I have to do," Alit said. Looking into Raka's face he said with a smile, "Have I wearied you with my cares, my friend?"

"I am very glad you have confided in me," Raka answered. What have I said? he thought in the same moment with a start. You trust in me and what do I do with your trust? he thought. No woman is of such importance as to come between us, he thought again and for a few seconds he felt that he could cast the restless passion for Lambon, and all its blindness, aside. It is not the woman that matters, he thought a moment later. It is honor, Alit's and mine.

Alit reined in his horse and at once it began grazing at the edge of the road. Raka's horse snorted and followed its example without waiting for its rider's command. There was a moist smell of grass and green plants and the air had already a mountain keenness.

"Raka, my brother," Alit said, "it is long since we spoke together as we have today. I am going to ask you something now as we stand here in the sight of the Great Mountain. My answer to the Dutch may very easily mean war. And I do not wish to deceive myself—war with the white men is not a joke. It is perhaps the end. You know that I would never fall into their hands alive. Not one of my fathers has given himself up alive to any enemy. If the end came———"

"Yes?" Raka asked intently when Alit hesitated. "If the end came?"

Alit clasped his hands and lifted them to his forehead and said nothing for a few minutes, as his practice was when he concentrated himself to the utmost.

"If the end were necessary—and I called upon you—are you ready to die with me?" he asked.

A smile lit up Raka's face, the old radiant and triumphant smile. All was smoothed out and made simple and his heart beat freely and evenly.

"To die with you is the least you could require of me— my friend and brother," he said gaily.

*   *   *   *   *

"This jingle-jangle of the gamelan is enough to drive anybody crazy," Commissarius van Tilema said to Controller Visser. "Won't the blighters ever stop?"

Berginck, the Resident, sat at the table smoking a cigar. "It is easy to see you have not been long in Bali, Herr van Tilema," he said, laughing inwardly. Visser went down the steps and looked over the wall into the outer court of the puri. Below it sat the gamelan players doing their best to honor the exalted guest. Visser came back.

"If the Commissarius so desires I can tell the people to stop. But it is not very polite———"

"Then, in God's name, don't let's be polite," Van Tilema said irritably. "You can't hear yourself think. It has gone on now for five hours by the clock———" Visser disappeared once more. He went to the gamelan players and spoke to them. "The tuan Besar, the guest, wishes you to rest a little," he said diplomatically. "He, too, would like to have a little sleep in order to be fresher for the enjoyment of the dancing later."

The gamelan players looked straight in front of them; some kept on playing, others laid down their sticks. The anak Agung Bima bustled up. "Do you not hear what the great lord commands? You are to stop playing so that he can sleep," he shouted. "I will see that you have something to eat meanwhile," he said more amiably. The men squatted down comfortably and chewed their sirih.

"The guest wishes me to say also that he has never heard such a good gamelan in Java," Visser added in order to leave a good impression.

"We are only beginners and unworthy to play before the great lord," the drummer said politely. There was some laughter from behind. Although they all knew that there was an island called Java, they were not sure all the same whether it belonged to this world or whether the world ended beyond the sea that encircled Bali. Visser clapped the anak Agung on the shoulder and went back to the Commissarius, whom the Government of Batavia had sent to straighten out the tangled situation in Bali. Berginck and Van Tilema were now sipping the thick, hot coffee which four servants had put on the table with great ceremony. It was about the second hour, and the puri had settled down after the firing of the salute and all the tumult and the talking which had greeted the distinguished visitors. A large number of Balinese were still squatting round the house in which the guests were lodged, and staring at the white men as they drank their coffee outside.

"Can't they be sent about their business?" Tilema asked impatiently. "Or have they paid their money to have a look at us? I feel like a chimpanzee in a zoo."

The Commissarius was a tall, lean man with young-looking eyes, a light yellow moustache and good features. He had white hands and tapering fingers, such as you see in portraits by Van Dyck. As a rule the very picture of unruffled amiability, he was in a state of nervous irritability that day. He had had an unpleasant journey; he had had a rough crossing to Bali, and being pulled ashore through the surf had left him with qualms in the stomach. He still had a rather sentimental love of Bali, for he had spent some time there when he first came out, and even had some acquaintance with the language. Van Tilema had a capacious and methodical memory, and what he had once known he never forgot. In spite of this the efforts he had had to make for the last three days, first at Tabanan and now in Badung, to listen to Balinese and to make his replies in it had been too much for him. He was one of the most capable, circumspect and best educated officials in the colonial service, and though a young man, held a high position on the Council of India. It was believed in Batavia that it was only necessary to send Van Tilema to Bali in order to have all difficulties solved and every demand conceded. The Commissarius was of the same opinion; he had gladly volunteered for the job; he wanted very much to see Bali again and he was confident of success. He was inspired also by professional vanity. He knew no greater pleasure than pulling chestnuts out of the fire without burning his fingers. He had insisted on the Government's giving him the widest discretion, a discretion that did not preclude a friendly and accommodating solution. "I come as the dove with the olive branch," he explained to the Resident on his arrival. And now he had spent three days in the puris, accepting presents and hospitality, being honored in every way, received with bent backs and clasped hands—and he began to see that he was not advancing by an inch and that behind all this formal politeness there was a steely resistance. So it had been yesterday and the day before at Tabanan, so it was today at Badung. "What's that racket now?" he asked irritably, looking round quickly.

"It's the pigeons," the Resident answered with a smile. "They have little silver bells on their feet which ring as they fly."

The Resident is making fun of me, Van Tilema thought in exasperation. The Commissarius is losing his nerve, the Resident thought complacently. These gentlemen from Batavia might now see for themselves that it was not so easy to make a Balinese raja see reason.

The Resident had been aware now and again in recent months that he was getting older. The colonies used a man up quicker than life at home. Another half-year and he would have reached the age limit; then he would be given a minor decoration, a suave letter and his pension. He had a little house and tiny garden with a pear tree at The Hague, and a married daughter there and two grandchildren. Then the Tilemas and Boomsmers and the whole Government with the Governor-General at the top might play the fool with the Balinese to their hearts' content. I have had enough of it, the Resident thought to himself. Let others take a turn.

"What is the programme for the afternoon, Visser?" Van Tilema asked. "I'm pretty well at my last gasp and not very eager for another full-dress palaver. I must get used to all the officials here smelling of jasmine like the prostitutes in Singapore."

"Champak," Visser muttered. "What?" asked the Commissarius. "What did you say?" Berginck remarked innocently. Van Tilema raised his eyebrows. Visser hurriedly intervened. "There are no ministerial visits nor official discussions for today," he said. Visser propped his right arm on his left hand and pointed with outstretched thumb at the sky—in imitation of a Balinese telling the time. "When the sun is there, the Commissarius is awaited by the old lord of Pametjutan—provided of course he happens to be right in the head just then." Once more the Commissarius had the feeling that he was not being taken seriously. Bali is demoralizing to officials, he thought most unjustly. "What time will that be?" he asked impatiently. "Three o'clock, Commissarius," Visser replied smartly.

"And the old lord is properly crazy, is he?" Van Tilema asked. The Resident took his cigar from his mouth. "It depends, Commissarius," he said. "It's in his head, he has bad headaches and he believes that a worm inhabits his brain. At times his mind is clear and then it is damned clear. But when he's crazy, then he is very crazy indeed."

"Just like the young lord——" Van Tilema said sharply.

Berginck smiled affably, while Visser took out a paper; after consulting it he proceeded to read out: "At four o'clock we see a barong at Taman Sari. I asked the raja for that particularly as I was sure it would interest you greatly. Incidentally, the village has had a lot of bad luck, and they hope, by having their barong out———"

"Barong, barong," Van Tilema said, searching the well-kept files of his memory and finding no record. "I confess I have forgotten what a barong is," he said. "Perhaps there wasn't such a thing in my day."

"A speciality of Bali. Possibly they're not very keen to let us Dutch see it," the Resident said. "It's a mix up of trance, magic, kris-dance and all the rest of it. Visser is quite mad about it. Every village has its own barong—a sort of tutelar deity. Anyway, you'll see for yourself, Commissarius. I must say it's of more interest than most of the dances they do here."

"It occurred to me," Visser said, carefully picking his words, "that it might not be without a certain significance for the Commissarius to see a kris-dance. We are always in danger of being in error about the Balinese. They are so polite, so gentle, so submissive, with all the reckless gaiety of children. The barong shows one that all this can turn in a trice to cruelty, to frenzy—and it is important to remember that when dealing with the Balinese. Otherwise you may find all at once that you are out in your reckoning."

"So even the Controller thinks he can read me a lesson," Van Tilema remarked to himself with amused annoyance. Then glancing at Visser's animated, good-natured dog-like face, he acknowledged to himself that he meant well and forgave him. "I see—an educational outing," he said rather tartly. "Fine. It is not lost on me that you have made this arrangement for my especial benefit. If you gentlemen will excuse me, I will have a quick bath and change my uniform for this excursion to Taman Sari."

"What do you make of our tuan Besar?" Berginck asked his Controller as they crossed the court to the Chinese building, which was this time assigned them as their lodging. Visser was taken aback by this almost tactless familiarity.

"A well educated man and full of the best intentions. The Balinese are delighted that he speaks their language," he said discreetly.

"Yes, yes," the Resident replied, who himself knew only Malay and Javanese. "But will he pull it off?"

"I have had a word with the punggawa of Sanur," Visser said. "His opinion is———"

"The punggawa is in our pay, you know that as well as I do. His opinion counts for nothing," the Resident broke in. "But what is your own opinion? You know the Balinese better than any of us. Will Van Tilerna be able at this last hour to turn them from their folly?"

"The Council of India is against sending soldiers and warships here. Every shell costs lives and money, as every child knows. The Commissarius has an offer in his pocket which amounts to a concession; if Badung pays the seven thousand five hundred guilders as compensation the Government will renounce its claim to the cost of the blockade and all will be forgotten and forgiven. If the lord of Badung does not close with this offer, then I really doubt whether he can be quite right in the head," the Controller said in conclusion.

The Resident bit off the end of his cigar as he thought this over. "When you consider the universal love of peace and the reluctance on all sides to fire the first shot, it really makes you wonder where all the wars come from. Got a match for me, my dear Visser?" he asked in the same breath.

By the time the Dutch officials and the lord of Badung with his retinue arrived at Taman Sari the whole village was already astir. Sixteen lancers preceded the carriage and the people fell back to the sides of the road and went on their knees to greet the great lords. The punggawa, complete with servant and umbrella, awaited them at the entrance to the village and himself conducted the distinguished visitors to the Temple of the Dead, before whose chief gateway the barong dance was to take place. Men, women and children squatted in hundreds in a circle, with the usual array of women vendors and hungry, expectant dogs in the background. A bamboo platform had been erected for the lord and his following and for the Dutch there were chairs which the Chinese Njo Tok Suey had provided.

"Our old friend the gamelan once more," the Commissarius sighed before he had even sat down. The musicians of Taman Sari, wearing head-dresses adorned with gold, sat on the ground and played with all their might.

"If I have to listen to this for very long I shall fall into a trance myself. It acts like a narcotic. Don't you feel it too?" he said. The Resident greeted his superior's pleasantry with a smile. Lord Alit leant over towards them. "There has been much sickness in Taman Sari of late," he said in Javanese. "The village hopes to enlist the protection of the barong. Their barong in this village possesses peculiar power."

"Very interesting——"Van Tilema replied. The punggawa had placed himself close to the Controller, Visser, and he whispered in his ear from time to time. The boy, Oka, who crouched at his master's feet, smiled shyly as he offered him a coconut. The Commissarius smiled back and declined. There was a continual coming and going in and out of the temple gateway. Women bearing offerings passed through, old men kept a look-out behind the wall, young men with krisses at their backs came out and marched across, bending low, to the gamelan players, squatted down and silently chewed their sirih.

"By Jove—that's a fine fellow!" Van Tilema exclaimed.

The Resident followed the direction of his eyes and Visser beckoned to the man as he approached. It was Raka coming through the crowd, which quickly made way for him, showing not only deference to his caste but their affectionate regard for him. The lord smiled to him. Raka bowed ceremoniously, clasping his hands, and made as though to crouch on his heels below the platform. The lord quickly beckoned to him to join him. "This is Ida Bagus Raka," he said to the Commissarius. "The son of the pedanda of Taman Sari and the best dancer in all Badung."

Van Tilema looked graciously at the young man, whose dress and bearing marked him out from all the rest. "Will Ida Bagus Raka dance for us?" he asked politely in Balinese. Raka said no, with an embarrassed smile. "Raka is a baris dancer, he has nothing to do with barong," the raja said. "I see," the Commissarius replied in confusion.

The gamelan in the balé now stopped playing, and the sound of another one could be heard approaching along a path which led through a grassy clearing to the Temple of the Dead. The musicians walked at the head of a small procession which moved slowly towards the temple, carrying large, white and red sickle-shaped flags. Two men held up long-handled gilded umbrellas over a strange mythical beast, which was escorted by a number of men. Some women with flat offering baskets on their heads followed at an interval.

"The barong——" Visser explained. "It goes to the temple to receive offerings before the dance. The other dancers, too, have to make offerings and say prayers in case of accidents when they get going with their krisses."

The monstrous beast drew nearer and the afternoon sun flashed from its sides. It was a huge creature with a disproportionately small head carved in wood and painted red and black. Its jaws opened and shut and were furnished with grisly teeth. Arched above its head was something resembling the mountain of muscle on a buffalo's shoulders, composed of gilded and pierced leather scales, set with small mirrors and richly ornamented. As the barong approached the temple gateway, reflections danced over the gray walls at every movement of these pieces of looking-glass A heavy long-haired, yellowish white pelt covered the barong's body; and its hind-quarters and loftily curving tail were again all red and gold and looking-glass, and loaded with a great number of bells which tinkled at every step. Now although the barong advanced on the four bare and not too clean feet of two village youths, with human legs in close-fitting red and white striped trousers, yet it was so thoroughly beast-like in appearance and motion that the Commissarius looked after the strange creature with a smile of astonishment as it vanished through the temple gateway, which seemed too narrow to admit its mighty bulk.

"Looks crazy, that beast," he said approvingly.

"It is by way of being the tutelar deity of the village," Visser explained in a low voice. "Bung full of magical power. Now they are bringing the mask of Rangda——"

"Yes?" the Commissarius said, rather out of his depth, as a fresh group went into the temple carrying in their midst a small chest swathed in white.

"Something like the principle of evil, Commissarius. A representation of the death-goddess Durga, who in other manifestations appears as the wife of Shiva," Visser said.

"Oh, stop that," Van Tilema said pleasantly. "Indian mythology is too complicated for me altogether. And now that damned gamelan is starting up again."

Berginck laughed. He could well understand Van Tilema's aversion. "A regular sleeping-draught," he said. "We can doze off for an hour at least before the fun begins."

But Van Tilema was alive to the claims of politeness.

"Wonderful surroundings," he said to the lord. "The old trees —and that path through the clearing. Bali is wonderful."

Alit looked at him with mild surprise. "It is very good of you to praise our island, although it has nothing out of the common to show——" he replied courteously.

"There is Teragia?" Raka said.

"Who?" the lord asked, laying his hand on his friend's shoulder and then instantly withdrawing it again.

"I remember you once asked about my wife. There she is," Raka said.

Alit looked, but without curiosity. Teragia was ascending the steps to the temple, carrying a silver vessel of holy water and followed by a few girls with smoothly combed and flower-adorned hair.

"Is this show ever going to start?" the Commissarius said to the Resident.

Visser whispered to the punggawa, who then dispatched a youth, and soon after the gamelan ceased playing, only to strike up again at once in a different rhythm and style.

"Now then," the Resident remarked contentedly with half-closed eyes as he settled down to his cigar.

Next two men with long-handled umbrellas emerged from the temple gateway, and took up positions on either side of the steps near the stone demons who guarded them. Then the barong appeared. It stood waiting between the almost too ornate pillars of the double gateway glaring at the people below. Then it descended, now slowly, now with backward stampings, and traversed the dancing arena. Its bells jingled, its jaws opened and shut with a wooden snap and its red and white striped legs tramped forwards and backwards. It was the dance of a dangerous, malevolent and at the same time humorous beast, and it lasted a good long time.

Van Tilema sighed with relief when the barong finally retreated again within the temple. Now four dancers came out of the temple, wearing white, laughing masks, girls' faces of a fixed sweetness beneath round, peaked, gold hats. They had fans in their hands and they glided and zig-zagged over the arena, crossing in front of and behind one another.

"What do these affected ladies represent?" Van Tilema whispered; he was attempting in vain to recover his usually unruffled good humor.

"Some say butterflies," Visser whispered back, "and some say spirits who belong to the barong."

"I see," said the Commissarius.

The lord smiled to his guest. He found it astonishingly rude of these Dutch to talk together in their own language, and make contemptuous remarks about the sacred and solemn dance they were invited to watch.

"I am sure the dances in Holland are much more beautiful and splendid than ours," he said.

The Commissarius thought this remark delightful and began to laugh. He put his hand on the lord's knee and replied, "Holland has not had much time up to now to devote to the art of dancing. Perhaps that is still to come." Raka joined in his laughter; he found these white people comic and entertaining.

"I have been told that the Queen of the land of Holland is very beautiful. Does she not dance? And the princes and princesses of the court?" he asked, clasping his hands momentarily as he mentioned the foreigners' Queen. Even Berginck now started laughing. "Good Heavens, no!" he said highly amused.

Van Tilema was the first to recover his composure. "The customs of our country are very different from those of the Sultan's Courts in Java, Ida Bagus Raka," he said graciously. His mood had suddenly taken a turn for the better. The beautiful young dancer fitted exactly with the picture of Bali he had in his mind whenever he recalled his days on the island as a young official. "They are after all only children," he said in Dutch to the Resident.

After the white, laughing masks had glided to and fro for a long time, raising the dust in clouds with their strong broad boys' feet, four others emerged from the temple gateway.

"Djaoks," Van Tilema exclaimed, for his memory had suddenly begun to function again.

"Yes, Djaoks," the lord said, delighted that his guest showed some appreciation of what was going forward. These masks had large, round, staring eyes and moustaches, and they had peacock feathers stuck in their curiously shaped hats. They wore clumsily made gloves, from which long nails projected of a substance resembling mother-of-pearl, and altogether they made an impression of strength and malevolence. Between them and the laughing masks there developed a drama of menace and pursuit and sham fight, all represented in the elaborately stylized movements of Balinese dancing. This part of the performance also took a long time, and Tilema now brought himself to take a drink from a coconut. Gradually he became used to the gamelan which through endless mazes always returned to the same scrap of tune. He was quite affected himself when the rhythm altered again, and an almost imperceptible movement ran through the spectators. The barong appeared in the temple doorway and, descending the steps, mingled with the masked dancers. Its two attendants with the umbrellas remained standing at the foot of the steps.

"Looks quite a dangerous beast," the Commissarius whispered to the Resident.

Berginck nodded without taking his eyes off the barong. There was something savage, threatening and unbridled in the manner of its entry. Sometimes it stood completely motionless with its eyes fixed on one particular group among the spectators, until the children sitting in front wriggled in embarrassment and laughed uncomfortably. Then it suddenly plunged again, stamped in anger, shook itself till all its bells rang, reared up, snapped its gruesome jaws savagely, while the rather comic goatee depending from its chin jerked up and down. It stampeded the eight masked dancers and drew them hither and thither, raising the dust and giving every sign of animal strength and impetuous vitality. Van Tilema watched the beast's antics with fascinated eyes; he had quite forgotten that beneath its pelt there were only two village youths. But after a while his attention wandered and he looked again at Raka, whom he found particularly pleasing. A black head-dress whose edges had a pattern in gold was wound about his glossy hair; he wore a kain of dark wine-red in which a silver thread gleamed here and there, and a loin-cloth of brown silk encircled his remarkably slender hips and reached to his chest. He was not adorned with hibiscus flowers as the lord and most of the other men were; instead he had a single orchid in the middle of his forehead, which by its shape and the way it crept out beneath his head-dress suggested an animal rather than a flower. This scorpion-like orchid was indefinably in keeping with Raka's fine, arched nostrils and oblique eyes and long eye-lashes.

The sensuous outline of his lips made him seem to be always smiling in a half-mocking, half-mysterious way. Van Tilema watched him as he bent forward to take an unripe coconut from a servant's hands and offered it to the lord. Alit took it smilingly, lifted up the green shell and drank. Then he gave it back to Raka.

"Has this young man any influence with the raja?" Berginck took his cigar from between his teeth. "No political influence as far as I know," he said and replaced his cigar. Visser gave a gentle pull at Van Tilema's sleeve to distract him from his absorbed contemplation of Raka. "There are the kris dancers," he said. The Commissarius looked as he was directed, but saw nothing in particular. A knot of about a dozen men were squatting, rather drowsily it seemed, in the gateway of the temple. They all wore krisses and were stripped to the waist, but they did not differ in this from the rest of the spectators; the only difference was that their heads were bare. Most of them were young, although a few among them might have been twenty-four or so. They sat on their heels with one arm stretched out over their knees for balance and chewed as placidly as cows chewing the cud. Occasionally one whispered a word to another and was answered with a sleepy smile.

Time went on to the tinkle of the bells on the barong's body and to the interminable music of the gamelan. Already the trees that surrounded the open space were casting long shadows and beneath the wairingin that grew beside the temple wall it was almost dark. The eight masks sat down on the ground when their dance was over and the barong retired within the temple gateway, shaking itself in a threatening manner. A brief pause followed, during which there was a charming interlude that Van Tilema watched with much enjoyment. A crowd of people had assembled at the edge of the arena; they were on their way home from their labors in the fields, but they had not ventured to interrupt the dance. Now way was made for them and they looked, as they moved across the scene like a pageant of peasant life.

Men with sheaves of rice on poles over their shoulders, men with pitches of hay, children driving buffaloes from the pastures and more children with droves of ducks. Lastly there came a troop of women, carrying bundles of large palmleaves; their little daughters came scampering behind them with baskets of fruit, giggling nervously, for the gamelan had begun playing again and the show was about to proceed. Just as a new personage was making his appearance from the far side of the arena, some stragglers from the flocks of ducks came along and rushed quacking in all directions, making the children in the front row laugh loudly. An old man got up and chased them away just as the next scene of the drama commenced.

A being of alarming aspect, dressed in red and wearing a demon's mask, appeared on the scene and declaimed his set speech in a forced voice. Van Tilema smiled; he remembered those Balinese plays he had seen long ago and the natural tones of the voice he now heard brought it all back.

"This, I believe, is Rangda's daughter and she is going to meditate in the graveyard," Visser whispered as he encountered the Commissarius's eyes. But Van Tilema did not wish to be coached. He took another glance in the deepening dusk at the knot of kris dancers. They sat as before, as though the whole affair was no business of theirs. Tilema had heard and read wonderful descriptions of these kris-dances, though he had never had the opportunity of seeing one during his time in the island. It will, no doubt, be rather a fantastic affair, he thought sceptically. Turning to Berginck he discovered that he had fallen asleep—without loss of dignity, however, for his head was kept in an upright position by his uniform collar in spite of his closed eyes. The gaze of the Commissarius lengthened its range, and he saw that the lord was absorbed in a conversation with Raka. Tilema gave his mind up to the effort of understanding what they were saying. His Balinese was patchy, but he could just make out that the topic was the great beauty and enviableness of some possession or other. Whether it was a woman or a cock he was unable to be sure. As soon as Raka became aware that the white man's eyes were upon him he broke off, and taking a handful of maize-leaf cigarettes from his girdle he offered them to Tilema in a shyly amiable way. The Commissarius took one and bravely put the mouth-piece of straw between his lips in spite of its overpowering taste of cloves. Tours of inspection in the colonies brought with them all kinds of strange and dubious delights, for East Indian hospitality was lavish. He was already dreading the evening meal.

Meanwhile the barong had taken the stage once more, and appeared to be engaging in a violent and threatening dispute with the

Rangda's daughter. The jaw-clapping was louder than ever, so were the roaring and stamping, and when it stood at bay with lowered head and raised neck, there was something really menacing about the beast that made the flesh creep. Once again Van Tilema let his gaze wander; he looked at the spectators and was surprised at the placid cheerfulness with which the fabulous beast and its conflict with the female demon were regarded. Among the vendors at the back he saw men sitting on their heels, chewing, eating and flirting. There was even a small ring of gamblers, throwing down their kepengs on a board and bending forward to see the result of their throws. The children in the first row of the circle surrounding the arena had their usual, sleepy, dreamy smile, but some teased one another or sucked sugarcane or smoked cigarettes. Behind them, their mothers held their babies to their breasts, and only a few of the smaller and more timid children hid their heads in the sarongs of mothers or elder sisters, and of these some had fallen asleep. Behind, again, a group of girls was leaning one against another—as though posing for a sculptor, the Commissarius thought—and as the air had grown cooler two of them were wrapped in one shawl, which now and then bellied out like a sail. Behind the girls the young fellows of the village were crowded together, laughing and nudging one another with the very obvious intention of getting closer to the girls without being observed.

When Van Tilema's eyes had roved round the entire circle and came back to the arena he found that very little had happened there in the meanwhile; and so he sank into reflection. The gamelan was still playing, Rangda's daughter shouting her strident curses and the barong surging and stamping around her. Van Tilema reflected on his mission, and how he could best bring it to a successful conclusion. He began to compose in his head his speech for the conference next morning, frowned when he was stumped and smiled to himself when a good Balinese idiom occurred to him. It was essential to bring these folk to their senses. He stole a glance again at the raja. He looked limp and without energy. Opium, thought the Commissarius. Opium and keeping a harem and the lack of occupation. Not much of an opponent, he thought, and felt more hopeful. Suddenly a slight commotion aroused him from his reflections. "What's up?" he asked Visser. The raja was on his feet gazing at the barong, which was now being led to the temple by two men under the shelter of its sacred umbrellas.

"Nothing—only the front legs fallen into a trance," Visser said, laughing under his breath.

"How do you mean—a trance?" Van Tilema asked in a puzzled voice.

"I saw it coming," Berginck put in, although he had only just woken up. "That boy has been trembling the whole time." Raka turned to the white men with a smile.

"It will go on again at once," he said. "A friend of his is waiting to take his place."

The gamelan had not ceased playing, and Van Tilema was surprised at the calm way in which the little incident passed off.

"What sort of trance is it?" he asked.

"Nothing out of the way for a Balinese. A sort of catalepsy. There is a priest in the temple who will bring him round," Visser said. The barong was already emerging again from the temple, rattling his scales more violently than ever. He circled the arena, which he now had to himself, two or three times in a threatening manner. But now from the side opposite the temple two men appeared carrying an umbrella beneath which a new demon of hideous aspect advanced. This creature wore a mask with long tusks, bulging eyes and an immense long tongue hanging out of its mouth. Its head was furnished with a shaggy wig of goat hair which hung down to its knees. It brandished a dirty white cloth in its hands. The children cowered and looked alarmed as this personage came on the scene.

"Here we have Rangda herself," Visser said in an undertone. The Commissarius began to find the Controller's running commentary annoying. "I think we might insist on the conference beginning at eight o'clock. I want to get on to Kloengkoeng," he said to the Resident, without paying much attention to the new scene. Rangda, too, declaimed in hoarse, squeezed-out tones from behind her mask. Fresh flocks of ducks had appeared in front of the ring of spectators and their quacking joined in with comic effect. A vendor threw a stick at a dog which was trying to thieve the eatables displayed on her broad leaves and he yelped piteously. Visser bent down and picked up the pith helmets of his two superiors. "We had better get everything out of the way," he said. "It will soon get going."

What on earth is there to get going, Tilema thought to himself. Rangda stood there, clapping herself on the knees and leaning back in a fit of vulgar demon laughter. The barong tramped up behind her and pushed her in front of him by the neck with a wooderr clatter of its chops, and Rangda brandished her dirty cloth. Rangda's feet also were the dirty feet of a simple peasant; the nail of one big toe was torn and black. The little knot of kris dancers squatted as before in the temple gateway. The umbrella-bearers who had escorted Rangda stood at the farther side of the arena, and behind them were others also with umbrellas and sickleshaped flags, which they held aloft over a figure resembling Rangda but with back turned on the proceedings as though entirely unconcerned.

"Does it go on like this for ever?" Van Tilema asked. The Controller only muttered, "Durga—the goddess of death." Van Tilema turned to the lord to ask whether the conference could begin at eight. But the lord did not appear to hear him. He had one arm round Raka's shoulders, without, however, paying any heed to him; his eyes seemed to be fixed on vacancy. Raka himself looked as though he was asleep; his face had undergone a remarkable transformation—or so the Commissarius thought. Dusk had already fallen under the palms and the features of the onlookers grew dim; yet at this very moment Van Tilema clearly distinguished a beautiful young woman in the second row who was winding her little daughter's head-dress round her head and laughing as she spoke to her.

"Now," Visser said, "the barong needs help—against Durga."

Next moment a shout was heard and the kris dancers flew at Rangda in a wild charge, holding their curved krisses erect, death and murder and frenzy in their eyes. This mad onset was so sudden and had such an air of deadly earnest that Van Tilema felt for something to hold on by. "Nothing will happen," he heard the Controller murmur at his elbow and he was grateful to him this time. Rangda raised her hand and the men flung themselves in the dust and lay as though dead. They lay with legs sprawling just as each had chanced to fall, as though killed by some unseen weapon, and as the fallen lie on a battlefield. But Rangda, too, was the victim of some mysterious influence. Her limbs began to quiver and shake and she fell stiffly into the arms of her umbrellabearers. Several men sprang forward and carried the rigid human form away.

"Another trance—that's not in the programme," Visser mumbled. The barong, escorted by its two umbrella-bearers, now began to move in and out among the prostrate kris dancers. They rose one after another at the touch of the monster's feet. With kris in hand they staggered a few steps with hanging heads, and then suddenly turned the points of the double-edged, serpentine blades against themselves. Roaring and groaning each man threw himself on his own kris, ran themselves through the breast, leapt high as though in convulsions, only to plunge the kris deeper and more violently. This frenzy of destruction and suicide rose in wave after wave, ebbing and flowing again in crisis after crisis. Tilema discovered that he was gripping Visser in a grip of iron, while Visser murmured from time to time, "Nothing is happening—it's all in the game." Resident Berginck pulled hard at his cigar to keep himself in countenance, but his hands shook, for the sight was one of almost unbearable horror. "Not a drop of blood—not a drop," Visser murmured reassuringly. "They can't wound themselves as long as they are in the trance."

Van Tilema could in fact see that the bare brown chests of these frantic men remained unhurt by the thrusts they gave them. And the way the Balinese spectators behaved was incomprehensible to him. They crowded closely round the space where the men were raging and some even laughed. The children were still in front and had no intention of missing a moment of it. A priest in a white jacket and white headdress went calmly among the frenzied dancers and sprinkled water over them. A few other men threw themselves on one or other of the kris dancers, and after taking away his kris, guided his tottering steps to the barong, who stood quietly waiting. Those who waked from the trance wiped the streaming sweat from their faces on the barong's black, beflowered and rather comic beard and then vanished rather shyly among the crowd. Others raged on with increasing violence, as though they wanted to kill and flay themselves at any cost. And now a procession of girls came out of the temple, led by a tall thin woman; in silence they walked, with a step that was almost a dance, from one to another of the shouting, groaning and crazy men, trying to bring them out of their trance by sprinkling them with holy water. Van Tilema stared with a mixture of repugnance and horrid curiosity at these incomprehensible goings-on, until the arena became shrouded in a veil of dust; and it was only then that he was aware of what had been happening at his elbow.

Raka, the beautiful young dancer, with the orchid in his gold-patterned head-dress, to set off his handsome face, had fallen into a trance too.

The lord had tried at first to arrest the tremors of his friend by whispering calming words in his ear. Then he had held him in his arms when he shuddered more violently and threw himself about. Some of the lord's retinue helped to hold him, until he forbade them and let Raka go. With a sudden cry Raka shook the men off and with his kris drawn rushed to join the other kris dancers who were still surging round the barong.

The Commissarius went white, for as Raka, unconscious of what he did, flung him aside, the curved and snake-like edge of his kris whistled about his ears. The raja jumped from the platform where they were all sitting, and strained his eyes to follow Raka's movements as he joined the others in their whirling dance. His courtiers crowded round him, talking loudly. Even the Resident addressed him—in Javanese which in the moment of excitement no one could understand. Visser remained standing near the Commissarius, a little white himself, perspiring profusely and smiling a little wryly. "Extraordinary," he said as though to himself. "So far as I know, Raka has never fallen into a trance before."

"Can you explain the whole show to me, Controller?" the Commissarius asked, observing with annoyance that his hands shook, and that he had an uncertain feeling in his knees and a sort of cramp in his jaws.

"There is nothing to explain, Commissarius," Visser said. "It is Bali, that's all."

"And the moral?" Van Tilema asked.

"I don't follow you, Commissarius," Visser said with formality.

"No? I thought the story had a moral—for my benefit," Van Tilema said.

Berginck joined them in time to hear the last words.

"A kris-dance is not a political factor," he said curtly. "Such things have their place in ethnological studies but not in our files. Thank the Lord, I remembered to bring some gin with me to Badung. It takes a lot more than rice wine to help one swallow such entertainment. Don't you agree with me, Commissarius?"

There were now only three men still under the trance, Raka and two of the kris dancers; and darkness was rapidly drawing on. When neither holy water nor fumigation nor the touch of the barong sufficed to wake these three they werd disarmed. It took six men to release the kris from the grasp of Raka's clenched fingers. The barong turned about and retired with its two umbrella carriers into the outer court of the temple. The three unconscious men were carried in behind it. Teragia led one tottering form, one was supported under the arms by two relations and Raka had to be carried, for he was as rigid as a bar of iron. The prince was anxious about Raka and sorry for him, for he had never been taken in this way before and in him it was unbecoming. He puzzled over the significance of the occurrence, it seemed to him to fit in remarkably well with the alteration he had observed in him of late and he racked his brains for anything in the old lontars that might bear on it.

"What happens next?" he heard the Commissarius asking, and he recollected his distinguished guest.

"If it pleases my friend we can now return home," he said courteously. "I mean what happens now in the temple?" Van Tilema asked. The abrupt end left him unsatisfied. The people were already dispersing, and although they bent low as they crept away, owing to the presence of the raja, they were all the same perfectly cheerful and incomprehensibly unmoved.

"In the temple? Nothing worthy of mention. The dancers will be awakened from their trance," the prince said. He took some cigarettes from one of his courtiers and offered them to his guests.

"I suppose we are not allowed to enter the temple?" Van Tilema asked. "All the same I'd like to see what the end of it all is," he added in Dutch to Visser.

"If my friends would not find it wearisome——" the lord replied, and smiling with vacant politeness he conducted the Dutchmen up the steps and went before them through the temple gateway. He was eager himself to know how Raka was. The Commissarius clasped his pith helmet to his breast as though he was in a church.

In the outer court two torches were already alight. The barong stood with lowered head between its two umbrella carriers and a

mat was spread in front of him on which the young girls were preparing offerings. The lord stood some distance away with his guests
and looked on. The smoke of the torches made Berginck cough. A
temple priest sat in front of the mat trying to release the three men
from the trance with holy water and fumigation.

"The tall woman holding the youngest one is married to Raka,"
Visser whispered to the Commissarius. "He's a nice boy," Van Tilema
whispered back after looking at him. He was limp but not yet conscious; his head rested on Teragia's breast, and a hoarse sobbing and
groaning issued from his throat. A second lay rigid, with legs astride,
between the barong's front feet, the bare brown and rather dirty and
weary feet of a village youth, who was not at all sure he had not
in some magic way been transformed into a part of the monstrous
beast which was the divine protection of the village. Raka had been
laid in front of the priest; his body quivered convulsively and the
blood trickled from a scratch on his chest. His saput was awry and
his long hair, which had fallen down when he threw off his head-
dress, was covered with dust and sand.

The raja took quick puffs at his cigarette and Berginck breathed
in its aroma of cloves with a faint repugnance. Van Tilema observed
the raja out of the corner of his eyes. He was trying to be cool and
collected, but it was clear that the young dancer's trance upset him.
No wonder, thought the Commissarius, who was still feeling weak
in the knees.

The girls, after they had laid all their offerings on the mat, began
singing, in order to loosen the trance by the soft persuasion of music, and to guide the souls gently back to the bodies to which they
belonged. Teragia, too, sang, holding the young man's head on her
breast. She did not look at Raka, for she was bereft of any feelings of
her own and possessed solely by her magic powers. The smoke of
the two torches hung low over the ground, and whenever the singing
girls paused to take breath the cicadas could be heard all round the
temple walls. Raka began to utter deep groans as though overcome
with agony, and the priest held the brazier of glowing resin towards
him. Raka plunged both hands into the red-hot embers and appeared
to find some relief. The spasm slowly relaxed; he took deep breaths
of the holy fire and the groans died away. The other two dancers
came slowly to themselves. They opened their eyes and looked about

them, smiling in an embarrassed way before joining the other kris dancers, who squatted near a balé in the darkness, resting. Only Raka was still in his trance. The prince looked at him as he lay there limp and unconscious, and felt that never had Raka been so dear to him as now when he lay there helpless and deprived of his reason.

"He will come round in a moment," Visser said in a low voice to the Commissarius. The priest sprinkled Raka's forehead with water once more, and Teragia came and bathed his temples. Raka's face relaxed and seemed for a moment to be sleeping, then he opened his eyes. He sat up and looked about him in surprise. The women had ceased singing and at that moment the mask of Rangda was carried past in its white-swathed box. Raka stood up and putting his hands to his hair he bound it up behind his head. Teragia helped the priest to collect the sacred vessels and utensils.

"We can go now, if my friends agree," the lord said, turning to the temple gateway. Some of his retinue ran ahead with backs bent to scatter the children who were still crowding round outside. Van Tilema took a deep breath of the cool moist air given off by the trees. "Interesting, Herr van Tilema, don't you think?" the Resident said, as he wiped his face before putting on his helmet again.

"Decidedly. Extremely so. But tell me, my dear Berginck, how on earth is one to make such people see reason?" the Commissarius replied, deep in thought.

"I have been asking myself that question all the twelve years I have spent in Bali," the Resident replied blandly. The lord came to a stop when they reached the grass path leading to the clearing, where torch-bearers and lancers were stationed to await him. "Here comes Raka," he said. "Where are you off to, Raka?"

"To the river to bathe, your Highness," said Raka, bending forward as he stood still. Van Tilema looked at him with curiosity and astonishment. Not a trace was to be seen of the complete loss of consciousness and the frenzy in which he had been plunged a few minutes before!

"Is Raka not tired?" he asked in Balinese.

"No, tuan. I feel happy and relieved," Raka replied.

Van Tilema shook his head and smiled. "They call me a connoisseur of Bali in Batavia," he said to Berginck. "But I see now I don't know the first word about it."

The lord fell back a step. Raka was just behind him. "How did it happen, Raka?" he asked in an undertone.

"I don't know. I felt a great anger and that is all I know," Raka said. After a moment's hesitation he added, "Tell me—did I say anything when I was beside myself?" Alit looked round at him in surprise. "No, you said nothing, my brother. What should you have said?"

Raka looked fixedly at him for a long time and said not a word. The Dutchmen had already been lighted to the carriage. You have become strangely and greatly altered, the lord thought, but he did not say it aloud. "Ask me nothing, for I cannot tell you," Raka said. He turned away, stood still for a moment and then followed the other kris dancers to the river.

＊　　＊　　＊　　＊　　＊

When Raka was attacked by the first symptoms of the horrible Great Sickness he did not believe it, although he saw it with his own eyes and felt it on his own body.

It began almost imperceptibly with a slight affection of the skin on his left breast. A small mark formed which became gradually a brighter red; it looked unhealthy and mysterious and was no larger than a kepeng. This mark grew larger for a few weeks and then it remained the same size; there were no other symptoms to be observed and although he was worried he forgot it again.

Yet at this time he felt that his life had suddenly become insipid; it no longer ran fresh and clear in his veins as from a spring, but crept along muddily as the dyke water of a sawah and Raka did not know what to do about it. When he went to his secret meetings with Lambon he was overcome by a sudden zestlessness, as though being with his beloved was no longer a joy but a task. Lambon became angry and jealous. "Have you found another woman who pleases you more than I do?" she asked persistently. "Are you tired already of coming to me? Is it so far from Taman Sari to Badung that you are too tired to embrace me? Or perhaps you are afraid of old Ranis who keeps guard over me?" She plied him with these and all the other questions that a woman who is madly in love can think of to torture her lover. Raka left the ruined island where they had their meetings in an ill humor and he no longer went every day to find her there as before. Yet he felt the same longing and desire as soon as they had parted and his sleep was restless.

To calm himself he went to see Alit, for he sometimes thought that his joylessness and weariness were due to his having been compelled to betray his dearest friend. They smoked much opium together and for hours Raka forgot his cares. He had his pipe filled again so often that Alit smiled and took it from him. Yet as soon as the cheering effect of the opium passed off Raka felt as disconsolate as before. When they bathed together he was careful to hide the bad place on his breast with his arm, and when he bathed with the young men of Taman Sari in the river he concealed it too. He now wore his saput wound high up round his chest and, as the handsome Raka wore it so, it soon became the fashion with the young men of Taman Sari and the villages round about.

Raka was waiting for the diseased skin to heal. But it did not heal.

At about the same time as he fell into a trance at the barong dance at Taman Sari, his ears began to be affected. They were of remarkable beauty and now they began to swell at the edges. Raka made little of this symptom too. A poisonous spider has bitten me while I was asleep, he said to comfort himself. When no one was looking he felt them and they seemed his own ears no longer. They did not throb or pain him, but it was as if the coarse clumsy ears of a slave had been conjured on to his fine Brahman skull. At the thought that he might be the victim of an evil spell he felt more cheerful, for spells could be broken.

Without a word to anyone he went to the balian to ask his advice. He did not directly mention his ailments but said that he believed some sickness had been given him by enchantment.

"What sort of sickness?" Teragia's father asked him.

"I don't know," Raka said, looking at the balian with weary eyes. "I feel I am sick. I have pain now here and now there, and neither food nor sleep nor play with women are any pleasure to me."

At this his father-in-law looked earnestly in silence, for he was a good doctor. Raka had put on a short, black-and-white checked coat for this interview so as to conceal the sore spot on his breast and two heavily-stamened hibiscus flowers hung down over his ears. The balian asked him several more questions and then told Raka to have certain offerings placed on his house altar next morning and

to return to him with other offerings for the ceremony that was required for the breaking of this difficult and indefinable spell.

Raka went home deep in thought and the people in the village
street were surprised he did not call out to them or stop to have a
word with them as he usually did. At home he avoided his father—
why, he scarcely knew—and sat beside his mother in silence playing
with the edge of her kain as he used when a child. When her hands
wandered over his face to see why he did not speak he turned his
head so that she should not touch his ears. But her hearing was
keen for unspoken thoughts. "Why are you sad, son?" she asked.

"I believe a poisonous spider must have bitten me while I was
asleep," Raka said, "and ever since I have been sick and weary."

"It will soon be over," his mother said to comfort him. "Teragia
can make you a drink from roots that will drive the poison out of
your body."

"I will ask her," Raka said and got up to go and look for his wife.
He found her in the yard behind, sieving the unhusked rice in the
big sieves with her servants, making the chaff fly. "I want to speak
to you, mother," he said. He often called Teragia mother since she
had borne him a son. She left her work at once and followed him
into the garden, where she found him sitting on a block of unhewn
stone, of which his father was going to chisel the image of Cinthia
for the throne of Suria in the rice temple.

"I have been speaking to your father," he said, "and he wants
you to take him early tomorrow morning all the offerings required
for breaking a sickness spell. Your father said you would know just
what offerings were required."

"There are five different rice offerings and I shall also want a new
jar for my father to break over your head," Teragia said obediently.
She looked closely at her husband and gave a start. He was altered in
some indefinable way. She could not have said which of his features
had altered, but he no longer looked himself—he was no longer
Raka, the most beautiful dancer of all Badung. As soon as he looked
at her, she quickly turned her pained and anxious eyes away.

"My mother thinks you might make me a drink from roots to
drive the poison out of me," Raka said. His hands hung down slackly
and his eyelids were inflamed, as though he read too much, as his
friend Alit did.

"I can make you a drink from roots," she said shortly. She was sitting on her heels and now she got up and left the garden. Then she stopped and came back and squatted down again at a distance from Raka.

"I know that you have been love-sick for a long time, brother," she said gently. "Do you think the sickness comes from longing after a woman who belongs to another man?"

Raka gazed at her in silence. He marvelled, as he often had before, at Teragia's mysterious knowledge of hidden things. " Go into the house, mother," he said. "I think I can hear Putuh crying." Teragia went at once as he bade, and a little later he saw her standing beside his father with the boy on her hip. During the last months, ever since he had been distracted by his passion for Lambon, he had paid little attention to his son. Too little attention, he felt suddenly. The child had grown and begun to take notice of things. He had strong little legs and loved to stand on his mother's hips whenever he could. Raka looked on from a distance as Teragia put the boy down on the ground; he crowed for joy as he tried to walk with her hands under his plump little shoulders. When at last he fell over and tried to crawl, she quickly picked him up again, for it was not befitting the dignity of children as human beings to go on all fours, and it was never allowed. Putuh with exultant cries grasped his mother's firm, small breasts. Raka felt he would like to take his little son in his arms and rejoice in the warmth of his body. I must spend more time at home, he thought. I will play with my son and teach him his first words. Perhaps it would lift the oppression for a moment from his spirit. He got up and went across to him. The child stared at him as though he was a stranger; then a smile spread over his chubby face and he held out his arms to his father, and Raka held out his arms to his son.

It was at this moment that the full horror of his frightful disease came on him for the first time. I am unclean, he thought, and a cold shudder shook him to the depths of his being. He let his arms fall before they had touched the child, and turning round he went back into the garden and sat down on the stone. Teragia followed him with her eyes and then carried her son indoors.

Next day the offerings were offered up and Raka went to the balian and stayed with him for a long time. He was rather more cheerful when he returned, for the intricate ceremony with all its sprinkling and praying and the purification by water, fire and smoke had had a slightly intoxicating effect like that of the opium he smoked in the puri. There was a cock-fight at Sanur and he went, hoping to distract his mind. The oldest of his cocks won, but the triumph gave him little pleasure. Again he wore the short black-and-white checked jacket to hide the sore on his chest. On the way he stopped and felt his ears. They seemed to be rather less swollen than before. The sense of an improvement in his condition lasted for four days.

Then his hands became affected.

His fingers started hurting, not badly; it was only a dull and distant ache that lasted for a few hours and then went away and came back, went away and came back. The pain had gone altogether in a week, but it left his fingers stiff and curiously numb. Raka sat down on the stone in the garden; this was now his favorite haunt, for he could be sure of being unobserved there. He looked at his fingers and moved them to and fro. He practised movements of the fingers as he used to do as a child when he was being brought up as a dancer. They moved, but it was no longer the tumble movement of a dancer's fingers, that amazingly controlled vibration, bending and stretching and fluttering to order, that had made him the best dancer in Badung. They moved as the fingers of a man who had been ploughing all day in the sawah. Raka gazed at his fingers for hours together. In spite of their long nails they were his fingers no longer. Their shape was different—thicker and clumsier. He gazed at them and as he gazed he moved them about. Teragia went by with lowered eyes to pick flowers for the offerings.

She pretended not to see him so as not to disturb him and he hid his hands in his lap. When she had gone he began moving them about again. Then the pain returned.

Yet it was just at this time that hope was renewed. It seemed to him that the sinister and baneful bright red blotch on his breast was disappearing again. Whenever he looked at it there seemed less to be seen of it and its edges, which for weeks had been sharply marked off, became scarcely noticeable. Raka remembered having heard that hundreds of people in the villages about had had the first signs of the Great Sickness on them and that these had vanished again—a passing spell of no importance and no abiding force. His breast was healed, his ears no longer swelled and he no longer worried about them. But he practised his fingers in desperation and forced them to move freely, for the festival of the full moon was approaching when many dances took place.

It was at this time, too, that his lack of zest and joy gave way to an insatiable hunger for life. Although he lied to himself and would not let the hideous truth take possession of his thoughts, yet deep within there was the terror and the consciousness of being sick and unclean and shut off from all the joys in which other men took delight. It was as though he clung to all he had soon to surrender, to devour and drink in all the pleasures which would be taken from him. He went daily to meet Lambon and almost crushed her in his arms. He had no sense or discretion and would not see that she had to leave him for her hours of duty with the lord. He threw prudence to the winds and forgot that death was the penalty of love. When he was with Alit he smoked opium to excess and, as soon as its stimulus cleared his brain, he talked without end in a fevered rush of wit and fancy, to the astonishment of Alit, who often asked, "Do you want to drive Ida Katut from the puri in despair at finding you a better story-teller than himself?"

It was Lambon who first openly alluded to his malady. One hot and sunny afternoon on their island, when they were playing together like enamoured butterflies, she suddenly stopped short in a caress and ran her finger-tips over his breast. "What is the matter with your skin?" she asked, frowning. Raka pulled up his saput and tied it tight. The light was dim in the room, but the door was ajar to let in the air and there were also two openings in the wall behind which admitted a little daylight. Lambon gave the door a kick and the sunshine flooded the warm dusk within. Her fingers still toyed with the muscles of his chest. "Your skin was always as fair as the god Arjuna's," she said. "That is why I love you. I will not have it red as it is now. What have you been doing to your skin?"

Raka pushed Lambon away and got up and shut the door again. "It is the heat," he said hoarsely. "The blood is trying to get through my skin to cool itself."

"I want your skin to be beautiful and white," Lambon repeated obstinately. The air in the closed room throbbed with terror. " Muna has an ointment which makes any skin beautiful—I will get some from her," Lambon said. "Shut your eyes and don't say another word," Raka said in desperation. He would have liked to drink her up as he would drink a ripening coconut and throw away the empty shell when he had done with it.

He left the puri and went back to Taman Sari. He stopped at the edge of a sawah which just been freshly irrigated and looked about him. There was no one to be seen. Only two white herons stood fishing for eels at the farther edge. He untied his saput and bent over the water. He saw the sky reflected there and its pearly clouds; he saw himself, clearly yet darkly and in sombre colors. He could not make out what his skin looked like. He washed his numbed fingers and walked on.

When he got home he rummaged about in the large basket in which he kept some of his dancing robes. He was looking for a Chinese mirror which Alit had once given him, so that he could see to put on his Baris crown. As soon as he had found it he held it up to his chest. The round mark had vanished and now he knew why. All the skin up to his shoulders had become red and inflamed. The sickness and uncleanness had spread from within. Raka, after this discovery sat for a time with drooping shoulders and limp arms. Then he lifted the glass and looked at his face. His eyelids were slightly swollen, but otherwise it was the same as ever. He stroked his thick, arched eyebrows with the tips of his fingers and caught his breath; a few of the hairs came out and were left on his fingers. He stared at them for a long time and then puffed them away. Why does this happen to me, he thought, why to me, in the name of the gods, why to me?

At the festival of the full moon he led the village Baris dancers. It was fortunate that they all had to wear white jackets with long closely fitting sleeves. He brandished his spear in his right hand and a scarf in his left and made his stiff fingers move and quiver. It was a torture and he suffered an agony of dread because he was sick and unclean and ought never to have entered the court of the temple. But he still lied to himself without conviction and hoped against hope. Perhaps, too, he even had the childish thought that he might soften the hearts of the gods, who punished him so grievously, by dancing before them at the cost of such agonizing pain in his hands.

No one in the village noticed anything, so far as he could see. The days of the full moon were celebrated in the temple of the puri too, and on the following night a play was given there, in which he had to dance as Arjuna, the most beautiful of all the gods.

Raka avoided Lambon that day, but he spent a long time with Alit, smoking opium. So he was light of heart and almost without a care when the time for his dance drew near. He dressed in Alit's room in the old, intimate way and he took care not to let the lord see his chest.

It seemed to him that he danced better that night than he had ever danced in his life. He was alone with himself, enclosed in the blue veils that shut him off from the real world. He saw nothing— not even Lambon in her place among the rest of the wives. Those "other thoughts" took possession of him; his arms were like wings and his fingers were supple and he forgot his cares and laughed to think he had had the fear of being attacked by the Great Sickness.

This was the last time Raka danced. After this he danced no more.

The nails fell from his fingers and his fingers contracted. At first it was the left hand only and then the right went the same gruesome way. He slept no longer in the big house, where his son's cradle was, but in an empty balé near the rice barn. He had heard that the children of parents who were taken with the Great Sickness inherited the uncleanness in some mysterious way and so he kept away from his child, although he felt a great longing during these very weeks to hold his little son in his arms and to press him to his heart and to be consoled and comforted by his baby talk. When he went to Lambon—and the flame of his love still burned within him—he did not dare to be with her except at night and in utter darkness. He held her so tightly in his arms that it hurt her, but his fingers could no longer feel the sweetness of her body. By day he now always wore a black jacket with long sleeves in which he could conceal his hands and if anyone spoke to him he hid them in the folds of his kain.

But if people did not see his hands they saw his face. Even from the day of the temple festival the village had begun to whisper and the rumour went from mouth to mouth and spread from house to house. There were old people in Taman Sari who could recognize the Great Sickness even before the victims themselves were aware of it. It was as though they were alive to the peril of leprosy in advance and no least sign of it could escape them. Raka's eyebrows had not yet gone thin, but they had lost their glory and glamour. They were the eyebrows of a man marked down. His face was not yet swollen, but the fairness of his skin had taken on a reddish shimmer and no longer lay close and comelily over the bones, but loosely, with a gleam as though of sweat Raka was still beautiful, but he was not himself. He looked like a man marked down for the severest punishment the gods can visit on humanity.

When Bengek, the husky fisherman, was taken with the Great Sickness, the men stoned him out of the village and they burnt his mother's corpse without allowing him to take any part in it. They hunted and stoned him from village to village, and now he lived in the scrub on the lagoon where the river entered the sea—the uncleanest spot on the coast, where his own uncleanness could do no more harm. No one gave a thought to his fate or cared if he starved there or was devoured by rats, for the sooner he died the better. But when Raka showed the first symptoms of the sickness the whole village was seized with sorrow and no open mention was made of it. They loved Raka and could not believe that he could be punished in this way, any more than he himself could believe it. He was a Brahman and the son and the grandson of priests and it was inconceivable that he had to pay for the sin of a forefather. And his own life lay open before their eyes, unshadowed and kindly; and since the gods could not be unjust, the people of Taman Sari clung to the hope that it was a mistake and that the old men were deceived in their knowing whispers. The village reserved judgment and held its breath and waited. It was a reprieve they felt was owed to their love of Raka.

One night in the first week of the fourth month when Raka lay in great pain in his lonely balé—for now the toes of his right foot were beginning to contract—it happened that Teragia came to him. He saw her coming with the little coconut shell lamp in her hand, which she put down on the ground a little way off, as though she knew he did not want her to see him. Raka held his breath, rolled himself up in his kain and pretended to be asleep. Teragia came into the balé without making a sound and knelt down near him. He was sleeping on a mat on the bare rammed earth, not on a bamboo couch. For a while she said nothing and he heard only her quick, constrained breathing.

"I knew you could not sleep, brother," she said softly. "That is why I came."

Raka opened his eyes. At first he saw nothing, and then when his eyes got used to the darkness he saw Teragia's head above him; she had a light-colored shawl over her shoulders to protect her against the chill night air. He shrank into his kain to hide himself, but Teragia felt for his hand under the folds, and in spite of his resistance she took hold of his cramped fingers and enfolded them tightly in her large warm hands. After a minute or two something in him gave way and he relaxed and the fierce need of hiding away in secret left him and became a pain in his throat and a hot wave in his breast and he laid his head in Teragia's lap and wept.

She rocked him gently to and fro as she would a child and after a moment she asked softly, "Are you in great pain?"

He shook his head in her lap and went on sobbing; his tears were like a bath that washed him clean within. Teragia waited patiently until he was calmer, but it took a long time. She held his leprous fingers fast in the pressure of her large hands; they lay as though between the two halves of a coconut shell, as the ashes of a burnt body did before they were consigned to the river. Some semblance of peace came over Raka and he stopped sobbing. Teragia put her forehead on his cheek and began to speak; she was as near to him as on the night when she conceived her son.

"You have been avoiding your father for many weeks and you have been afraid of your mother's touching you. But it is time you spoke to them."

Raka thought over this for a long time in the darkness before he answered. "And what will happen to me after that?" he asked.

Teragia sat upright and let go of his hand. She began stroking his forehead as though he had a fever. "You must not think of yourself but of your father and the village. You will bring great misfortune on all if you remain here. You know that," she said. Raka made no reply.

"You are unclean," Teragia went on. "And you are making your father's house unclean and the whole village and the temples. The waters of the sawahs will be made unclean through your presence and the children will die and the people starve if Taman Sari has another bad harvest."

"What shall I do? What shall I do?" Raka whispered.

"You must not wait for the village to cast you out. You must go of your own accord," his wife said.

"You are hard, Teragia," he said, filled with bitterness.

"Yes, I am hard," she said, and went on stroking his forehead.

"Why does this happen to me, why to me?" Raka whispered. "Can you tell me that? Why to me? Why just to me? What have I done? Why do the gods punish me so terribly? Why have they made me a leper and unclean for ever?"

Teragia wound her arms about his shoulders when she heard his despairing cry and held them so tightly that it hurt. It was some consolation to him. "I do not know," she said softly. "I have asked the gods, but they give no answer. You must bear it."

"Bear it for ever and ever," Raka repeated. Teragia knew what he meant. Whoever died of the Great Sickness might not be burned and his soul, unreleased and unclean and pestridden, had to remain on the earth and never find rest. Raka, her beautiful husband, an outcast and an exile for ever and ever, a soul condemned and deprived of all hope of ever being born again.

"Will you speak to your father tomorrow?" she asked again and so often that he felt she was made of stone.

"Yes," Raka whispered. "I will speak with him."

She could feel his body relax in her arms as soon as he had made this resolve.

"The village will decide where you may build yourself a house," Teragia said. "They love you and will make it as light for you as possible."

"Have I to give up everything and see no one again?" Raka said as though to himself—his parents, his house, his son; the puri, the dances, the temples, the cock-fights, the festivals; his friend Alit—and Lambon, his beloved; give up his whole life, his radiant glamorous life, and say good-bye to it all.

"I shall go with you," Teragia said. "The child can stay with your parents. I weaned him as soon as I recognized your sickness, so now he needs no mother."

"You will come with me?" Raka said in amazement. He had forgotten Teragia when he enumerated all he had to give up. Yet she would go with him. She was hard and heavy and stern and had large hands and wrinkles round her mouth and she could neither play nor laugh. But she would go with him—the unloved wife, while the Beloved stayed behind and was lost to him. "I do not want you to come with me if I am cast out," he said. "I do not need you."

"Who will cook your food?" she asked, and now in the darkness and in the midst of misfortune she smiled. She leant over him and without his saying anything she found the place on his shoulder that had begun to hurt again. He sighed as she felt it and then resigned his outcast limbs to the firm touch of her large warm maternal hands.

Muna, the slave-girl, ran through the courtyards with her headdress awry and kain flapping and the men shouted witticisms after her whenever a glimpse of her legs was to be seen; but Muna heard nothing as she ran on and on, through courtyards and doors, scattering the fowls as she went, and on beyond the little balés where the slaves lived, until she reached the wall behind which was the ruined house by the water. She thrust aside the creepers that overhung the entrance and though she was in such haste she now stood still a moment to get her breath.

On the other side of the ditch Lambon sat with flowers in her hair, deeply absorbed in the task of sharpening a long thin wand. She was dabbling the soles of her feet in the water, from which rose a smell of reedy decay. When the wand was pointed to her satisfaction, Lambon put her tongue between her teeth and started hunting the few dragonflies which had settled on the water-lilies. It was a foolish proceeding, for there was plenty to eat in the puri and the favorite wife of the raja had no need to eke out her meals by catching dragonflies. But Muna knew well why Lambon did it; she had been waiting there day after day in vain and had to pass the time in some way or another. When she had caught a couple of dragonflies she gave up the pursuit and threw her wand into the water, where it floated idly on the surface, and sat down again with the two dragonflies in the palm of her hand and then forgot all about them. Muna imitated the call of a betitja and Lambon looked up.

"Will you not come back to the house, mistress?" Muna begged. Lambon shook her head. Muna measured the ditch with her eyes, took a run and jumped across. Lambon looked at her with mild astonishment: the little slave crouched near her and tenderly embraced her knees.

"Why should I go back?" Lambon asked impatiently. "No one misses me and the lord has been shut up with the pedanda for the last three days and will see nobody."

Muna choked back a sob. "Raka will not come any more, little mistress," she said.

Lambon gave a start and pushed Muna away. Although Muna had backed her up in all her secrets, smoothing her path by bribing the old Harem attendants and doping them with opium, so that Lambon could steal away unobserved, and although it was understood between them that Lambon went to meet a man, yet Raka's name had never been uttered.

"Do not wait any longer, Lambon, for Raka will never come any more," Muna said again, almost chanting the words.

"Did he tell you to tell me so?" Lambon asked in terror. "Or have you found out that he goes to someone else?"

"Little mistress," Muna said miserably, again embracing Lambon's knees, "little mistress, Raka is sick. He will never come any more. He has the Great Sickness and they have cast him out of Taman Sari. That is why the lord is shut up with the pedanda and will see no one."

Lambon closed her eyes. Everything turned round and round and for some time there was a rushing sound in her ears, as though she was standing under a waterfall. But she came to herself again and pushed the slave-girl, in whose arms she found herself, away. "You are lying," she said loudly. "It is not true."

Muna said no more. She merely looked at Lambon, who saw now that her eyes were brimming with two heavy tears which slowly rolled down her cheeks and were licked away by her tongue as they reached her mouth. Though she cried she did not cease to smile and to cling to Lambon's knees. Lambon felt that her heart would fly from her breast as a bird from an open cage. She drew in her breath with care.

"Tell me all you know," she said.

"No one believed it at first," Muna said, taking breath for her announcement. "It seemed too frightful that it should come to Raka of all people. His forefathers were Brahmans and priests and nothing is known of any guilt to deserve such heavy punishment. But nevertheless it is so, and at some time evil must have befallen which now the gods bring home to Raka. It was noticed first at the Full Moon Festival of the third month, and then it got worse and worse and the people of Taman Sari came together and the Council decided to question him. They went to his father, the pedanda, and asked to see Raka, who by then was in hiding. That was nine days ago, mistress——"

Lambon nodded. Feebly she moved her fingers in her lap and reckoned: it was eleven days since her last dark night with Raka. Eleven days of frightful impatience and uncertainty and waiting.

"And then——" she said.

"When he came from his balé they saw that he had the Great Sickness and that they would have to send him away from the village, although it made their hearts ache, for not one wished ill to Raka. But Taman Sari has been punished enough already and the people are afraid of the gods, and rightly, and so they could not turn their heads away or make their eyes blind to spare Raka. I hear that the pedanda himself agreed with them and bade Raka leave his house at once. It is particularly serious for the house of a priest to be made unclean in that way. But they say that his father went with him when he left the village and embraced and blessed him before they parted at the cross-roads, caring nothing for the uncleanness. They did not have to burn the balé where Raka slept, but only to lay the proper offerings on the floor for the bad demons, and the pedanda remained for three days in prayer and meditation. Then he and his house were clean again and he speaks no more about his son. The people of Taman Sari were very sad, too, for a whole day, but they try to forget and they say it will be a good rice harvest. There was far too much sickness and misfortune along the coast, but now the gods seem to be appeased."

"And Raka?" Lambon asked softly.

"Raka?" Muna said. "They say he does not look so horrible as other lepers. He has not lost his eyebrows. They say he stood by when the chief men of the village spoke to his father, but he himself did not say a word. They say he said good-bye politely to all as though he were just going for a walk or to Kesiman and that he turned round at the cross-roads and waved his hand and smiled until they were out of sight."

Lambon pondered over all this for a long time. Muna's eyes filled with tears again, but Lambon did not cry. It was as though so great a disaster could not find its way into her little head.

"And where is he now?" she asked.

"The Council of Taman Sari assigned him a place south of the village and his father promised him wood and bamboo to build a balé But the council of Sanur would not agree to his settling there, for the water runs from Taman Sari to Sanur and their sawahs would be unclean if Raka lived higher up there. All the five coast villages have united in sending him where lepers belong. He is building his house there."

Lambon shuddered. She knew the river mouth with its stagnant, unclean, brackish water, its prickly scrub and sand dunes, where the mosquitoes hung in clouds all day and ghosts and strayed souls gathered by night.

"And he is all alone there?" she murmured.

"Not alone," Muna said. "Bengek, the fisherman, lives there, too, and he is trying to dig the ground and to grow something." She hesitated a moment before adding: "And Teragia, his wife, has gone with him."

"How have you found out all this?"

"Old Ranis heard it in the market. Everyone is talking about it. Puglug, who comes with things to sell from Taman Sari, told her and many others have confirmed it word for word."

"Yes, Puglug always knows all the news," Lambon said, smiling wanly as her thoughts went back to her brother's wife. It was all very far away and much had happened since she left her family. It was only now she grasped what Muna had started by telling her. "And you say Raka will never come here again?" she whispered. Muna embraced her knees afresh and more tightly than before.

"Little mistress," she said, "little mistress, don't you understand yet? He is unclean. They would stone him if he came to Badung. You must not think of him again or the gods will be angry."

"Should we, too, make offerings to be clean?" Lambon asked in alarm.

"I know nothing about those matters and we cannot ask anyone either," the slave replied.

"No, we cannot ask anyone," Lambon repeated. She had forgotten her family and the household in which she grew up, but now she felt homesick for them. Puglug and her aunt—they were never at a loss over offerings. She went on thinking it all over in a daze.

"And did he say good-bye to no one in the puri?" she asked.

"No, only to his child and his parents so far as I heard."

"Not even to the lord?" Lambon insisted.

"How could a leper speak to the lord? Perhaps he sent a message of farewell to our master by his father," she added.

"Do you know anything about that?" Lambon asked quickly.

The slave put her lips to her mistress's ear. "They say the lord wept when he heard about it—Oka told Ida Katut," she whispered.

Lambon opened her hands and looked at the crushed dragonflies which all the time had been clenched in her fist. Then she laid her hands wearily in her lap. "What am I to do now?" she asked, almost crazed with sorrow.

"Forget," said Muna. "The days come and go, the water flows by and you will soon forget."

Lambon shook her head violently.

"Yes, yes," Muna said. "I know how it is. I, too, was fond of a man—Meru, the sculptor, your brother. But he gave me up for Bernis the shameless, and then I thought I should die for the pain in my heart. Now, I cannot remember even what he looked like or the sound of his voice."

Lambon considered this, but it was no help to her. She reflected. "Perhaps I might ask if the lord would see me," she said shyly. Muna peered into her face in amazement. "He wept—should I not be with him when he is sad? I could fill his opium pipe and that stills pain," Lambon went on.

"Would you like some opium?" Muna asked, for she had quick perceptions. Lambon had never yet smoked.

"Yes. Get me some opium," she said.

"And now come back, little mistress," Muna begged. "You will get the heat sickness sitting over this stagnant water. I will bring you opium and I will ask Oka whether the lord would see you. Perhaps the pedanda may have a farewell message for you from his son—"

"What a liar you are," Lambon said with a smile as she released the slave's hands from her knees. "I will come soon. Leave me here alone a moment longer."

Muna gazed at her and sighed. She looked round and found a half-decayed board which she laid across the ditch. "There, is not that better?" she asked as she stepped across the bridge.

"No bridge is needed now," Lambon said, and for the first time the whole extent of her unhappiness came over her. When Muna had vanished through the leafy doorway she sat on, transfixed and turned to stone by grief. She stretched out her foot and kicked the board into the water. It splashed her kain and she wiped the drops away. She found the dead dragonflies in her hand and slowly tore them to pieces—the wings, the long gleaming bodies, the heads with their jewelled eyes—and threw them into the water. Then she put her arms round her knees and buried her head in the dark cleft between them. She longed to cry. But no tears came.

The Srawah

WHEN the people of Taman Sari had finished building their rice temple and had dedicated it anew with a great festival; when the eleven-storeyed tower of the coral temple at Sanur was completed; when the villages of the coast had burned all their dead, surrendered all their unlawful possessions to the gods and driven out their outcasts, then a good time came. Everything had been done to ascertain what the gods required and to carry out their wishes and now they were satisfied and blessed the coast villages with good fortune and rich harvest.

The rats disappeared from the sawahs and the rice flourished. Where usually a sheaf of seed yielded forty-five sheaves at harvest time, they could now hope for sixty, so laden were the ripening ears. The coconut palms bore rich clusters of fruit and the squirrels had retreated northwards. Rain came down from the Great Mountain as often as it was wanted and the streams carried rich mud to the valleys. A few old people and a few children, who were no older than the dew on the fields, died, but all the other sick got well and there were enough hands for the work in the fields and for threshing the rice. The children's thin arms plumped out again with flesh and their fine round little bellies were a joy to see when they collected in troops about the gateways.

Also there were many more sons than daughters born at this time, and there were many birthday feasts when the whole village cooked and ate heartily and drank tuak or sweet rice-wine, and even the dogs got fat from the leavings of the offerings and the feasts.

Pak had his full share of the general prosperity and this he found only right. His plates were let in to the base of the new high altar of the temple and formed one of the chief decorations there. He had made the gods a present of them and it was only just that the gods should thank him as they saw fit. Pak loved to stop at the new shrine on the way home from his sawahs, letting his buffaloes graze outside, while he knelt before the shrine and gazed with satisfaction at his plates. It seemed to him that they shone with growing beauty and that their roses bloomed with ever fresher tints.

His labors in the fields were rather lighter now, for his brother Lantjar was big enough to help him and Meru went with Rantun when she herded the ducks. His blind brother, too, loved the new temple; he loved to sit there while his quacking charges revelled in the mud of the sawah. Sometimes he passed his fingers over the stone figures and the ornamental work of the gateway and the carvings of the door of the Gedong shrine, for even he had helped with advice when it was being restored. He had developed a sense which replaced his eyes; he found his way all about the village and he also employed his nimble hands in making clappers for scaring birds from the sawahs or toys for little Siang. The children loved his company, particularly quiet little Madé, the second-born, and she was his guide whenever he needed one. Klepon was now a sturdy little bare-legged girl and Rantun, who was entrusted with her up-bringing, sometimes put a small, empty plate of woven leaves or a scrap of sugar-cane on her shaven head—to start her education in good time. The old grandfather sat looking on and shaking with laughter at the earnest endeavours and sad mischances of his little granddaughter.

In other ways, too, the household enjoyed peace and concord, and for this there was a particular and joyful reason. Sarna, before her sickness, had announced with pride that she was once more expecting a baby, and no one doubted it would be a son, for she was the sort of woman who always had boys. She made a good deal of fuss over her pregnancy, for she often felt so bad that her stomach rose in revolt; on other days Lantjar had to climb the trees and bring her all the sour, unripe fruit he could find. Pak laughed good-naturedly and was well content to watch his second wife rounding out daily in fruitful motherhood. Puglug, too, was indulgent to her younger sister and only laughed at her moods and complaints. Puglug was amazingly silent all these weeks and sometimes sat quite still with her hands in her lap and a secret smile on her plain honest face. As she said nothing Pak noticed nothing. His aunt had to open his eyes for him. "You had better ask your brother Meru to make a second cradle for you," she said.

"Why? What is the joke now?" Pak asked, taken aback.

"Have you no eyes in your head?" the aunt exclaimed, bent double with laughter, and the old man came up, too, and laughed at his son's denseness; even Klepon and Siang joined in, though they did not know what the laughter was about. Puglug alone kept her composure; she stood there silently smiling to herself. It took some time before Pak grasped that the visits of politeness he had been paying her had borne fruit and that she, too, was expecting a child. He was very glad; it was part of the general fertility. He patted her on the shoulder as soon as they were alone and said, "So you mean to give me another little girl, mother. What a lot of women I shall have soon in my household to thresh my rice!"

As the two wives were now in the same case they became more friendly and more like sisters, for they were expecting their babies in the same month. When Pak attended the meetings of the Subak or the village council, of which he was now an important and respected member, he was greeted by all kinds of flattering jests about his two wives. "I hear that both your cows mean to calve at the one time," Rib, the wag, said, and Pak replied with ready wit, "You are envious, are you, because your ducks lay no eggs?"

Sarna gave birth to her child in the first week of the fifth month, and it was a son as expected. Although this child was not so long in coming into the world, he was the cause of quite as much agitation and crying aloud; and Pak worked hard to support and assist his wife and was bathed in perspiration by the time the child appeared. Once more Sarna was too weary to clean up the room herself and Puglug, in spite of her pregnancy, knelt down and washed the mother and the baby and the rammed earth of the floor, on which it had been born. Pak hit on a fine name for this son too; he called him Lintang, the little star—since he had already begun finding names for his sons in the sky. The aunt, however, grumbled and said that such high-sounding and arrogant names might harm the children.

Two weeks later Puglug came home from the market earlier than usual, put her load down in the kitchen, changed her good new kain for an old one, walked rather heavily to the house and laid

herself down on the floor, which she had previously swept. When
Pak came home after taking his best cock to the market to show it
off to the other men, he found Puglug already in silent labor. The
only sign of her pains was the drops of sweat on her face and she
smiled grimly when Pak sat down behind her to help. This was the
sixth child to be born in his house and he was a practised hand. The
women who were present chaffed him good-humoredly and the old
midwife, who was there on this occasion also, said with a titter, "If
I die one of these days Pak can take over my job; he is as good at
it as I am."

By sunset the child lay there on the ground and Pak found to his
unbounded astonishment that Puglug, too, had borne him a son. It
was the last thing he had looked for from his first wife and it took
his breath away. The women laughed aloud at the dumbfounded
look on his face and showered congratulations on him and the
child. Sarna was as much astonished as he was. She cried out in her
surprise and delight and knelt beside Puglug and shook her and
shouted in her ear that it was a son, a fine plump boy, a son—as
though Puglug did not know it herself. Sarna bathed the new baby
and washed Puglug, but then Puglug got up and cleaned the room
herself, for this was a point of honor with her on which she would
not give way.

Pak went about the yard boasting and joking. "Now I shall have
to starve in spite of my two wives," he said, "for they have both
taken it into their heads to bear me a son at once, so they are both
unclean and there is no one to cook my food."

It was not so bad as all that, however. Rantun, without a word
said, filled the place of both mothers and did their work and she
could already carry three coconuts on her head or a medium-sized
jar of water.

"I don't know what name to give the child, mother of my son,"
Pak said to Puglug. "You have thrown me off my guard and confounded me."

"We might call him Datang—he who has come," Puglug suggested, for she was a simple-minded woman of no great education.

"Not good enough for my youngest son," Pak said, and began
racking his brains for a fine name. He looked up at the sky for inspiration, but nothing would do. Bulang, the moon, was at best a girl's

name and Mendung, the cloud, sounded sadly. Ciangelala, the rainbow, was not pleasing, for many people called a rainbow simply the louse of the sky. It was not until two days later that Pak had a happy thought. It came into his head of its own accord as he was breaking down the western sawahs for the second time with the lampit. The earth sucked and lay flat, the mud splashed up and spattered him and the buffaloes, and the smell was pleasant to his nostrils and the field was full of strength and the promise of fertility. And so Pak went home at noon and said to Puglug, "We will call our son Tanah, the earth, and I do not know of a better name."

When three months had passed and it was time to celebrate the birthdays of both children—it was an economy to do it on one day—there was another surprise in Pak's household. Meru took Pak aside and said with some embarrassment, "Could not my wedding take place on the same day and then we could entertain all our guests at once and have the pedanda to invite only once?"

It then came out that Meru had come to terms with Dasni and Puglug said she had known it a long time ago and it was a very good thing. Pak suspected that she had had a finger in the match and on further consideration he commended her for it. It was true that Dasni was dark of face and had pimples and large, heavy breasts, but that did not matter since Meru could not see. Besides, he had enjoyed plenty of beautiful girls while he still had eyes to see them, and Dasni was a distant cousin and so did not need to be carried off and it cost nothing to marry her. And as she was skilled at weaving baskets and mats and used to selling sirih, she would bring money in and also undertake the labors for which the aunt had long been too old. And so everything was arranged for the best in Pak's household.

When all the festivals were over and paid for and he counted up the savings he had buried in his floor, it appeared that the family was possessed of no more than fifteen ringits. That was not much and once more Pak had to put aside all thought of buying himself a kris or even of having his teeth filed, although both were very necessary for a man of his standing. And if the old man were to die one of these days, as he sometimes announced as a probability, there would not be enough money to bury him in a becoming manner and to entertain the village suitably. Pak looked about for a quick way of making money and thought: My cock will earn me all the money I want.

It happened most fortunately, as one among the many other blessings that fell to Pak's lot ever since he gave his plates to the temple, that one of his cocks grew into a fine fighter.

It was one of the three young birds that Sarna had begged of her father, a fine cock with white plumage, strong legs and the tiny sprout of a comb. Pak's father, who knew more about cocks than any man in Taman Sari, had had his eye on this cock from the first, when he was so young that his voice broke whenever he crowed. He had sat on his heels by his cage for hours observing him, taking him out and examining his claws and his neck and talking to him; and he had mixed his food for him with great care in accordance with most particular prescriptions. Twelve grains of maize with water at morning, six at midday, together with a strengthening mixture which he himself prepared with cow dung and pepper. He had massaged his muscles, cooled his feet in the stream that ran past the house or in the dew of the grass, and hardened off the soles of his feet.

When the cock was full-grown the old man called to Pak one day and said, "I think this bird will win you many a fight. He is a genuine Srawah."

"That's not possible," Pak said. "How should Wajan, who is so avaricious that he counts the grains of rice his children eat, give me a genuine Srawah as a present?"

"Wajan knows nothing of cocks, but I do," the old man said. "I have examined him feather by feather and point by point and I tell you he is a Srawah. There is not a feather on his body that is not either black or white."

Pak took the bird from the basket and weighed him on his hand and looked him over and excited him and took great delight in the bird. He was a beautiful bird, white with a few black down-feathers. In the afternoon he took him for the first time to the plot of grass in front of the town hall, where the men always squatted to appraise each other's birds.

"What sort of a one have you got there?" they asked him.

"Nothing out of the way. He's too young to fight yet. My father-in-law gave him to me," Pak said.

"Is it a Srawah?" an elderly man, who was nearly as knowing as Krkek, asked.

"I don't know enough about cocks myself to say," Pak said with boastful modesty. "My father seems to think he is a Srawah."

"Where did he come from?" another man asked, taking the cock from Pak's hand and holding him up in the air.

"From Bedulu, I believe," Pak said.

"Then it certainly is a Srawah," the elderly man insisted. The wag, Rib, who came up just then, looked at the cock and asked, "When are you going to kill your cockerel and make satté of him?" They all laughed loudly and Pak joined in. "If you were not too stupid to know east from west you would be able to see perhaps that he is a Srawah," he said, for he was long past the stage of merely laughing in admiration of Rib's jokes; he could now answer back and turn the laugh on to his side.

"If your cock is such a wonderful bird, you had better hide him before his Highness, the anak Agung Bima, catches sight of him and takes him for the puri," Rib replied.

"It is a Srawah and the best cock I have seen for many a long day," said a very old man with no teeth, who had been squatting near saying nothing, with his prim of betel and tobacco inside his lower lip. Pak took his cock home again, full of pride and joyful anticipation; for a Srawah was the descendant of an invisible, divine cock, and recognizable by particular marks; and this one could not fail to win fights and bring him in money and do him honor.

From now on there was another source of joy and hope and importance in Pak's life besides his ripening sawahs and his growing children, and this was the young cock. He left it to his father to mix his food and to oversee his upbringing, but he himself fed him, so that the Srawah should take to him, and he spent a great part of his free time gazing at him, pampering him, carrying him about, showing him off, boasting of him and slowly preparing him for his first fight.

The Srawah had not a single defect and he grew larger and more pugnacious daily. He had a fine broad back and his muscles, which Pak massaged daily, were also broad and firm, as they ought to be. He was given no grain now but only chopped dried fowl, flesh and bone and particularly the legs, mixed with water, so that the strength of the other bird should pass into him. His middle claw had twenty-one rings in the skin, the sign of a conqueror, and when Pak lifted him up and put him down he could feel the springiness with which the bird always jumped from the ground again. There was also a tremor in his shoulder muscles and sometimes, too, a throb in his throat after crowing, such as only particularly good fighting-cocks made.

"You will win me many fights, Srawah, for you are strong and beautiful," Pak whispered to him, and he stroked the cock's feathers for half-hours together; the cock liked this and Pak's hands, too, were soothed and happy.

Every second week he threw him into the water and left him to swim to make his feet flexible, and on the cocks' birthday, which was celebrated throughout the whole country, he laid the prescribed offerings on the top of his hamper. He did not allow the cock to remain on the place when Meru was newly married, for a fighting-cock might neither have hens of his own nor come anywhere near such uncleanness if he was to keep his strength. So Pak put his cock in Wajan's charge for forty-two days and went there daily to feed him with his own hand, and to see that he was put out on the grass in his basket so that he could eat as much of it as he wished.

Waian looked at the cock and was annoyed that he had given away such a fine bird. "Will you exchange your cock for three co-conuts?" he asked. "I am willing to have him back though he has faults of every kind."

Pak merely laughed at this offer, and he was glad when the forty-two days had passed and he could take his cock home again. Now, too, the bird was old enough to learn how to fight in earnest and how to protect the vulnerable spot under his wings. Pak tied a kepeng round his neck by a cord so that it hung over his breast. As he could not endure this he sprang into the air and raised his spurred heels, and thus learned the movements which served at once for attack and defence.

And now when Pak took the cock at noon to the open space in front of the village hall, where the men tried out their birds, there was not one that his cock was afraid of; on the contrary, he drew himself up and lowered his head and his neck distended with valiant breath and he showed eager lust for battle.

And so when there was to be a three-day cock-fight at Sanur the old man said, "This time you must let your cock fight and he will certainly win."

Pak took his cock from the basket and stroked him. "Cock," he said, "now the time has come for your first fight and you will certainly win, for there is not a cock as fine and brave as you. When you have been victorious I will buy you a red rice cake such as you have never eaten in your life— that I promise you." The cock listened attentively, standing quite still and erect between Pak's knees, and then he made a contented cluck in his throat and Pak was sure he had understood.

During the last three days before the fight many people came to Pak's yard to ask his father's advice. Pak took out the flat wooden bowl where he kept the sharp spurs, nine in number and of various shapes and lengths. They were polished and in fine order, for the old man kept them oiled, as they ought to be, with the oil from a shadow-play lamp, which was mixed with the sharpest spices, so that the sharpness of the spurs matching the sharpness of the red pepper might speedily slay any opponent. Pak's father had a small jar of this oil by him, and he gave some of it to the other men, too, as a gift or in return for a present of fruit or rice.

Pak, as well as his cock, grew more and more excited as the day of battle drew near. Pak stroked his feathers until they shone and he himself put on his best kain, and with the cock in a bamboo hamper set off accompanied by his father. As they went along between the sawahs they saw other men all going in the same direction with their hampers, and there was a feeling of great festivity and excitement in the air. On the way the old man impressed on his son again and again what he had to do. "You must pit your cock only against a pure white bird or, failing that, only against a Buwik, speckled with all colors, although such a Buwik would be a dangerous adversary. And don't forget either that you cannot win unless you start him from the north-east corner, and you must on no account let yourself be hustled into any other quarter. I once knew a cock who was the very image of yours; he belonged to the old lord of Pametjutan. He fought for ten years and was never beaten. I hear he's alive still, and they give him rice and look after him well in the puri, although he is so old, for he was worth a fortune to the lord in his best days."

"If my cock wins today I am going to buy him a red rice cake. I have promised him that."

"He is going to win," the old man said.

The cockpit at Sanur was a large square building whose floor rose in three wide steps, so that each row of spectators could see over the heads of those in front. In the middle, and slightly raised above the ground level, was the four-sided battleground. The air circulated freely since the building had no walls; it rested on posts and between the lower and the upper roof there were again posts, so that the building was both airy and well lighted. Women vendors were encamped all round, but only men were allowed inside to watch the fights and boys who were old enough to herd buffaloes. On one side there was a dais for the lords who had announced their intention of being present, and in the northeast corner there stood a small altar of bamboo with offerings for the demons who delight in battle and seeing blood flow; for cock-fighting was not only a pleasure and a recreation but at the same time a holy and necessary offering. If these demons were not placated with a few drops of the blood of cocks, then blood-lust and anger would enter into men, and they would begin to fight and slay one another and then blood would flow, not in drops, but in floods and torrents.

Opposite the seat of the lords was the place for the judge. An elderly man took his seat there with a shallow vessel of water in front of him and one half of a coconut shell with a hole in the bottom. Next to him another man sat with a small gong. The fighting had been in progress for hours, but Pak, in obedience to his father's advice, had bridled his own and his cock's impatience. The earlier fights were of small importance and were not for cocks such as his. Nevertheless, the building was crowded and the whole neighborhood echoed with the crowing of cocks in their hampers. Gamblers shouted their bets and held up their money, and bets were often taken from one side of the building to the other. The owners of the cocks that were fighting at the moment squatted in the ring, and other men at the corners with their birds in front of them were waiting to match them. Others again whose birds were to fight next were already busy binding the fine sharp two-edged blades to their spurs, carefully winding the shaft of the weapon with a long cord, so that the blade stuck out firmly at a killing angle from the fighter's spurs.

At the very moment when Pak and his cock and his father reached the balé and were looking about for a place, the attention of the spectators was taken from the cocks by the arrival of the lord of Badung, accompanied by his retinue. The punggawa greeted him and was invited by the lord to take his place beside him. The keeper of the lord's cocks put down the hampers and took the birds out. "Mbe!" the spectators exclaimed as each fighting-cock appeared. Every one was a picked bird, fine, strong, quivering with courage and lust of battle, crowing, flapping its wings, dancing with impatience and hardly to be held back. The punggawa, too, had two servants with four of his cocks and these also were splendid birds. A little old man crouched at the lord's feet— Ida Katut, the story-teller. He was clasping a dark-brown hamper to his breast and from it, rather later, he tenderly drew a white cock who gave every sign of courage and pugnacity, although he was small. Pak's father leant over to his son and said, "That little white one has won fourteen fights already. He has a scar on his right leg. Can you see it?" Pak gave only a fleeting glance; his eyes were glued to the lord's cocks. Mine is quite as beautiful, he thought, with a sudden rush of pride, and his heart glowed within him. He opened his hamper from which the head of his impatient Srawah had been darting again and again and balanced him on his hand. The sudden swell of pride was as suddenly dashed. No, he thought, my cock is not half as good as the lord's ones. He was better than most in Taman Sari, no doubt. He had looked magnificent on the grass plot in front of the village hall; but now that Pak was forced to compare him with the finest birds of Badung, he shrank at once and Pak's courage failed him.

"I will wait a bit and see first how the other cocks shape," he whispered to his father. The old man raised his eyebrows in assent without taking his eyes from the ring. "Would you like to bet?" Pak asked, knowing that his father had not a kepeng. He took a little string of kepengs from his sirih pouch and gave it to his father. Pak had dug up five ringits' worth of money from under his house when he set off for his cock's first fight; yet he was not so sure now that he was going to win a great deal.

He put the cock back in the hamper for the time and gave his mind to the ring. The tumult in the balé was just reaching its height, for two red cocks were about to be let go by their owners and the last bets had been taken. Money was tossed on the ground and money was passing from hand to hand until it reached the taker. Bets were shouted on all sides with cries of even money, two to one and five to one. The moment the cocks were let go, silence fell. Pak had merely shaken his head in response to any bet offered him. His money was not to stake on somebody or other's red cock. He was keeping it for his own bird, who stuck his head out from time to time and crowed a challenge followed by the little gurgle that promised victory. The two red cocks stepped round each other for a moment, and then sprang up with a flutter of their wings and their steel spurs cut the air. At the very first encounter both were wounded. One of them appeared to have had his right leg sinew severed, for he sank to the ground and blood trickled from him. The other was bleeding, too, from the left wing, but he could stand. As neither renewed the fight the gong sounded, and at the same moment the judge put his coconut shell into the bowl of water. It filled and sank. He took it out and put it in once more, and when it sank for the second time the time was up, and the gong was again struck.

During these brief moments a few more bets were made while the owners of the two cocks, after retiring to their respective corners, tried every means of restoring their birds for the next round. But they did not seem to have much success. When the gong sounded and the cocks were put into the ring again, one of them sat down as before and the other stood still and showed no fight. The coconut shell was again dipped, while the spectators abused, encouraged and derided. When the gong was struck again without battle being joined, the two cowards were put in a basket together and so compelled to fight. This time the cock with the wounded leg decided to attack. He flew up—and now there was profound silence—his spurs flashed and the other cock collapsed. The basket was removed, again the gong sounded and the coconut shell sank below the water. As neither now got to his feet, the fight ended in a draw and the spectators greeted this conclusion with good-tempered burble and laughter. The two men took up their cocks, one wounded, the other dying, and went away. Pak's father looked round at his son and smiled. Pak raised his eyebrows. He was glad he had not betted. The lord, whose light skin was set off by a black jacket, had paid little attention to this fight. He was talking earnestly to the punggawa. From time to time Ida Katut clasped his hands before venturing to interpose a jest which the lord acknowledged with a distracted smile. More and more men arrived and more and more cocks. A serried rank formed at the back of the highest step, everywhere the spectators were squeezed closer and closer together and the hot air scarcely stirred.

Pak made two bets; he put fifty kepengs on a tailless cock and two hundred on a Buwik and won both times. He got terribly excited when one of the lord's cocks fought a cock from Kesiman, but he did not dare to bet. The cock from Kesiman looked a splendid bird; the lord's cock had fought many a battle and had the advantage of experience, but his years began to tell. Pak fancied the cock from Kesiman. But though he put up a gallant fight, the lord's cock won and Pak released the breath he had held throughout the third round. Once more he was glad he had not betted.

Thus hour after hour went by, and the sun was already in the third quarter of the day when Pak took out the Srawah and pushed his way through to seek out an adversary for him. By this time the heat and the excitement had reached fever-pitch and the bets rose in proportion. Men who had lost all their money were throwing down rings and krises, and the crowing of the cocks and the shouted bets were equally loud and piercing.

As soon as Pak put his cock down on the ground and stroked his neck feathers upwards to rouse him, he could see, as the bird sprang up with a thrust of his strong legs, that his Srawah excited admiration. He was beside himself with the lust for battle. He sunk his head and wanted to fight every cock that was shown him. But Pak knew that he must match him only against a pure white one or else a Buwik and he refused all others. After looking all round he saw a man from Taman Sari who had a good white cock. The two birds had often tried each other's mettle in sport on the grass outside the village hall, and Pak was sure his bird would win if he fought this white one. His owner, however—Limbak was his name—had a firm belief in the strength of his own bird and was in any case a boaster and a gambler. He had often chaffed and annoyed Pak by crying down his Srawah. Pak exchanged a glance with his father and waddled, still squatting, up to Limbak. "What do you say to it?" he asked. Limbak displayed his white cock and they both held their birds fast to prevent them going for each other on the spot. Both were eager to fight; there was no need to rouse them first. Several men squatted near and gave their opinion, but Pak was now so excited that

he didn't hear anything that was said to him. Limbak took hold of
Pak's Srawah to size him up and Pak took Limbak's white cock and
stroked his neck feathers and let him bounce up from the ground.
He could tell by the feel of him that he had not such good muscles
or as good a wind as his own bird. He felt sure of victory and felt
with one hand for the money in his girdle. But Limbak, though a
braggart, was no fool. "No," he said, giving Pak his bird back, "not
today. Next fight if yours is still alive." A few men laughed.

Pak had to look about for another opponent. The Srawah was
so full of fight and impatience that he nearly burst. He flapped his
wings, crowed challenge after challenge and Pak could feel his heart
beating under his fingers.

"Show your cock," someone said behind him. When Pak looked
round he found himself face to face with the punggawa, the most
powerful man in the five coast villages. He had left the elevated
seat that befitted his caste and in the heat of battle had come down
among the common people and he had a Buwik in his hand. While
Pak was still staring at the punggawa and his speckled cock, his
Srawah sprang up with lowered head and wanted to begin.

"A good match," the punggawa said. He gave his bird to Pak and
took hold of Pak's to test him. Although two other cocks were fighting in the ring at the moment, many eyes, as Pak could feel rather
than see, were turned from the contest and fixed on him and the
punggawa. There were cries of "Let them have a go at one another,"
and "That will be a good fight!" and "Pak, the punggawa will have
roast fowl tonight!" The last was in Rib's voice, and Pak turned
angrily round and saw the broad grin on the face of his humorous
friend. He was still holding the punggawa's cock and the punggawa
was holding his. Never had Pak had such a cock in his grasp. All
that his own cock had this one had, too, and he had twice of it.
His muscles were even harder and broader, the air quivered in his
breast, his legs were as springy as bamboos and his courage beat out
of him like the heat of a fire. Pak looked about him in a daze, for
cries of encouragement and warning flew about his head. He looked
for his father and saw the old man's eyes far away in the throng. But
he saw also that the old man was standing up and looking across to
him, and that he raised his eyebrows and dropped his eyelids and
this clearly meant: Yes, let them fight.

"Right," Pak said to the punggawa, forgetting in his excitement the polite forms of address due to a man of his station. There they sat man to man on the same level, on the floor of the cockpit, and it was no time for formalities.

"Twenty-five ringits," the punggawa said. Pak fell steeply from his height.

"I have not got them, Highness," he said, and taking back his Srawah, revived his courage by the feel of the bird's strength.

"Five, then?" the punggawa asked. Pak nodded.

"Who will put twenty-five ringits on the Srawah against my cock?" the punggawa shouted. Pak felt as though he were whirling in the rapids of a river in the rainy season. Suddenly there was silence.

"Let me see your cock," the lord said from his lofty seat, and stretched out his hand. Pak did not understand what he meant. Somebody gave him a dig in the ribs. "His Highness the raja wants to see your cock," Rib shouted somewhere behind him. The anak Agung Bima, whom Pak knew, came down and took his cock from his hands. Pak felt bereft when it was taken from him. He followed him with his eyes as the anak Agung Bima carried him off and handed him to the lord. The lord weighed him on his hand, rubbed his neck feathers up the wrong way, stroked him, looked at his feet, made him spring up from the ground and then held him down. The cock struggled and was not polite to the lord, for he loved his master, Pak, and could not bear a strange hand on him.

"Fifty to your twenty-five," the lord called out to the punggawa, and the cock was passed from hand to hand back to Pak. The officials and courtiers who sat behind the lord now began talking all at once, and a ring set with rubies was thrown on the ground. It rolled past Pak, who stared at it in amazement. The real betting had not yet begun; this was only the prelude and the excitement rose higher and higher as the two adversaries armed with their spurs were matched against each other. Pak held his cock and his heart throbbed right up in his throat.

Suddenly he was overwhelmed by a pang of fear. If he let his beloved cock loose on the other, there was no certainty he would be victorious. He might be dead in less time than it took a bored coconut to sink in the water. It came to him in a flash that his cock would lose and be killed. He looked round about him, and back at

his own bird, and it seemed very small and young. He looked at the
punggawa's. It was a gigantic bird and it seemed to grow larger and
more formidable the longer he looked at it. He clasped his cock to
his breast.

"I am afraid," he said.

"What of?" the punggawa asked.

"I am afraid. My cock is no good, Highness," Pak said. The punggawa looked at him for a moment, shrugged his shoulders and
stood up. Someone picked up the ruby ring. Pak's cock crowed. Pak
looked for his hamper and was overcome with shame. He wanted to
bundle his cock inside and go home.

Jokes and jeers were showered on him from all sides. The lord,
who had been laughing a moment before, looked annoyed. But Ida
Katut restored his good humor in the nick of time. He drew his little
white cock from his hamper and clambered down from the dais to
the edge of the ring.

"Twenty-five ringits to my lord's fifty," he shouted. "And no one
shall say we are cowards, my cock and I."

Everyone laughed, the lord too. It was comical to see how the
little man puffed himself out, strutting like the hero of a shadow-
play, and how his little white cock copied him, flapping his wings,
extending his lowered head with the obvious intention of making
short work of Pak's Srawah.

"Done, my friend?" Ida Katut asked Pak.

"Yes, sir, if it pleases you," Pak said in confusion.

They were surrounded by a ring of men and a moment later they
sat in a corner binding the spurs on to the feet of the cocks. Pak
went over in his head all the advice his father had given him—the
north-east corner, the broad short spur, and not to forget to breathe
his own strength into the cock before the fight began. Ida Katut
meanwhile provoked more laughter by arming his little cock with
the largest and most formidable spur he could find in his wooden
box. It was of serpentine shape like a tiny kris and it gave the little
white cock an extremely warlike air. In spite of this Pak felt completely confident. When their turn came they took their birds into
the middle of the ring. Both were mad to fight and now the spectators began betting.

And now Pak noticed that not everyone was betting on his fine large cock; the little white one had the reputation of being a great fighter and a sure killer, as Pak's father, who knew everything, had told him beforehand. The betting was fast and furious, voices rose, money flew through the air and there was great excitement. Pak put his hand to his cock's breast and felt it beating fast and hard against his little ribs, and he rubbed up his neck feathers to excite him still more. He blew his breath into his eyes and beak and let him go. His five ringits lay beside Ida Katut with Ida Katut's five on top. There was a lot more money on the ground, and as the fight started Pak felt his heart beating like a drum in his chest.

The two cocks circled round, with heads sunk and bent legs, watching each other. Suddenly the little white one flew up and attacked the Srawah. The Srawah, too, sprang up and defended himself. The spurs flashed, a few white feathers flew and again the cocks faced each other. Neither had gained any advantage. At the third encounter there was a murmur from the onlookers, and Pak was aware that now his cock was wounded in the right leg. There was a trickle of blood but he did not seem to notice it, although he limped as he turned in a circle with lowered head watching the other cock. The little white one was a dangerous opponent; how dangerous, Pak saw only now. He was experienced and cool-headed; he meant to kill and he knew how to wait for the right moment. He flew up the fourth time and when the spurs flashed past each other in the flutter of feathers the onlookers shouted "Got him!" But they were mistaken.

The cocks separated again and Pak's Srawah limped on his wounded leg and sat down in dejection. The plumage of the white one was bloody, but it was the blood of Pak's cock, not his own; and yet neither was seriously hurt. As the fight was not resumed, the gong was struck and Pak took up his bird and hurried to the north-east corner where he was relieved to find his father waiting for him. The old man took the cock from his hands, bathed him quickly and skilfully in the bowl that was there ready, massaged the wound with the tips of his fingers, stroked his plumage and gave him to Pak to breathe into, for Pak was young and he was old and had not much strength to give.

The cock was ready even before the gong sounded, and although he limped it seemed that a waxing rage of battle had only now come over him. The moment Pak let him go he fluttered up over the white one and again a murmur went in a wave through the balé. This time the Srawah had taken the white one off his guard and his left wing hung down. Though both were wounded they felt nothing and had no thought but to fight to the death. Pak's cock limped and Ida Katut's could scarcely fly up any more, but they went for each other, in the air too, and aimed blows at each other with their little swords with the greatest gallantry and the utmost contempt of death. At their fifth encounter Pak saw that his cock struck the other beneath the wing. "Got him!" shouted the onlookers, and the judge struck the gong. Then both cocks fell back on the ground, and the white one lay there as though dead with a trickle of red on his breast. Pak's cock lay down too, seeming now at last to be aware of his wound. The gong sounded and the judge put the coconut on the surface of the water. "Get up, get up," Pak implored his cock, for only if he got up before the next gong was he the conqueror. "Get up, have courage, get up," shouted all the men who had put their money on the Srawah. The lord sat bending forward gazing with a thoughtful smile at Pak's bird.

Ida Katut's cock now moved his head and with a tremendous effort raised himself a little way. At the same moment Pak's cock sprang to his feet—his legs, Pak knew were stout and strong—and drawing himself up on his uninjured leg, so that the other had no weight to carry, he remained standing. Ida Katut's brave little white cock let his head fall and died; the Srawah remained standing. It was his first fight and no one could tell him what the gong meant. But he was a genuine Srawah and a descendant of the divine cock, and victory was in the marrow of his bones and in his blood.

The coconut sank for the second time. The gong sounded. The cock stood erect a moment longer and then, amid laughter and applause, flapped his wings and uttered a loud victorious crow, followed by the gurgle which only the best cocks can boast.

Ida Katut gave a sidelong and rather sorrowful look at his dead bird, and then pulled the twenty-five ringits he had lost to the prince from his girdle with many farcical groans and laid them at his master's feet. The lord laughed. He no longer looked at Pak's cock. Pak took up his ten ringits, feeling sorry now he had not wagered fifty. He picked up the dead cock by the legs and lifted up his own with care. The Srawah had sat down after his crow of victory, and was now bleeding faster. The next fight was on as Pak went away followed by shouts of congratulation from a few of his Taman Sari friends.

"I ought to have let him fight the punggawa's cock after all," he said to his father.

"That is so," said the old man.

Pak felt the cock's heart beating against his finger-tips and he loved him greatly. The courageous and excited little heart grew slowly calmer. The old man took hold of him, looked at the wound and tried to stanch the bleeding. Pak was rent to the heart, as he had not been since little Siang's sickness. His cock came next after his children. "Cock, my beautiful brother," he whispered to him, "you fought well and you are the bravest and strongest of them all. You won and you will win again. And you shall have the rice cake I promised you."

He stopped at one of the vendors' and bought one of her rice cakes for two kepengs, baked with oil and palm sugar. He and his father bathed the wound in the stream, put the cock in the hamper and carried him home.

The old man made an ointment of cow dung and the wound healed in three days. Pak buried his ringits. He was happy and could scarcely wait for the next cock-fight. There was some to-do with the women over the dead and conquered cock, for they wanted to cook him and make a fine dish of him; but Pak insisted on cutting him up, muscle and bone and valiant little heart as food for his own Srawah, so that he might acquire the strength of this good cock whom he had conquered. And the Srawah danced and leapt in his cage whenever he caught sight of Pak, so fond was he of his master. Moreover, Pak heard later that the punggawa's speckled cock was defeated by a red cock of the lord's and slain, and again he thought: I ought to have let him fight.

From now on, Pak went to every cock-fight in the district, even as far as Kuta and Badung. The wild excitement and joy and pride of these fights became part and parcel of his life, and a temptation he could not resist. Although before this Puglug had always grumbled over the cocks, both to herself and out loud, she was polite and even amiable to this one. For not a fight went by without Pak's coming home with money in his girdle, and his courage rose with every victory, and he staked and won larger and larger sums. The cock became such a pet in the family that Pak and his father had to keep a sharp look-out to prevent the women and the children giving him grains of rice on the sly, which would have made him soft and pampered.

With a good harvest, three sons in the family, money under his floor, his joy in his cock and general good fortune and prosperity, Pak's life would have been crowned with complete content, but for the ever new requisitions levied by Badung on the people of Taman Sari—not on all of them, but on those who belonged to the puri and were in a sense serfs of the lord of Badung. In ordinary times this serfage was hardly noticeable, but now the Dutch ships lay in the roadstead and the foreigner's cannon stood on the beach and the rumour of a war with the Dutch daily gained ground.

Pak was a serf. His father in his youth had been a servant in the puri of Pametjutan. That was how he had got the two western sawahs. Pak himself had had occasional service to render to the lord of Badung as porter, for which he had been almost too liberally rewarded with the two eastern sawahs. When he surrendered his sister to the puri he had been given the new sawahs. Nevertheless, he always had that bitter taste in his gullet whenever he was reminded of the lord; for Meru his brother went about, a blind man with a stick, and Pak was the serf of the man who had had his eyes put out. So now when officials from Badung came and armed the men of Taman Sari who belonged to the puri, with krisses, lances and rifles, Pak, though he could not refuse to receive the weapons, felt no inclination to fight. He was a peasant of low caste and not a warrior of the caste of the Ksatrias. It is true he had wished for a kris all his life and he wore it for show at the cockfights; but he put the lance away in the balé where all his other implements were stored. The rifle, in the use of which two of Molog's soldiers instructed him, he handed up again, after thinking it over, to the punggawa.

"Highness," he said, "I am a simple man and it seems to me that evil spirits and demons are concealed in this thing. I have small children in my household and I am afraid this rifle might kill them without anyone touching it and—as I am told—even from a distance. If there is war with the white men and my lord calls on me I can always come and get it."

The punggawa smiled instead of being angry. As Pak was not the only one who looked askance at these newfangled weapons, many other rifles were handed up and were stacked in an empty rice barn in the punggawa's yard.

It frequently happened, however, that Pak was summoned to Badung to undertake various tasks and he grumbled under his breath. He labored on his sawahs and gave half the yield to his lord. Half of his sweat and his labors and the ache in his thighs and back were for the raja's benefit. "It is not right that he should call us away from the fields as well to mend his walls and dig his ditches," Pak said, and all the men of the villages throughout the country said the same. The truth was that the puri of Badung had for years been relapsing into a state of splendid decay, as had all the other puris of Bali, with great holes in the ground into which people stumbled at night, broken-down steps, gaps in the outer walls, roof-timbers eaten away by ants and sun-dried bricks crumbling into dust; and now it was being repaired under Dewa Gdé Molog's sharp eye. Scarcely had Pak finished one bout of these wearisome labors and got back to his fields when he was again ordered back to Badung.

This time it was not so bad. He came home pleased and excited. But as usual Puglug knew all about it without his needing to open his mouth. "Shall I never in my life be allowed to have any news to tell?" he said with annoyance. "I have been ordered to lead two pack-horses when the lord goes to Tabanan."

Puglug, who was only waiting to take the words out of his mouth, now broke in volubly, "On the second Wednesday of this month there is to be the burning of the body of the father of the present Raja of Tabanan and the preparations have been going on for the last three months. They say at the market it will be the most splendid cremation ever seen in this part of the island for ten years past. Thirty-three thousand ringits are being spent on it, and I should dearly like to go and take Rantun and Madé. with me, for they will never again in their whole life have the chance of seeing such a splendid sight, I dare say."

"Thirty-three thousand kepengs?" Pak asked.

"Ringits, ringits—thirty-three thousand ringits," Puglug said. "There will be guests from all the puris, but no white men, as there were at the last cremation of a lord at Karang Asem, for there is enmity between the Dutch and the lords of Tabanan. The white soldiers have made a camp at Ketewel, so perhaps on second thought it will be better not to go to Tabanan with my daughters, in case of war."

"The lord of Tabanan has not invited you," Pak said, for his tongue had become nearly as sharp as Rib's. His father chuckled to himself. "How many of the old raja's wives are going to be burnt?" he asked, spitting out his betel juice.

"None. It is old-fashioned and not done any more, father," Puglug said. "But there will be six separate gamelans playing and dances all day long and a big cockfight the day before. There will be enough to see if one had six eyes in one's head instead of two."

"Some people talk as though they had six tongues in their heads instead of one," Pak said pointedly. It was only when he had released this barb that the meaning of Puglug's words reached him. "A cock-fight—at Tabanan?" he asked thoughtfully.

"You had better ask cleverer people than me," Puglug said, affronted, and went off with her water-jar on her head and little Tanah on her hip.

Pak's father, with increasing age, had acquired the habit of falling into a silent abstraction, from which he unexpectedly emerged with all his wits surprisingly about him.

"What is there old-fashioned about wives being burned with their husbands so that they may enter the heaven of Shiva at the same time as he?" he asked briskly. "When the father of the lord of Pametjutan was burned, twenty-six of his wives went with him, two of his half-brothers and several of his courtiers. It was a very fine burning."

Pak was not listening; he was lost in thought. "Lantjar," he said to his younger brother, "you shall come with me when I go to Tabanan, you can carry the cock."

"What will you bring me back if your cock wins?" asked Sarna, who was sitting on her heels not far away. She giggled and gave Pak an alluring look out of the corner of her eye, for she was not aware herself how fat she had grown, but Pak was, and also that she had a disfigured lobe to her ear.

"Five kepengs' worth of pegnut medicine," he replied pointedly, and Dasni, Meru's wife, laughed out loud, for it was well known that pegnut medicine was for hot blood.

"You sometimes talk as though you had forgotten that I might have married a raja," Sarna said to Pak. As she said this the old man once more joined in the conversation. "The old Raja of Tabanan was a great lord," he said. "It would be a scandal if he were burnt without his wives and I do not believe it will happen."

When Pak arrived at Tabanan with the baggage-train of the lord of Badung he marvelled yet again over the way his father always knew everything beforehand and was always right. As he squatted near a sirih seller he overheard people saying that three of the favorite wives of the dead raja had expressed their desire to be burned with him. He gave only half his mind to it, for on the other side of him there was talk about the cock-fight for the following day. "Last time the Raja of Kloengkoeng won over four hundred ringits," said a tall man who had squatted beside him to buy cooked rice. "He is expected early tomorrow morning and he is bringing his cocks with him, for it is going to be a great cock-fight."

"The Raja of Bali has the best cocks in South Bali," Pak said proudly. "He has brought twelve cocks and not a single one of them has ever had so much as a scratch."

"They are not going to let the wives be burned," a young fellow with his mouth full of rice said at Pak's elbow.

"And who is to forbid it?" asked the sirih seller, rolling tobacco in a leaf.

"The Dutch. They don't like wives having themselves burned," a middle-aged man put in, as he squatted down and joined the group.

"The Dutch have nothing to say in Tabanan nor in Kloengkoeng either," the tall man said.

"Do you come from Kloengkoeng, friend?" Pak asked.

"Yes, from Kloengkoeng. And you?" the tall man replied.

"I come from Taman Sari on the coast of Badung," Pak said.

"What is your caste?" the middle-aged man asked. It was the usual question between strangers.

"I am of no caste and the lord has given me some sawahs," Pak said humbly.

"And you?" the old man asked of the tall one.

"I am a smith from Pandjar Pandé," he replied.

"Has the master-smith come for the cock-fighting too?" Pak asked much more politely, for the guild of smiths enjoyed the highest esteem. Their daughters might not marry with any higher caste, but only another smith—so proud were they.

"Yes," the smith said. "I have brought two cocks and I mean to let them fight. And you?"

"I have brought one—a young bird," Pak said with becoming modesty.

"The cremation tower is as tall as a coconut palm," the young fellow said, "and five hundred bearers have been appointed to carry it. I am one of them."

Pak paid seven kepengs for the food he had had and went away in the smith's company. The town was already full of the noble guests and their retinues and though night was drawing on new arrivals kept coming in. The streets were thronged; torches flickered amidst the dimmer light of many oil lamps. Joyful anticipation shone in every eye and much tuak was sold and drunk. Everyone wore his best kain and even Pak wore his kris in his girdle. An immensely tall scaffolding of bamboo rose into the night sky in front of the lord's puri, hung with matting, which concealed the cremation tower. Pak looked up at it with awe; he looked forward to the cremation, even though the cock-fighting next day aroused a keener excitement. The sky was clear and thickly set with stars.

"Where are you spending the night?" the smith asked in a friendly way.

"I have left my brother and my cock in the puri of the gusti Oka," Pak said. "Our raja is staying with him because he's a cousin of his, but the puri is not large and probably we shall have to sleep in the open."

"I should very much like to see your cock," the smith said, and Pak realized that the tall man was one of those to whom cock-fighting was all in all.

"Come along then," he said, feeling flattered.

They made their way through the strange and overcrowded town and arrived at the puri of the gusti Oka, who was an official at the court of Tabanan, and after some difficulty found young Lantjar with the cock in the crowd outside the wall. Many of the porters of the lord of Badung's baggage-train were already asleep on the ground, rolled up in their kains. Big fires had been lighted and many torches were burning to keep away the evil spirits. There was

a smell of smoke and horses and crowded humanity. Here, too, the
men were hemmed in by a crowd of vendors, who had come to
make money from places as far off as Mengul and Badjra. Some of
the men from Badung had brought their cocks with them, for they
could not forgo the pleasure of having a cock-fight of their own.

"There is all the difference between looking on while others eat
and filling your own belly," said the smith, who seemed to be a
well-spoken and sensible man. Pak found his brother by one of the
fires; he was sitting on his heels, sleepy-eyed, and chewing. He had
grown into a good-looking young fellow and the girls were already
beginning to give him sidelong glances. Pak had decked him out in
his own second-best head-dress for this great festivity. The basket
containing the Srawah was behind him in the flickering dusk on
the trodden grass at the foot of the puri wall. Pak was pleased. He
had given him strict orders not to be parted from the cock, for he
had a suspicion that in this strange town, to which crowds had been
drawn for the festival, every other man might be a thief. A cock like
his was more than likely to attract attention and be stolen.

"This is my brother Lantjar," he said to the tall smith, "and here
is my cock."

The man from Bandjar Pandé squatted down at once beside the
basket and inspected the Srawah. The cock was sleepy and distracted
by the smoke and the smell of strangers and the reflected light that
shone in his eyes from the walk of the puri. But as soon as he recognized Pak he began to dance as thought it was broad daylight.

"Could you take him out?" the smith asked. Pak observed with
pride the look of admiration in the face of his new acquaintance as
he put the cock in his hands. The Srawah resented the touch of a
stranger and struggled. The smith laughed. "I'll put my money on
him tomorrow," he said, and he could not have paid him a higher
compliment.

"Your cocks are much better, I am sure of that," Pak replied with
equal politeness.

"Listen," the smith said. "This is no bivouac either for you or your
cock. You come with me to my uncle's house; he is the chief man of
his district and there is plenty of room at his place. You can count
on a mat and a handful of rice for your brother and yourself there
and your cock will be glad of the company of mine."

Pak was just going to accept this tempting offer when terror gripped his heart. Perhaps this smith was one of those very thieves he was afraid of. He was being invited to spend the night in a house he knew nothing of and then when he woke up in the morning his cock would be gone. With a heavy heart he remembered that he was fat from his own village in a strange land, where even the very air had another taste.

"No, we had better stay here," he said almost gruffly. "The overseer might come looking for me."

The smith looked at him with a smile and said, "As you like, friend. Peace on your staying."

"Peace on your sleep," Pak called after him. He regretted his refusal a little. He edged nearer Lantjar, stared a while longer drowsily into the fire, heard the burbled voices and, a little later, the jingling bells of a train of pack-horses passing by and fell asleep.

He was up early next morning, for the kulkul seemed to be beating in every corner of the town. Lantjar rubbed his eyes and wondered where he was when he saw the unfamiliar palace wall and the strange trees above it. Pak first went to the stables in the puri to see to the feeding of the two horses in his charge. He asked one of the servants who were hastening to and fro where you bathed at Tabanan and set off there with Lantjar. He carried the cock himself.

The gamelans were already beginning to play here and there; processions of women, too, could be seen going to the temples with pyramids of offerings on their heads. They found the bathing-place and its little temple, but had to wait their turn, there were so many men there already. When they were clean and refreshed Pak took out the food for the cock from his sirih pouch, mixed it with water and fed the Srawah. He found a grassy place where he put him down to cool his feet and eat his fill of grass, bathed his breast and murmured flattering words in his ear. The cock listened with attention and beat his wings. Pak squatted a long time by the side of the road, for though many men passed by and many admired his bird it seemed to him too early to enter the lists. If the Srawah saw the other cocks he would want to fight at once and his excitement and impatience would only tire him out. He spent nine kepengs on rice and hot roasted nuts for Lantjar and himself and then they went to find a place for themselves.

The first man to greet Pak was the smith. Pak saw at once that he had been wrong in taking the tall man for a thief. The smith was gorgeously dressed and wore a magnificent kris such as only a man of the guild of smiths, whose privilege it had been for centuries to manufacture the sacred weapon, could possess. The smith was shown great honor by all. His uncle, a gray-haired man with the large, bold eyes of a noble, appeared to be a man of importance in Tabanan. Pak felt it was an honor when the smith beckoned to him to take his place beside him. Each looked at the other's birds and Pak found that the smith possessed two excellent cocks, a Buwik and a tailless one.

"It is a pity our cocks cannot fight one another today," the smith said, "but it is not the day for it."

"That is so," Pak agreed. His father had impressed upon him that he had to seek out a red cock or a brown one with yellow neck and that on this day his cock was to fight from the north-west corner.

An enormous crowd of men had collected—one whole side of the balé was occupied solely by lords and their dignitaries. The finest cocks of all Bali were to be seen, for there were lords who had come even from the north to take part as guests in the cremation and they had brought their cocks with them. Not far from the Raja of Badung, Pak observed a fine-looking man with fiery eyes who was talking to the young lord with great animation.

"That is the gusti Nyoman of Buleleng," the smith's uncle said, for he knew most of the nobles by sight.

"Nyoman the traitor," muttered the smith. Pak looked at him with astonishment. The lord of Badung did not seem to be in as good spirits as the other raja. "Is your lord sick?" the uncle asked. "Opium," Pak replied, who had heard this from Puglug. He swallowed. It was extraordinary how he got that bitter taste in his mouth whenever he saw his lord.

This was the proudest and happiest and most deliriously exciting day Pak had ever lived through since his first son was born. His Srawah fought the lord of Badung's red cock —and won.

He scarcely knew himself afterwards how it happened. He had arrogantly refused various matches, which for one reason or another did not appeal to him, and then when the keeper of the lord's cocks held the red one out to him he did not dare say no. He looked at the

Srawah and he saw that he wanted to fight the red one and conquer him. Terror and courage laid hold on him at once. And he accepted combat. It was the same red cock that had killed the punggawa's white one, before whom Pak had beaten a retreat that day. He had been jeered at and mocked. His cock was a good one—as good as any lord's cock. He took on the match and won.

Pak never forgot his excitement as the clamor broke out behind him and the men jumped to their feet and the bets got bigger and it dawned on him that this was the match of the day. When he released his cock for its battle with the lord's, his arteries were so full of throbbing blood that he felt as if his chest would burst. He staked twenty-five ringits himself—a fortune. Thousands of ringits were laid against his cock, money enough to buy a whole kingdom. There stood his Srawah, white with his black down-feathers and he himself was but a man of low caste. Many of the lords of Bali with all their households betted against him—but the smith had put a hundred ringits on the Srawah. When the fight began and the clamor ceased on the instant, Pak felt that his heart had stopped, to beat no more.

There were five rounds in the fight, for neither cock could wound the other. Five times the coconut shell sank and five times the gong went for the next round. Five times Pak carried his cock into the corner, talked to him, bathed him, breathed his strength into him, encouraged and implored him to fight, to conquer, not to leave him in the lurch. The ring was strewn with feathers white and red. Some of the lords jumped down from their platform and crouched on the ground to get a better view. The lord of Badung crouched beside Pak, the peasant, and shouted for excitement. Pak could hear himself shouting too.

In the sixth round the Srawah killed the red cock.

Pak was bathed in sweat when he bore his cock away. He had to be careful not to drop the ringits he had won. He nearly cut himself as he untied the spurs, his hands shook so. His cock's heart beat so violently that he feared he might after all collapse and die of a burst heart, merely from the excitement of the fight and his victory. My cock has beaten the raja's, he told himself. My cock has beaten the raja's, my cock has beaten the raja's. He bought him a rice cake and sat down beside his basket on the grass. My cock has beaten the raja's.

That night he accepted the invitation of the smith of Bandjar Pandé and spent the night at his uncle's house. There was plenty to eat and they sat up late listening to the story-teller the uncle had engaged for the entertainment of his guests. Lantjar's eyes grew round, for he had never heard such wonderful tales. Pak tried to pay attention to them, but his thoughts wandered. My cock has beaten the raja's, he thought. He bent over to Lantjar and said under his breath, "Now we can both have our teeth filed. I have enough money to entertain the whole village."

The smith had brought a fortune back from the fight. He had put a hundred ringits on the Srawah and thirty on his own bird, the tailless one. On the other hand, he had lost twenty-five when his Buwik was killed. Pak could tell that the smith was a very rich man, for he seemed to think less of his winnings than the pleasure of the fight. Sometimes a shadow crossed his face and then Pak knew that he thought of his cock that had been killed and was grieving for the loss of him. Once during the evening, when Pak had already drunk a good deal of rice wine, the smith sat down beside him and said, "You don't want to sell your Srawah?"

"No," Pak said, clear on this one point in spite of the fumes of the wine. He fell into a deep sleep in a balé with bamboo screens round it. The premises were crowded with guests and there was room found for all. The town resounded with dancing and music.

The cremation took place next day. When Pak with his new friend the smith arrived at the puri he saw more people collected than he had ever seen before in one place. The gamelan played without a break. The lofty tower was stripped of its coverings and was a magnificent sight—eleven storeys, all lavishly adorned. Pak had to bend his neck right back to see the top of it. Three smaller towers stood beside it for the wives.

"There is the beast for the burning," the smith said, pointing to the lion which stood beneath a gilded roof carried on pillars covered in red. It was a magnificent cremation beast, gilded and adorned. Balés had been erected outside the wall of the puri and there the noble guests sat waiting, the men in one and the wives in another. Pak craned his head, for it occurred to him that Lambon might be among them, but he could not see her. "My sister is our lord's favorite wife," he confided to the smith. He had quite forgotten this honor that had been done him and it was only the sight of the wives in all their glory that recalled it to him.

"Then it is only right that your cock should beat his," the smith said. "You have won twenty-five ringits from him." "I shall win a lot more," said Pak. He was puffed out with pride. "That was only a beginning."

The smith, as though he had his doubts about the Srawah's future, made no reply to this. Pak looked again at the tower. "There they come," he said impatiently.

A lofty bamboo bridge crossed the wall of the puri to carry the corpse, so that its uncleanness should not contaminate the palace gateway. The bridge rose steeply to the highest storey of the cremation tower. Voices were hushed as the corpse was carried up there and everyone craned his neck. The gamelan droned on solemnly. The bearers ran hither and thither, swarming like bees, brown-legged, with their kains girt up as though for labor on the fields. They were young men, picked for their strength—hundreds of them, it seemed to Pak.

"I don't know whether you can count on your cock winning very often," the smith said. "Every fight costs him a lot. He spent much of his strength yesterday. Here come the wives."

Pak was rather annoyed that his friend should doubt his Srawah. "My cock has strength enough for fifty fights," he said, and then bent his eyes on the wives. They crossed the bridge and then waited until they could mount their towers, which a whole crowd of bearers were carrying on long poles, a tower to each wife. Pak could not see whether they were beautiful, partly because they were veiled by their long hair and partly because they were surrounded by relations who followed them into the tower. "They are not very beautifully dressed," he said with some disappointment The wives were dressed in white, plain white breast-cloths and white kains, but their hair was unbound, as the princesses wore theirs in old times.

"They are dressed as becomes those who die of their own free will," said an old man who had overheard Pak's remark. "They are no longer young," the smith said. "But still vain all the same," Pak said laughing. Daily life with Puglug and Sarna had ended by teaching him something of women. The white-robed wives had bright combs and mirrors in their hands and were busy combing their hair, to make it as smooth and beautiful as they could before offering themselves up to death.

"It is not my place to advise you," the smith said, resuming the previous topic, when the towers had formed up in single file and little more was to be seen of the women in them, "but it might be as well to sell your cock before he begins to lose."

Pak nearly lost his temper, but instead he laughed. "Do you want to buy him?" he asked right out.

The smith looked at him as though to say: Not bad for a peasant. "Perhaps," he replied.

"I am not selling him," Pak said. At this moment the tumult of the bearers rose to the highest pitch. Their faces were smeared with soot and lime and they shook their fists to menace the invisible spirits that might bar their way. The swaying towers were raised shoulder-high and then steadied again. "The young Raja of Tabanan is up there with his son," the smith said, pointing up to the top of the high tower. The crowd now surged along behind the funeral procession to the cremation ground. Pak saw little of the procession which preceded the towers. He only heard the shouts of the bearers and the drone of the gamelan music.

But now and then he caught a glimpse of the splendor—lancers, ministers, nobles, women bearing offerings. Even the favorite horse of the dead raja was there too. Pak could hardly breathe for the pressure of those behind. The road was a solid mass of people winding on, head by head, like the scales of a brightly-colored snake. "It is not far," the smith said to comfort him. Pak laughed back. No more was said about the cock. As they drew nearer to the cremation ground they felt the heat beat in their faces and from time to time their eyes watered and they coughed with the smoke.

"We shall be best up here," the old man, who belonged apparently to Tabanan, said. They followed him up a narrow slippery path and from the top they could, as he had said, see the whole scene. "Why is the fire alight already? The beast has not arrived yet," Pak said. There was a pit surrounded on all four sides by a wall above which flames leapt up and it was from these that the heat and smoke came.

"For the wives," the old man said. "Here comes the beast, too."

A bamboo bridge hung high above the flames, protected from the fire on the underside by green leaves. Pak found it all he could do to stand fast on the slippery ground with the crowd surging behind him. The smith put his arm round his shoulders and in that way they held their ground. Meanwhile, the whole procession arrived below. The pedanda with his tall crown was borne on a chair. A long serpent of richly decorated cloth bound his chair to the lofty tower that followed it.

When the procession came to a halt, the pedanda rose to his feet and taking a long bow shot four arrows to the four points of the compass. He hit the head of the serpent with a flower that fell from an arrow in its flight.

"Suppose I offered you forty ringits for your cock," the smith said. Pak swayed slightly on the edge of the smooth descent and leant close to the tall man's shoulder. Forty ringits was a huge sum. He had never heard of such a sum being given for a cock.

"The cock will bring me in more than forty ringits if I let him fight," he said, drawing in his breath.

"You know best what he is worth to you," the smith said reasonably. Below them, the serpent was now released from the pedanda's throne and wound round the beast which had been borne along in the procession, a large and splendid creature. The smoke from the fire became unendurable. Shouts and laughter arose when the bearers carrying the tall tower turned about and danced backwards and forwards; they turned the great swaying structure round three times to confuse the evil spirits; for they are stupid and can only go straight forward. Then they set the tower down on a bamboo bridge leading down to a roofed platform of earth, on which the lion had already been set down. The relations of the dead raja, his son and grandson, who had accompanied him thus far on the topmost storey of the tower, carried the white-swathed corpse down over the bridge, supported by many men. They all now crowded round the lion, which was opened and made ready to receive the body. The smith shouted something in Pak's ear, but Pak could not hear what he said, for the noise was louder than ever. The fire roared, the burning bamboos crackled loudly, women sang, the gamelan played, the bearers shouted at the tops of their voices and Pak's head was dazed by all the clamor and the smoke. "What did you say?" he shouted back. The smith signed to him that he would wait till the noise died down. The body was now deposited in the lion; the pedanda said a prayer and poured holy water into the beast in torrents. The relations crowded round and offered their gifts to the dead raja. The gamelan stopped playing and the singing, too, ceased. Pak dried his streaming eyes on a corner of his kain.

As there was nothing in particular to see at the moment the smith resumed his discourse. This smith was an obstinate fellow—used to bending iron.

"It is possible you may still win two hundred ringits with your cock—if the gods so will it," he said. "It is also possible he may be killed in the next fight. Then you will be sorry you refused forty ringits for him. Forty ringits would buy you a sawah."

Pak felt uneasy when he heard this. That is so, he thought. If the gods willed, my Srawah might be killed in his next fight. Forty ringits would buy me a sawah. "What heat," he said rather querulously. A fire had now been lighted under the cremation beast and with a loud crackling noise its bluish flames licked the lion, in which the soul of the dead raja was to find release. The clamor broke out afresh as the bearers of the three smaller towers approached and began turning this way and that in the open space. The tops of the towers, on which were the wives and the small escort of relations who bore them company, swayed to and fro. When the spirits had been sufficiently led astray the towers were taken in their turn to the bridge which spanned the square of flame on tall bamboo posts. The wives and their relations descended from the towers and walked to the middle of the bridge where a small shelter resembling a balé was ready to receive them.

"It must be hot there," Pak said.

The old man who had spoken to him before joined in again. "They are the raja's first wife and his two favorite ones among the others," he said. "Four-and-twenty wives he had and only three go with him. Their resolve does them credit."

"What are they doing up there now?" Pak asked him.

"They are waiting for the lion to be burnt up and the raja's soul released so that they will be ready at the right moment to accompany him to heaven."

"Shall we wait any longer?" Pak asked the smith rather impatiently. It was not very pleasant standing there in the mud with the smoke and the jostling of the crowd.

"You don't see such a fine cremation every day," the smith remarked politely to the old man. He, however, in the manner of old men, praised former days at the expense of the present.

"It was better in the old days—three wives are not enough for a great raja," he said.

The red and gold decorations on the lion were black and the beast was a mere skeleton of charred woodwork. Its head toppled off into the fire as men with bamboo poles wound in black and white cloth stirred and poked the blaze.

"My father, too, tells of great cremations with many wives," Pak said politely.

"It is only a silly craze of mine, I know," the smith said, "but your cock takes my fancy. I'll give you fifty ringits for him."

Pak had wavered at the offer of forty, but when he was offered fifty it suddenly occurred to him that the smith was trying to take him in. It came into his head that the cock was worth even more—a hundred, two hundred, any sum. He had beaten the lord's cock, he thought again with an echo of the pride and joy he had felt the day before. No amount of money in the world could buy him this sensation.

"You are rich and I am only a poor man," he said politely, "but I would rather keep my cock."

"Now they are going to jump down," the old man said. The three wives emerged on to the bridge in their white robes. They were giving the last touches to their dresses and their hair, for they wished to look their best when they appeared in heaven. Those behind Pak surged forward, to be pushed back with all his weight. Suddenly the flames shot up, as great jars of oil were poured on to them. Two of the wives stepped to the edge of the bridge, exchanged a smiling glance and put their hands to their hair. Pak observed that each held a dove. They both jumped down at the same moment, and as their bodies fell vertically through the air the doves flew away.

"Mbe!" the old man exclaimed with satisfaction, "there go their souls to heaven to find their happiness."

The third wife had meanwhile stepped to the edge of the bridge. She did not smile and her eyes were closed. The fire roared below and she hesitated for the twinkling of an eye. Then she jumped and the dove flew away. "She was afraid," the old man said contemptuously.

The crowds began to disperse at once. There was a noise like a thunder-clap from the puri and Pak gave a start and gripped the smith's arm. "Cannon," he said with a laugh. "Shall we go now?" Pak said, coughing. The gamelan had struck up again to conduct the guests back to the puri. The relations of the wives had left the bridge and smilingly joined their companions.

"I'll make you a proposal," the smith said when they had joined the crowd on the road which was now streaming back to the puri. "I have taken a fancy to your cock. Yesterday I made a hundred ringits by betting on him. I will give you those hundred ringits for him. Don't be a fool. Give him to me."

Pak hesitated for one second only. "Not for a thousand," he said. Never had his cock been so dear to him as now. The smith gave no sign of his disappointment. He clapped him on the back and laughed and they parted the best of friends, after Pak had gone to fetch the Srawah from the house where he had spent the night.

Next morning they set out on the return journey to Badung, and Pak congratulated himself on having news to tell which for once in a way Puglug did not know already. Towards noon they made a halt at a spring to drink and water the horses. Pak sat by the roadside with Lantjar and took the cock out to give him an airing. The anak Agung Bima, who had chosen Lambon for the puri, came strolling up and stood beside them. Pak folded his hands politely. "Is that the cock that killed our lord and master's red one?" the anak Agung Bima asked.

"It is, your Highness," Pak said with a modest air, although he was puffed up with pride.

"A fine cock," the anak Agung said. He bent down and lifted the bird from the grass with his own hands, ran his fingers through his plumage and felt his weight. The cock crowed, flapped his wings and struggled. The anak Agung held his feet and counted the rings on his middle claw. "A genuine Srawah," he said with awe. Pak nodded. "I have been offered a hundred ringits for him," he said. It was more than he could do to keep it in.

"The lord has taken a fancy to your cock. He does you the honor to accept him," the anak Agung Bima said. He beckoned to a man and gave him the bird to take away.

Pak was left with the empty basket by the side of the road. His gullet was bitter as on the day when the eyes of his brother Meru were put out.

The End

A MOTOR-CAR went at full speed along the Konigsplein in Batavia. The dust swirled up in Boomsmer's face and he took out his handkerchief and held it in front of his face. Nevertheless, it went too slow for him. The gravel of the approach to Government House crunched under the wheels. The white building and its pillared portico glared silently in the sunlight. Boomsmer jumped out and ran up the wide steps. It was cool here on the clean flagstones. Boomsmer looked at his dusty handkerchief, wiped the sweat from his brow and then dusted his shining black shoes. He wondered next what to do with the dirty handkerchief and then, making a ball of it, threw it, after glancing round, into a dark corner beside the steps. Then he went through the folding doors into the vestibule of the Council room.

Van Tilema was standing looking out through the lofty window. "Here you are—at last," he said almost rudely as Boomsmer made his bow. "The others are all in there."

"I have come as fast as a motor-car could bring me, Herr van Tilema," Boomsmer said in an injured tone. "I'm still feeling shaken all to bits." Van Tilema turned on him with a face that showed his ill-humor.

"What is all this we hear, Herr Resident?" he said without offering Boomsmer a seat. "It is incredible—three widows burnt! Three innocent women! We are not in the Middle Ages!"

Boomsmer let his hands fall to his sides. "I felt like having a stroke when Gusti Nyoman told me about it."

"The Governor-General is beside himself," van Tilema went on, pointing at last to a chair. Boomsmer sat down, bending only from the hips. "Appalling that such a thing should happen in a Dutch colony."

"They are still cannibals in Borneo," Boomsmer said in his injured voice. "What can you do with these fools of natives?"

"What you should do is your own affair, Herr Resident," van Tilema said. "It is out of the question for such things to be tolerated. The Government appointed you as Resident of Bali because you were a young man who had grown up with the modern ideas that inspire our colonial policy. The Governor-General was convinced that you would administrate Bali in accordance with his views. And now this happens the moment you have taken up your post! It was the Government's belief that many of our difficulties in Bali were to be imputed to the fact that the worthy Berginck was too slack—owing to his age. But I must say this for him: Nothing of this kind would have happened in his time. Three women burned! Do you understand what that means? Can't you see how the English press would seize on it and trumpet it abroad if it got wind of it!"

Boomsmer pushed out his lower lip. The English could mind their own business, he thought. The English had been rammed down their throats ever since the Boer War. He had had enough of them. Yet when he thought of the widows being burned he felt a sensation of nausea—as though he actually smelled the charred human flesh. It was revolting, cannibalistic and not to be tolerated: in that, he agreed with the Government. His indignation rose as he thought of it. Van Tilema, when he saw how red in the face he was, signed to a servant who was squatting in a corner and the kipas began to fan the air.

"I regret that I was unable to prevent this shocking occurrence, Mynheer van Tilema," Boomsmer said. "I entirely agree with the Government that such doings cannot be tolerated. They not only violate the treaties concluded with South Bali but are in flagrant contradiction with those dictates of humanity endorsed by the Government of the Netherlands. In my opinion it is the last straw."

"Yes—or the spark in the powder cask," van Tilema said.

Boomsmer's heated face cleared. It positively bloomed above the tall collar of his tunic. "His Excellency General Veldte has intimated to me already that action must be taken. I should be overjoyed, van

Tilema, overjoyed! Regrettable as the occasion is, I should welcome it if it meant that we at last employed force to establish our rule over South Bali in accordance with those humane and civilized principles which are constantly being set at naught by these scoundrelly rajas. It is high time," he said, getting up in his excitement and pacing to and fro, "it is high time to vindicate our honor. The Government has endured it too long, far too long."

"You are an idealist. All our younger officials are great idealists," van Tilema said with scarcely perceptible irony. He was a man of taste. He liked good books. He was writing a book himself about Javanese architecture. Tall talk was repugnant to him. "When I joined the service in Bali as a young man we were still all realists. It was impressed on us all that the Government had no money to spare and was out for profit. Copra, harbor dues, imports and exports—in the tradition of the old Company. We were merchants. Now our policy follows a new fashion—ethics, humane views, high principles, the rights of the native population and so forth. I quite agree. I have had quite enough of the rajas and it is high time we taught them a lesson. I could never stand those gentry and their households and satellites. I am all for the simple sudra—the peasant. The real Bali is to be found in the village community and its ancient laws. I believe in guns, as you do, as a means of clearing out the rajas and restoring to the villages the influence they had in the old days. The mere thought of women being roasted alive makes my blood boil. As far as that goes we see eye to eye, Herr Resident."

Boomsmer looked at his watch. "I think it is time we went in," he observed. He felt with disquiet that he was sweating at every pore. It was his pride to appear perfectly cool in any climate. He felt for his handkerchief and then remembered that he no longer had one. As soon as the Commissarius turned away he quickly wiped his brow with the back of his hand. Now his hand was moist and he had to wipe it on the lining of the pocket of his white tunic. Meanwhile, his forehead was perspiring once more. "Pretty hot in Batavia today," he said with a conciliatory smile.

"Think so?" van Tilema said with raised eyebrows as he opened the door.

The Council room was a large and lofty room, now in semi-darkness owing to the drawn curtains. A life-size portrait in oils of the Queen in full regalia hung on the wall. There was a large table surrounded by chairs. The green baize tablecloth had had to be forgone, as the mould of the tropics always ate it away. There was a carafe of water on the table and a large glass jar with a lid containing cigars. Several men were standing about in the room—General Veldte, with a blond, pointed beard, turning gray, and one or two members of the Council of India, of which van Tilema was a member. The new Resident of Bali and Lombok was greeted with varying degrees of disesteem. The General merely gave him a nod, for they had already had a word together on Boomsmer's arrival in Batavia.

"Well, Boomsmer, this is a nice business in your part of the world," Mynheer De Voogt, who had known him from his earliest years, remarked.

"For the last time," Boomsmer replied grimly. The door in the opposite wall was opened by a servant and Arnheim, the Governor-General, entered the room. The Governor was a man of medium height with gray hair and his eyebrows were so close to his vivacious brown eyes that they, too, looked dark. His movements were quick and abrupt and gave the impression that he was always in a hurry to dispose of the matter before him in order to proceed to others of greater importance. He was popular, although he had the reputation of being an autocrat. Perhaps he was, but he always took the responsibility for his decisions and if anything went badly he never put the blame on his subordinates.

The company greeted him respectfully but without ceremony, since the cigars on the table implied that the sitting was not of an official character. Most of them were longing to smoke, but they had waited for the Governor's arrival. Arnheim went quickly to his seat at the head of the table and sat down. The kipas were set in motion. "Good morning, gentlemen," the Governor-General said, looking round in good humor. "Are we all here? Kuiper not here yet? I think we may begin without him. Cigars? Cigarettes?" He started the glass jar, which looked like one of those jars for cheap sweets in a confectionery shop, on its course round the table. "Will anyone have a drink?" he added, making it clear that the members of the Council were there only as guests and not really for a conference.

The Governor-General himself took a cheroot no bigger than a cigarette and began speaking at once.

"I have summoned you, gentlemen," he said, obviously in the best of spirits, "to tell you that the expedition to South Bali is a settled thing. Our troops will be ready to embark on the tenth of September. General Veldte has laid his plan of campaign before me and will be glad to give you all the necessary information. I only wish now to sum up once more the reasons for this decision, every aspect of which has been debated by the Council of India."

The gentlemen smoked and the kipas wafted the hot air from one end of the room to the other. There was an atmosphere of drowsy and relaxed attention such as prevails in a class-room when the master talks and the pupils are not called upon to open their mouths.

"The territories of Badung, Tabanan, Bangli and Klungkung have for years past given us more than sufficient grounds for taking action against them. They have signed treaties which they had made no attempt to carry out. Our protests have received rebellious and contumacious answers. A few days ago the lord of Badung announced his final refusal to pay the sum demanded of him. Tabanan has backed him up and if we do not show our fist we shall have Buleleng up in arms as well one of these fine days. In South Bali things are done that we cannot shut our eyes to. The rajas continue to execute their cruel mockery of justice; they have heads and hands cut off and keep their subjects in dread of tortures which it makes one's hair stand on end even to hear of. In Bangli a man was executed by dragging him over thorns and broken glass until he was dead. In Badung a man's eyes were put out for some trivial offence. You all know what occurred over the wreck of the *Sri Kumala*, and no redress has been made. If the Government has tried again and again to employ peaceable means, the South Balinese owe it principally to Mynheer van Tilema, who has again and again put in a good word for them." The Governor conveyed this official reprimand with a smile; and the Commissarius acknowledged it by rising half-way from his chair. This was merely a by-play, for the two men were fast friends.

"And now," the Governor-General proceeded, raising his voice, "and now there is this horrible, this inconceivably horrible occurrence in Tabanan. Gentlemen, we live in the twentieth century; and in our close proximity, under the sway of our own Dutch Indian Government, innocent women are murdered, slain in the most gruesome and barbarous fashion. This shocking affair, which should never have been allowed to happen, shows us that not a day must be lost in sending our troops to Bali. It is our duty to administer our colonies in such a way that we can look the world in the face with a clear conscience. It is our duty to disseminate Dutch ideas and Dutch progress throughout the island. It is our duty to protect the rights of the natives and at the same time to root out the cruelties and dark superstitions and customs which cause them so much suffering. You will agree with me, gentlemen, when I say that nothing must prevent us from carrying civilization and enlightenment to the colonies which form a part of the great kingdom of the Netherlands."

A murmur of assent went round the table. Boomsmer poured himself out a glass of water. Van Tilema looked at a fly that had settled on the portrait of the Queen. He knew it all already.

"Some will ask whether the cost and the risk to our troops are justified by what we stand to gain," the Governor went on with a quick observant glance round the table. "Well, all I have to say to that is that it is not a matter of gain—not of gain to be reckoned in so many sacks of coffee or rice or in guilders. Our gain is a spiritual, or, if I may so put it, an ideal gain. It is our prestige, the respect shown us by the world at large and an extension of our own power and influence with which we are concerned. It depends on our colonial policy whether we stand on an equal footing with other Powers who also have great colonial possessions." (England again, thought Boomsmer.) "We all know how much needs to be done in the islands for the advance of civilization and enlightenment. Step by step we must further the work of civilization. And our next step must be the complete subjection of Bali."

A murmur of enthusiastic approval greeted this conclusion. The Governor leant back and lit a fresh cheroot from a match held out by his neighbor. He had apparently said all he had to say.

"Your Excellency," van Tilema said when silence had fallen, "I believe I speak for us all in thanking you for your statement. We are all in full agreement with your views and are ready to uphold them in the Council of India. We love the Colonies and we wish to justify our pride in them. As for myself, I have a particular feeling for Bali, which—I freely admit—may perhaps be a trifle sentimental. But for that very reason I will do anything to make a recurrence of the scandalous and horrible events that have occurred in Tabanan impossible."

"My heartiest thanks, Mynheer van Tilema," the Governor said in conclusion of the proceedings. "I knew we should all be of the same opinion, gentlemen."

Before the Governor had time to rise from the table, Boomsmer was on his feet. "Your Excellency, General Veldte, gentlemen," he said hastily, "as Resident of Bali I have one word to say. Deeply as I deplore the inconceivably terrible triple murder at Tabanan, I am almost glad of it since it has tipped the scales in favor of military action. I thank your Excellency for his intention of making Bali a part of the great kingdom of the Netherlands, in spirit and in fact, and if necessary with sword in hand."

He sat down and felt in his pocket, but finding no handkerchief there looked round the table with a rather sheepish smile. The Governor got up and gave him a casual nod. Van Tilema blinked his eyes when he heard the big words that came so easily and unprompted from Boomsmer's mouth whenever he opened it. "You must excuse me, gentlemen, I have to be at Buitenzorg by two," the Governor said, reaching the door before the words were out of his mouth. As soon as he had gone they all began to talk at once as they left the room.

"I'll make a job of it in fourteen days with three battalions," General Veldte said. "I shall take three companies of engineers too, for bridge-building and so on. I'm glad the Governor has put his foot down at last."

"We have native agents in all districts," Boomsmer explained to De Voogt. "And we have detailed reports of the number of arms in the puris. I have made sketch maps of the most important strategic points; they are being printed at the present moment for the use of our officers."

"Well, what do you make of it, Van Tilema?" a short stout councillor asked the Commissarius. "Is this expedition against Bali only a holiday outing? They say the Balinese are dangerous enemies."

Van Tilema shrugged his shoulders. "I am no prophet," he said. The little councillor held him by a gold button of his white tunic.

"I can tell you one thing, Van Tilema," he said. "Those three widows they burnt came in very handily for the Governor. The troops were, practically speaking, already on the march."

"If it had not been this cremation affair, it would have been something else," the Commissarius replied. "Where there's a will there's a way."

It was cool on the broad flight of stone steps. Their voices echoed, though they spoke in undertones. Boomsmer's dirty pocket handkerchief still lay in the corner. He paused, fell behind the others and then quickly bent down and stuffed it into his pocket.

Why should I throw it away? he thought. It is quite good and the dhobi can wash it.

✳   ✳   ✳   ✳   ✳

There, where it entered the sea, the river was broad and level and stagnant and a brackish smell rose from it. When the tide was out there was a sandy marsh between river and sea, with pools that oozed away and bred clouds of gnats. The ground was barren and nothing grew there but harsh grasses and prickly cactus bushes.

Now and then bits of red coral were washed up into the dead river bed; they looked like pieces of raw flesh. No birds sang there and no palms grew and there was no shade.

When Raka and his wife took up their quarters there, they found they had an undesired companion—Bengek, the husky. He had never been a beauty, but now the disease had made him more hideous than ever. Teragia shut her eyes when she first caught sight of him. Yet after a time she grew accustomed to him and when he was in great pain and went to her she comforted him or cooled his hands and feet with bandages of clay. He called her mother and Teragia soon put up with his dependence on her, just as she did with the three starving dogs which had likewise attached themselves to her.

Raka was at first nauseated by Bengek, but it was soon apparent that he was already more at home with the place and the fate to which they were both condemned, and he was serviceable. He had a boat and though his hands were of little use now in pulling in the net or raising the anchor, yet now and again he brought back a fish and shared it with them. The worst they had to endure at the outset was the lack of water, for the stagnant river water was infected with all kinds of sicknesses and fevers. Teragia summoned up her old powers. She was unclean, since she lived with a man who was unclean, and she did not know whether the gods had taken her gift away. But when she paced the ground with closed eyes she was aware of water trickling far below. She told the men to dig for the spring. It was hard work, for Bengek's hands were mere stumps and Raka's fingers hurt him as they contracted more and more. Also the Great Sickness oppressed them with an unremitting weariness. Probably both men would have died of starvation if they had not had the woman with them; for Teragia did not take the sickness and she gave them daily something of her own strength and courage. They dug and found water where Teragia had said. They built two balés, one for themselves and one for Bengek, who up to now had slept on dry twigs like a wild bird. Raka obtained bamboo and wood from his father. Servants of the priest's household brought it to a certain spot and left it there, and Teragia fetched it as soon as they had gone. The spot was some way beyond the last of the Sanur sawahs. The ground was flat and arid and the sea winds swept over it. Nothing but the short harsh sea-shore grass grew there. There was a solitary stone figure belonging to a temple that had long since sunk into the ground—a raksasa, one of the guardians of the temple, whose weathered, lichened face had taken on an evil expression. There, on certain days, rice was left for the outcasts and a little yarn, too, so that Teragia could weave kains for them, and a few other of the barest necessaries of life.

Nevertheless, their hopeless existence had its rays of hope. "I have heard that even those who were sick as we are have sometimes got well again and been taken back into their villages," Bengek said in his husky voice. He still wore flowers he found in the seaside grass behind his ear.

"If the gods will it, we shall get well again," Raka replied. He still could not believe in the fate that had overtaken him. Sometimes he had the hope that one morning he would wake and find himself healed and spotless and leave these days behind him as an evil dream.

"We must build ourselves a house-temple," he said, and Teragia rejoiced that this thought should come to him and fell in with the proposal eagerly. So the two men began to dig up clay and shape bricks which they dried in the sun. They searched for white coral stones on the beach for the walls and drift-wood for the shrine.

They could only work for short spells before they were overcome by fatigue and pain. The building was slow. Teragia helped them and worked as though she was a man herself. It never occurred to Raka that she was a woman. An unloved woman is not a woman. Lambon was lost and came to him only in his dreams at night. Teragia, too, had a lost love of which she never spoke. She was heart-broken for her little son, for Putuh, whom she had forsaken in order to go with Raka. Often they sat long hours together without uttering a word. Raka thought of Lambon and Teragia thought of Putuh.

Bengek dragged a plank from the beach that smelt of decay, and laughed. "A long time ago there was a Chinese ship wrecked near here," he said. "Nobody thinks of it now."

"I remember it," Raka said. He smiled as he thought of the Chinaman he had carried ashore on his back through the surf.

"This is a plank from the ship," Bengek said. "It will do well for the back wall of the shrine."

"We ought to make a garden," Raka said one day. "Palms and fruit trees and hibiscus. And we ought to plant a wairingin tree near the shrine to keep off all the evil spirits that haunt this spot."

They could feel the evil spirits at night even though they were invisible. They were all round the place and made their sleep broken and their dreams heavy and their hearts oppressed. Sometimes mysterious lights flickered to and fro across the river. Teragia contrived to scratch a letter on a piece of bamboo and left it at the foot of the raksasa for the servants to find when they came next with the rice.

"To our father, the pedanda, Ida Bagus Rai of Taman Sari," the letter ran, "We, the outcasts, beg the pedanda to send us seeds and fruits of all fruit trees, but above all cuttings from a wairingin tree, so that we may try to grow them and improve the place where we live. We beg the pedanda's forgiveness for the uncleanness this letter brings into his clean house. Joy and peace to the pedanda, his house and the child in his house."

When Teragia went next time to fetch the rice from the stone image, the letter had gone. A week later, the coconuts, seeds and young shoots Teragia had asked for were there. She waited until the two servants were lost to sight among the rice fields and palm groves that fringed the horizon and then bore off the welcome load. The pedanda had sent no answer to her letter and Teragia ached with longing for her child. Perhaps he is sick, she thought. He will be talking by now. He can walk like a man. When will he ask after his parents?

All three set to work planting and sowing. The ground was barren; the river had deposited all its mud on the sawahs and brought only sand and rubbish as far as this. But with the water Teragia carried from the spring and the ashes of the grass and weeds they dried and burnt and the offerings they made to the gods, the seeds pushed through the soil and the offshoots grew. A little green and shade rose about their balés.

"We will have a sawah too," the men said after a time. Man is a hardy plant; and these men were as tough as the prickly scrub that grew in the sandy soil. They went out and as they had no plough they began turning the soil with their maimed, cramped hands. Sometimes they never spoke a word all day, but at other times Bengek relapsed into his old volubility and asked Raka question after question. It was odd, too, that he still respected the caste of his fellow sufferer. He crouched down before Teragia, and clasped his hands when he spoke to Raka.

"Do you know why this misfortune has befallen you?" he asked while they rested from digging.

"It was the gods' will," Raka replied.

"Why did they will it?" Bengek persisted. "If the gods are just, as they are always said to be, why do they inflict such punishment on a man like you?"

"I make atonement for the guilt of a forefather," Raka said.

"You?" Bengek asked in amazement. "You, Raka?"

"The guilty are punished for seven generations and even longer. Much may have happened in that time. Perhaps one of my forefathers swore a false oath."

The time when he had refused to acknowledge his fate was gone by. Now he bore it.

"Yes, the gods are just," Bengek said. "They afflicted me with the Great Sickness because my mother was a witch."

Raka looked at him with weary surprise for making this open confession. But Bengek was wholly absorbed in what he wanted to say. Probably he had had this load about his neck all his life. Now that he was an outcast he could speak of it—to Raka, who like him was an outcast.

"She was a witch and she sold her descendants to the powers of evil. My life was false and accursed from the beginning. I have lived alone so as not to hand down the curse to children and grand-children. I wanted to leave the country and exile myself to another island where no one would know me. I had money buried under the wall to get me away from my mother, the witch. But she went at night to the cemetery and made offerings and uttered incantations and the evil spirits showed her where my money was hidden. She stole it and though I looked everywhere I could never find it. When I threatened her she laughed at me. One night she changed herself into a ball of fire, I have seen her fly away over the sawahs. She was a witch and I killed her, to prevent her causing still more misfor-tune. I poisoned her with bamboo leaves, and when she was weak I asked her where the money was. I could feel the Great Sickness coming on me and I wanted to give the money to the gods, so that they might relent and turn the affliction from me. But the witch died without telling me where she had hidden it. When she was dead I began searching. Every hand's breadth of ground I turned over, but I did not find it. Then the men came and drove me out. The gods are just, Raka. That is so."

When they had dug the ground, they led water from the river to this sawah of theirs. There were many days when Raka could not walk, for his feet were very sore; his face on the other hand was still beautiful and the least affected of his whole body. Teragia made him wooden crutches—crutches for Raka, the dancer.

"How long will it be before we die, Raka?" Bengek asked as he bent over the soil.

"I do not know," Raka said.

"Are you impatient?" Bengek asked.

It was a strange question and Raka considered it for a long time. "It will be no better for us when we are dead, my friend," he said at last.

"That is the worst of it," Bengek said, "being unclean for ever and ever."

Raka said nothing to this. With difficulty he cut a hollow bamboo to the right length and gave it to Bengek to put in the ground.

"Can we never be born again?" Bengek asked again.

"They who have the Great Sickness may not be burned. How shall their souls be freed?" Raka said. He did not say "we," he still shut his eyes to his fate.

"And is there no remedy?" Bengek asked.

Raka smiled. "There is a story in an old lontar book," he said, "of a king whose brother suffered from the Great Sickness. He was a soldier and came home from a war in which he had been victorious. He was very proud as he entered the puri with many lancers and much glory. But an old woman went up to him and put her arms about his hips as a lover might and all saw that she was a leper. Thus he got the Greak Sickness and was cast out. They built him a balé all by itself in the farthest court of the puri and let him stay there, as he was the brother of the king. When the time came and the king died and was burned, the leper left his balé and leapt into the flames after the king. And his soul was freed and rose to heaven."

Bengek considered this for a long time in silence. "What good is that to you and me, my friend?" he said. "There will be no fire for us to jump into. We have not even got coconut shells to burn in order to cook our food."

Raka looked up and saw Teragia coming. She was tall and lean and her face was seamed with the wrinkles that sorrow and destitution had engraved there. She helped him on to his crutches and led him home. She stood by him and though he had never loved her, her presence was meat and drink to him.

"I will ask your father for seed for the sawah," she would say. "I have woven you a new kain. The wairingin stock is putting out branches. We must make ready special offerings for the New Year festival. You men might make a little gamelan with keys of bamboo." They were lepers, cast out and accursed for all time and beyond, but life went on. Teragia could detect its current in them as she could the trickle of a spring beneath the soil.

She engraved another letter on a piece of bamboo.

"To the pedanda, Ida Bagus Rai, our father.

"Will the pedanda in his goodness send us rice for the men to sow in the sawah they have got ready without plough or lampit, with the labor of their hands? The wairingin stock has taken root. Raka is resigned to his fate. Only my heart is sick and cannot cease thinking of the child in the house of the pedanda, our father. The pedanda will forgive his unclean daughter, Teragia."

Many days passed after this letter was dispatched and nobody appeared over the flat waste of sand near the image of the raksasa. Their food gave out. The two men put out in the boat and exerted themselves to the utmost; but their fingers were too clumsy for the fine arts of fishing and they came back empty-handed. Teragia looked for grubs at the river mouth. She found a few and caught four dragonflies and two butterflies. She cooked them all and gave them to the men with the last grain of rice. Bengek ate eagerly. Raka pushed the leaf towards her with what was left of his meal. She went outside and turned her back and ate thankfully. Two more days went by.

On the third day towards noon Teragia saw a figure come over the flats and sit down beside the raksasa. She put her hand over her eyes and waited for this person to go away again before she went to fetch the food. But the person did not go. When Teragia looked again she could not recognize who it was, but a voice was wafted by the wind over the flat ground and pierced her to the heart. The air was still, for though the waves beat on the shore and the grasshoppers chirped, this was a sound that never ceased and Teragia no longer heard it. What she had heard was the voice of her child.

She got up and went to find Raka, who was sitting near the half-finished house-temple—for though the sick men had courage to start on many things, they lacked strength to finish them. She called out to him, "My brother, our son has come, he is playing beside the raksasa. Let us go nearer so that we may see him."

Raka looked at her in amazement, but he shook his head. "I cannot go, mother," he said. "He must not see my uncleanness. He must know only that his father was Raka, the dancer." Teragia laid her hand on his shoulder to console him before she went.

She ran over the expanse of tufted grass until she was near enough to see the image of the raksasa clearly. The stone demon was sunk in the grass on the far side of the wide river bed and the sun gleamed on the wet sand. Teragia was still far enough away not to hurt the child with her uncleanness and yet near enough to look at him and hear his voice—faintly but recognizably. Again she put her hands over her eyes and squeezed the tears from her eyelids, so as to see clearly.

She saw that the figure beside the raksasa was not, as she had supposed, a servant girl, but the pedanda, Ida Bagus Rai, himself. The cleanest man in Taman Sari had come to this foulest spot to bring comfort to her heart. Putuh, her son, stood between his knees.

Teragia crouched down on the river-bank and looked across at the child. He did not see her and the pedanda made no attempt to point her out to him. He made no sign of having seen her and he did not call out to her. He merely sat there talking to the boy. The boy was strong and naked. His head was shorn and the lock on his forehead cut. He wore anklets and bracelets and a little metal casket round his neck to protect him from evil spirits. Teragia herself had put his navel cord in it and tied the little box round his neck. That was long ago, Teragia thought. He could run about now and he talked and babbled eagerly to his grandfather. He fell down when he ran after a butterfly, but he did not cry. That is Putuh, my little son, my princeling, my beautiful little bud, Teragia thought. Her eyes were glad and her heart drank healing in.

She sat on one side of the broad river-bed and the priest sat on the other. His hair was combed straight back and adorned with flowers. It had gone white. When the sun began to sink he got up, put the child on his hip and disappeared along the way that led to the rice fields, the palm groves and the world of men.

*   *   *   *   *

The orderlies let the champagne corks go with a pop and a few of the ladies screamed as if they were being tickled. The farewell committee in white lace dresses with puff sleeves and large low-crowned hats were red in the face with excitement. The embarkation of the troops was an event to celebrate. The orderlies filled the glasses with a practised hand acquired in the military casino at Surabaya. The ladies raised their glasses and after sipping them offered them to the officers. The bands of both battalions were playing, that of the 11th below on the pier and the 18th's on the deck of the *Van Swoll*. Lieutenant Dekker, in his new blue uniform, took his wineglass from the hand of a girl in pink. She had a garland of moss-roses on her wide-brimmed hat of yellow straw with a long ribbon of black velvet hanging down behind. Lieutenant Dekker did not know her name, for he had only just reached Surabaya from Holland; but she seemed to him, owing perhaps to an unusual exaltation of his spirits caused by the farewell party, to be a girl of exceptional beauty and charm. The girl took a bunch of flowers from her black velvet waist-band and stuck it firmly in his shoulder-strap. Lieutenant Dekker bent down to enable her to reach up without having to stretch. He wondered whether officers who were going on active service were justified in stealing a kiss when they wished to so much as he did. He took the girl's hand with the idea of leading her to a quieter corner of the deck. But there was no such corner. There was not a quiet corner in all *Marinelaan*. Not only were the two bands playing at once— one the "Gladiators' March" and the other the *Oranje* anthem—but two speeches were also being made at the same time, one below on the pier, where the troops were drawn up in a square, listening with set faces to a company commander who was addressing them on the eve of their departure, and the other on the deck of the transport where the lady president of the committee was in full cry.

"For the welfare of our colonies . . . you go to the war in the cause of the Netherlands . . . to fight for law and order—not to lay down your arms until. . . the rebellious enemy must be chastened . . . your good rifles . . ." The officer had a fine commanding voice, but in the general hubbub only scraps could be heard.

Above, the president of the committee made a carefully composed farewell speech which she had committed to memory days before, after many fair copies had been written out. Shrill and yet shy, grilling in her tight corset, a champagne glass in her gloved hand, she stumbled through the greatest moment of her monotonous colonial existence.

". . . when you come back victorious . . . your mothers will be proud of you . . . no danger will deter you from chastising the enemy . . . every woman and girl of Surabaya wishes you a glorious victory . . ."

"Hip-hip hurrah!" burst from the ranks with amazing precision. They were strong, hardy-looking fellows, mostly fair-haired, wearing wide-awake, turned-up straw hats, whose brims could also at a pinch be turned down. Their blue uniforms were clean and their buttons shone. Part of the native troops, Javanese and Ambanese, had already embarked at Tandjon Priok. The *Van Swoll* was for the officers and men of the 18th Battalion and the engineers. She was not really a warship, but one of the mail-boats which were taking part in the transport of the expeditionary force.

"And when do you expect to be back again?" the girl of the moss roses asked.

"In two or three weeks," Dekker replied. "May I write to you perhaps in the meanwhile?" he added with a beating heart.

"That would be delightful—but are there post-offices in Bali?"

"All that will be arranged, of course," Dekker said proudly. He felt that he was marvellously fitted to play his part in a campaign, and absolutely in his proper place. "I am jolly lucky to see active service the moment I come out," he said enthusiastically.

"Yes—but it is a pity I got to know you today," the moss-roses remarked. "Now I shall worry about you."

"Not really?" Dekker exclaimed delightedly. "Then I shall have to write to you every day. May I?"

"You don't even know my address."

"No—but I know your name—Brigit—"

"Brigit what?"

"That I confess I don't know. But I heard your mother call you Brigit."

The band was playing "William of Nassau." The men clattered on and on up the gangway and vanished below. Farther out in the roadstead lay the smaller vessels; and natives, impressed for road-making and porterage, were being rowed out to them. They were singing uproariously. The laughter and talk on board the *Van Swoll* became deafening. The champagne, the heat of the afternoon sun, the music, the speeches and the war-like elation proper to the occasion all went to the officers' heads. Fathers, colonels with paunches, tightly buttoned into their service uniforms, were embraced by wives and children. Javanese girls craned their heads through the grating of the *Marinelaan* for a last glimpse of their Dutch sweethearts. A few of the soldiers below were drunk and, poking their shaven heads out of the portholes, they shouted unintelligible ribaldries across to the quay. Cheers were raised, officially and spontaneously, for Queen Wilhelmina.

"And you must stop the Balinese being wreckers and burning women," Brigit said to Lieutenant Dekker.

"We'll make short work of them, you can count on that," he assured her. She looked at him with admiration. Every woman looked at every man with admiration. They were heroes and they wore smart, new blue uniforms. Every woman was a beauty in the men's eyes—for they were leaving them for the great adventure of war.

"And do us honor over there among the savages," said the president of the committee, who was overcome by all the champagne she had drunk in the flush of patriotism. "All ashore, all ashore," the N.C.O. called out as he made his round of the ship, followed by two trumpeters.

"And when I come back?" Lieutenant Dekker asked breathlessly.

"I shall be there—down there beside the lamp—waiting," Brigit said.

At the last moment he took courage and kissed her after all. It was a thoroughly incompetent kiss, the kiss of a beginner, which alighted on her cheek instead of her lips. Nevertheless, Brigit made a great deal of it and closed her eyes as though she was going to faint. Dekker suddenly felt that his uniform was too tight for him in all directions. The last he saw of Brigit was her slightly crushed puff-sleeves, as she followed her mother down the gangway. The two bands now played turn by turn, now the one on deck and now the one below on the quay. The cable was let go—to the accompaniment of such wavings and shoutings and weeping and laughter that there could scarcely have been a single inhabitant of Surabaya left at home. The *Van Swoll* swung slowly, very slowly, from its berth on the *Marinelaan* into the bay where the other ships lay one behind the other. Two torpedo boats escorted the transports that were leaving Surabaya that evening. The flagship, the *Wilhelmina*, was already at Buleleng. The *Both* and the *Bromo* had sailed that morning. It was now after four o'clock, and as soon as they left the harbor and stood out to sea a light breeze sprang up. But the sea was calm and as smooth as oil as far as the eye could see.

Lieutenant Dekker stood at the taffrail until the quay became a tiny streak and then vanished from sight. The sun was level with the water in a sparkling track of flame. The band stopped playing, but occasionally there was wafted from the shore the tum-tum-tum accompaniment which was all that could still be heard of a military march. Life was glorious. Lieutenant Dekker, twenty-five years old, champagne within and the campaign before, felt like the hero of a novel. When night abruptly came down he retired to his cabin.

It was very small, with two bunks one above the other. His servant had carried down his small case, to which his water-bottle and sword-belt and other articles of his equipment were strapped. It had a warlike air. A lean man, enterprising, with a resolute nose and spectacles that seemed out of place on it, was already in the cabin.

"I am Pastor Schimmelpennick," he said. "Do you mind if I take the bottom bunk? I'm not a very good sailor."

The lieutenant looked at his cabin companion and saw the chaplain's badge on his open uniform collar. "I much prefer the top one—to escape the cockroaches," he said amiably. The pastor was white in the face, but he smiled bravely. Dekker was a little disappointed at having a pastor foisted on him instead of being with a fellow-officer. He was the youngest officer in his battalion and little acquainted with the others. He found many of the older officers very underbred, but they made a great deal of their experience in colonial warfare. They wore long beards and Dekker thought this unsuitable in officers, and it made them look older than they were. Many were pot-bellied from drinking too much beer during a long period of peaceful garrison life.

Dekker himself was slim and he had a small, turned-up moustache, of which he was all the more proud because he had only recently acquired it.

He rummaged about in his small trunk and pulled out a little book that every officer had been given; it contained information about the strange island they were bound for. He then went on deck. The sea still looked smooth but the ship had begun to roll. Dekker sat down near a lamp in the saloon and began to read. "The Balinese is cruel and cunning in spite of his apparently gentle disposition." Beer and cards were already in full swing at the far end of the saloon. At another table there was a party of officers swopping stories. After a time Dekker grew restless and went out on deck. Black velvet on her hat and round her waist. What charming taste she showed! Three other ships with their chains of light preceded the *Van Swoll*, all bound for adventure. The soldiers sang between decks. The two torpedo boats, which had accompanied the flotilla so far, now fell back. Suddenly there was a report like the sound of guns; but it was only rockets discharged from the torpedo boats as a farewell salute. They were red and green and their reflections in the water were like long brightly colored snakes. Dekker was moved; it was glorious to be facing danger.

"... and promise me to beware of bad water," his mother had written from Enschedé. "Uncle Pieter says you must always wear flannel round your stomach at nights, the tropics are treacherous ..."

More rockets. "For the soldier's life is free—" the men sang below. Brigit de Haan, 43 Kaliasin, Surabaya.

The pastor was asleep when Dekker climbed into his bunk. There were no blackbeetles up there but plenty of ants. In the morning when he looked through the porthole the coast of Bali was in sight. It looked much the same as the coast of Java.

＊　　　＊　　　＊　　　＊　　　＊

The shore was crowded with people who were all intent on watching the eleven warships drop anchor off the coast of Sanur. It was high tide and the waves ran high. Sometimes a gigantic green wave rolled in and hid the ships with its white foam. Women, children and grandfathers had all left their villages so as to miss nothing. They squatted on the sand, the elders chewing sirih and the children smoking cigarettes or sucking sugar-cane. They were all afraid, but curiosity won the day. Sarda, the fisherman, who had good eyes, counted the guns that stared at the land from the decks of the two great gray ships. "I can see four on each," he announced. "They look out of their holes like dung-beetles."

"They have twelve in the puri of Badung," Krkek said thoughtfully.

"Will they shoot?" a woman asked as she drew her shawl anxiously over the baby sucking at her breast.

"Why should they shoot?" Krkek said. "They will not shoot at us. We are only peasants and have nothing to do with them. Badung town is far away and those big ships cannot get to land. If the white soldiers had any sense they would have little prahus instead of ships that look like elephants and cannot come inshore."

"What do you think they will do?" Pak asked his father. The old man sat on his heels on the beach, chewing and shading his eyes with his hand, for they could not see into the distance.

"I do not know, my son," he said, after taking time for reflection. Pak was disconcerted. It was the first time the old man had had no answer to give.

"Have ships like this never come before to fight against the lord of Badung?" Pak asked.

"Never to Sanur," his father replied. "When I was a child they came to Buleleng and many people died."

A circle gathered round the old man to hear what he said. "We peasants have no quarrel with the white men," Krkek said. "No one will die on our coast." The rice had to be planted in many sawahs, the sharing out of the water was all arranged, and if all was not done to the day and hour confusion would follow. Krkek, the head of the subak, wanted peace and order in his district. "There is no use in sitting here, staring at the foreigners' ships," he warned them. "The chief thing is not to get behind with the work on the land."

"What are we to do in the fields now?" Rib asked disrespectfully. "The sun is retiring to its house and it is evening."

"There are flags of red and white and blue on every ship," Sarda announced, still giving the rest the benefit of his keen sight.

"What can that mean?" some of the others asked.

Pak's father gave his mind to the problem. "They mean to say that they honor our gods," he said at last. "White for Shiva, blue for Vishnu and red for Bramah."

Pak was proud of the old man and most of them accepted his explanation with respectful attention. Others laughed. A few vendors had appeared on the beach, mostly hard-working women such as Puglug and Dasni. But the men were too excited to squat down by them and eat rice. "Here comes the punggawa," Krkek said, and they all turned their eyes on the road that led from the village to the shore.

The punggawa was accompanied by several servants, including his umbrella-carrier, and the people crouched down respectfully with folded hands to greet him. What surprised them was that one of his servants walked in front of the punggawa waving a piece of white cloth from a bamboo pole. "Is there some magic in the white flag?" the women asked in whispers. Krkek gave the explanation.

"No," he said. "It is a sign that we mean peace."

"That is so," was murmured on all sides. They felt much consoled now that the punggawa was among them, bearing the flag of peace.

After the punggawa's servant had gone far out on the wet sand waving the white flag, a boat put out from the largest of the ships. The men all crowded to the spot it was seen to be making for. A white flag was flown from the bow of the boat, too.

Some fishermen helped to beach the boat when it reached the shore. The rest of the men squatted respectfully in a long row on the beach with their wives and children behind them. Some of them recognized the man who got out of the boat and went up to the punggawa. He was no Dutchman but the gusti Nyoman of Buleleng. Nor were the crew that rowed him ashore Dutch but Javanese in uniforms, which in spite of their dark skins made them look like Dutchmen.

After the punggawa had greeted the gusti and exchanged a few words with him, something unexpected occurred: the punggawa, without servants or umbrella, stepped into the strange boat. The gusti sat down beside him, one of the Javanese gave orders and the boat was pushed off. Soon they saw it rising and falling among the breakers, whose force had now diminished, and reaching the big ship.

"What is the meaning of that?" Pak asked in dismay. "Have they taken our punggawa prisoner?"

"We must stay here and see what happens," Krkek said.

They all squatted down again and the whole shore was fringed with a long line of men, silently waiting. Now, too, a few went to buy sirih or food and the vendors made a few kepengs. It got cooler and quite dark. The Great Mountain far away held the light longest and then it, too, vanished from sight. The ships were now lighted up. Some boys of the villages brought maize straw from the fields and made a fire. No one thought of going home.

It was pitch-dark when the boat returned and brought them back their punggawa. All the men crowded up to pull in the boat and help him ashore. He went to the fire and they saw that his face looked serious.

"People," he said, "it will be best if you go to your homes now. Nothing will happen to you if you do as I say. I am riding at once to Badung to carry an important letter to the lord. When I return I will tell you what you are to do next. I warn you not to do anything to rouse the anger of the Dutchmen, for they are strong and have many guns. Now go home, and peace on your sleep."

The people dispersed quickly, murmuring in low voices. They were in haste to reach their homes, for it was dark and some, such as those who came from Taman Sari and Renon, had a good distance to go.

"What does it all mean?" Pak again asked his father. Suddenly the land in which they dwelled had become strange and eerie. No one knew whether offerings ought to be made, or of what kind, to ward off an evil they felt was in the air, but of which they knew too little to be able to say in what shape it would descend upon them.

"The punggawa is right," the old man said. "It is as on the day of Njepi when heaven is cleansed and all the demons come down to earth. Then, we, too, stay in our houses and whoever ventures into the streets is punished. It is like that now. If the Dutchmen come to our villages and find the streets empty they will go back to their ships as the demons have always gone, thinking there were no people in Bali."

Pak found this enlightening. They finished their journey in silence. They left the oil lamp burning all night, but nothing untoward occurred, although the people of Taman Sari often waked and listened. It was a night like any other: the dogs barked and the cicadas were loud.

Early next morning the kulkuls beat an urgent and persistent summons. Pak hurried to the town hall without even going first to bathe. The wide village street was full of men hurrying through the half light, winding on their headdresses as they went and making brief remarks. When they reached the village hall they found the street and the grass in front of it, where usually the cocks were paraded, crowded with lancers on horseback. They recognized the Dewa Gdé Molog, the captain of the lord's warriors. The horses neighed and bit each other, and the dust rose in clouds as they pawed the ground. Molog came forward to the edge of the large balé, and the people of Taman Sari crouched down reverently almost under the horses' hooves.

"Men of Taman Sari," Molog shouted in his powerful voice, "the lord of Badung has sent me to make it known to you that the Dutch mean to invade our country. You are called upon to give your last drop of blood in its defence. All the men of this village who live on the rice of our lord and master have been given weapons and instructed in the use of them. Use them now against the enemy as our honor and safety demand."

The men were as still as death when they heard this. The Dewa Molog took a kris in its scabbard from the hands of one of his warriors and held it aloft. Then he drew the weapon from the scabbard and pointed it to the four quarters of the sky. It was Singa Braga, the Sacred Kris of the Lion and the Snake. Not a sound was to be heard but the barking of the village dogs.

"This is the proclamation of the lord, your master: Follow the Sacred Kris and defend your country," Molog cried. He pushed the sword back into the scabbard. Then he cleared his throat, for he had over-strained it during his ride from village to village, proclaiming everywhere the call to battle. The men of Taman Sari maintained their embarrassed silence. They were still squatting there when Molog and his mounted men had vanished in a cloud of dust on their way to Sanur.

"Where is the punggawa?" some of them asked at length. "He must decide what we ought to do."

When they came to the punggawa's house in Sanur they found that he had not yet returned from the puri, and also that Molog had left a strong detachment of warriors armed with lances, krisses and rifles posted in the palm grove behind the punggawa's house. The men were uncertain whether to feel that this was a protection or a menace.

They stood about irresolutely for a time, not knowing what to do next. The punggawa had told them to keep within doors, but they felt safer when they were all together. No one thought of going to their sawahs that morning. Finally, Krkek and a few other of the more level-headed men of the village called a meeting of the council and they all returned to the village hall of Taman Sari, the great balé with its two-tiered roof supported on posts, where they had always so far solved all difficulties that threatened the village.

There was a brief discussion in the laconic style of peasants confronted by an unexpected problem. The wealthy Wajan was in favor of abandoning the village and going into hiding if the Dutch invaded the country.

"Hide where?" Rib asked, with a flicker of his customary frivolity. "We are not squirrels, to creep into coconuts."

Pak had the extraordinary sensation of thin cords being strained round his chest. Krkek in his sensible way finally summed up what was in all their minds. "What concern of ours is a war between our lord and the Dutch?" he said. "We do not want a war and fighting is not our business. What are the people of Badung to eat if the peasants go to war instead of growing rice? The plough is more important than the kris."

"That is so," the men agreed.

Pak had something to add to this. "If the Dutch offer violence to our women or injure our children, then we will fight; but if they only march through our village on their way to Badung, then we will stay in our houses and not stir," he said out of the oppression of his heart. The raja put my brother's eyes out, he took my best cock away from me: I will not fight for him, he thought dumbly.

"We'll fight like armadilloes," Rib said, and the assembly dissolved in a fit of laughter. Poke an armadillo with a bamboo pole and he will roll himself up and sham dead: you may step on him and roll him over and he will not care.

At noon the kulkul beat again and the men hastened to the house of the punggawa at Sanur, whither it summoned them. They now all had krisses stuck in their girdles and no children were to be seen in the village street. They crowded into the courtyard and crouched there with clasped hands; there were so many of them that they could not all find room and there was a dense crowd outside the gate, too. The punggawa looked tired, and the state with which he usually made his public appearances seemed to have wilted during the night.

"Men of Badung," he said, "I will now tell you all that has occurred. I was yesterday on the ship which carries the great lords and rajas of the Dutch and I spoke with them. They mean no evil. They love you and will take you under their protection. Their quarrel is only with the lord of Badung. They gave me a letter to him and I took it to Badung. In the letter they offered him peace for the last time and demanded his submission. I spent the whole night in discussion with the lord and his counsellors. The old tjokorda of Pametjutan was also present and the pedanda, Ida Bagus Rai, the holy man, to whose advice the lord listens. The lord refused to submit.

"Men of Badung, I am now going on board the ship of the white men to take them this answer. Then they will land and make war." The punggawa looked from one to another of the men who were immediately in front of him. Their faces had that sleepy expression which they took on only in moments of the closest and most anxious attention.

"This war," the punggawa went on, "will be worse than anything you can imagine and many will be killed. Is it your wish that I tell the Dutch that the five villages of the coast desire to be at peace with them?"

At first there was silence, and then a murmur, and finally an old man, the head man of the village council of Sanur, spoke up: "It shall be as the punggawa has said—that we desire to be at peace with the Dutch. But, master, there are many men in the five villages who belong to the puri and eat the lord's rice. These men are in duty bound to fight for him. What shall they do?"

"That," the punggawa answered, "is for each man to decide for himself. I hold no man back who wishes to fight for his lord. I myself shall hang a white flag before my house and whoever is afraid of the Dutch can come into my courtyard and be safe. Those who mean to fight have nothing to do with me; they must join the warriors of Molog, the captain, and put themselves under his protection. And now I advise you to go to your fields. If the Dutch find you peaceably at work they will do you no harm."

With this the punggawa turned about and went into the house without waiting to hear what the men had to say to it. They hung about for awhile in the road in front of the house, and then dispersed and slowly made their way home.

"What shall you do, Pak?" Sarda, the fisherman, asked, as they reached the outskirts of Sanur where their ways parted.

"I don't know yet. I must ask my father," Pak said. He was utterly worn out and dazed by all the talking that had gone on that day.

"My family has been given three sawahs by the lord," Sarda said. "I can hardly do otherwise than take my lance and go to Molog."

Pak looked at the fisherman in amazement—Sarda, his friend, who had helped him to carry off Sarna; Sarda, with whom he had often drunk palm wine, who sat side-by-side with him when they played in the gamelan, and who took one end of the pole when they carried the gong—Sarda meant to fight and Pak did not. He put his hand on his shoulder before they parted. He did not know what to say.

When he got home he squatted beside his father and ate the rice his second wife brought him. The women had their children close round them and were eager to hear what Pak had to tell. But they were too polite to ask. Pak was exasperated by them, nevertheless. "Go into the kitchen and don't all sit round me like croaking frogs." When the women had gone the men of the family were left sitting together— Pak and his father and uncle, blind Meru and young Lantjar. Pak had his youngest son on his knees. When he had told his news they all sat and chewed in silence. At last the old man spoke.

"I cannot understand what you tell me, my son," he said. "The punggawa holds his office from our raja and is a relation of his. How can he tell you to keep peace when the lord calls on you to fight?"

"The punggawa is our friend and does not wish the villages of the coast to come to harm. We ought to be grateful to him for not forcing us to fight," Pak said, though the thought of this had never occurred to him.

"A rumour has come to me on the wind that the punggawa is a friend of the Dutch and is in their pay as the gusti Nyoman is. Perhaps he is a traitor as the other is. Who has told you that his advice is right?" the old man asked obstinately.

Pak folded his hands and replied, "The raja put out the eyes of my brother, your son. He has taken my best cock from me. I will not fight for the raja."

"We are all the lord's servants," the old man replied. "My father served him and I, too, and you. The sawahs whence our rice comes belong to the raja. We belong to the raja. When he sends out the holy kris to summon us, we must go."

When the old man had said this he spat out his betel-juice and looked straight in front of him. An oppressive silence weighed on the rest. The cocks crowed from the back of the yard. The women in the kitchen had never kept so quiet. The old man got up and crossed the yard and disappeared behind the rice barn. After a while they saw him coming back again; he had a lance in his hand and his kris in his girdle. He stopped in front of his three sons and looked at them all in turn. Meru raised his face to his father, for he could feel his eyes resting on his head.

Pak folded his hands and asked in the ceremonious style used to a superior: "Whither does my father mean to go?"

"To join the raja's warriors," the old man answered. "Peace rest with you."

They bowed themselves with hands clasped and looked after him as he left the yard by the narrow gate. Pak felt as desolate as he used to feel when a child if darkness overtook him out in the pastures with the buffaloes.

Nothing unusual occurred that night and the next morning began as any other morning did—with the crowing of the cocks, with the sound of the besoms as the women swept the yard, with the barking of dogs and the blazing up of the kitchen fire. The women did not indeed go to the river for water, for Pak had bidden them keep at home. They got what water they needed from the narrow watercourse that ran through the village and the cocks were put out on the strip of grass outside the gate as they always were. After doing nothing for an hour Pak grew impatient. He considered taking out his buffaloes and going out to the sawahs, which it was time to plough the second time. He stood at the gate of his yard to find out what the other men were doing. The street was quieter than usual and not a woman or child was to be seen. A few men passed by and Pak called out to them. "Are you going out to work on the sawahs?"

"We are not sure," they replied. They were as undecided as he was. Pak turned back into his yard, busied himself in his barn and rubbed his buffaloes down with wisps of grass—an attention they accepted with surprise. It was fortunate that so sensible a man as Krkek had the biggest say in the village. He sent the subak's runner to tell the men to go and work on the fields as usual. There was no danger. Pak took out his buffaloes with a sigh of relief, gave the women strict orders to be prudent and left. He felt a little anxious about his father.

He ploughed without paying proper heed to the work, and his furrows were not as straight as usual. Yet after a time he felt the healing of the earth and the air of the sawahs, as he always did, and his cares passed away as the little cloud over the palms to the north. The tjrorot beat his little bamboo kulkul. When the sun was straight above his head the big kulkul in the village beat, too. Pak wondered whether to go home. Everything was upside down. In the ordinary way every man knew what he had to do: when to work, when to hold festival, what offerings to make, and what customs to obey. Ever since the menace of war with the Dutch, everything had been uncertain and Pak had been called upon to make decisions which were beyond the power of a simple man like him. For example, he had told Meru that very morning not to drive the ducks out on to the pastures. But then he saw the duck-herds were out and the ducks joyfully plunging their beaks into the mud and he felt he had perhaps been wrong. His ducks were hungry and possibly they would turn on each other in their pen and peck each other to death. How was he, who did not even know what to do about his ducks, to know what to do when it came to fighting the Dutch? When the holy kris called, one had to go, his father said; and his father was wise. It was the first time in his life that Pak had gone against the old man. His throat was filled with bitterness, his tongue and his gullet were bitter, and his mouth. I will not fight, he thought once more. My brother has had his eyes put out and my cock has been taken from me. I will not fight.

He saw Lantjar come running between the sawahs, breathless and stumbling as he ran. "The Dutchmen are here," he shouted from a long way off. "News has come— they have left their big ships and are coming ashore in many boats—thousands of soldiers with rifles and guns. What are we to do?"

Men were hurrying past from the other sawahs and more messengers came running from the village. "They look like raksasas, with beards and enormous eyes. They have huge horses with them, bigger than have ever been seen. They cannot speak to us, but they threaten us with their rifles. The women are crying for fear in every house."

Pak dragged his plough out of the wet earth and his buffaloes from the field. He was ploughing the new sawah and he was glad it was not far away from the village. Lantjar helped him with the beasts. All the men hurried from the fields. In spite of his haste Pak halted for a moment when he reached the rice temple and, leaving Lantjar in charge of the buffaloes, he went in. He knelt down before the chief shrine and gazed at his plates. He felt sure the gods would protect him in return for his gift. He wanted to pray, but he could not think of a word to say by way of prayer. He could only crouch there with hands folded on his forehead and lay open to the gods the wishes of his heart. Protect my house, my family, my children and my fields. When he left the temple he had no more fear.

Just as they reached the outskirts of the village the mounted lancers broke from the bamboo thicket by the stream. There were many more of them than on the day before. Pak realized that a large number of men had joined the lord's warriors, men who went as his own father had, when the holy kris called. He looked for the old man among those who followed the riders at a slower pace on foot. But he could not see him for the throng; his buffaloes tore along for home and the water splashed up in his eyes as they forded the stream. The fighting men vanished in the direction of Sanur.

The village had become so strange a place that it might not have been Taman Sari at all; Pak felt like the man in the fairy story who opened his eyes and found himself on an unknown island. There was a wild rushing to and fro in the streets; the people were scurrying hither and thither as senselessly as frightened hens. Women wept and children screamed, making such a clamor that the unfamiliar noise that came rattling from Sanur was scarcely audible. The brilliant light of day was thick with dust. A procession of women carrying offering baskets came walking through the distracted crowds on its way to the village temple. They were right: it was necessary to pay honor to the gods. A little farther on Pak met the pedanda, Ida Bagus Rai. He strode calmly on with his long staff in his hand, followed by two pupils, as though he knew nothing of strife and fear. A few people made him a fleeting obeisance with hands folded.

Pak took courage and addressed the priest in spite of the unmannerly rudeness of doing so. But the extraordinary events of the day seemed enough to excuse him.

"Pedanda," he said, "my old father, whom the pedanda knows well, has forsaken us. He has gone out to join the raja's warriors. What shall we do so that nothing shall happen to him?"

"Your father is a loyal servant," the pedanda said kindly. "The gods will protect him. And you—are you afraid?"

Pak let his eyes fall. The pedanda smiled. "If there is danger, bring your family to my house," he said. "I will gladly take them in, I have been a friend of your father's for many years. They will be safe with me, for my house is under the protection of the gods."

Just as Pak was about to thank him there was a clap like thunder. The report was so tremendous that Pak felt the air rush against his ears as though to burst his head. It was answered by a prolonged and piercing scream from the women and children in the road. Pak found himself clasping the priest round the knees with his head buried in his kain as if he was still a child himself. "It has begun," the pedanda said, still smiling as before. "The Dutch cannon," He released himself gently from Pak's grasp and walked on.

When Pak got home with his buffaloes the news that Sanur was in flames had already in some inexplicable manner come to Puglug's ears. "The Dutch have set fire to the village and everyone is dead— they have not left one alive," she said, and her lips trembled. Sarna threw her arms round Pak's neck without shame, as though they were behind closed doors in the intimate seclusion of her house. He shook her off.

"Have the cocks been fed?" he asked. Meru, the blind man, shook his head. Pak went to fetch the cocks from the roadside and fed them. For some reason it comforted his wives a little to see him doing it.

There was a particularly tall palm in the garden and Pak climbed up it to see the burning of Sanur. But Sanur was not burning. There was only a little smoke in the north-west corner of the large village where the Coral Temple stood. Nor were all the people dead, for now the first fugitives arrived, with children, buffaloes, baskets and cocks, and told what had happened.

The raja's soldiers had lain in ambush behind the palms near the beach in order to fall on the enemy as soon as they came ashore. This was an act of reckless daring, for there were only about a hundred men of Bali against thousands of soldiers. But their warlike ardour boiled up and could not be restrained. Also the Molog himself, their captain, was at their head to lead them.

The foreign soldiers shot from their boats, and their rifles shot so swiftly that each shot mowed down several men. Molog's men shot, too, but their rifles did not shoot straight and they seized kris and lance meaning to fall on the enemy as they landed. The sand of the shore was whipped with the bullets of the Dutchmen, according to the fugitives, and the warriors kept to the shelter of the palms. The sight of the strange soldiers and their immense horses, as they drew near the shore in their boats, was terrifying. But then three men advanced quite alone up the beach towards the raja's warriors. One of them was the gusti Nyoman of Buleleng—he had a drawn kris in his hand. The other two were the tall white men whom the lord had always called his friends. Dewa Gdé Molog recognized them. The gusti Nyoman called out to the warriors in a loud voice to lay down their arms and no harm should come to the village. Molog replied with a shout: his soldiers rushed from their cover with loud cries, their curved krisses in their hands, and fell headlong as though Durga, the goddess of death, had lain her finger on them. But two Dutchmen fell also with blood flowing from them. The others lifted them up and carried them back into one of the boats. The rest of the warriors retreated. Then came the great thunder-clap and the largest of the gray ships was suddenly wreathed in smoke. The shots from its cannon had hit the Coral Temple and destroyed it. The shrines and thrones of the gods fell in ruins. Fire broke out and the new eleven-storeyed tower and even the exposed roots of the wairingin tree were turned to charred embers.

The people of Taman Sari heard this account with shudders of horror and fear, but with the liveliest curiosity notwithstanding.

They crept out from their houses into the street and surrounded the fugitives and asked them a thousand questions. When they heard of the destruction of the temple they could not at first believe it. "Mbe!" they exclaimed, "how is it possible to destroy a temple? How can the gods permit it? Mbe! Mbe!"

Most of the fugitives had relations in Taman Sari. Dasni's parents and brothers and sisters were among them and they led a worn-out cow by a rope. Suddenly there was a shout of laughter and they all turned round. It was Rib. They looked at him in astonishment. "And here have we been taking offerings and keeping festivals in the Coral Temple for years and now it appears that it was never a holy place at all!" he cried out, laughing till tears ran down his cheeks. At first they looked at him in astonishment, and then they all laughed to They understood what he meant. Rib was right. "There were no gods in the Coral Temple—if there had been it could not have been shot to pieces," they shouted. "If it had been a holy place nothing could have destroyed it!" In spite of their fears they all laughed at the thought of it.

"No gods have ever dwelt in the Coral Temple and we have been fools enough to go on making offerings there," they cried out one to another. The longer they reflected on the absurdity of having paid honor to a temple in which obviously not a single god had ever taken up his abode, the more ridiculous they found it. And so it came about that the fugitives were conducted to the several houses with loud laughter and shouts of mirth.

"The cannon cannot do any hurt to our rice temple," Pak said when he reached home. "It is holy and the gods visit it every day."

The first Dutch soldiers to enter Taman Sari arrived towards evening. At their head rode a man with gold decorations on his coat, a captain as Molog was. His horse was even bigger and more alarming than the accounts had led them to expect. It was twice as big and tall as the horses they had in their country. The Dutch soldiers, too, looked as though they had twice the strength and courage of the men of Bali. One or two discharged their rifles, for the fun of the thing apparently, for no one was killed, and the reports had the festive sound of Chinese crackers on days of teeth-filing or corpse-burning. The people of Taman Sari could not refrain from hanging over their walls and devouring the foreign soldiers with their eyes. It was only when they heard shouts from the northern exit of the village, and when their own mounted lancers clattered through the place and when darkness came down without an end to the shooting, that fear overtook them.

Pak sat on the steps of his chief house and brooded. He missed his father's advice. His heart was sore for the old man and at the same time he felt that he himself was too stupid a man to be the head of the family in such distracting times. I can labor in the sawahs like a buffalo, 1 am all right for that, he thought sadly, but my head is empty and I do not know what to do. Shall we stay here within our walls, he thought, or shall we flee? The responsibility for Dasni's parents and family and cow weighed on his mind as an added burden.

Puglug came from the kitchen bringing him his rice and a hard-boiled duck's egg and stayed squatting near him while he ate.

"The punggawa has taken all the rifles which he has kept hidden in his rice-barn and laid them before the captain of the foreign soldiers," she said. "There were twenty. He has hung a white flag on the tall pole and a second white flag at his gate beside his bird-cages, so that the enemy on the big ships shall see them and not shoot at his house. The punggawa is a friend of the Dutch and it is safe at his house. Hundreds of people have taken refuge there already."

Pak threw away the emptied leaf. "Wife, where do you hear such tales?" he asked indignantly. "Is there a bird that flies about and tells you all it sees?"

Puglug was affronted and got up and went. She came back again, however, and said, "You have children, sons and daughters. I thought you would be glad to know of a safe place." And with that she returned to the kitchen. Pak went on brooding.

Perhaps, he thought, it would be safer at the punggawa of Sanur's place. But how shall we get there? It is getting dark and it is a long way. The sawahs may be thronged with soldiers—or else evil spirits may be lying in wait for the souls of the slain. What would the old man do, he thought, racking his brains. He would not go to the punggawa, whom he called a traitor. Suddenly he found the answer and his face cleared. He went to the women and sent the little girl to summon the whole family.

"Get ready," he said when they were all assembled. "We are going to the home of the pedanda, Ida Bagus Rai. He has offered us the protection of his house because my father is his friend. Hurry up, we must get there before dark."

"Shall we take rice with us? Shall we be there a long time? Do the buffaloes come, too? And the ducks and the cocks?" the women all asked at once. Pak stopped his ears. "Take the children and leave the animals here," he said. "I will come back first thing in the morning and feed them."

"Lantjar can get down some coconuts and papayas, so that we shall not go empty handed," Sarna said, remembering her manners. Pak gave her a smile for this excellent idea. Rantun put her arm round Madé and led little Klepon by the hand. The aunt carried Siang, and Puglug and Sarna each had a little son on her hip.

When they were all ready the first bats were on the wing. They hesitated in the gateway, for just as they were going through they heard the tramp of soldiers' boots and the Dutchmen appeared in a cloud of dust. "Through the garden and along the stream," Pak said. They all turned back and crossed the yard, past the house altar where their aunt had laid offerings, through the dusk of the palm orchard and over the bamboo fence that bordered the stream.

Dasni's parents insisted on dragging their cow along with them after all; it splashed through the brook and mooed loudly, for this was strange water. Dasni led Meru, and Lantjar made a way for the three little girls under his outstretched hands when they reached the bamboo thicket. Here it was quite dark. Pak went ahead on the moist slippery ground. Glowworms hung on the leaves and little Siang grabbed at them. When they got to the edge of the bamboo thicket they saw the open sawahs before them as a patch of light under the dark arch of the leaves. They hurried on to get out of the darkness. Suddenly Pak stopped. Only the cow splashed on through the water.

Heads and shoulders, soldiers in blue uniforms, started up from the standing crops in the sawahs. They were so far away that they looked quite small—but they laid their rifle butts to their cheeks. Pak's wives screamed. He hurried them back under the bamboos. There was a rattle and a whistling sound. Now the cow, too, stood still. Pak was astonished to find his knees shaking. He held his breath and stood there in the darkness with his family behind him. He could not see the soldiers from where he stood, but he heard them approaching. They made a great trampling as they trod down the rice and a smell of leather and unfamiliar sweat was wafted from them. A captain on a white horse was framed in the leafy archway where the bamboos ended. They could see him, but he did not see them because they had shrunk back into the darkness and did not stir. The captain turned his horse, called out to his soldiers and they ran after him, through the stream and over the fence, and vanished into the village palm plantations.

Pak waited a long time before he moved. When the last sound had died away he crept out. It seemed to be safe now. He beckoned to his family to follow him. The cow again plodded through the water. Pak waited at the edge of the trampled sawah until they had all assembled. His daughters were still missing. They waited for them, but they did not come. "Rantun, Madé, Klepon," Pak called out. A whimper from the bamboos was the only answer. "They are afraid," Pak said with a smile, though his own lips trembled. He went back along the narrow path beside the stream to fetch them. He could not see them but he heard Madé crying. "Be quiet," he whispered into the darkness, "or the soldiers will come back." The crying grew louder. Now he heard someone breathing behind him—it was Puglug, who had followed him to find her daughters. "Be quiet," she whispered, too. She parted the bamboo branches and pulled Madé out. Pak felt about for the other children. He got hold of the edge of a kain; it was wet from the stream that flowed over it. "What is it?" Puglug whispered. "I don't know," Pak replied.

But he knew already. His eyes had grown accustomed to the darkness. He saw his little daughters. They lay on the ground. They were limp and motionless. They did not stir. They made no answer. Rantun's head was in the water and Klepon was clasped tightly in her arms.

Pak bent down and lifted the two children up. He carried them out of the thicket into the light and laid them down in the trampled rice haulms of the sawah. They were dead.

*   *   *   *   *

Lieutenant Dekker had distinctly seen the flash of lances among the palms before he gave the order to fire; yet nothing was to be seen of the enemy when he and his men entered the plantation. He had the place thoroughly searched, for he had been sent out with his twenty men to patrol the district for ambushed natives. Not an enemy, not a lance to be seen. He dismounted and let his horse graze the short grass among the palms. He was glad of the dusk. He closed his eyes, which were fatigued with dust and sunlight, and again he saw lances. He saw the beach as it had first met his eyes on landing—with the gleam of lances concealed behind the palms and the half-naked natives charging the soldiers, with their snake-like blades drawn. Dangerous and cunning, so it said in the hand-book. The country was made for ambushes.

These brown-skinned men could lie hid in the ricefields, in their dense plantations, which at first he had taken for the jungle, and behind every palm; and they might be concealed in their odd-looking huts. There were walls everywhere as though these villages had been built on purpose for defence and surprise. The inhabitants were neither to be heard nor seen, but Dekker felt them on every side of him. His men, who under the sergeant had scoured every corner of the palm grove, now returned. "All clear, sir," the sergeant reported smartly. He was an old, seasoned colonial soldier with a yellowish-white goatee. Dekker had a faint suspicion that, as a second-lieutenant in a brand new uniform, he was not taken quite seriously. He had had a great idea of himself and his leadership when he had set off on his white horse at the head of his men. But the first three hours of the campaign had made a lot of difference. He had twice lost direction, though any Javanese convict or navvy could tell it by a glance at the sun. He knew now, too, that a horse was merely a ridiculous encumbrance in the rice-fields. It sank in the mud, stumbled over the banks, fell, shied at snakes; he cursed both it and his hot tunic and felt the sweat streaming down him. Never again on horseback, he swore.

He was very thirsty. For the third time his hand went to the water-bottle at his belt, though he knew it was empty. The murmur of a stream could be heard from the edge of this plantation and it aggravated the sensation of thirst.

"Don't drink that water," he called out sharply when some of his men went towards the stream. It said in the hand-book: "Officers are strictly warned against letting their men drink the river water in Bali. The water is full of impurities, and epidemics are one of the greatest dangers threatening the expedition. Drinking water will be supplied in sufficient quantities to each unit."

"Three of the men are footsore, sir," the sergeant said. "They want to bathe their feet."

Dekker looked on with envy as the men took off their boots and socks and bathed their feet in the stream. As an officer he could not follow their example. He could not ask the sergeant for a drink from his water-bottle, although he had seen the men sharing theirs. He turned about quickly with a feeling of lurking eyes behind a trunk. Nothing. No eyes, no lances, no enemy. He had always imagined that on active service there was an enemy opposed to you whom you attacked and conquered. Here the enemy was at his back and unseen. It was uncomfortable.

He heard a bugle call in the distance and felt relieved. It had a familiar sound of garrison life. The men pulled on their boots and socks. It was dark by now. Dekker took out a cigarette, but his parched mouth made it tasteless. He threw it away and passed his tongue over his lips. "We'll go back, sergeant," he said. The sergeant approached his officer when he was addressed in this informal way. "We ought to have had a couple of Ambonese with us," he said, looking up at the palms.

"Why?" Dekker asked. Orders had been given to employ only white troops in all operations that threatened danger. He had been proud when the captain of his company detailed Dutch soldiers for his patrol.

"You are thirsty, sir," the sergeant explained. "If we had one or two colored boys with us they'd have been up there in a flash and brought down a few klapas for you, sir."

"Brought what?" Dekker asked.

"Klapas—coconuts, sir."

Dekker had a small Malay dictionary in his kit as well as the hand-book. He was not yet quite at home with the language, for what he had learned of it in Holland in preparation for colonial service did not sound quite like the Malay spoken by the troops. He was always caught tripping by the scraps of Malay that people in the colonies interspersed with their Dutch.

"Give the order to march off," he said.

The sergeant barked out the order, Dekker mounted his peevish nag and rode beside the sergeant. He ought by right to have ridden ahead, but the sergeant had a better sense of direction. Dekker took out his hand-book and examined the rough sketch maps, and then put it back again. They came to a village street. All the villages looked alike with their endless walls and gates and curiously exotic temple doors, and the thick foliage of tall trees meeting over the roads.

"Patrol—halt!" the sergeant ordered.

"What is it?" Dekker asked with some agitation. The sergeant saluted: "Requisition, sir," and leaving the men and the officer where they were he tramped noisily in at one of the gates. Dekker got ready to give the order to fire in case anything happened.

Nothing happened. The sergeant reappeared with three large, green, coconuts. They were already cut open. He gave one to the lieutenant and the others were passed from hand to hand. Dekker had never tasted anything so good as the cool clear liquid. It soothed his dry and dusty throat and he drank it to the last drop. The sergeant looked pleased.

"Patrol—march," he said. "I paid them three kepengs, sir."

When they reached the camp at Sanur the troops were just beginning their evening meal. The labor corps, impressed for the campaign, had done good work in this short time: tents and camp beds had been put up and lamps of the kind called company lamps were alight everywhere. The General and his staff were even installed in a proper house—not a Dutch house but in something that at least had walls and a door. The welcome smell of food steamed from the large stew-pans and the men were lined up, dixies in hand and broad grins on their faces.

Lieutenant Dekker made his report to the Captain, had a word or two with some of his comrades and went to his tent. He was tired out—more tired than he had realized. It was only at the sight of that wretched affair called a camp-bed that he felt how leaden his legs and how hot his eyes were. His Javanese servant was squatting smoking outside his tent.

"Minta makan," he said, proud of being able to order his meal in Malay. The boy went off noiselessly. It was comfortable in the tent and the lamp was lighted. The air now was quite chilly. The pastor lay on his bed reading with his tunic unbuttoned.

"Well, what have you been up to, my friend?" he asked, pushing his spectacles on to his forehead.

Lieutenant Dekker was rather annoyed at the prospect of being saddled with the pastor for the whole of the campaign. He had even gone so far as to mention the matter to the first-lieutenant.

Schimmelpennick was a very good fellow, but he made it so very clear that even a pastor could be a very good fellow. Besides, he was not at all robust. He had been horribly sea-sick during the landing, though he had certainly borne it like a hero. He did not seem to feel the heat, which Dekker found intolerable. On the other hand he was always feeling cold and complained of it bitterly. Now he had another grievance.

"My Jongos hasn't come yet with the barang-barang," he complained. "I shall have to sleep in my clothes, that's all. Very unpleasant."

Dekker pulled off his boots and eased his toes.

"C'est la guerre," he said aptly.

"What? Yes—you're right there," the pastor replied.

The boy brought the food—meat and potatoes and a thick sauce smelling of onions. Dekker ate hungrily. "Minta minum," he said, feeling thirsty.

"That's just the snag," Schimmelpennick said triumphantly.

"Something has gone wrong with the water ration. They said we had oceans of water sent on shore from the warships. No doubt, but where has it got to? Not a drop to be had in the whole camp."

"We must send a few Ambonese up the coconut palms for klapas," Dekker said, with recently acquired wisdom. He felt a longing for their cool liquor.

"Some of the men gave me water from their own water-bottles," the pastor said. "What fine fellows they are, such a wonderful spirit of comradeship and so grateful for any little joke one makes."

Dekker took off his tunic and unbuckled his revolver. "Where can one get a wash?" he asked. He was dog-tired.

"Wash? Campaigners don't wash," Schimmelpennick replied gaily.

"I might have a swim in the sea, perhaps," Dekker said. The thunder of the waves could be heard distinctly.

"Don't do that," Schimmelpennick said. "Sharks, barracudas, sword-fish, very poisonous."

The boy came in once more and put down a tin pot of coffee for his officer. Dekker drank greedily while the pastor looked on.

"Delicious, I expect," he said rather enviously.

"It's liquid, anyway," Dekker replied.

He lay down on his bed and shut his eyes. He saw lances, palm jungles, naked brown natives, sword-blades, lances, ambushes, water and again lances.

The pastor sat up again. "I've had my disappointments, too," he said. "It's Sunday tomorrow. I wanted to give the men the word of God. Out of the question. I went to the General. Wouldn't hear of it. They have to be on the march tomorrow. I'd like to know what I'm here for."

"For the dead," Dekker said. "To comfort the wounded."

"Comfort, yes," the pastor said. "We have had two slightly wounded cases today. One is Mohammedan. The other did send for me and do you know what he wanted? Gin. That's what he wanted." He lay down and took off his spectacles. "Shall I put the light out?"

"Do," Dekker answered drowsily.

"I am told there's malaria here too," Schimmelpennick said anxiously. I must write to Brigit, Dekker thought sleepily. "When we got near the land, naked savages armed with lances charged from their ambush," the letter began.

❊   ❊   ❊   ❊   ❊

The puri in Badung was burning in several places. The Dutch had shelled the town and the neighborhood with their howitzers and large parts of the puri were destroyed. Only the north-east wing, with the house-temple and the ajacent courts, were still undamaged. There were also one or two balés in the southern courtyards still intact and in them the wives and their servants were huddled together. Many of the slaves and servants had run away. On the other hand there was a constantly increasing stream of people pouring into the puri—fugitives from the villages or families who acknowledged their attachment to their lord. For two days there was much crying aloud and weeping to be heard, but now there was silence.

The people of Badung had had four days of the fighting, fighting such as they had never known. The rifles of the Dutch shot swiftly and reached far. It needed no courage to discharge them as it did to attack the enemy with kris and lance. It was clear to everyone, too, that the Dutch as enemies had no manners. In the wars between the various Balinese states certain polite formalities were always observed.

Fighting began early in the morning and there was a truce when the sun was at its height for rest and refreshment. But the Dutch, once they had begun shooting or marching, gave them no rest. They had besides a crafty way of fighting. They never came from the direction they were supposed to, but sent their soldiers off on long wearisome round-about marches so as to take Molog's fighting men by surprise where they were least expected. They felled coconut palms which had taken many years to bear fruit and made bridges of them instead of fording the rivers. They trampled down the sawahs with their heavy boots and the hoofs of their horses, instead of marching along the roads, and they broke down walls for no reason. Their strength and ruthlessness made them invincible. All in the puri knew that the battle was ended. Messengers came to say that the foreign soldiers had shot the puri in Kesiman to pieces and were now encamping there for the night. There was nothing to stop them now between Kesiman and Badung.

As the lord's chief house had been burnt to the ground and the smoke and smell of fire there was almost unendurable, the lord had installed himself in a balé near the house-temple.

He had returned late in the afternoon from Kajumas, where he had spent some time with his soldiers to inspire them with fresh courage. On the way home, covered in mud and sweat—for he and his small retinue had had to avoid the roads and steal through the sawahs for fear of falling into the enemy's hands—he had bathed in the river as any peasant might. When he got back he went to his wives to console them. Then he sat in the open balé and told his boy, Oka, to give him his opium pipe. He looked utterly exhausted while he smoked, but there was a smile on his pale lips. A light tinkling sound came from the air and he raised his sad, smoke-inflamed eyes. The pigeons were wheeling in the sky; the sun glanced on their plumage and turned it white and silver. The little bells on their feet rang out and their white feathers shone against the smoke-gray sky. The lord followed them with his eyes. They did not return as usual to settle on the roofs. They forsook the place that hope had already forsaken and disappeared into the sky.

A procession of women came through the main entrance, bearing presents in baskets on their heads and led by Bijang, the hundred-year-old mother of the old lord. Lord Alit got up and went to meet her. He greeted her with hands clasped and gave her his support. He saw that she was dressed as though for a festival. Her bare arms and shoulders smelt of sweetly scented oils and looked like old parchment.

"Are you tired, child?" Bijang asked, laying her hand on Alit's knee after he had led her to the balé. Her women remained crouching in the court below.

"No, mother," he said.

"Your uncle and father, the tjokorda of Pametjutan, is very sick and in great pain. He could not come himself so I undertook to be his messenger," she said with her confiding smile. Alit looked at her attentively.

"What have you resolved upon, child?"

"The end," the prince answered. A silence followed. The crackling of fire could be heard from the other court.

"I am rich," Bijang said after a pause, touching her great-grandson's knee. "I will gladly give you all the money the Dutch demand from you. You can send it this very night to Kesiman to their captain. Then they will return to their ships and Badung is saved. What do you say to that?"

Alit looked with a smile into the old lady's small wrinkled face. "No, mother," he said, "it would be dishonorable."

"I know nothing about that," Bijang said in a chant. "I am only a foolish old woman and know very little. There is great lament in the puris. Even the cows are lowing after their shot calves. It is not good that such unhappiness should be, when money can remedy it."

"Money is no remedy," the prince said.

Bijang was silent. Then she said, "I will let my son know what you have resolved. If it is the end, then we will die with you." Beneath her aged skin there was the face of a young girl, gently, almost gaily, smiling. She pointed into the court. "My women have brought you some fruit and offerings for your altars. They wish to ask you whether they may stay in your puri, for their balés have fallen down."

"They are welcome," the lord said. After a moment's hesitation he added, "Tell them they must make white dresses and jackets, as though they were men."

Bijang bowed her head. Only those who dedicated themselves to death wore white robes. "I will tell them," she murmured. She got up, declined Alit's help and looked at him almost archly. "It is time for me to go to heaven, but you might have stayed here a little longer, child, you are young and the world is a beautiful place for the living."

"My soul is old and longs for rest," Alit replied seriously. Bijang merely said politely, "May I now conduct my women to yours, for there is not much time for them to make their dresses."

"Peace on your way," he said,

"Peace on what you do," the old lady replied.

He looked after her as she walked away leaning on her stick and followed by her women. "Tell old Ranis to send Lambon to me," he said to Oka.

No fresh shells fell into the puri and the fires had burnt out in many places after they had devoured all there was of wood or thatch. When Lambon came the lord drew her between his knees, as though she were his child, not his wife. She stayed crouching there, saying no word, feeling safe, making no sound except for an occasional convulsive sob, for she had wept a lot and been in great fear. Alit put his hands on her head and stroked her hair. It was warm and smooth. He said nothing. He sat and stroked Lambon's hair without knowing it: he was lost in thought. Oka had fallen asleep on the ground at his feet. Lambon, too, fell asleep at last with her head resting on his knees. He sat there for a long time; then he woke them, taking care that their souls should have time to return to them. They looked up in surprise and smiled.

"Lambon," he said, "I want you to go to the women and take them this message: Early tomorrow will be the last assault and a great battle and the end. All who wish to leave my puri, wives, servants and slaves, are free to go. Those who wish to face the end with me must make themselves white dresses and jackets, as though they were men, for it is permitted them to die with the men and enter heaven. Tell them that."

"Yes, your Highness," Lambon whispered with bent head.

"I shall not see you again, Lambon," Alit said, looking down at her. She still had the fragile daintiness of a child. "You were always dear to my heart, little sister. I wish you happiness if you return to your father's house."

Lambon cleared her throat. "I will stay with my master," she said in a hollow voice. Alit turned away from her. After a moment's pause she folded her hands, bent low and went.

"And you, Oka?" the prince asked.

"I, too, will stay with you," the boy said. "Shall I have a kris of my own?"

"Yes, you shall have a kris. You may take one of mine," Alit replied with a smile.

Oka's face beamed with pride and delight and he rose on his toes like a fighting cock.

"Wait for me here, I shall want you," Alit said as he left him. He walked quickly to the large balé in the outer court, where all his courtiers and counsellors were awaiting him. Although it was evening the light was still so strong that the flames of the fires could hardly be seen. They appeared only as a blue vapour with wreaths of smoke curling up into the still air. The Dutch had begun shooting again, but their guns shot wide of the mark.

✳   ✳   ✳   ✳   ✳

So many families had sought refuge with the pedanda, Ida Bagus Rai, in Taman Sari that the people sat closely packed on the ground, men and women and children, with their belongings they had brought with them. Here and there they had lighted small fires over which they cooked a simple meal. The children were laughing again after the terror they had been through or playing quietly for fear of annoying their elders. Mothers were singing lullabies or telling stories in low voices to keep the younger children quiet. The pedanda's blind wife, tall and erect in her black kain, felt her way among the crowd to ensure that all found room. Dasni, Meru's wife, sent Lantjar home again to fetch mats, for they would add greatly to their comfort. Puglug sat beside her with a fixed smile on her plain face; she had lost two daughters, but it would not have been polite to let her sorrow be seen. Also little Tanah was at her breast, sucking vigorously, and in spite of her grief she was penetrated by a glow of joy. Dasni's mother was on the other side of her, murmuring those consolatory words which the old and experienced always have at their command. "Believe me, you will soon forget. Children are born and children die. I have had six and only three are alive at this day. If you asked me the names of the dead ones I could not tell you them. The passing of time is like running water: it washes everything away." The old lady's ceaseless murmur of consolation finally sent Puglug to sleep.

Pak was with the men; he was rather silent, but not so unhappy now as when he carried the limp bodies of the children out of the bamboos. The village had buried its dead after sending envoys to the Dutch, offering its submission and asking for a truce in which to dig the graves. Since then not a shot had been fired along the coast and the main body of the enemy had marched inland towards Badung. Nevertheless very few of the people ventured back to their homes.

Early in the afternoon the guns on the shore and in the ships had thundered out and you would have thought every house in Sanur and Taman Sari would have fallen in ruins, but now there was peace. Some of the men had even begun gambling, tossing their kepengs down on the mats and making their bets. It turned their thoughts from their troubles and that was a good thing. The pedanda sat at the far side of the courtyard on the balé near the house-temple and meditated. He looked as though he were far away and had no idea that his courtyard was full of a homeless multitude.

A peasant came in at the gateway accompanied by his son, a boy. He was wearing a large-brimmed hat, although the sun was no longer strong. The child had a roguish, dirty face and the peasant's feet were coated in mud.

"Where is the pedanda?" he asked. "I have a message for him."

One or two men pointed towards the balé where the priest sat lost in meditation. "Where have you come from?" they asked the new comer. "From Badung," he replied. "How are things there?" they asked again, but the man did not answer. He went up to the bamboo fence which separated the courtyard where the temple was from the outer one. He stood there waiting with the boy at his side.

"I have a message for the pedanda," he said after a while. The pedanda looked up from his meditation and saw the man standing there. It was unusual that a man should stand in a priest's presence. "Enter," Ida Bagus Rai said as he stepped down from the balé and went to meet him. The man clasped his hands fleetingly as he met the priest. "This is the message," he said in an undertone. "Tomorrow there will be a great battle in Badung, the last onset and the end. The pedanda is requested to make offerings and to pray."

A few men and children were crouching pressed up against the bamboo fence listening; but they could hear nothing for the man spoke under his breath. The pedanda led him quickly away by the arm. "Come into my house, stranger," he said. The people in the yard looked after them in amazement.

When the door was shut behind them the priest smiled. "You will make a bad sudra, lord," he said, "if you do not bow before the pedanda."

He himself bowed, for though he was a Brahman and the lord's friend and teacher, honor was due to the lord's station. He looked the young lord up and down, observing his girt-up kain, his muddy feet and the sickle in his girdle. "What is the meaning of your disguise?" he asked. "Why do you come to my house unattended?"

"Can you not guess?" Alit asked.

"Do you mean to flee? But whither? When the enemy have taken Badung, they will turn upon Tabanan and Bangli and Klungklung. Where can you hide from their rifles?" the priest asked sternly. "And have you forgotten what the old books say? The Ksatria who shuns battle is without honor,"

"I do not mean to flee," the prince said, smiling. "Did you not understand my message?"

The pedanda looked serious. "I did understand it. I will make offerings and pray. I will be with you when the end comes. Did you come yourself, alone and disguised, merely to tell me that?"

"I want you to show me the way," Alit said.

"You know your way. Your way is right," the priest replied. The lord hesitated as the priest said this and then laid his hand beseechingly on his knee.

"You must show me the way to Raka," he said softly. "I cannot send a messenger—he is unclean. I must go to him myself."

There was a long silence after this. Ida Bagus Rai reflected on the enormity of the lord's coming in disguise on the last night of his life to visit his friend—a leper.

"I cannot conduct you to him," he said sternly. "His presence is an uncleanness."

"I know," Alit said. "But I am beyond all that. Tomorrow is the end—cleanness or uncleanness makes no difference to me now. You will find this, too, in the books: For the enlightened all is one! The Brahman and his holy prayer; the cow, the elephant and the unclean dog; he who is without caste and devours dogs' flesh—they are all only one. And," he added, looking the priest straight in the eyes, "does not the end make everything clean?"

After a long silence the pedanda replied, "Good. I think I understand you. Now go before the people in my courtyard notice you. I will meet you at the southern end of the street."

Only a few of the people looked at the man from Badung as he made his way between their mats and left the yard. They paid little attention to him, for messengers were always coming and going in these troubled days. The lord with Oka by his side walked quickly through the village and waited under the wairingin tree that stood at the south end of it. None of the enemy's soldiers were to be seen, but far away an unfamiliar bugle note could be heard. Taman Sari was strangely empty and silent. In spite of the war it had a peaceful air. Alit took a deep breath. The scanty clothing of a casteless peasant sat lightly on him. After awhile he saw the pedanda approaching. He was alone and without his priest's staff. But—and the lord smiled with pleasure at the sight—he had put on a new white linen kain and a new, closely fitting white jacket. They went along together without saying a word. Oka ran along now in front and now behind, singing to himself. He was happy to escape for a few hours from the confinement of the puri and the drowsy fumes of opium.

"How fresh the air smells," Alit said after a while, breaking the silence. They went along between the flooded sawahs, which gave a perfect reflection of the sky, with the green tops peeping through. Some, however, had been hideously trampled and laid waste by the marching soldiers. When they came to some fields where the ripening ears showed the first glint of silver the lord let the spikes slip through his hands as he went.

"I feel happy," he said. "It is a joy to be walking through the sawahs again like this."

He smiled as he thought of it. "I don't believe I have done it since I was Oka's age," he added.

They reached the bank of the river and waded across and climbed up the other side which was fringed with palm trees. It was darker under their shade though the sky was still bright above. When they left the palms behind and were in the open again they could see the expanse of the sea, ringed with white surf. The Great Mountain rose far away, clear of clouds. The western sky was green and a first star rose out of the sea. They did not meet anyone at all and the peacefulness of the scene was profound.

The pedanda, white-haired and robed in a white kain, went first. The lord followed him. As he went along with a light and regular tread the words of the old books rose to his mind and accompanied his steps. He who is wise of heart sorrows neither for the living nor the dead. All that lives lives eternally. Whatever has existence can never end. Life is indestructible. It can never by any means be lessened or altered. Only the outer shell, the perishable, passes away. The spirit is without end, eternal, deathless. He looked up. The flying dogs, borne on large heavy wings, came through the air, bringing the evening with them. The ground began to fall gently to the sea. It took a long time to reach the end of the last sawah. After that the open country lay before them under the sky, loud with the chirping of thousands of grasshoppers.

The pedanda stopped and pointed across the river whose wide sandy bed stretched in front of them. "The unclean live over there," he said. "I must wait here."

He sat down to meditate beside the image of a raksasa that had sunk into the ground. The lord looked round for Oka. "Stay here with the pedanda," he told him gently. He himself went on without pausing, crossed the river and went towards some low shrubs among which he caught sight of some roofs.

Teragia was coming from the spring with a water-jar on her head. "Come no farther, stranger," she called out. "Unclean dwell here."

"Greetings, Teragia," the lord said, without stopping. She looked at him in astonishment as he approached. Her face was tanned with the sun and lined with care and so impassive that he did not know whether she recognized him or not when he stopped in front of her and took off his hat and threw it down on the grass.

"Where is Ida Bagus Rai?" he asked. "I have a message for him." He gave him his full title, as though Raka were still the darling of all. Three lean dogs came and sniffed at him without barking.

"In the house," Teragia said. "Go in, if you are not afraid of the uncleanness."

"I have put all fear away from me," Alit replied as seriously as though he were addressing another man. She was so tall he had to look up when he spoke to her. The enclosure with its unfinished walls and its two small balés was clean and tidy. Raka sat in one of them on a mat, with closed eyes, doing nothing. The lord had felt afraid of seeing his friend's beautiful face again, blotched and swollen with the Great Sickness. But it was not marred; it had only become strange and other than it was before.

"Raka," he said in a voice not quite his own. Raka opened his eyes and looked up.

"Alit," he cried. He corrected himself with a hasty movement as though he had only now recognized the lord and clasped his hands humbly. "Tjokorda, your Highness," he whispered. Then seeing that he was disguised he asked quickly, "Are you in flight?"

"You, who know me better than anyone, ought not to ask me that," Alit said, smiling. He was still searching for Raka in Raka's face, but the darkness came quickly down and obliterated the features of the seated figure.

"I have sent messengers through all my kingdom to say to all that tomorrow is the end. Offerings will be made in every temple. Anyone who wishes to die with me may come to my puri. I could find no messenger to come to you. Therefore I came myself," he said, still standing in front of the crouching man. He was thinking of the promise they had given each other on their way to Batukau and he knew that Raka was thinking of it too.

"A sacrificial death is the cleanest thing of all," Raka whispered, raising his hand. "And I of all things am the most unclean."

Alit now saw that Raka's hands were deformed and his fingers no longer like those of a human being. As he got to his feet his crutches, which he had propped against the edge of the balé, fell with a clatter to the ground. Alit was filled with pity and yet he shuddered. Only the shell, the perishable, passes away, he thought again. Comfort and certainty were in the old books of the Mahabharata, wisdom that foresaw all and gave an answer.

He bent down to his friend and touched his shoulder with the tips of his fingers. He could feel that Raka trembled. "Sacrificial death makes the unclean clean," he said. "That is why I am here to point you out the way. Tomorrow we shall enter heaven together."

As he raised himself he felt Raka touch his feet. He forced himself not to shudder at the touch. Raka without a word laid his forehead on the lord's feet.

Teragia's long shadow fell over them. She was there with a lighted lamp in her hand. When Alit turned to go she lighted him as far as the river. She stayed there until he had forded the sandy river-bed and reached the raksasa. She saw the white figure of the pedanda as he rose to his feet. He unwound his white kain, took off his white jacket, took his kris from his girdle and put them all down beside the image of the demon, just where rice and fruit had always been put for them. He went away clothed only in a loin-cloth as the lord was.

She waited a long time until they had vanished from sight and then she went to fetch the clothing. The kris had a scabbard of tortoise-shell. The hilt was of wood and on it was carved the veiled widow. Teragia went back and helped Raka to put on the dress of those who were dedicated to death. She herself still had a white kain left over from the days when she prayed the gods to enter into her. She was inexpressibly happy and thankful. Raka was happy too. She could tell it by the way he discarded his crutches and set out only with the support of her shoulder. She did not take a torch to light their way for fear they might be recognized and driven out. They went in darkness, slowly and painfully and thinking only of reaching Badung before the first glimmer of dawn.

Whenever Teragia turned round she saw the three famished dogs at her heels. Behind them a crouching figure stole along—Bengek, the husky, the unclean, the son of the witch. He kept out of their way and thought they could not see him, but they had seen him from the first moment when they left the river mouth. She secretly smiled her rare, unwilling smile.

"Bengek wants to die with us," she said to Raka. "May he do that?"

"Who am I to stand in the way of his being born again?" Raka said gently.

They got to Badung in the fourth hour of the night. No one recognized them although they reached the shattered wall of the puri among a crowd of people all going the same way. The gate by which Raka had gone to his stolen meetings with Lambon swung open in desolation. They crouched down not far from it and waited for the morning.

Messengers had gone in haste to all the villages of the kingdom with the message: Tomorrow there will be a great battle and the end. Many of those who belonged to the puri came and some did not. And not a few who were neither related to the lord nor bound to him by any sort of service went nevertheless to Badung to die with him. For death has a mysterious power of seduction, as wine has, or love. They came with their wives and children, with the old men and grandmothers of their families, clothed in white if they had any white linen and, if not, in the gaily colored kains of the simple people. Every man had a kris and many of the women and boys had them too. They streamed into the puri and squeezed their way as near as they could get to their lord or to Molog, the captain of the warriors, and said, "You summoned us and we are ready to die with you." No one felt any fear, all were merry and in festive mood as though they had come to witness a cremation. The children did not cry; they leaned against their mothers and fell asleep or if they could not sleep their eyes sparkled with excitement and the reflection of the fires. No torches were needed in the puri, for the fires blazed up now here, now there and lit up the courtyard.

No one smoked opium or drank palm wine that night. Sacrificial death is clean and holy and must be met with an unclouded mind and open heart. No one wept, but now and then a sound of laughter was heard from the huddled dwellings where the lord's wives lived. They were the scene of feverish activity: The slave girls were cutting out long strips of linen and stitching the little men's jackets in big hurried stitches. The women laughed as they put on this unusual dress. Tumun, who had formerly been a prostitute at Kesiman, gave free rein to her vanity on this day of days. She shaved her eyebrows by the light of an oil lamp and fixed gold ornaments to her temples. Muna, the slave-girl, was busy beautifying Lambon, so that in heaven as well she should be the raja's favorite wife. With jokes and flatteries she combed Lambon's luxuriant hair and put little splinters of wood sprinkled with scented oils behind her ears. Every mirror was brought out and in front of each a woman turned herself this way and that in her new white robes. Muna herself, frivolous little slave-girl though she was, had resolved to die with Lambon. It was astonishing how few of the wives and servants and slaves had left the puri. The women whom Bijang had brought along were less lively. The tjokorda of Pametjutan, to whom they belonged, was old and sick and moody and often clouded in mind, and perhaps they were not so very delighted by the thought of being married to him in heaven and for all eternity. Messengers hurried between the two puris, bringing articles of clothing and adornment. They brought news too. The old tjokorda, it was said, had left his sick bed and clothed himself in white. He could no longer walk, but a chair was ready in which, when the moment came, he was to be carried out to meet the enemy. Bijang was keeping him company and telling him stories to pass the time. She already had a kris in her girdle to complete her male attire, the messenger said, and she entertained her slave-girls by showing them how she would kill herself. She had decided to die in her puri, since she was old-fashioned and thought it undignified for a noble lady to show herself to foreign soldiery, even though it was only to be killed.

A fresh onset of festal gaiety swept through the women's quarters when Ida Katut made his appearance with a command from their lord that they should put on all the finery they possessed. The little story-teller had for long enjoyed the dubious privilege of taking liberties with the raja's wives and behaving as though he was not a man at all but a gelded buffalo; and so it was his office on this occasion also to hand over the krisses which the lord sent for his wives. They were not particularly choice ones, for these had all been allotted to the men and boys of the court; but they were highly polished and sharpened. The slaves put them in their mistresses' girdles and Tuman made great play with hers and swaggered about like a prince in a fairy tale. Ida Katut himself wore an enormous kris at his diminutive back and was tremendously busy. Oka ran about with him and he, too, had a kris at his back. He was too impatient and excited to sit still and begged the little story-teller for one fairy tale after another to pass the time. After Ida Katut had gone the women opened their baskets and chests and took out their gold crowns, their rings and bracelets and adorned themselves as though for the festival of the New Year.

As the night wore on more and more people crowded into the puri until there must have been thousands assembled there. On this solemn occasion the four castes kept more strictly apart than they usually did. The simple people, the sudras and rice cultivators, the servants and all the casteless artisans who belonged to the lord assembled in the now ruinous outer court, marvelling at its desolation and not venturing to enter the inner courts. The warriors of the Ksatria caste, who had come with all the members of their families from the smaller puris and noble houses, surrounded Molog, their captain, who gave his orders in a loud voice. The cannon were examined and dragged into position, new emplacements were made if the old ones had given way and rifles were issued and the warriors mustered. They, least of all who were assembled in the puri, gave any thought to death, although it was their trade. The relations of the lord, all the distant uncles and cousins, the children of half-brothers, descendants of wives without caste who yet were of the blood of the tjokordas—all these assembled round the house where they supposed the lord to be. Gusti Wana, the first minister and all his dependants was among them; he wore hibiscus flowers and fine beaten gold in his head-dress and was more talkative than usual. There, too, was Anak Agung Bima, with his youngest grandson in his arms, and the chief overseer of the lord's sawahs. All the dignitaries of the court were gathered here and all their relations and the servants of their relations and the servants' families. The whole network of relationships that spread through the country from the puri after the manner of the roots of a wairingin tree was to be seen there in all its ramifications. They were all there ready and glad to die with their lord, while the free men of the villages slept peacefully in their homes with their wives and children.

In the fourth hour of the night the pedanda, Ida Bagus Rai, arrived from Taman Sari accompanied by a pupil carrying the holy
vessels. All made way for him reverently, for he was one of the wis-
est and holiest men in the land. He, too, was clothed in white and
the people did not know whether this was merely in token of his
priestly dignity or whether it was because he had decided to share
the lord's end. His hair, too, was white and gleaming and adorned
with rare orchids and yellow, white, red and blue flowers for each
of the great gods. He wore a kris in his girdle, a simple one with a
scabbard of woven bamboo and a plain wooden hilt. He asked the
servants and courtiers where their lord was to be found and, as no
one could tell him, he went past the pond to the courts in the north-
east of the puri where the watercourse surrounded the island on
which the house-temple stood.

Lord Alit was kneeling before the great shrine of his holy forefathers, lost in meditation, his hands clasped on his forehead. The
pedanda knelt down on the mat beside him and put his hand on his
shoulder. "Are you praying, my son?" he asked gently.

"I am praying the mighty fathers of my race to tell me whether I
have chosen the good way," Alit said. His eyes shone hot and dry in
the light of the two oil lamps which hung before the shrine.

The pedanda set out the sacred vessels on the mat and signed to
his pupil to leave them. He took his bell out of the box and put on
his tall priest's crown. He washed his mouth and his feet and sat
cross-legged before the altars. "I will call on the gods for you and
they will answer you," he said.

Offerings lay on every throne and the fading flowers smelt strong
and sweet. The smoke of sandalwood and resin rose from the bra-
ziers and mingled its scent with that of the flowers. A murmur,
subdued by the distance, came from the crowded courts. The stars
moved across the sky, hour by hour, a cool wind got up and swept
away the smell of burning and made the flames leap up. The night
passed, the kulkul beat, the cocks crowed. The last night before the
end was over. The darkness was already growing pale in the east
when the lord and the priest got to their feet and left the temple.
Many of the people in the courtyard had fallen asleep leaning
against the balés and at the foot of the walls, tired out with the exertions and agitation of the previous days. The fires had burned down.

The prince and the priest made their way among the exhausted and sleeping people to the gate leading into the outer court.

"Peace on your way, my master," the prince said as though he had already put off his exalted rank.

The pedanda smiled, though there was still the absorption of long prayer in his eyes. "I am staying with you," he said, "and with those whom you take with you into the heaven of Shiva," he added and his smile took on a deeper meaning. The lord smiled too, for they both thought of Raka. When he went into his house to clothe himself in white and to put the sacred kris, Singa Braga, in his girdle, his mind was wholly at peace. The ancient words of the holy writings echoed in his heart and gave it calm and certainty:

Happy the warrior to whom the just fight comes unsought. It opens for him the door of heaven.

Six cages containing little gray doves hung from the roof of the balé. Alit opened them one after the other.

Without honor is he who casts off duty and obedience. To lose his honor is worse for a man of noble blood than to die.

The doves cowered down when he put them on his hands; they hesitated to take flight into the darkness. So he threw them up into the air.

The end of birth is death. The end of death is birth. So it is ordained, it was written.

The day dawned to the accompaniment of the thunderous report of a Dutch gun.

*   *   *   *   *

"I can't sleep. Can you?" Pastor Schimmelpennick asked as he sat up in bed. "Every bone in my body is aching."

Dekker rolled over and looked irritably at his tent companion. "I had just got off to sleep," he said reproachfully.

"It's morning at last, thank God," Schimmelpennick said, putting on his spectacles and taking out his watch. "Four thirty-six. Let's hope for a better camping place tomorrow."

Dekker pushed his hair from his face. He, too, was now aware of aches and pains in the back from the day's marching and a night on straw. The company lamps were all alight, for a rumor had reached them at midnight that the Raja of Badung was planning a fierce assault and the battalion had been given the alarm. The men were sleeping on the ground beside their piled arms. The officers had been allotted the huts of the puri of Kesiman—in so far as they were not shot to bits. Dekker looked about him.

"Nice pig-sties, these palaces," he said with repugnance.

The pastor smiled to himself. "You are right there, my friend," he agreed. "A pigsty and nothing more. Those fellows in Java are big swells in comparison."

Dekker lay down again and closed his eyes. The straw scratched his neck and the earth floor of the hut was lumpy. He tried to find hollows to fit his bones, but it was useless. Nevertheless, he fell into a doze after a time and was nearly asleep when a loud report, immediately followed by a second, woke him up again.

"The big naval guns," the pastor remarked with satisfaction. "Rather different from our little twelve-pounders."

"Haven't heard anything of them for long enough," Dekker said. The four days' campaigning, with all its experiences and exertions, seemed like years. He had a beard starting to grow and his nose was peeling with the sun. The bugles sounded reveillé.

"Now for it," he said with an uneasy feeling in the pit of the stomach as he buttoned up his tunic.

"Are they going to give us any breakfast, I wonder?" the pastor asked.

"Something or other's wrong with the rations," Dekker said. "I'd like to know who gets the makanan sent from the ships."

The confusion of a camp roused in the half-light of dawn filled the courtyards. Men starting up from sleep, coughing, fumbling, cursing and laughing, staggered to their feet and finally sorted themselves out. The pastor sat with the handbook to Bali on his sharp knees and studied a poor map of the puri of Badung. The naval guns continued to rend the air. "If only I don't have diarrhoea," he said, clasping his round paunch.

"Why, do you feel bad?" Dekker asked unconcernedly.

"A bit cold and queer in here. Perhaps it's that emergency ration of last night."

"The grub was all right," Dekker said; he was tired of his companion's little troubles.

"Well, of course, if you like pork and beans out of a tin," the pastor said in an aggrieved tone.

"Why have they stopped firing, I wonder," Dekker said. The sudden stillness after the shattering reports made an impression of vacancy.

There was a smell of men and boots, of paraffin lamp-soot and smoke. The dawn-sky grew lighter. "Oh, well— God be with us," the pastor said as he got up. "God be with us"—that was what was always written on the fly-leaf of his mother's household account books at home in Enschedé. Enschedé. was far away. "My left foot has gone to sleep," Schimmelpennick complained. Most of the lanterns were now extinguished, but here and there in the yards fires for cooking had been kindled. Coffee was dished out and the men surged round, a confused mass of gray in the gray light. "Here—I say," the pastor said as the Javanese servants pushed by to get their officers' breakfasts. Dekker drank his coffee in silence. His sergeant came to make his report—No. 4 platoon ready to march off. Dekker buckled on his short sword and felt what an important person he was. Half an hour later they were on the march.

The 18th Battalion led with the band. The Dutch soldiers sang. The artillery followed with the howitzers, covered by two companies marching on either side of the road, leaving a cloud of dust in their train. The Ambonese, who followed with the reserve companies, marched without discipline and out of step. They had a sleepy look, although they had no rivals when it came to fighting. Dust settled on blue uniforms, dust coated eyelashes and choked throats. The smell of humanity mingled with the strong sweet smell exhaled from the trees that rose above the walls on both sides of the road. The line of the march to Badung went over Tanguntiti and progress was extremely slow. Here and there a brown face peered over a wall and vanished again in terror as soon as it was seen. Then the flanking companies were ordered to break down the wall to protect the troops against the risk of an ambush. Now and then the native labor corps threw a bomb over the walls into the dense foliage of the palms.

Lieutenant Dekker was riding with the 11th Battalion through Sameta when they had the order to halt—why, they did not know. Although it was not yet nine the heat of the sun was intolerable as soon as they stood still. Time seemed to have come to a stop. Rifle-fire could be heard a long way in front; then it ceased again. The naval guns still rent the air from time to time. They moved forward again slowly. Dekker still had the unpleasant sensation of being ambushed at any moment. He rode his charger and was quite glad to be on horseback again. Two days of skirmishing and footslogging had blistered his feet and every step was an agony. He suffered from the mosquitoes as well. They fell with avidity on his fair skin and seemed even to inhabit his uniform. The romantic notions he had had of active service when he parted from Brigit were years behind him. He had even ceased to write letters. There was nothing heroic to write about; the dangers he still felt to be lurking on every side were imaginary. There were said to have been seven casualties in the four days, but no one had seen them. The medical detachment and its colored stretcher-bearers ambled along unregarded with the baggage train. Water and rations were the chief topic of conversation. Poker was played in camp just as it was in the casino at Surabaya. An Ambonese in the 3rd Company had attacked a Javanese with a knife and had been flogged. The Javanese was back in the ranks. Dekker now had his doubts whether a second-lieutenant could distinguish himself sufficiently in this campaign to earn promotion.

There were several halts and then the rattle of rifle-fire could be heard ahead. Dekker saw a few half-naked brown bodies lying in the road with their lances beside them. He turned his head away, for it was the first time in his life that he had seen any dead. They marched on; this was the stretcher-bearers' job. Word came from the staff that the enemy had withdrawn into the puri of Badung and was making a stand there. The orders were to encircle the puri and to attack it from all sides at once. The third and fourth companies of the 11th and two companies of the 20th were detailed to proceed by a side road that led off in a southwesterly direction. Two howitzers and six sharp-shooters accompanied them. For a long time they could still hear the band. Then they were among the sawahs. Dekker once more cursed his horse. The first-lieutenant rode ahead with a captain and they were both smoking. Dekker was surrounded by the steam of the perspiring men. "Have you get a cigarette, sergeant?" he asked, for he had none left of his own. The sergeant produced one from inside his cap. It tasted appalling, as was to be expected.

The naval guns had ceased to fire. "Halt," came from in front. The sharp-shooters dropped to the ground and loosed off at a party of men with lances who had been seen in a field of rice. Dekker saw with relief that the captain and the lieutenant had dismounted and were leading their horses. He, too, jumped off his horse and gave the reins to the sergeant. He had scarcely been a moment on his feet before they began to cause him renewed agonies. "What are those signals the natives keep on sending?" he asked the sergeant. "I can hear them the whole time."

"Signals, sir?"

"Yes. Tom-toms or kulkuls, as they call them. Drumming on bamboos."

The sergeant listened. "That is a bird," he said with a grin. "I don't know what it is called."

They had reached the first house in the town of Badung, when a shell landed not far from them. Trees crashed and the earth flew up behind the walls of one of the houses. For a few minutes they all lay flat and took cover. The sergeant had pulled his young officer down as the shell whistled over their heads. "Blast them!" he cursed. Dekker felt his knees tremble; he had the wind up. The horses broke loose and galloped off in terror.

"That was my first," Dekker said to excuse himself, as he got on to his feet again with a smile and wiped the soil from his face.

"And one of ours too, sir, damn them," the sergeant said. "If the marines don't stop chucking these things about, they'll kill some of us instead of the enemy."

But no more came over. Probably the staff had some means of signalling to the warships. All they heard now was the roaring and crackling as the puri collapsed in flames. The smell of burning was almost intolerable when they emerged from a narrow avenue of palms and found a shell-shot wall not far ahead.

The captain summoned his officers and briefly explained the situation with the aid of the map he had torn out of the hand-book. They were on the north side of the puri. A second detachment was advancing from the south. The main body was marching by the main road from Kesiman which led to the main entrance of the puri. The artillery was to take up a position at the cross-roads where the main road to Badung turned off. There they were covered by a smaller puri, Tian Siap or Tain Siap, if the howitzers were called on for a preliminary bombardment. The two companies of the 11th Battalion were to advance to the north wall of the puri and then make contact with the rest of the Battalion. The buglers sounded a signal and were answered from no great distance. The officers gave their platoons the order to march. They could not see very much now, although the sun had been blazing away out among the rice-fields.

A ditch separated the road they were on from the wall of the puri. Clouds of smoke drifted over them and obscured their view. On the right, the road was fringed with trees behind which walls and dwellings lay concealed. The ground was soft and covered with grass.

There was not a sound to be heard behind the wall of the puri except the crackling of flames and the crash of falling roofs. It might, for all they could tell, have been utterly deserted. Perhaps its inmates had all fled, or perhaps they lay in hiding, ready to rush out and massacre the Dutch soldiers. It gave Dekker an eerie feeling. His men, too, had become silent; they marched on along the wall in a chastened mood and as noiselessly as their heavy boots allowed. The only sound was the bugle calls. They approached nearer and nearer to the answering bugle without seeing anything of their own men. Suddenly a puff of wind blew the smoke aside and the tops of the palms stirred. Their way on was barred by a wairingin tree over whose roots the men had to go in single file.

They reached the end of the wall and turned the corner. Now they were on the west side of the puri, in the middle of which, as Dekker knew well from his frequent study of the map, was the main entrance. Soon he saw the lofty gateway. Here the main road made a clearing and the sun could be seen in spite of the smoke. The shadows of the palms were black and sharp on the bare ground. Dekker took hold of his field-glasses, and so did the captain. The bend in the road from which they expected to see the main body approaching could not be more than a kilometre away to the north. There was nothing to be seen; the silence that greeted them was incomprehensible and shook the young lieutenant's nerves.

Suddenly there was the report of a gun inside the walls of the puri, immediately followed by a second. "Company—halt!" the captain shouted. "Company—halt!" Dekker repeated in a trembling voice.

He gave a look at his men. His ear-drums were still throbbing. No one was wounded. The smell of powder smarted in his nostrils.

The troops ahead of them had halted. And now the Dutch howitzers replied from Tian Siap. It's begun at last, Dekker said to himself.

It was then that people were seen emerging on to the top of the steep steps leading down from the gateway of the puri to the road below. They were clothed in white and adorned with flowers. Their tread was sedate and they had lances in their hands. Behind them were bearers carrying a man shoulder-high on a decorated throne. They set the throne down. For a moment the man was quite alone on the topmost step. Then a procession of other men came out one after another and ranged themselves behind the solitary figure. Dekker let go of his sword-hilt. He could not understand what it all meant. It looked like a scene on the stage. Yes, that was it—it was exactly like a scene at the opera in Amsterdam, to which he had been occasionally. The men were dressed up and they moved with slow and measured steps, just as though they had no idea that the Dutch faced them with guns and rifles and sharp-shooters, and that their palace was surrounded and that a war was on. The man who all this while stood alone and parted from the rest—the raja, he heard the Javanese soldiers mutter—raised his clasped hands to his brow and he stood thus for several minutes. There was still the same air of complete unreality about it. It's not possible, Dekker thought; people don't do that, dress like that and behave that like unless they are opera singers. Yet a very real force emanated from the lord's attitude of tense concentration. The men on the steps before and behind him stood as motionless as bronze statues and the Dutch soldiers did not move either.

Suddenly the lord raised his head and in a flash he had drawn the kris from the scabbard that projected behind his shoulders. He held it outstretched above his head and it flashed in the sun. An unearthly shout broke from the men around him. The next moment they charged the Dutch, kris in hand.

"Fire!" the captain shouted. "Fire!" Dekker roared in his unpractised voice of command. The men fired. A few of the Balinese fell and lay where they had fallen. The rest charged up the main road towards the turning from Tian Siap where the howitzers were firing and the bugles blared. The two companies of the 11th followed at the double. The whole scene was wrapped in the smoke and dust that hung like a curtain between them and the wild rush of the white-clad figures and almost hid it from sight. Dekker ran in front of his men between the shell-shot walls on either side of the road. A party of men armed with spears dashed out of one of the doorways. Dekker was surprised to find that he had drawn his short sword. A bayonet flashed past him into the stomach of a Balinese. When he looked about him he found that he was separated from his company. It looked as though the Dutch would give way before the mad assault of the Balinese. Dekker shouted a command. He saw one of his men fall and noted the astonishment in his face. The other officers, too, were shouting to their men and they re-formed their ranks. And now they had joined up with the main body.

Gun- and rifle-fire swept the Balinese as they came round the Tian Siap turning and charged straight for the Dutch troops. The lord was the first to fall. The rest ran on over his dead body in a wild onset and when they fell, still more came on. A mountain of wounded and dead was piled up between the puri and the Dutch troops. Meanwhile the gateway disgorged more and more of them, all with krisses in their hands, all with the same death-frenzy in their eyes, all decked out and crowned with gold and flowers.

Three times the Dutch ceased fire, as though to wake these frantic people from their trance or to spare and save them. But the Balinese were set on death. Nothing in the world could have arrested them in their death-race, neither the howitzers nor the unerring aim of the sharp-shooters, nor the sudden stillness when the firing ceased. Hundreds fell to the enemy's rifles, hundreds more raised their krisses high and plunged them into their breasts, plunging them in above the collar-bone so that the point should reach the heart in the ancient, holy way. Behind the men came the women and children, boys and girls with flowers in their hair, mothers with infants in arms and old slaves with white hair and girlish breasts. They were all decked out with flowers whose scent mingled with the smell of powder and the sickly odor of blood and death that soon filled the air.

Here and there, priests were to be seen among them, going calmly to and fro among the dying, and sprinkling holy water on their quivering bodies. The raja's wives had gold crowns on their heads, on which flowers of gold nodded and their hands and arms were loaded with jewels, which they tore off and threw to the soldiers with a look of contempt in their large, unconscious eyes. Some Javanese and Ambonese left the ranks to seize the jewels, but were hounded back by their corporals. Some of the officers turned their heads aside or put their hands over their eyes. Dekker, for one, was unable to endure the sight of men killing their wives and then themselves, and of mothers driving a kris into their infants' breasts. He turned away and vomited.

Soon the whole road was filled with the dead and dying and the front ranks of the Dutch soldiers were faced by the frenzied Balinese. It was only a man here and there among these white-robed natives who actually attacked kris in hand, but it was done with such a furious lust to kill that the soldiers gave way before the onslaught. The sharp-shooters picked them off one by one, after coolly taking aim. And still the puri disgorged fresh victims, who streamed out as a river from a sluice.

Farther to the west the puri of Pametjutan went up in flames. When a detachment was sent there, another procession came out to meet them. The old lord was carried out on a chair borne shoulder-high. He was dressed in white like the rest, and his bloodless face was white, too. His dignitaries and officials and servants followed, many of them as old as their master. Lancers went in front and some women and many children followed behind. When his chair was set down he stood erect for a moment while his men charged the Dutch, kris in hand. Fire was opened on them and the old lord fell; soon he was covered by those of his following who were shot or who died by their own hands. The bugles sounded and the companies turned about and returned to the main road at the double. The slaughter there was not yet at an end, although the ground was covered with the fallen. There was still a remnant pressing on between the white soldiers and the brown Balinese, determined to follow their lord to heaven.

Dekker forced himself to look. He saw a woman snatch a kris from a boy's hand, stab her infant to the heart and then herself. A man stepped over her body; he was a little old man of almost comic appearance and he was brandishing a large kris in the act of killing the boy. Dekker drew his revolver and fired at the old man. He scarcely knew what he did, but he wanted to save the boy's life. He was a beautiful child, slender, large-eyed and he smiled all the time.

When the little old man fell the boy took the kris and killed him with it, for Dekker's revolver-shot had only wounded him. Dekker's hands and lips trembled. "Such things don't happen, it's not possible, it can't be," he muttered. He felt ill and the sight of the death of the old lord of Pametjutan had made him vomit a second time. The boy withdrew the kris from the breast of the little old man, who still seemed to be laughing. Dekker saw it with the clearness with which things are sometimes seen in dreams, everything was sharply outlined in black with a curious greenish edge. Blood ran from the kris in the boy's hand. As he raised it Dekker rushed forward among the falling Balinese, between bullet and kris, to save the boy's life. He closed with him and tried to wrest the kris from his grasp, but the slender youth had an unexpected and unbelievable strength. He defended himself and brought the kris down on Dekker's shoulder. Dekker tightened his grip on his revolver and shot the boy in the hand. But he had already turned the kris on himself and fell limp and bleeding on Dekker's breast. "Serves you right," Dekker said, overcome by rage and pity at the same time. He opened his eyes and found the boy's unconscious body in his arms. Again he felt ill, his stomach heaved, everything heaved, the green edge on things vanished, everything went black and he knew no more.

When he came to himself without knowing how long he had been unconscious he felt himself swaying in a measured swing. At first he thought he must be in the *Van Swoll* again, but then someone bent over him and said, "Well, that's a fine way to behave."

He was on a stretcher with a stretcher-bearer behind and before, whose tread gently swayed him to and fro. There was a smell of powder and battle. He was familiar with it by now. His left shoulder hurt him and his tunic stuck to it. When he turned his head to see what was going on he found that there was another stretcher being carried close beside his. It was the boy for whose sake he had plunged into the mêlée. Apparently they had reached the dressing station, for the stretchers were put down in the shadow of some bread-fruit trees and the boy was laid on the grass beside him. It was a strange feeling to have the warm, living body of his little enemy so close to his own. The boy sat up cross-legged and let his head sink on his chest; probably he felt dizzy, as Dekker did, too.

"The little heathen is bleeding, the plucky little chap," Schimmelpennick said pityingly. Dekker looked at the boy. His eyes were shut, but he was smiling. He had slanting eyebrows and a little dimple in his right cheek and an unusually beautiful mouth. There were flowers in his hair, and the smell of flowers about him conflicted with the iodoform of the dressing station.

"Are you in pain?" Dekker asked in Dutch.

The boy opened his eyes, smiled and raised his clasped hands to his shoulder. There were cuts on his chest and arms, and his right hand was grazed by Dekker's bullet. He answered in a low voice in Balinese.

"Are you in pain?" Dekker repeated in Malay.

"No, tuan," the boy answered.

Dekker could not take his eyes from the boy's face. It was the first time he had seen a Balinese face at close quarters and he was astonished and almost dismayed by its beauty.

"What is your name?"

"Oka is my name, tuan."

"Oka," Dekker repeated. Feeling slightly ill again he closed his eyes quickly. The bread-fruit trees above were beginning to turn round when he sank back and looked up.

"Water?" the pastor said, holding a water-bottle to his lips. It brought Dekker round.

"Is there actually water?" he asked in astonishment.

"Yes, the ration party seems to have discovered where Badung is at last," Schimmelpennick said cheerfully. Dekker drank eagerly and then held the bottle out to Oka. The boy shook his head. "The Balinese won't drink after anyone else," said a Javanese soldier who was sitting on the grass with a sprained foot. Dekker longed to show Oka some little attention and he saw the look he gave the Javanese soldier's cigarette.

"Smoke?" he said in Malay. Oka nodded. The pastor produced a large cigarette-case. "The last one, unfortunately," he said as he offered it to Dekker. Dekker lit it and after one eager puff he handed it to the boy. Oka took it thankfully and then shyly offered it to Dekker again.

"Little friend—Oka—friends we two," he said in the little Malay he knew. He put his arm cautiously round the boy's shoulders and felt a warmth of tenderness he had never known before. His own shoulder hurt him, but he was happy. They smoked their cigarette turn and turn about while waiting for the doctor—the second-lieutenant of the 11th Battalion, and Oka, the boy from the puri of Badung.

The fighting was over. The puri was burnt almost to the ground. The staff stood on the watch-tower on which was the kulkul of Tjan Siap. General Veldte looked down the road through his field-glasses at the heaps of dead. Stretcher-bearers were turning the bodies over to see if there was still life in them and carrying away the wounded.

"They don't utter a sound," the General said thoughtfully, without taking the glasses from his eyes.

Van Tilema was on a chair behind him, smoking hard and looking very white. "They have a sort of bravery and pride we shall never be able to understand," he said wearily.

"No pleasure to us to have to fire on such fellows," the General said, "but if we hadn't they'd have made short work of our men. They were mad."

"The holy madness," Visser said from behind. He had been promised the post of Assistant Resident of Bali for his services and because his native spies had done such good work. He felt sick at heart.

"Do you remember taking me to that kris dance, Visser?" Van Tilema asked. "I believe they were in a trance today, too, to behave as they did. I even believe they were glad to die."

"Let's hope so," Visser said curtly. Boomsmer, who was near the General, cleared his throat. "I shall never be able to understand it," he said, "women and children—and old men, it's too horrible to be believed."

Van Tilema turned to him. "It's a lesson to us all, Resident, how we ought to treat the Balinese. Hats off to such a death as theirs."

An adjutant came up the bamboo ladder and saluted. He carried something in a blood-stained white cloth.

"The body of the raja has been found, your Excellency. Here is his kris."

The General took the kris out of its wrappings, and they all bent over to look at it as Veldte drew the blade from the scabbard. It was a beautiful serpentine blade, with a keen edge. A lion and a snake were engraved one on each side of Singa Braga, hair and scales inlaid in gold. The hilt, too, was of gold and set with Indian gems of many colors and irregular shape.

"That is Singa Braga," Visser said. "The holy kris."

"Bullet holes," the General said, stroking the blade which had been pierced in three places by bullets. "A fine trophy." "We'll put it in the museum at Batavia to commemorate a gallant enemy," Van Tilema said, pushing the blade back into the scabbard. The General took off his hat and bowed his head. Boomsmer turned quickly away, tears started to his eyes.

*   *   *   *   *

The last shots fired in Badung were those fired over the graves of the four fusiliers who had fallen on the Dutch side. The bands played a funeral march; the General made a speech, and afterwards Pastor Schimmelpennick took his turn and exhorted the troops to honor the memory of their dead comrades and to serve the Dutch Government as loyally as they had done.

The Balinese collected their dead on the afternoon of their last assault, and burnt them all at the same time so that their souls should enter heaven together. There were many dead—no one could say how many. Puglug brought home the news that there were over two thousand, but Dasni contradicted her and said that there were six hundred at most, according to the account she had heard. Sarna rebuked her, for in her opinion it was rude of her to imply that Puglug was a liar and a story-teller. Dasni begged pardon and admitted that there were two thousand, or at any rate a thousand. Sarna insisted on Puglug's being treated for the time with particular respect and consideration, because she had lost her two little daughters in such a heart-rending way. She even went so far as to ask Pak to sleep with her more often so that she might have another child and forget her loss. And Pak, who was himself still upset and sorrowful, went that night to pay his first wife a visit in the big house.

Whatever the number of the dead in Badung, it was certain at least that scarcely a family had not someone to mourn for. Round the kitchen fire at night they told of the finding of the dead and how they had died—the lord and his uncle pierced with bullets, and all the retinue of both courts had fallen close behind their masters, covering the bodies of their lords with their own. The Dewa Gdé Molog with many other Ksatrias had been blown up by the bursting of the cannon when it was fired as the signal that the end had come. Very few of the women and children had bullet-wounds; they had killed themselves with their krisses or been killed by their husbands and fathers. The women as they whispered together in the kitchen spoke of Lambon and her beauty even after death. She and Tumun, the prostitute, and the slave, Muna, had all died by the same kris. Bijang had been found in the smoking ruins of the puri of Pametju-tan, leaning against the wall and slain by her own hand.

It had been hard to find the old man, Pak's father, for he was merely one of the servants, and had not even had a white kain to put on. But he, too, was dead, run through by a bayonet. Pak would not rest until he had found him, and was sure his body was burnt and his soul free to enter heaven in company with the more exalted souls of the nobles. There was much mourning for the pedanda, Ida Bagus Rai, for he was a man of great holiness and Taman Sari was lost without him and his counsel. Not far from the pedanda were lying the bodies of the unclean ones, Raka and Teragia and Bengek. But this was spoken of only in a whisper. No one could understand how it came about that the lepers were permitted to take part in this holy sacrament of death and the End. But they were all pleased, since they had loved Raka and revered Teragia.

"It was the gods' will," the people of Taman Sari said when they heard of it. "They carried Raka and his wife to the puri to cleanse them, and free their souls from the curse and the spell that came down to them from their forefathers."

"And as for the husky one," the aunt said in a whisper to the other women, "we can be glad he was burnt with the rest. Now his soul cannot plague the village as an evil spirit and an unseen demon as it would if he had to die unclean."

All the women stood at their doors when the Dutch soldiers marched through again on their way to Sanur. They held out baskets of coconuts and fruit as a sign of submission and peace; and the soldiers ate and drank and patted the children and laughed at the girls' naked breasts.

Slowly the villages forgot their fear. The peasants emerged again from their hiding-places and saw to their beasts and their houses. Krkek called a meeting of the subak, for the distribution of the water had fallen into utter confusion and the fields had to be cultivated.

Pak took out the buffaloes and went to the sawah to resume his ploughing where he had left off when the Dutch landed.

It was a fine day, sunny, but yet with a cool breeze blowing over the fields from the sea. The tjrorot called and the herons stood fishing for little eels at the edges of the sawahs. Birds sang in the bamboo thicket where Rantun and Klepon had met their death. The women bathed and washed and laughed in the river. Lantjar helped with a second team and Meru sat on a bank and made a show of herding the ducks. It was the second ploughing, and the earth was more obedient to the plough. The mud covered Pak's legs to the knees in a cool crust. Blok, blok, blok, the soil said. He had made an offering to Sri, the rice goddess, and prayed for a good harvest. His children were dead and his father gone to heaven, but his sawahs were still there. It happened as the gods willed and what they willed was right.

Madé, his second-born daughter, came out at midday with his food and he took her between his knees and stroked her head. He cut her a fine bamboo wand to catch dragon-flies with. Soon the time would come to make kites for his little boys. The ploughshare cleft the mud and the furrow was straight and good; the sun shone and ripened the western fields while he ploughed and planted the eastern ones.

On the way home he gave the buffaloes into Lantjar's charge and went once more into the rice temple. It was unhurt in spite of the shooting, for it was a holy place and the gods loved their new shrine and came there daily to rest unseen. Pak knelt and put his clasped hands to his forehead. He was only a simple man and too stupid to pray. He did not give thanks for anything and he did not pray for anything; he only felt that there was meaning in everything and that things happened as the gods ordained. He was glad of his rice for his evening meal, glad to have Siang and Lintang and Tanah to carry in his arms, glad to caress his cocks and to sleep with his wives. He was glad to beat the gong in the gamelan and to discuss the weighty village affairs with the other men, and to thatch his walls with fresh straw; and he was glad to rest and glad that the war was over. His children were dead and his father had been killed, but his heart was filled with a contentment the white man does not know.

"Sign here," Boomsmer, the Resident, told the Chinese,

Kwe Tik Tjiang. The merchant of Bandjarmasin read through the receipt which the Resident had pushed towards him.

"I, the Undersigned, hereby acknowledge the receipt of 7500 (seven thousand five hundred guilders) from the Dutch Indian Government as compensation for the loss of my ship the *Sri Kumala*, which was wrecked off the coast of Sanur on the 27th of May, 1904, and plundered and broken up by the inhabitants of the province of Badung.

Buleleng, January 2nd, 1907."

The Chinaman dipped his brush in the Indian ink which the Assistant Resident, Visser, pushed towards him and carefully delineated the intricate signs which formed his name at the foot of the receipt.